BROOK
HAROLD

BROOK
HAROLD

Jamie Edwards

BROOK HAROLD

This is a work of fiction. All of the characters, names, incidents, organizations, and dialogue in this novel are either the products of the author's imagination or are used fictitiously.

iUniverse books may be ordered through booksellers or by contacting:

iUniverse
1663 Liberty Drive
Bloomington, IN 47403
www.iuniverse.com
844-349-9409

ISBN: 978-1-5320-7600-8 (sc)
ISBN: 978-1-5320-7601-5 (e)

Library of Congress Control Number: 2019907006

Print information available on the last page.

iUniverse rev. date: 05/13/2021

CHAPTER ONE

WHERE IT ALL BEGAN

After my Parents moved from New York to Kentucky, Mom slipped into a severe depression. Coming from a busy city where everyone was always in a rush. Coffee shops, shopping, and restaurants all in a walking distance of my parent's apartment. To a small, laid back town in a middle of nowhere. All the bigger malls, the fancier restaurants were at least an hour maybe more away. She would occasionally run into town but most shops were ma's and pa's, family owned shops. Nothing fancy and everyone was in no rush. Everyone knew each other by name, plus everyone knew each other's business. Nothing stayed a secret in that town. Because it was a small town, Mom got bored. Dad tried to get her out of the house. He mentions more than once about going to either Louisville or Lexington. But Mom didn't want to dump me on my grandparents. So Dad mentioned, what about a girl's weekend with my aunt? She wasn't a fan of that either; it worried her that dad wouldn't know how to take care of me.

I recall several months my Parents argued over these topics. The more they argued, the less Mom preferred to be at home. She figured if she wasn't home, they wouldn't quarrel.

There were countless times Dad put me to bed. When I woke each morning, Dad already taken off for work and Mom was on the couch passed out drunk.

With me being only one, I couldn't fend for myself. I went hungry a lot of days. But Dad always made sure I had dinner and if I was awake before he went to work, he fed me breakfast.

I remember I woke to my Parents arguing, which was common. So I hid under my covers.

But this one night, they were louder than usual.

After I heard a loud crash, curiosity got the best of me. However, if I knew what I would have seen when I left my room, I wouldn't have left the safety of my bedroom.

When I walked into the living room, Dad was on the floor with the end table knocked over plus the lamp and he had a bloody nose. It confused me. Because I never saw that part of their arguments.

I noticed Mom looked at me; I looked at her but her expression gave me chills. Her eyes were black, filled with hatred. Her look scared me to death.

Dad told me to go back to my room but fear froze me.

To this day it still gives me chills and I can still picture it like it happened yesterday.

The next day Dad struggled to explain it but I was too young to understand what a love affair was. He tried to explain it by saying Mom was kissing another guy. Yet he still lost me.

Since I am older, I know what he meant, and it makes my blood boil. But, it also breaks my heart knowing what Dad went through.

Even though Dad was living in hell, he was the strongest person I knew. Going to work full time, coming home to take care of me and the house, and dealing with Mom. Dad was in pain, but rarely did he complain. I wanted to grow up to be like my Dad. He was my hero.

My parents divorced in November before my second birthday.

I spent my birthday with Dad and my grandparents. Mom didn't want to come. She didn't want to be in the same room with him.

Dad was out of the house by January. And left me with Mom. It confused me why Dad was leaving me. I thought I made him upset.

I understood why Dad left when I got older but it also pissed me off. Why the hell would you leave your kid with your ex wife who abused you?

Back then, I felt scared to be alone with Mom. And I felt sad because my hero left me.

As weeks passed, I became Mom's target. But with being little, meant I could get away from her quicker. I always hid under my bed. There were many times I fell asleep under there.

Though that only worked for Mom, I also was her boyfriends target. It was harder to get away from him. The both of us never had that father, son relationship. I was…. His toy..

Anyway. A year after Dad left, he came back for me. But I had mix emotions. Like, feeling confused, feeling upset. I had to live in hell for a year. Dad only had to deal with Mom but I had to deal with her and her boyfriend.

But I was excited, I didn't want to live there anymore.

I was three and couldn't pack well. I needed Mom's help, but she sat on the couch smoking her weed instead.

Though my pacing bugged her, she yelled at me to sit down. She frightened me, so I listened right away. So, I went to sit at the dinner table, where I stared out the window. I am not positive if I blinked.

When I saw Dad pull up, I ran like the wind to greet him outside. I gave him a big smile. Back then I didn't understand why Dad gave me an uneasy smile while getting out of the car. Like I do now.

He was angry at Mom because she beat me up. Actually, Willie (Mom's boyfriend.) did.

Dad and I went into the house, he told me to go wait in my room for him.

My parents haven't seen each other or talked to each other for a year. And what was the first thing they do? Argue with each other. This time it was about how Mom has been treating me.

It was three o'clock, by the time Dad and I left. We stopped at a burger shop ten minutes from Mom's.

A waiter showed us to our table, while he was asking if he could bring us anything, we locked eyes for a moment. I gave him a nervous smile which he returned with a dark smile.

If I knew Mom's boyfriend worked there, I would have begged Dad to go somewhere else or go home and eat.

After Dad gave, our waiter, Mom's boyfriend, the order, Dad tried to make conversation with me.

I wondered if Dad forgot what age I was. Sure, I may have been advance in my speech but didn't mean I could hold a whole conversation.

Leaning in toward Dad, I told him quietly and hastily,

"Daddy. We should have gone to your home. People are looking."

I remember his surprised look he gave me before he let out a sigh.

Dad leaned back in his chair. "Brook, It's okay. Don't worry about it."

But that didn't comfort me. It made me worry more. I had bruises on my face and I wanted no one to think my Dad did it. So I pulled my hooded part of my hoodie over my head.

"Daddy. Everyone is looking. Are you not scared?" I trembled.

Dad told me not to worry about it. And that we will take it one day at a time. He even apologized for leaving me. Because he didn't think Mom would beat her own child.

Well news flash, she did. And even brought her boyfriend on board.

Willie our waiter came by to drop off our water and to take our order. But he still gave me that dark smile. I tried to avoid eye contact with him. However, I find it funny how blind Dad was. If I was a parent, I wouldn't like if some random guy kept smiling creepy at my child.

Dad order two cheeseburgers with fries. While waiting for the food to come, Dad and I continued to talk.

Because I didn't feel comfortable being in public plus with Willie around, I gave Dad short, to the point answers.

After we got done eating, Dad paid for the bill and Willie told us to have a nice day but he kept on staring at me.

He scared me, so I moved closer to Dad.

I was the happiest kid to be back on the road again. No more Mom. No more Willie. To this point, I was free. I could get my life back on track. Work through things I witnessed with my parents arguing and what I went through.

I was even more thrilled to be pulling up to Dad's house. Where I saw an older lady.

She was about five feet tall with grey wavy hair.

"Who's that?" I asked.

"Brook, meet your Grandma Duke." Dad replied.

When Dad got out of the van, he walked over towards Grandma. Five minutes passed till Grandma came to get me out of the car.

"Hi Brook, I don't know if you remember me. But I am plus rest of the family will help your dad take care of you."

I remembered who she was. I felt angry at her. Like why didn't she tell her son to come get me. Was the whole family hoping that my mother wouldn't put a hand on me. Like she would be magically cure of her mental sickness?

I gave Grandma a disgust look as I turned away. I heard her sigh. When I looked back, I saw Dad standing by the van with a disappointed look.

He thought, he hoped that I would go to Grandma with open arms. I couldn't when I felt like Dad's family betrayed me.

Dad singled me out of the van as he grabbed my bag with the other hand.

I remember when we went into the house, Dad told me it was safe to remove my hoodie. If Grandma weren't at the house, then sure. But she didn't get a good look at me while we were outside. One, it was getting dark, two, Dad didn't have the dome light on in the van plus my hoodie was still up.

So I took my chance, put my trust in Dad. I was feeling tense while removing my hoodie. After I did, Grandma I remember her gasped as she covered her mouth.

She looked me over more than once. Like she wasn't trying to miss a bruise. I felt uncomfortably that I gave Dad an annoyed look.

Grandma looked at Dad and gave him a disgusted look as she told him, "Outside now."

After they went outside. I felt like I could breathe. I already had a long day. So when Dad came back in, he told me that Grandma left and asked if I wanted to turn on a movie. But back then, I didn't know if I could say no to him. While living with Mom, I could never say no without being in trouble. So I told Dad yes. But we didn't get far into the moving when Dad picked up on my tension. So, he turned it off, and we talked.

"Brook. Your mom is ill. It is nothing we did. She thinks different from we do."

I remember staring at Dad with a confused look. I didn't understand what he meant. But, I am sure it was hard to explain.

Because he wasn't getting anywhere with the conversation, he decided it was bedtime.

I was more excited about sleep than Dad was. See, while I was at Mom's, I didn't sleep well. So I hoped that I would get sleep being at Dads. However, I panic because I didn't have a bed there. Dad only pack one bag of my stuff and left the remaining behind. But he reassured me by telling me he or like his sister set up my room here.

A new place, a new room, and a new bed. That's a lot to take in when your only three years old.

The house was old and creaky. Between the odd noises and the shadows that lurked in the corner of my room. I didn't get sleep the first week while I was there.

I remember a morning when I woke up to the smell of pancakes. the sun shining into my room; It put a smile on my face.

Because Dad chased away all the "ghost" and kept me safe from all the strange noises. And I woke every morning feeling safe and to the smell of breakfast. My hero was back, and I didn't want to lose him again.

But it was also the day I got to meet rest of the family. Dad turned on a movie for me, gave me some toys and he cleaned the house. But no matter what he was doing, I kept a close eye on him.

It was around dinnertime when the family showed up but I was in the living room playing with toys and I wasn't paying attention. I stopped playing when I heard people talking behind me.

They confused me because I didn't understand why they were looking at me. I understood later why they were staring at me. Because I still had marks on me from Mom and her boyfriend beating me.

"Brook, I want you to meet Aunt Natalie and Uncle Jason. Aunt Natalie will watch you while I go to work." Dad said.

Dad and Aunt Natalie have similar looks with their blond hair and blue eyes. Except Dad was short stocky with a crew cut and a five o'clock shadow. Aunt Natalie is more on the heavier side with shoulder length hair, she had pinned back.

Uncle Jason's beard was fuller than Dads plus he was taller than Dad. Uncle Jason also had brown shaggy hair with brown eyes.

I shifted my eyes to the floor as I replied,

"Oh." Turned focus back to them. "Hi."

Said hi to Grandma again, got to meet my Grandpa.

He was bald with blue eyes, same body type as my Dad. Because he was older, he used a cane to walk around.

It was one of the best days of my life I haven't had in a while. And before I knew it, it was dinner time then bedtime.

Dad noticed that I have been having nightmares since I arrived. So he put me in therapy. I learned how to coupe and Dad learned how to help me.

Though I got diagnosed with, panic disorder, social anxiety disorder. GAD (General anxiety disorder), PTSD (Post-traumatic stress disorder).

While I was in therapy, Dad focused only on us, work, and therapy. He had to learn how to help but, he also was learning new things.

I went to therapy once a week up till my birthday in November.

Four months in when Dad saw I was getting better. We spent more time with the family. And because it was my first summer with them, they wanted to make it special and they did. They had the whole summer planned out. We went to playgrounds, the beach, the zoo, and taught me how to ride a bike. And if it was stormy outside, we went to the mall, to the movies, to the library, or simple stayed home and had a cookout.

Then November came, they made my birthday special. Plus, we celebrated the long haul through therapy. A week later it was Thanksgiving then Christmas. Aunt Natalie and Grandma showed me how to make Christmas cookies.

I remember laying on my bed on New year's Eve. I was a different boy then when Dad came to get me from Mom's. I had a wonderful year, life was great. And I prayed hard that I wouldn't have to go back to Mom's.

It was 1998, and I promised myself to make it the best. A new year, a new life. I may have only been four years old, but I also went through a lot compared to other kids my age.

I remember one day; I was sitting on the window bench watching the snow fall while I played quietly. Then Dad came to sit next to me.

"I have a late shift tonight. You will stay with Aunt Natalie's through the night. But first, we are going outside to play." He said with a smile.

I gave Dad a worried look. When I had to stay away from him for a night, I always went into a panic attack. Fearing the worse he wouldn't come back for me.

Now I laugh at myself worrying over something so small. But to my four-year-old self, it scared me.

I turned my worried look into a smile. Because I got to play outside with Dad before work.

You know when you're having fun, time seems to go by faster? Well, I had so much fun with Dad the time went by fast and we had to get ready.

When we got to Aunt Natalie's house. I hung on to Dad and wouldn't let him go.

"Brook, we go through every time. And I pick you up every day after dinner. Except for tomorrow I have a day off so I will get you after breakfast."

After Dad left, I felt sad, but I went to play with Aunt Natalie's dog. A Golden Retriever named, Princess. Played with her for a little, played with toys, and then it was dinnertime.

After eating dinner, and washing the dishes, we turned on a movie.

I remember trying to stay awake so I could watch the movie but I kept going crossed eye. I did finally fall asleep. And I woke screaming. I kept repeating, no, while I gripped the couch.

When I looked up, I saw Aunt Natalie standing in front of me. She knew what was going on. She read the terror that run across my face.

She pushed her hair behind her ear as she sat down next to me. Put her left arm around me and asked,

"Honey, do you want to talk about it?"

I didn't reply for five minutes. I stared at the ground in a daze.

Going to therapy helped me. I have only been away from Mom's for a year. Days were better for me then nights.

Dad knew it, Aunt Natalie knew it, and so did my grandparents. It concerned them all. They brought it up to my counselor, but he told them, continue with therapy and helping me through the hard times.

When I looked up to Aunt Natalie, I cried. And she held me tighter and kept on telling me how the whole family loves me and they are here for me and they will never leave me again. I eventually fell asleep.

But Princess woke me by licking my face. Though, Dad was already there, talking to Aunt Natalie. I could hear them from the couch.

I remember thinking, now what and that I felt ashamed of what happened the previous night. I thought about getting up and going to the kitchen but I waited on the couch for them to come in.

When they came in, Dad asked about last night.

"Can I ask what you had a nightmare about?"

I did not want to answer his question; I shook my head no.

"Okay. You're doing so good. I don't want to see you have a relapse."

I looked at him with an annoyed look as I asked,

"What is a relapse? I don't understand."

"It means going backwards. It will be okay. I promise." He smiled.

That summer, we did the same things as last year except for this time, because I am older, we went to the Kentucky derby. Which I thought it was cool. Watching the horses run made me what to run with them. When you run, you get this feeling you're free and I like that feeling. Mainly because I always ran away from Mom or her boyfriend so they could hurt me.

Fall came, and I played in the leaves. Halloween I dressed up like a horse. So I could run like them.

Then November came. Dad got a paper in the mail, stating that he needs to go to court on January 20 with Mom, to file for custody.

So, the family made sure that my birthday, Thanksgiving, and Christmas was extra special. And we all prayed that Dad will get custody. Because we didn't know if Mom changed or not. I recall over hearing Dad talking to his sister and parents saying he will do 50/50 custody if Mom has changed. But we all doubt it.

When the day came for Dad to go to court, Mom showed that she didn't change. But she told the judge an incorrect, sorrowful story, stating that Dad kidnapped me and she wants full custody.

But what the judge did wrong, she let her emotion decided for her. And because of her choice, I half to live in hell. But back then, we were all hoping she changed. Plus the judge put a retraining order on Dad till I was eighteen years old. That is 13 years of me not seen my dad.

We grabbed my stuff from dad's, said our goodbyes then Mom and I were on our way home. It made me sad to leave Dad and his family.

Chapter Two

Mom and I plus Willie

"Honey, I work Monday through Thursday, nine AM to four PM. You will go back into daycare. Willie will pick you up around, 2:30 and bring you home. From the time you get home, I want chores done. If the chores aren't done, there will be consequences. When you're finished, I want you to start dinner. Plus I want obedience, no talk back. Understood?"

"Willie?" I asked.

Mom glanced at me through the rearview mirror and replied,

"Yes. Willie, my boyfriend. Remember?"

"Yes. Surprised you're still with him." I replied sounding annoyed.

"But you do you understand the rules. Right?"

"Yes, I understand." I grumbled.

When we got home, Mom took me out of the SUV and with my things. Then we walked into the house.

I stood there at the entrance, looked around as I took a deep breath. I was back at Mom's and feared for my future.

"Brook, please go put your stuff in your room. I am going outside for a cigarette."

I looked up at her, gave her a nod then she walked outside.

I walked towards my room, walked in, and looked around. Not being at Mom's for two years, I figured she would have done something to my room but she didn't. It looked the same. Bed made, toys on the ground and the closet door opened. It reminded me like the time froze.

"Brook, honey, the house hasn't changed. Everything is still in its place. Look, the house needs cleaning, I will allow you to work on that. You have rest of the night and tomorrow before I bring you to daycare. If you don't finish all the work before we leave tomorrow, you will have double work when Willie drops you off. Plus, he's coming with a six-pack because I need a drink to relax."

I found it funny she knew what I was thinking. And she was right, the house didn't change. Only the atmosphere.

"That's why you had a cigarette. Why are you stressed if you won the battle?" I gave her a sarcastic smile. "I mean, I am glad you're giving me permission to clean the house tonight but aren't we both sharing the chores? Plus, it's my first day back. So relax a little. Why are you still with that jerk? He is half the problem that tore this family apart." I replied to her.

Mom stood there giving me a disbelief look.

With a scoff, she told me,

"Brook, I bring home the paycheck, you do the chores. And that "jerk" as you call him, has being here for me when your dad wasn't. Plus, I haven't had a drink or any drugs for thirty-six hours. I had to look decent for court. Remember?"

As soon she got done talking, I heard the entry door close. A two minutes passed when I saw a guy standing behind Mom. She looked over her shoulder than gave him a smile. He returned the smile then looked at me.

I remember Willie clear as day. I remember I felt angry. I didn't want to deal with him.

"This can't be Brook, could it? The last time I saw you, you were hiding in your sweatshirt trying to avoid looking at me. How did your Dad not notice that your guys waiter kept on smiling and looking ONLY at you, Brook." Willie told me with a hint of a taunting smile?

Then they left my room. But I watched them walk towards Mom's room.

The only thought popped in my head was, Mom hasn't changed and I shouldn't trust either of them.

It was five o'clock P. M by the time I wander to the living room than the kitchen to look around at the mess. Wash dishes, take out trash, wash and dry laundry and vacuum. My five-year-old self thought it was a huge task, so I cut the chores in half.

So, I went throughout the house and gathered the garbage and the dirty dishes. Took the garbage outside, started a load of clothes. Then washed the dishes.

I got all that done in two hours plus I could do the vacuuming in the morning.

I figured I should get ready for bed. Because I didn't know if Mom wanted me to make her breakfast or not. Plus, I still had chores to finish.

I went to tell Mom what I got done and told her I was off to bed. Mom told me she started work at 9:30 in the morning.

I had to get used to sleeping at Mom's house. Her house made less creaking noises than Dad's. Newer house verse an old house. Instead of being afraid of the shadows, the thought of Mom or Willie hurting me, frightened me more.

My alarm went off at seven A.M. I remember hitting the snooze button then rolling to my back and stared at the ceiling. It disappointed me I woke up at Mom's. I was hoping it was a bad dream and I would have woken in the safety of Dad's arms. So much for dreaming.

I got up, got dressed; walked out of my room towards the laundry room to start another load.

Walked towards the kitchen, grabbed the vacuum out of the hallway.

After vacuuming, I figured I could start breakfast. Instead, I stood in the kitchen perplexed. I did not know how to cook. So, She got cereal.

"Good morning Brook, the house looks nice. I have work at 9:30. We will leave after we get done eating." Mom told me.

"Where's Willie?" I asked.

"He's already at work."

Because we got done eating early, Mom wanted me to do the breakfast dishes before we left. I didn't understand why. She would make me clean the house when I got back from daycare. But I figured it was a smart choice not to argue with her.

After I did the dishes, it was around 8:30 we left. We only drive for a minute then we showed up at a house. It confused me then because I thought Mom was dropping me off at daycare. But this looked like

someone's house. But I learned you can have a in home daycare.

While we walked up to the door, a lady greeted us with a warm smile.

"Hello Suzie." Then the lady looks at me." Wow, this must be Brook. My I haven't seen him since he was little." The lady said.

"He has been at his Dad's for two years." Mom replied.

"Wow! Has it been that long? How is Nathaniel? How did court go?" The lady asked.

"You know what, Nathaniel didn't want him." Mom wept.

I shot Mom a disgusted look. She looked at me and patted my head to keep me quiet.

Her remark pissed me off. She is playing with June's emotion's, (The daycare lady.) Like she did with the judge. Dad wanted me but Mom had to make him look like the bad guy.

"For real? Oh, wow. That's, um, that's surprising. I was positive he would want Brook." The lady said in disbelief.

"Yeah, me too." Mom said while she was rubbing her left arm. "Look, I got to run. Willie, my boyfriend, will pick him up after work. Around two."

She leaned down to give me a goodbye hug. But I felt uncomfortable. I haven't lived with Mom for two years and when I did, she only abused me.

The daycare lady knelt down to my level, we both looked at each other.

She had brown skin instead of white like mine. Her hair was black, long and wavy. Her eyes were golden brown, hiding behind her hot pink glasses.

"Brook, I know this is all confusing to you, and you may not remember me. I am June. Come on, I will show you the toys and rest of the kids."

We walked into the living room as she called over a little girl.

That was a little taller than me and her skin was lighter than her moms but still dark compared to mine. She had hair like her mom except for the color. She had chocolate brown and her eyes were emerald green.

"Hillary, do you remember Brook? We haven't seen him for two years. Please make him feel welcomed."

I stood by the window by Hillary; I watched June walked into the kitchen.

And Hillary went to go play. When she wandered off, I sat down in the corner by the window. I was a shy child. I didn't know how to play with other kids. When I lived with Dad, I had no one my age to play with. The only time I played with kids my age was at the playground.

Anyway, twenty minutes passed and Hillary walked up towards me.

"Come on Brook, come play." She told me while she was trying to get me up.

I replied to her in an annoyed voice,

"No! I don't want to play, I want to go home."

I faced the wall because I didn't want to play.

"Brook, the other kids think your weird. I do too."

I looked back at her as I replied in a irritated way,

"So? Leave me alone!"

I turned from her. Then I overheard her telling the other kids I am shy and I don't know how to play with other kids.

She drove me nuts, but I also thought she was cute.

I got up to go to the kitchen. When I walked in, June asked me, how everything is going.

"I want to go home. Not to my mom's, I want to go to my dad's." I told her sounding upset.

"Oh hon. I am sorry. You will feel hurt and angry for a while but you will get pass this. Plus, I am sure it's hard being here." She replied.

"Yeah. Also, I am not in the mood to play with other kids. I want to be alone."

"Do you wanna talk about it?"

My thoughts were; Sure, I could tell her that my Mom lied in court and played with the judges emotion to get what she wanted so the judge based her decision from her past.

I shook my head no. Even if I told her that, would she believe me?

When Hillary walked into the kitchen, I grumbled.

I went to go sit the corner again. To think about: Mom, her boyfriend, Dad, and my future. I had a lot to think about.

"Brook?"

When I looked up, I saw Hillary looking at me.

"Yes?" I replied.

"I am sorry for teasing you."

I gave her a smile; she returned the smile.

For the remaining of the time, I kept to myself. Then, it was time to go. June called my name to let me know Willie was here.

Oh goody. Was my thoughts. Hoping I didn't have to deal with him.

I got up, got ready to leave. When I walked into the kitchen, I looked Willie over.

His brown shaggy hair, along with his five o'clock shadow with his piercing dark blue eyes. He stood there with his arms crossed his chest with an amused smile as he looked at me.

I gave him a half-hearted smile.

We told June bye and Willie thanked her.

Once at home, Willie unlock the door to go inside.

"Okay, here is the list of chores from your mother. She expects you to get them done before she gets home." Willie told me.

I look at him with a surprised look and replied,

"Chores? What chores? The house looks clean." I read over the list. "Is she serious?! I am five." I told Willie.

He shrugs his shoulders with a reply,

"I know. But it's your Mom's house rules, so follow them."

It shocked me. I cleaned the house last night and this morning. What more did she want?

"Well, I need to get going to my second job." Willie told me.

I quick glanced at the clock and replied,

"Wait. It's 2:30, and my Mom wants this down in Two hours and a half. Plus, your leaving me alone? You can't leave me. I am five, remember?"

Willie nodded at me with an annoyed look as he replied,

"Yes, Brook. I know you are five. You keep reminding me. I need to get to work. Like you do, buh-bye."

With a disbelief look on my face, I watched Willie walk out of the house.

I had two hours and a half to impress my mother. I couldn't finish all these chores in that short time frame. But I knew standing there in shock was wasting time. So I worked hard and did the best I could do.

I got most of the chores done minus laundry and dinner. So, I went to sit on the couch to take a break, then I looked at the clock, 4:15 P. M

Never mind. I had to get back up. Walked towards the laundry room to start another load. Walked back towards the kitchen to start dinner. Except I still didn't know how to make dinner. I made peanut butter, jelly sandwiches.

I set the table, made dinner, and put it on the table.

Glanced at the clock, five o'clock P. M. Looked at the door, then switched my focus to the table.

Then I heard Mom open the door. I closed my eyes, reminded myself to breathe then opened my eyes. I looked at her, cleared my throat and said,

"Hi Mommy. Dinner is ready. We are having PBJ's." I looked away from her. I felt ashamed because I didn't know how to cook.

I wanted to prove myself to her. ever since I was two. I felt like I wasn't good enough for her. And I was causing her to be mean.

I looked back at her, waiting for her feedback. Kept my eyes on her while she walked around the breakfast bar. When she stopped in front of the table, she gave me a smile; I returned the smile.

"Sit down. We need to talk."

I sat down across from her and replied,

"Yes? Got everything done that you wanted me to do. I am still finishing the laundry."

"I appreciate that. Plus, Willie will need to teach you how to cook." She picked up the sandwich and looked at it in disgust. "Because I don't want peanut butter sandwiches." She gave me an unhappy look while putting the sandwich back on the plate. "Anyway, Willie called me after I got off of work. You were questioning him?"

I exhaled while pushing my plate away. Not questioning him, was questioning Mom.

Leaned back in my chair and looked away from her.

"Yes, I questioned. But I wasn't being rude or anything," I looked back at Mom, "I am five, Mom. One, I shouldn't be alone by myself. Two, at my age, I shouldn't be doing all the chores you told me to do in that short time frame." I replied to Mom.

Mom shrugged her shoulders and got up and walk towards the hall. She turned to look at me as she replied,

"I am not hungry."

I sat there staring at my plate. Thinking our talk could have gone better.

I got up to get the kitchen re-picked up. After the kitchen, I went to finish the laundry.

"Brook,"

I turned to look at Mom.

"My friends will be over in a half an hour."

I nod in agreement. Then she left the room.

My first thought was; I am going into the closet.

In the past when Mom had her friends over, she would put me in there.

But the house was clean; the laundry almost finished. I went to sit in my room till Mom called me or came to get me. After sitting for three hours, I heard a knock on the door.

It was eight o'clock P. M. I went to go open my door and there stood Mom and Willie.

I gave them a confused look as I asked,

"Can I help you with something?"

They both smiled

"My dear Brook, Come out here, please." Mom told me.

And the fun begins, they already had a drink or two.

I nodded and followed them out to the living room.

When we walked into the living room, everyone stopped and looked at us.

"We won the battle!" Willie told everyone sounding excited.

And every one in union told Mom and Willie, congratulation.

"Let me introduce him to y'all, this is Brook Harold. If you need any help with anything, call his name." Mom added.

"Because we own him!" Willie said while excited.

They own me? I felt concerned. I didn't know what they meant back then.

I watched Mom and Willie walk away. I stood there unsure what to do. Should I stay or should I leave?

A few minutes passed, when one guy answered that for me, as he was hollering at me.

His rough voice startled me and I gave him a nervous look instead of helping him.

"Hey, stupid boy, instead of staring at me, go get me another drink. Annie, (My Mom's nickname.) said we can control you." This guy demanded me.

This guy's appearance showed that he was tough. Had a leather jacket on with a purple dress shirt tucked in his dark blue jeans. His voice was deep and raspy along with his piercing dark blue eyes. He had a Mohawk that was jet black.

I gave him yet another nervous look and replied with,

"Y-yes, sir."

While I was walking towards the kitchen, I thought to myself that's not exactly what Mom said..

Grabbed the beer walked it back to this guy.

Lucky me, I became the snack/drink delivery boy until one - thirty AM. I would rather be in the closet. At least I could sleep.

Never mind for sleep. Who needs sleep? Not Brook Harold that's who. I thought to myself.

Mom only wanted me to be her little puppet.

before I could go to bed, I had to make the guest beds. It was 2:15 A.M by the time I made it to my room. But I didn't go to bed, I sat on my bed thinking about my future?

I woke up looked around. My light is still on. I don't remember falling asleep. I looked at my clock, eight o'clock A.M.

Got out of bed; walked out to the living room, everyone was still asleep.

My cooking skills hasn't approved since yesterday. And I don't want to give Mom and her friends cereal nor PBJ's.

I walked into the kitchen thinking what to make.

Dad made pancakes a lot while I was there. Maybe I could try making them from memory of helping Dad.

I attempted but nope. I set off the smoke alarm by burning the pancakes instead.

I stood there covering my ears unsure what to do because I couldn't reach the smoke alarm.

CHAPTER THREE

COOKING LESSONS

"Brook Harold Susie! What the hell are you doing?!" Mom questioned me in a panic.

I stood there watching her take down the alarm.

I did a quick glance towards the living room, realizing that everyone was staring at us with a furious look.

Looked back at Mom while uncovering my ears, as I replied,

"I-I-I was t-trying to m-make b-breakfast, that wasn't cereal nor peanut butter sandwiches."

Mom gave me a cross look, while she told me,

"Willie needs to teach you how to cook. Look, go into your room. I will figure out breakfast."

I gave her a nod and went to my room.

If there was one way to ask for a whipping without asking, set off the smoke alarm while everyone has a hangover. You'll get your butt kicked.

I sat in my room for two to three hours. I figured everyone went back to bed.

When Mom came into my room, we gave each other the same tired look.

"Everyone left." She clicked her tongue. "Um, the house needs cleaning and we will talk later. When I am in a better mood."

After she left my room, I looked out my window.

What is her better mood? I thought to myself.

Anyway, I went to go clean the house.

Four maybe five hours later, I got the house cleaned.

I ate nothing all day, and it was dinner time. Yet, I had to do more cleaning before I could eat.

When Mom said my name, I spun around in surprised. I was thankful she ignored how quick I was to answer.

"Because you do not know how to cook, Willie and I are going out for dinner. "Mom said.

"And what can I have for dinner? I haven't eaten all day. I have been helping you or in my room." I told Mom.

"That's a shame. Oh, please clean my room. Plus, we will talk when I get home."

I stood there watching her walk out with Willie. Jeez Mom, thanks for caring. Wait a minute, If she and Willie were in the room all day, why didn't they clean it.

I went to do Mom's room. But when I walked in, it looks like she had a tornado go through it. Clothes everywhere, empty beer cans, and what's this? Needles? Okay? Why do they have needles?

First the house, now her room. What's next? The yard?

I took almost two hours to get Mom's room done. Two hours!

I finally got around to dinner. And it was the best damn delicious peanut butter, jelly sandwich. Screw Mom and Willie with their fancy dinner. I worked hard for this sandwich.

Around eight o'clock PM, I was thinking Mom and Willie should have been home by now. Unless they are sitting at the bar, then they will come home late. Because that's what happen in the past.

I went to turn a movie and lay down on the couch. I am so tired I thought to myself as I closed my eyes.

I heard a faint voice calling my name. Trying to wake myself for two minutes, or at least what it felt like.

When I opened my eyes to see Mom looking at me. I groaned and asked,

"What?"

"Sit up." Mom told me, sounding eager.

"What time is it?"

"Midnight."

"Then why are waking me? I am sleepy."

"Darn. Get up."

I gave her an angry look and replied,

"All right, all right. I am up. What do you want?"

"I want to talk. How are you? How was your day?"

I gave her a skeptical look, and asked,

"Are you okay, Mom?"

She chuckled to herself as she looked away.

A minute later, I saw Willie come stumbling in.

Oh great, they are both drunk. I groaned while rolling my eyes in disgust; I got up walked towards the hallway, throw my hands in the air, and told them,

"I am going to bed you two are on your own. Goodnight."

I hurried to my room as fast as I could.

Shut the door behind me and leaned against my door.

I can hear them laughing from the other room. Sigh.

I slid down and sat there waiting for them to go into Mom's room.

Half an hour passed when They walk past my door.

Thank goodness, they went to bed. That's one thing I didn't miss when I lived at Dad's.

Mom coming home drunk.

I didn't know it then, but I was becoming their little servant.

The next morning I rolled over to look at my clock; nine o'clock A.M.

I didn't want to get up, but I knew I had to, because I had to make breakfast.

Which I still don't know how to cook.

Did they want cereal? No. Did they want peanut butter, jelly sandwiches? I doubt it.

They could make their own damn food.

I got up and made myself a bowl of cereal. Then turned on the T.V.

An hour later I heard one of them walking down the hall.

"Brook Harold. Where's breakfast?"

When I look over towards the hallway, I saw Willie.

"I don't know how to cook. Remember? And I was positive you two didn't want PBJ'S or cereal." I replied to him.

21

"(Sigh). No, we don't. I will have to teach you how to cook. Because, we can't live off of peanut butter sandwiches nor cereal. But your Mom and I will go out for breakfast first. Once we get back home, your classes will begin." Willie told me.

I nodded as I watched him walk away.

Joyous. Willie teaching me how to cook. This should be fun. Note the sarcasm.

Half an hour passed, and they walked into the living room.

"Brook, honey. Please clean my room, again." Mom told me as they were walking out.

I sat there staring at the T.V as I heard the door shut.

"Great! I am hoping it won't take me as long this time." I said to myself out loud.

When I walked into Mom's room and look around, it wasn't that bad. Since I cleaned it the day before.

On the positive note, I took less time cleaning it.

So, I went back to watching T.V. for an hour.

After I got done watching T.V, I went to sit at the kitchen table waiting for them to come home. Thinking they should be home soon.

Yeah, three hours passed before I heard them pull up.

"Okay, Brook, we stop at the grocery store to get supplies, so Willie can teach you how to cook." Mom told me sounding all excited.

I sat at the table, resting my chin in my hands, I gave them a tired look. Mom wandered towards her bedroom, then I re- look at Willie.

"All right lets get started." Willie told me.

I still sat there looking at him for another five minutes. Just looking him over.

I got up and walked towards him.

The first hour in, I am sure we were both thinking what's the point of these lessons, because it was hopeless. Or at least my thoughts were this. We weren't getting anywhere.

"The cooking lesson isn't hopeless Brook. So stop thinking it. You are stupid that's the problem." Willie replied.

Again with the mind reading. First Mom, now him.

I shot him an enraged look, while I replied,

"I will not be the greatest chef within an hour. I am trying."

We both sighed and Willie told me,

"Fair enough. But you need to learn."

"How's it going with the lesson?"

When we both looked over, we saw Mom standing by the breakfast bar.

"Your son is dumb. To be honest," Willie let out a long sigh. "I believe we are not getting anywhere." Willie told Mom.

"I am not dumb nor stupid. I need practice more than cramming it all in one day." I told him while clenching my teeth.

Willie looked back at me while replying,

"Right. Look, Brook, I need a break."

My thought was; He needed a break? It has only been an hour; I needed the break. So, we took a break... Clear my throat. Correction, Willie took the break. I got sent to do chores.

I chuckled to myself with a hint of a smile. Go figure.

According to Mom, the house was a mess. In surprise, I looked around the living room, I don't know where she could see this "mess" but I went to go clean this "magic mess."

I walked around the house looking busy, till Willie came out to finish the lesson.

"Okay, we will start at the top. Again. Because your Mom distracted me." Willie told me.

I rolled my eyes at him. Because making out with your girlfriend is much more important that teaching me how to cook.

"And this time around, no name calling." I replied to him with a smile.

"Whatever. Let's get started."

So we tried again and this time we got somewhere.

"We got somewhere, four hours later. But we got somewhere. I will go check on your Mom." Willie told me.

I looked away from him to look at the clock then re-looked back at him and asked,

"Dinner? It's two hours pass Dinner."

"We got left overs from your mistakes."

"True."

"So, figure something out. You're a smart boy." He said with a hint of a smile.

I watched him walk down the hall towards Mom's room.

"So, figure something out. You're a smart boy." I mocked him.

If I was so smart, then why did he call me stupid? I had to figure out what to make. There was a mixture of breakfast, lunch, and dinner. I made them a buffet. They can figure it out. It's all the mistakes I made.

Twenty minutes later, I saw Mom and Willie come down the hallway.

"Dinner is ready." Then I looked away, and I looked back up at them. "Bedtime snack is ready." I said with a nervous laugh.

Standing by the sink, I watched them get their plate of food. I bit down on my bottom lip while I watched them take their first bite.

"Not bad for beginners. Thank you, Willie for teaching my impossible son how to cook." Mom said.

"It was my honor to help." Willie said with a smile.

Then they both looked at me with a smile. I sighed in relief.

"If you don't need me any more, I will be in my room." I told them

"Honey, if you want some, grab a plate." replied Mom.

In surprise, I stood there looking at both, and asked,

"Are you sure? I don't want to be a bother."

"Come sit down Brook Harold. That's an order." Willie told me firmly.

How was that an order? I thought to myself.

So, I grabbed a plate and sat down with them. Because it was an order. Yes, still mocking Willie.

When we finished eating, Mom mentioned that they were planning to go see a movie after lunch tomorrow.

So they wanted lunch made early. Then they went to their room.

And I got the kitchen re-picked up plus the living room. After cleaning, I went to bed. It has been a long day.

The next day, Sunday morning, I tried to make breakfast. This time, the way Willie taught me.

Except, I set off the smoke alarm.... AGAIN!! Why I would I learn anything.

I covered my ears, and I saw Willie come out this time. I looked at him and mouthed the words, "Sorry."

Willie sighed, took down the smoke alarm and asked me,

"Brook Harold!? For real? I," He pointed to himself. "taught you how to make them, not burn them."

I uncovered my ears as I put my arms to my side while looking down at the floor.

I felt ashamed. Willie spent half the day teaching me and I failed him.

"(Sigh) I will make breakfast for your Mom and I." Willie told me.

I looked up at him while I replied,

"What about me? Do I get breakfast?"

I watched Willie looking around the kitchen and handed me a box of cereal.

"Cereal? I get cereal?" I asked while taking the box out of his hand.

Willie gave me a big smile then proceeds with making breakfast.

I couldn't complain, I got out of cooking.

I ate my cereal while Willie finished up cooking.

"Can you pick up the kitchen?" Willie asked me.

I gave him a confused look then gave him a smile.

"Mm-hm. Yes, I can." I replied to him.

"Thank you."

I watched Willie grab the tray of food while leaving the room.

While I put my bowl in the sink, I realized there was a note on the counter for me.

It read; what to make for lunch and the chores for the day.

After breakfast, I got half the chores done.

Then Willie helped me with lunch. After lunch, Willie and Mom were about to leave.

"Thank you for lunch Willie and Brook." Mom told us with a smile.

"Don't expect us for at least six hours. We are planning to grab dinner after the movie." Willie told me.

I nodded in agreement.

After they left, I finished the chores.

Then went to watch a movie I fell asleep to.

When I woke up, I looked at the clock then realized it was dinnertime. Got up made myself food.

By six thirty PM, Mom came home.

"Hi Brook. Where's the list so I can do a look over?" Mom asked me.

I handed her the list. But Willie is not here.

"Mom, where's Willie?" I asked

"He's at his apartment." Mom replied while she was looking at the list.

"Oh, didn't know he had his own place."

"Yep. He is waiting for the lease to be up, so he can move in here."

"Oh. Okay."

Then Mom walked away to look around the house while marking off the list.

About ten minutes later, Mom walked back into the living room.

"Everything looks nice. Though, you need to learn how to dust a little better."

I gave Mom an annoyed look, as I replied,

"Again Mom, I am five. I am trying my best."

"Try harder. I want none mistakes. I don't want to follow you around the house making sure your picking up after yourself. Got it?"

"Are you serious? I am trying. I have only been here for at least three days. Give me time. Plus, if I am doing all the chores, why would you have to follow me around the house to make sure I am picking up after, "myself"?"

Mom gave me a surprised look and replies,

"I had to right now! You didn't do the dusting, Brook! I don't want to come home to a messy house. And leaving dust everywhere, is being messy."

"It went from being, you left dust to you never dusted? Help me understand, do you want me to be perfect? That way you won't have to follow me around the house?"

"Yes! Not one mistake, Brook Harold. It's your job to keep up the house not mine. Willie and I pay the bills, pay for the clothes on your back, and the food. That's what my daddy always told me."

"Then don't worry about the house. Stop over reacting, Mom! Remember I am five. Give me a break. Dad wouldn't care if the house is mess.. But then again, you don't care about me. Like Dad does."

At that moment, she struck me. I guess I said something to piss her off.

"Don't you ever compare me to your father! He ran away when times got hard between the two of us. And if he cared for you so much, then why the hell are you living here!" She told me in a stern voice.

"Is this how your daddy treated you too? By slapping you?" I asked while I gave her an angry look.

Then she stormed off.

Again with the whole trying to prove to her I can do it..

CHAPTER FOUR

IT STARTS. AGAIN

The next morning I went to daycare with a black eye.

With my hoodie up, I walked in keeping my focus to the floor.

"Hi Suzie. Hi Brook." June greeted us as we walked in.

Standing by Mom, still looking down, I replied with a,

"Hi".

"Again, Willie will pick Brook up anywhere around two o'clock. Thank you again." Mom told June.

Then Mom got down to my level and whispered,

"Please remove your hoodie and have a nice day. I love you."

She gave me a kiss on my head while she was getting up.

I shot her an enraged look while she was leaving.

I walked into the living room and scanned the room. Then I noticed a new kid, or at least to me.

We made eye contact then I immediately looked away. Hoping he wouldn't walk up to me.

"Hi! I am Jeorge, (George). Who are you? I haven't seen you here before." He told me.

I glanced at him, then looked away, and replied,

"Same. I am Brook."

"Um, what happened to your eye, Brook?" Jeorge asked me.

When I heard his question, my eyes widen, my heart stopped. I was trying to pull over my hoodie more, so I could stay hidden.

"I... Um... I fell." I replied.

I then hurried away from him.

Because I was looking down, I ran into Hillary. I groaned at the sight of her.

"Brook, Hi!"

I watched her smile disappear to a trouble look.

"What happen to your eye?"

"Oh, my god. You too? I fell, okay. Everyone is this room, I fell! Don't ask me about it!" As I growled at everyone.

I realized that my action surprised all the kids.

Then June called me into the kitchen.

Great, I mumbled to myself.

I walked into the kitchen to see what she wanted.

"Brook, I only heard Hillary and Jeorge ask you, not the other kids. Plus, you can't tell me you fell or you won't be acting grumpy. So, what happened, honey?"

I gave her an annoyed look, and replied,

"Have you thought maybe I don't feel good? (Sigh) Like I told Hillary and Jeorge, I fell."

I looked away from her because I felt my eyes getting watery. I was trying to blink the tears away.

"Brook. (Sigh), Brook, please look at me."

I looked back at her and replied along with sniffles,

"Can I go now?"

She told me to go play.

I got up from the kitchen chair and walked towards the living room.

When I walked back into the livingroom, I saw Hillary and Jeorge plus the other kids looking at me.

"What?" I asked them with a sniffle.

"We are all worried." Replied Hillary.

I gave her a cross look, while I replied,

"You sound like your mother. (Sigh) I am fine. I want to be by myself."

I walked over to the corner window to sit.

Where I was re-thinking about last night.

She didn't like me telling her the truth. That's why she slapped me.

I looked at rest of the kids.

June was right. Only Hillary and Jeorge asked, not the other kids.

When I first saw Jeorge, I thought he looked and sounded funny.

At different times, Hillary and Jeorge were trying to get me to play, but I didn't want to play. I was happy playing by myself.

When June called us in for lunch, I was supper excited. Not for lunch but I get to go home in two hours.

After lunch, June turned on a movie for us. While all the kids gathered in a group, I kept to myself.

"Brook, why don't you join the group?"

I looked up at June and replied,

"I don't want to. I don't want to be here. Plus, I want to go home."

I turned my focus back to my hands.

"You've had your sweatshirt on since you gotten here. You must be warm."

I looked back at her with a stern look, with my teeth clenched, and replied,

"I don't want my sweatshirt off. I don't want to be in the group. I also want to be by myself."

I changed my focus to the T.V. After watching T.V. for a bit, Hillary walked up to me.

I grumbled while I asked her,

"Yes?"

"Do you want company?" She asked me.

"Sure, but I am not talking."

We sat together watching the movie till forty minutes into the movie. Then Hillary got up to sit with the group again.

I thought she would never leave.

By the end of the movie, June came to let me know Willie was here.

Finally! I hurried from the corner where I was sitting, to the kitchen.

"Let's go, right now. I am ready." I told Willie

Willie looked at June for an explanation.

"He didn't want to be here. Plus, He has been grumpy and keeping to himself. He also ate no lunch." June told Willie.

"Ah. I see. All right. Thank you, June. Come on Brook, lets get you home."

While Willie was helping me into the car, he asked me,

"Are you that eager to get home?"

"No, and yes. Everyone was asking me about my.." I looked away from Willie. "My eye."

"Oh. Did you talk back to Su, err, your Mom?"

I gave Willie a disgusted look, and he laughed to himself.

When we got home, Willie gave me last weeks speech. Blah blah blah. Can we move on now?

How exciting, more chores.

"You better get this list done or the kids will ask you what happened" Willie told me.

I looked down at the list in my hand, I replied,

"Hm, I can only use, I fell once."

When I looked up at Willie, he was laughing to himself.

"Yes?" I asked

"You fell? That's a lame excuse."

"Should I have said my Mom hit me?"

"No. That would be a bad choice. Look, I got to get to work. See ya later."

I waved him out with a reply,

"Yeah, yeah. Bye."

I walked around the house to see what I had to do.

I swear, this lady must purposely make a mess so I will have something to clean!

Any-who, I got to work right away.

Cleaned the bathroom, living room, and kitchen. Did the laundry, plus the dishes.

This time, I made sure I left no dust behind. I chuckled to myself while I smiled.

I trained myself that speed and accuracy was my friend. It was the only way I could get her ridiculous list of chores done in a short time.

Dinner time was always fun to plan. Trying to decided what to make them.

Spaghetti, that was easy. Plus, it's not peanut butter, jelly sandwiches.

I chuckled to myself, yeah.

If Mom is not happy about it. (Minute pause) Then she might have to tell me what she wants. But I was proud of myself.

At five o'clock P.M, Mom walked into the house. I was in the kitchen smiling at her while she shut the door behind her.

Mom looked around the room, then back at me and asked,
"What?"

"I made you something that is not a peanut butter sandwich nor did I burn the food." I replied to her with a smile.

"Good. I will be right back, let me go change out of my work clothes."
"Okay."

After she left the room, I dropped my smile. I was still not happy with her. She shouldn't have hit me. I only told her the truth.

Sigh, I sat down at the table waiting for her to come out of her room. After five minutes, when I saw Mom walking down the hallway, I rose to my feet.

She gave me a smile; I returned the smile, and we both grabbed our plates then I sat down. Mom grabbed her whiskey before she sat down.

"I got everything done that you wanted me to get done. Is there anything else I should take care of?" I asked her.

"I will have to look over the list after dinner, then let you now." Replied Mom before she took a drink.

"Okay."

We finished dinner, and we sat at the table longer. Mom lit a cigarette while she finished her drink.

A few minutes passed then Mom went to check off the list, like yesterday.

I re-picked up the kitchen, plus got the dishes done.

I was drying the last dish, so I can put it away, I saw Mom leaning on the breakfast bar. But she looked puzzled, I asked if everything was okay.

I saw her write something down, then she walked around the breakfast bar towards me.

Mom showed me the list while she was pointing to it and told me,
"You never cleaned my room."

I looked at her puzzled then back to the list, while I replied,

"I... It.. It was never on the list." I looked back at her, "Now it is, because you wrote it there."

"Oh?" She looked at me with a surprised look. "Are you telling me I am lying?"

Before I could speak, she grabbed me by my shirt and spun me 180 degrees and tossed me into a counter. I let out a yelp as I slid to the ground.

She got into my face, shoved the list at me.

"It says it right there! Do you see it?! Do you?! No!" She shoves the list even closer to my face.

I had tears running down my face; I kept trying to look away, but she kept forcing me to look at the list.

"Look, Brook Harold! Look! It says to clean my room!"

I saw her bring her hand up; I closed my eyes tightly and pleaded for her not to hit me again.

"God Brook, we went over this yesterday!"

I heard her grumble, so I opened my eyes to look at her. When I did, she was looking at me with fire in her eyes with her arms crossed.

Mom's glaring felt like forever. In reality, it was only five minutes.

She told me in a quiet voice,

"Look, I need my weed plus another drink. Please go clean my room."

I watched her grab her things while she was leaving the kitchen.

Still crying, I sat there for two minutes. To calm myself down so I wouldn't go into hyperventilating.

When I looked over towards the table, I saw that she dropped the list on the floor. I reached over to pick it up. I looked at it for a moment, then got up.

On my way out of the kitchen, I put it on the counter.

I walked into Mom's room, looked around.

I didn't know what she was complaining about; the room isn't that messy.

"The room looks nice honey." Mom told me while patting me on my head as she walked past me.

I felt confused. I didn't clean her room yet. Nor was she outside that long to have a smoke.

I watched her collapse on the bed while she closed her eyes.

"If you don't need me, I will be in my room."

"Brook, before you leave,"

"Yes?"

"What do you mean by your comment of, don't hit you? Would I ever hit you?"

I looked at her with a puzzled look. I knew better not to argue since she already threw me into the counter plus she has had two drinks.

"No, ma'am." I told her with a smile.

I walked out of her room towards my room.

Before I entered my room, I saw Willie walk in the house.

"You okay? You have a grumpy look." Willie asked me.

I gave him an angry look while replied,

"If you want to know any information, go talk to your girlfriend."

I walked into my room and collapsed on my bed.

Before I went to live with my Dad, Mom's beatings, her threats didn't bother me because I had hope. Those past days, I lost that hope.

CHAPTER FIVE

BAD DAY FOR ALL THREE

January ended. February came and went, along with March, April, and May. Then it was June.

Still taking care the house, no heavy beatings, only slaps to the face or backhand.

Occasionally will show up to daycare with a black eye or a fat lip, sometimes both. Hillary and / or Jeorge would ask me what happened. I always got grumpy with those two goofballs. Then June always brought me into the other room, to ask me what's wrong. When she asked me, I fell apart.

The question I always asked mom but got no answers was, if you're going to beat me up, why send me to daycare?

Anyway, depending what Mom told me the previous night, I would get up a little extra early the next day.

I remember one morning was not my morning. Because everything that could go wrong, did.

First, I woke up late. I had to be up at six o'clock A.M, but I got up at six thirty.

That morning I had to be up early to clean the house before daycare. Why? Because Mom was dumb and had a party on a work night.

Second, when I went to turn on the dryer, it wouldn't start! I tried to see what was wrong with it but after fumbling with it and still couldn't get it going, I left it for Mom or Willie.

I figured one of them had to call the repairman. I still had to clean the living room, the kitchen, and make breakfast, within a short time.

Which I could handle if Mom wasn't so damn prissy and if her expectation weren't so high.

I got the cleaning done, but it wasn't perfect. I had to start breakfast. Though, what I wanted to make is out of my reach.

So, I had to grab the step stool from the closet, bring it back to the kitchen. So I could grab the oatmeal from the top shelf. Even with the stepstool, I was still too short. I stood on my tippy toes to help, but I pushed the oatmeal off.

I stood there looking at the mess in horror. Like what would Mom do if she saw this mess?

I had to stop staring and get this cleaned up. I hurried off the stepstool, rushed to put it back in the closet, I grabbed the broom and dustpan and rushed back to the kitchen.

Even though I was going fast, I wasn't fast enough. I heard Mom walking down the hallway.

I froze. My heart raced, my hands sweated while holding onto the broom.

I dropped the broom and dustpan and dropped to my knees. Thinking it would go faster if I used my hand. "Brook Harold Susie! What the hell are you doing?!"

I closed my eyes tightly. I thought it was a good idea till Mom yelled at me. Stupid logic of mine.

While getting up, I told her,

"I-I was trying to grab the oatmeal from the top shelf, and I pushed it off by mistake."

"This house needed to be clean this morning, Brook Harold!" She growled at me while clenching her teeth.

I slowly backed up till I ran into the table which was behind me.

Mom's blood-shot eyes had fire in them while she stared at me.

I took a deep swallow as I replied,

"I am s-sorry, Mom. Minus the mess on the floor plus the dishes, it's clean."

I looked at her briefly then changed my look to the floor.

A moment passed before I looked back up at Mom while she was grabbing the belt.

I remember I felt helpless. My heart raced harder.

With a grim look, Mom told me to turn around and lean over the table.

I gave her a fearful, pleading look. She signaled me to turn around with her finger.

I closed my eyes as I exhaled while turning around.

I felt her lifting my shirt up. Not even a second later, she struck me.

I let out a whimper. Each sting was torture. I felt like my back was on fire.

I kept doing quick and short breaths as the tears ran down my face.

I yelled at Mom to stop.

When she stopped, I turned to face her.

"I am. I am s- sorry." I told her through sobs as I dropped to the floor. I sobbed at her feet. I begged for mercy.

I was on the floor for; I am guessing for five minutes before Mom told me to stand up.

I got up off the floor still crying as I asked,

"Yes?"

I watched her walk back and forth. Like she was thinking of what to say.

"You can't go to daycare now. (Sigh) Looks like you're on your own today, kiddo. Plus, make sure this house is clean by the time I get home."

"Y- yes ma'am."

After mom left the room, I went to clean up the oatmeal. It was hard to do with my whole body shaking. I took ten minutes to get the mess picked up.

"Bye sweetheart. Have a good day." Mom told me while she was leaving the house.

Still sitting on the kitchen floor, I thought to myself; she looked awful happy.

Because she looked happy, I questioned myself. Did I make it up in my head? Is this a nightmare?

I went to sit on the couch to think. To get my head clear.

The six months living with Mom, she never used the belt on me. The worst she has done was giving me a black eye or a fat lip, or a bloody nose or all three. Sometimes she would push me into the wall. But never whipped me before.

To be honest, she overreacted that morning for it being spilt oatmeal. She didn't even let me explain myself.

I was nervous to see Mom later that day. I was afraid that she would strike me again.

I thought about laying down for a nap. I was up late with Mom and her buddies then up early. Plus, the whipping drained me.

When I laid down in my bed. I couldn't get comfortable. I felt like my back was still on fire. Every way I laid it stung.

When I found a comfortable spot, I stretched with a yawn as I closed my eyes.

Two hours later, I woke from my nap. I groaned, my back was so sore.

I figured I should go pick up the house again. Even though it's clean, but I needed to stay on Mom's good side. But, before chores, I needed lunch.

When I walked into the kitchen to make a peanut butter sandwich... I soon found out we had no peanut butter. So I went to go find something else to eat, but that idea ended too.

Since Mom had to go grocery shopping, I started chores.

I did a deep clean of that house. I vacuumed every room. I scrubbed the bathroom floors, and the kitchen till the floors shined. I did the dishes. Clear throat. Because I never got them done this morning which was half of Mom's issue.

Any way, I was feeling proud of myself. The house looked clean. Except the laundry wasn't. I figured I would tell Willie about it but when three - thirty rolled around, he never showed. So I had to tell Mom about it.

I figured I should make dinner better than I had in the past. That way I could tell her about the dryer. Hoping she wouldn't kill me.

Dinner was ready by four - fifty and I sat at the table playing with my hands till she came home.

Mom always got home at five o'clock expecting dinner to be on the table. At five, not a second passed five. If dinner wasn't on the table when she walked through the door, oh hell, it would piss her off.

I was super nervous to tell Mom about the dryer. I would have told Mom before she left for work but if I got a whipping because the house wasn't clean. my young self had thoughts racing through my mind.

It was five o'clock P.M when I heard Mom pull up. I went to look out the kitchen window because it didn't sound like her car. That's because she had Willie's truck.

When Mom walked in, I was still by the window. We looked at each other, and then I looked out the window.

"My dear Brook. How are you?"

I looked back at her while I gave her an angry look.

"What is the look for?"

"I gave you a look because I am still not happy. I am angry. I am scared. Mom, you have never come at me like that before."

"Oh. I am sorry." Mom clicked her tongue. "Look, I had too much to drink last night, and I woke with a pounding headache. I haven't felt good all day. Yes, the house was clean," She looks around the kitchen / living room. "It looks re-clean, but the kitchen wasn't. There was cereal on the floor and the dishes were still dirty."

I shrugged my shoulders as I replied,

"I am sorry. Wasn't' trying to make a mess. I was trying to make breakfast. To be fair, I was cleaning the mess up," I pointed to Mom. "When you walked in. I even tried to explain to you. But you didn't care for what I told you."

Mom replied with a tired look,

"I am not hungry. Eat, don't eat. I don't care. I will be in my room. Willie will be here soon."

Humph, whatever. I thought to myself.

An hour passed when I realized I forgot to tell her about the dryer.

"Brook Harold! Where is your Mother?"

I turned around in surprise to see Willie standing behind me.

"In her room." I said as I pointed down the hall. "P- plus I need to talk to you." I anxiously told him.

"Don't move. I will be right back." Willie told me with a stern voice while pointing to me.

"Oh. Okay."

I wasn't certain if I should move or not. So, I stood in the living room waiting till he came back out. Because I didn't want to get into trouble again.

But if I knew I would have been standing there for almost two hours, I wouldn't have.

When Willie came out, he gave me a confused look and asked,

"What are you doing, Brook?"

I looked at him and replied,

"You told me not to move. And the way you came into this house yelling my name, I wasn't sure if I should."

Willie laughed to himself and replies,

"Brook, move. Get lost."

"Okay."

I headed towards my room when I remembered I needed to talk to him.

"Oh, Willie?" I said as I turned around to look at him.

"Hm. What?" He replied looking tired.

I gave him a nervous smile and told him the dryer was not working.

"What?! The dryer isn't working?" Willie asked.

"I couldn't' get it to turn on. I figured I should leave it alone for you or mom to take care of."

"Great!" He threw he hands in the air. "First the car now the dryer. Sigh. Okay, thank you."

That is why Mom had his truck.

After I got to my room, I looked at my clock and was grateful it was almost bedtime.

An hour later, Willie called me from the other room.

I wandered to the living room to see what he wanted.

"Yes? What can I help you with?" I asked

"When did the dryer stop working? Do you know? Mom asked me.

I looked over at Mom while I replied,

"Yes, ma'am. I couldn't get it to go before you got out of bed."

"Why didn't you tell me this morning about it? We could have gotten it fix sooner."

"I would have told you but I got into trouble because I spilled the cereal and because I didn't get the dishes
done."

"Why didn't you tell me when I got home?" Asked Willie.

I looked over at Willie and replied,

"You came in yelling my name like I was in trouble. I said I had to talk to you. No, I didn't tell you right away but after you came back out to the living room, I told you."

I was getting nervous with all the questions so I started to tap my foot.

"Well, Brook," Willie said while getting off the couch. "You could have told one of us sooner so we won't be in this mess." Willie chuckles to himself. "But, in reality Brook, you are in the mess. Why you may ask because we both have had a long day at work. We are both tired from last night."

"We also had too much to drink since Willie has gotten home." Mom pitched in with a giggle.

I looked over towards Mom then back at Willie.

"Yes, I could have told Mom this morning. But Mom, I got." A short pause while I looked away. Then I looked at her. "I got a whipping because of dump cereal. What would you have done if I told you about the dryer?" I looked over at Willie. "Willie, you didn't walk in here all nice asking where Mom was. Again, I told you about the dryer. I am sorry that I didn't tell you both sooner." I told them both feeling tense.

"Because you didn't want to tell us, you are now in trouble." Willie told me while backing me into a corner.

"For what?! Because I didn't tell Mom right away? And I didn't tell you right away?" I asked in a panic as the sweat dripped off my forehead.

Willie gave me an evil grin. I stood there in fear looking at him.

When I looked down, I saw him taking off his belt.

"NO! I already had that done. Want to see my back for proof?" I told Willie while trying to take the belt away from him.

But we played tug of war with the belt instead. I eventually got it.

"Brook. Give me the belt." Willie demanded me.

I shook my head at him.

"Give me the damn belt Brook Harold!"

I still shook my head no at him. My heart raced faster than before.

"Fine! I don't need to use the belt." At that moment, Willie threw me to the ground and kicked me.

I was trying to protect myself from him.

I laid there crying. The pain was excruciating!

The only thing I wanted him to do was to stop. The pain was so intense. The only thing I could do was cry out in discomfort.

"STOP WILLIE!" I cried to him.

I still kept trying to protect myself from him.

When I looked up, Mom appeared to be calm and unemotional. Which made it only worse.

I gave her a pleading looking, but she walked away.

"MOM!" I cried out for her.

How the hell can she let her boyfriend do that to her son!? She needed to protect me from that bastard. When she walked away, she betrayed me.

The pain became so unbearable that I zoned out. I didn't know how long he kicked me for.

When I knew he stopped kicking me, I looked at him with a questioning look. Then he started to punch me!

What the hell was his problem? Was he that mad that I didn't tell him or Mom about the dryer? Was he waiting for a day where he could beat the shit out of me?

By the time I re-opened my eyes, I saw Willie standing over me holding his hand.

I felt like the blood in my throat was suffocating me so I tried to cough. I moaned with every cough. It hurt like hell but I had to breathe.

After my coughing fit, I tried to sit up. I was laying in a pool of my blood. When I sat up, the blood dripped off my face.

I cried out in anger.

"What have I done to piss you off? The dryer?! No, I did not tell Mom. No, I did not tell you right away. But I told you!"

"Lack of communication Brook Harold! Your Mom plus I had a bad day at work. Remember me telling you that! Also, we are both drunk. While we may grab a beer or a joint to relax, you get to suffer! So, this is your bad day."

I continued to cough up blood, when I gave him an enraged, disbelief look. I turned my focus from him and laid down.

CHAPTER SIX

DAYS AFTER

Tuesday:

The next morning or I believe it was the next day.

I remember bits but it's like trying to put a puzzle together. You know the picture is there, but it's not whole till you put it together. I was missing information to put the puzzle back together.

I remember I moaned as I looked around the room. I figured I was still in the living room.

Laying on the floor, I covered my face with my hands. When I removed my hands, they were bloody. Wonderful. I thought to myself.

I tried to roll over to my stomach. Keyword, tried. But it hurt like hell.

Five more attempt at rolling over, I finally did.

I was trying to get up, but my whole body trembled. I was too weak to stand up, so I laid back down.

I remember feeling a sharp pain in my side while trying to breathe; so, I could only take little breaths.

I closed my eyes; I was trying to replay what took place last night. I remember I was talking to Mom and Willie about..... About what? In that moment, I was trying to put the puzzle together.

I then heard a faint voice getting closer. I barely opened my eyes to see a figure of a person standing next to me. Then I re-closed my eyes.

"How are you feeling?"

I shook my head no.

At that moment, my guess it was Mom, but I wasn't sure.

"Do you know who you are? I want you to say your first and last name."

I tried real hard to speak, but I only mouthed the words, "Brook Susie."

"Good. Do you know who I am?"

I squinted my eyes to look at this person. Again, I tried real hard to speak, but I only could mouth the words,

"Mom?"

"Yes. It's me. You don't look so hot. Here, let's get you up and into the bathroom."

The little strength I had, I got to my feet, with Mom's help.

My whole body was shaking. Mom had one hand on my back and the other holding my hand.

My side was killing me while I took a step.

"Come on Brook. You made it only two feet."

Two feet felt like a mile.

"Mom? I asked with a low, scratchy voice.

"Yes?"

"I. Am. Too weak." The moment I told her. I dropped to my knees.

My head was throbbing, the room was spinning.

(Groan) I grabbed my head while I laid back down as I closed my eyes.

Fell back into thinking about last night. What were we talking about?

Then some pieces of the puzzle were coming to me.

The dryer, it didn't work. The cereal. The dishes. The whipping.

My breathing got heavier. My heart raced. The talk between Mom and Willie. The corner.

I gasp. Willie! My eyes popped open as I looked around the room in a panic. I didn't see Mom anywhere.

I tried to get back up. (Moan) I had to tell myself to push through the pain. I got on my hands and knees, though; I felt my whole body shake. Come on Brook, get up. Ignore the pain. I kept telling myself.

I gave it all that I had left to get up on my own two feet.

Standing there, I felt real unstable. I leaned over on the armrest of the chair.

I then heard the front door open. Feeling afraid, still with a low and scratchy voice, I asked,

"Mom?"

Then Mom came into the living room.

"Brook! What are you doing?" Mom asked in a panic as she rushed over.

I flinched and gave her a fearful look while I replied,

"I was trying to make it to the bathroom. But I am too unstable to walk there by myself."

"(Sigh) Come on, sweetie. Let's get you to the bathroom."

Every step was agony. The bathroom was too far away.

My side was killing me. (Groan) Little steps Brook. Little steps. I told myself.

"Almost there, Brook. Ten more steps." Mom told me.

More like 50 miles to go.

I shook my head, no while I stopped.

"Yes, you can. One step at a time."

I took a deep breath, (OW) then continued to walk.

Made it to the bathroom. Finally. Mom directed me to sit on the toilet.

I went to sit down. After sitting, I grabbed my head while I watched her gather things.

"Sigh. Why don't you bring me into the hospital? Instead of treating me yourself." I mention to her.

"I don't need to bring you there when I have a degree to treat you myself."

"I want to make sure you know what you are doing."

Mom gave me an annoyed look and replied,

"Brook. I treat people for a living."

I looked away from her.

"You're Mother is an awesome nurse."

I let go of my head and looked over where the voice came from. Since I can't' see clear yet, I squinted my eyes to see who it was.

"Willie?" I asked.

"Hi, Brook. How are you feeling?" Willie said.

"What are you doing here? You did this! Get away from me!" I told him in a panic.

My heart raced, my breathing changed. I felt queasy. My eyes got watery.

"Brook? Are you okay? It's only Willie." Mom asked.

"NO! He did this to me!" A brief pause as I realized. "You both did this!" I said while I cried.

"Hon, you got to calm down. I need to bandage your wounds." quietly, Mom told me.

"Get away from me!"

Willie was at the door, looking at me. Mom was standing by the sink. I felt trap; they scared me.

"Brook, your Mom is trying to help you," Willie said.

"You both hurt me! Why would you want to help me?"

They both looked at each other, then looked back at me.

"Are you both feeling guilty?"

"A little. I never wanted it to go this far." Mom told me.

I shook my head at them while giving them a fearful look.

"I want to be alone. I don't want to bother anybody. Can I please leave?"

Mom and Willie looked at each other again, then back at me.

"After I get you cleaned up. Then you can go."

Not like I could escape. I nodded in agreement.

Mom used sterile wipes to clean up my head. I jerk away from her because those wipes sting.

"Sorry. You got a nasty cut on your head. How is your vision?" Mom asked.

"Is that why my head is killing me? My vision is still blurry." I replied.

"The cut on your head could cause pain, yes. Your left eye is swollen. It might take time for your vision to come back. More so in that eye. Your nose looks fine. It worried me because how much it was bleeding."

"It wasn't only my nose that was bleeding, Mom. But yes, that hurts too."

Mom did a quiet laugh while she smiled.

"I know, sweetie. You have a beautiful fat lip though."

"Thank you Mom, I can feel it."

"Now, let's look at your side. I want you to take off your shirt."

While I was taking off my shirt, I moaned. Little breath, I kept reminding myself.

"The pain is sharp and hurts like no other." I told Mom while she was feeling my right side.

"Yes. You got two broken ribs." Mom replied

Great, I thought to myself.

After Mom looked at my side, she looked at my back.

"Your back looks fine. Not too much damage from the belt. There you go, kiddo. All fixed up."

I got up, and I hurried past Mom and Willie to get to my room. Once in the hallway, I looked back at them. They both smiled at me. I turned from them and continued to limp towards my room.

When I got to my room, I looked at the clock. Seven clock P.M. It has been 24 hours since it happened.

I let out a groan as I carefully laid down in my bed. I laid my head down on my pillow. Grabbed my head while I closed my eyes.

Wednesday:

I remember waking up from a nightmare. Franticly looking around my room, feeling worried, but saw no one. I sighed in relief.

I got up to get a glass of water then went to the bathroom. Once I got into the bathroom, I stood on my step stool to look in the mirror.

I was in shock when I first looked into the mirror. I removed the bandage from my head; I study my face. I understood why I had a headache and couldn't see that well. My whole face looked like a marshmallow. All puffy.

I then looked at my right side, then back at the mirror.

My emotions were running high that my breathing changed. I started to cry.

I slammed down my fist on the countertop while I shouted why?

I was so angry at Mom and Willie. How could? How could they?

Again, did I get this harsh of a beaten because I didn't tell them about the dryer sooner? Because I spilled cereal? The dishes?! I was only five years old. No five-year-old should have gone through what I did.

I sat on the bathroom floor and cried hysterically.

My head pounded, so I grabbed it. Like that would help.

I felt sick to my stomach. I crawled over to the toilet and hugged it. After throwing up more than once. I laid down on the floor and fell asleep.

I stirred from my sleep because someone was calling my name.

When I opened my eyes, trying to focus. Mom and Willie were standing there looking down at me.

I jumped to my feet in a panic.

"Yes? What time is it? Want me to go make breakfast? What do you want?" I asked in a panic.

"Slow down bud. Your Mom and I wanted to know why you're sleeping in the bathroom." Willie asked.

I looked at him while I replied,

"Oh. I didn't feel good."

"Are you feeling okay?" Mom asked me.

I looked at them both very confused. What type of question was that? Are you okay? Um, no.

"Do I look okay?" I sounded annoyed.

They both shook their head no at me.

My point exactly. I didn't look fine. I looked like I got into a fight with a bull.

"Look, hon. We need to get to work. We will grab breakfast on the way out. After work, we will stop at the store to pick up more groceries. So, don't bother making dinner. Get the list done that I set on the counter for you." Mom told me.

I nodded in agreement.

I followed them out to the kitchen. After they went out the door, I locked the door.

I couldn't believe what they put on the list.

They wanted me to clean up the blood in the living room. I looked at the bloodstain which there is a trail all the way to the bathroom. If I bled that much: one, I shouldn't be doing the chores. Two, I needed to go to the hospital.

Rest of the list was of the normal.

To be honest, I didn't want to do anything. My side hurt and my head is killing me. Another reason why Mom should have brought me in.

But with happened the other night, I needed to stay on their good side.

I figured the bathroom would be easier, so, I will start there.

47

I had to ignore the pain I felt to push through my chores. I got them all done. I had to do the fun part now. Getting the blood out of the carpet and rugs.

I used a cleaning scrubby thingy to scrub the blood stain.

After five minutes of scrubbing it, it didn't look better. It looked worse.

I didn't know how to get blood out of the carpet. I still don't. But it didn't make me mad. They wanted it clean, but they never gave me any instructions.

I kept on scrubbing but it wasn't getting any better. After fifteen minutes of scrubbing, I gave up. I was getting tired, my side hurt and head is killing me. Plus, my hand hurts from me slamming it on the counter. I left a bruise by doing that.

I went to go lay down. But laying down still hurt.

Sigh. I laid there thinking about Dad. Aunt Natalie. How I miss them. I was happy there. I had nothing to worry about. They loved me. I am not loved living with Mom and her boyfriend.

It scared me to live with them. I was afraid they would beat me again if I couldn't get that stain out.

I remember I was about to close my eyes when I heard the phone ring. At first I didn't answer it.

I popped my eyes open when I heard a familiar voice telling me to pick up. I hurried out of my room as fast as I could.

"Hello?" My voice was Shakey while I answered the phone.

"Hi, Brook. I hoped that your mother wasn't there. I know I shouldn't be calling but I had to hear your voice."

After I heard his voice I got teary eyed while I smiled to myself.

"Hi, Daddy. I don't care."

"I would take that risk of me getting in trouble to make sure you are okay. Are you okay?" Dad asked.

Trick question. I could have told him no. That Mom and her boyfriend beat the shit out of me. But I figured what's the point. She would deny all of it.

"Yes, I am okay. How are you and Aunt Natalie? I miss you guys." I asked

"We are good. It's good to hear your voice. But I have to go now. I love you. Keep your head up, kiddo." Dad told me.

"I love you. Bye."

I hung up the phone with a smile. After I got off I realized I was hungry. But we had nothing in the house to eat.

I went back to scrub the spot. After ten more minutes of scrubbing, it didn't matter. I felt like I was making it worse. The house was clean minus that spot and the rugs.

I went to take that nap again. Because I was restless, I ended up laying there thinking.

While I laid there, I heard a car pull up. Didn't think much of it. Figured Mom and Willie came home early. Till I heard a knock. I had dragged myself out of my bed. Before I opened it up. I check to see who it was first. It was Hillary's Dad.

"Hello, Bryan," I said to him after opening the door.

He gave me an uneasy look before replying,

"Hello, Brook. Is your Mom home?"

I took a second to reply to him. I was trying to figure out what to say.

"She is sleeping at this moment. She is not feeling well."

"Okay. Well, hope you both get better soon. My wife and daughter misses you at daycare. How are you feeling?" He asked.

Felt nervous as I replied,

"I am okay. I miss June and Hillary too."

"Okay. Well, let your Mom know I stopped by."

"I will. Bye-bye." I said while I was shutting the door.

He didn't believe me and it didn't surprise me.

I went to stand by the stain. Staring at the big, evil red stain.

My eyes followed the trail to the bathroom. I am still trying to figure out the trail. If I bled that much, they should have brought me in.

When I lived with Dad, I fell down and hit my head; he brought me in to get stitches.

Mom and Willie didn't want to get charged for child abuse. That's why they didn't bring me in.

Anyway, I couldn't figure out how to get the stain out. I tried everything I could think of.

Because scrubbing the stain hasn't helped.

Sigh. I kept trying to scrub it clean. I scrub and scrub. I have spent most of my day scrubbing it!

I sat by the couch, with my knees close to my chest while I was resting my chin in my hands looking at it.

Thinking, I hope I don't get into trouble. This could be a test and I was failing it.

After a few minutes sitting there. I heard a car pull up. I hurried to my feet to go look out the window.

When I saw who it was, I looked at the clock. It's only four-fifteen. Why were they home? It was to early for them.

I went to open the door for them.

"Hi, Brook. How are you?" Mom asked.

"I am okay," I replied with a puzzled look.

"Look, you got the list done," Willie said when he looked at the list while he walked into the living room.

"Brook?" Willie asked.

The way he said my name, I knew I he saw the floor.

I gave Mom a nervous smile then turned to look at Willie and replied, "Yes?"

"Brook, what didn't you do?" Mom asked.

I turned back at Mom and gave her a nervous chuckle. I looked back at Willie, gave him a smile.

"I couldn't get it out. To be honest, I sat there scrubbing it and scrubbing it. You told me to clean it. You didn't tell me how to get it out."

I then looked back at Mom.

"I don't know Sassy. (My Mom's other nickname.) Do you think we should do something?" Willie asked my Mom.

"Hm. Perhaps we should give him a break this time around. But it's up to you." Mom replied to Willie.

Willie and Mom were using their eyes to talk to each other. Like they were telepathically talking to each other.

I kept looking back and forth between them trying to catch what they were saying.

Shortly after that, Mom said she is going into her room. I felt scared after she said that.

I watched her walk away.

"Mom? Mom?! Please come back!" I said with a quiver.

I turned to look up at Willie. I had a fear written all over my face and I am sure he saw it. He stood there looking down at me with an evil smile.

My thoughts raced. What does he want? Why is he staring at me? What more does he want to do with me? I didn't need another beating. My body hurt everywhere. I felt sick to my stomach. Which could have been from my migraine or because I haven't eaten.

I wish he would say something. Do something. Willie stood there scared me enough that I kept on crying.

"Brook, why are you crying? Are you a baby? Only they cry, not young boys." Willie said.

"Because I am scared. I don't know why you are staring at me. What are you going to do? Whatever it is, get it over with." I replied to him through sniffles.

"What gives you that idea I will do something?"

I looked up at him.

CHAPTER SEVEN

UNHAPPY

"Well, Brook?"

I looked away from him.

"Are you not answering because what I am holding?" Willie asked me.

I nodded and replied,

"You never had time to use it on me the other day because - because I took it from you. My thoughts are that you are back to get your fun out."

I looked up at him.

"My fun?" Willie gave me a smirk with a chuckle. "Whipping you is not my type of fun. Now, what I did to you on Monday night, yes, that was fun. What I am doing right now is also fun. Why? Because I love to terrorize you. I love how you become real still and quiet. I can see how your whole body shakes with fear. Your face shows that your mind is racing with thoughts. Because you do not know what is coming up next. That is why it is fun to intimidate you."

After Willie said it, he pushed me into the wall.

My anxiety skyrocketed. I gave him a fearful look. I cried out of control.

"Please, Willie. Please. I don't know what I did. But whatever I did, I - I am sorry. Please don't hurt me. Please." I was pleading to him.

Willie gave me a dark smile, I never seen his eyes this black before.

"See, like that. I don't have to lay a finger on you anymore, Brook Harold. What I did to you the other night has made you terrified of me. You were never this afraid of me. What's wrong? Don't trust me?"

Willie cracked the whip. I flinched, I covered myself, and I begged to Willie not to hurt me. He laughed.

"Wow! You are such a sissy. I haven't touched you. I only cracked the whip. Like this."

He made that noise again. I closed my eyes in fear of him hitting me.

"Stop your crying Brook Harold." After Willie said it, he left the room.

I slid down the wall, sat on the floor sobbing.

After I sat there for about ten minutes, I had to tell myself to get it together.

"Are you done crying now?"

I turned around in surprise to see Willie standing there with a smirk on his face.

"You know," Willie walks up puts one of his hands on my face. "It's hard to see your beautiful blue eyes when your eyes are bloodshot red." Willie removes his hand, then points at me. "I want you stop that crying now."

I shrugged my shoulders at him and asked in an upset way,

"Is there something you want?"

"Yes, I want you to put away the groceries," Willie said with a smile.

I nodded at him while I replied,

"Have you guys eaten dinner yet?"

"No, but we will go out to eat."

If he only wanted me to put away the groceries, what was the whole point of him being a jerk.

After putting the groceries away and Mom and Willie leaving, I made myself food.

I was happy that Mom bought more groceries. When I got done eating, I went to turn on a movie.

After the movie, I looked up at the clock; it was seven - thirty, bedtime.

I headed towards my room when then I stop short of my room; I realized that Mom and Willie haven't made it home yet. Which means they are sitting at the bar. Yay me.

The last time they went out and got drunk, they came home and woke me. Because Mom had to talk.

I took a shower before I put pajamas on. I have been wearing the same bloody sweat pants since Monday. Gross I know.

Tuesday, I was trying to get off the floor and comprehend what happened. Which took all day.

And Wednesday, I needed to get that stain out of the carpet. Which I never could.

Anyway, took my shower. Which it felt good but also stung.

Thursday:

I was stirring in my sleep when I heard a faint voice calling my name.

When I opened my eyes enough to see who it was, I grumbled.

"Yes, Mom? What do you want?" I asked.

"How are you?" Mom asked.

I sighed in disgust and I pulled my blanket over my face.

"So?" Mom asked while she removed my blanket.

"I am tired, it's midnight. You woke me up. Again! Why do you must bug me after you come home?!" I replied.

Mom shrugged her shoulders while she replied,

"Willie was telling me you are jumpier than before. Willie show me, I want to see."

I looked over at Willie. I gave him a pleading look.

Willie, smiled and ignored my look and cracked the whip.

I flinched at the sound.

Mom laughed along with Willie and she told him to do it again. So he did.

I closed my eyes and asked,

"Please stop."

"All right, all right. We will let you go back to bed." Mom mentioned.

She then looked at my alarm clock to make sure I set my alarm for the morning.

"You'll have to get up and make breakfast. This time not spilling it. Goodnight." Mom said before kissing my forehead.

After they left my room, I mocked Mom quietly..

"Oh please Willie, show me how you torment my son."

Oh, my god. Mom had Willie wrap around her finger, it was pathetic.

I was up at Seven sharp. Went to the bathroom. Then went to the kitchen to start breakfast.

I had to find something within my reach so I wouldn't drop it.

I thought about making Mom and Willie eggs and pancakes. That's within my reach. Though, with my luck, watch me drop the eggs or the pancakes mixer.

I set the table while the eggs and pancakes were cooking.

"You didn't drop breakfast again, did you?"

I turned to around to see Willie smiling at me.

I gave him an annoyed look with a reply,

"No, I didn't. But it's done."

"Good," Willie said.

"Brook. You are going to daycare today. You should go get ready." Mom gave me a disapproval look on how I look. "Like, take a shower. Because you need one." Mom told me while she was walking into the kitchen.

"Are you sure? As far as daycare. I mean." I asked

"Yes. You are no longer sick." Mom said with a smile.

"Sick? Okay, I will go get ready then. Wait. Do I get food?"

Mom gave me a disbelief look.

"Okay. Never mind. I will go get ready."

Don't worry Mom, I don't need food. Feeding your kid is optional. And I took a shower the previous night. Not that she knew about it but a shower isn't going to get rid of the bruises and cuts.

Sick.. I was never sick. She didn't want to admit that she allowed her boyfriend to beat the shit out of me. Which June would see when I go to daycare.

Took my shower Again.. Brushed my teeth. comb my hair.

"Why are you wearing your hoodie? It's the month of June." Mom asked me.

"Because, I want to." I told her.

"Whatever, at least you look better. We got to go."

I nodded at her while I replied,

"I'm ready. But I never got the breakfast dishes done."

"I know. You can take care of it later. We have to drop my car off at the shop before work." Mom said.

"Okay."

We got into the car to drive the silly minute. When we arrived, June was outside waiting for us.

"Hello, Brook. We missed you. Hope your feeling better. Susie, are you feeling better? When Bryan stopped by to talk to you, Brook told him you were sick."

"Yes, Brook mentioned that. I was asleep when he came by. I am doing better, thank you." Mom replied.

Which was a lie to both. I never told Mom, and she wasn't sick.

"Good to hear. What's the plan for today as far picking Brook up? I see that Willie is with you." "Yes. My car is having issues and we are bringing it to the shop. The plans for picking Brook up will be like normal. Willie will pick Brook up after work then drop it off and go back to work."

After Mom spit that out, June and I looked at Mom in surprised.

I turned to look at Willie, who was in Mom's car, he was holding his hands over his face. I looked back at Mom and June.

"Willie drops him off where when he goes back to work?" June asked while giving Mom a confused look.

"I... UH. N- no. I mean Willie goes to both jobs then picks Brook up." Mom told June sounding nervous.

"Okay. So I will see Willie at two?"

"Yes. Yes, I, we got to run. Talk to you later Brook, honey."

I told Mom and Willie bye. I followed June into the house.

"Brook! Hi! I missed you." Hillary said while she hugged me.

Not trying to show my discomfort but her hugging me didn't feel good. It felt like someone put a rubber

band around me.

"Yes, I missed you too. Now can you let go of me?" I asked.

"Oh." Hillary giggles. "Yeah."

"Bookie!" Jeorge (George) said while running up.

"Bookie? My name is Brook." I told him.

Jeorge laughs to himself and replies,

"I know. But it's like a nickname for you."

After I told Jeorge I like the nickname, he gave me a big smile.

The other kids never played with me like Hillary and Jeorge did.

"Brook, let's take off your hoodie. It's warm outside and I don't want you to get overheated." June told me.

"We will not get into this again. You like to tell me every time I am over about removing my hoodie. So, no." I grumbled to her.

June gave me a surprised look.

"I know, I don't want you to get to warm, that's all."

I gave her an annoyed look.

"Okay, okay. I will let you be." June told me.

"Thank you. Now, if you don't mind, I will be in my corner." I told her.

I went to sit in my spot while I watched the other kids play.

"Come play with me. You can't sit in the corner all day." Hillary told me.

"I am fine. Go play." I replied.

"Brook."

"Hillary," I said with a smile.

She gave me an annoyed look. Then a ball appeared in front of me, I looked down at it. When I looked up, Jeorge was smiling at me.

"You two won't stop bugging me till I come play, right?" I asked.

They both nodded.

"All right. I will come and play."

They both squealed in delight.

The time went by faster with me playing with them verses me sitting in the corner.

"Kids, it's lunchtime. After lunch, we will go outside." June told all us kids.

I was super excited for lunch; I felt like I was starving.

I followed the kids to the dining room. Sat at the table.

June made us ham sandwiches.

I sat there inhaling half of my sandwich. It tasted so good. That I was about to finish my other half when I realized that all the kids plus June were watching me eat.

Clears throat. "I am done eating. Thank you for lunch." I said while pushing my plate away.

All the kids looked shocked and June had a worried look.

"Brook, if you are hungry, eat," June told me.

"No. I am done. Thank you. May I be dismiss?" I asked.

"Yes, you may. After the other kids get done, we are going outside." Said June.

Outside time:

June convinced me to remove my hoodie. Although she had an uncomfortable look when she looked me over. I think she saw the ashamed look on my face that she gave me a reassuring smile.

It was nice being outside. Taking in the fresh air. All the different smells from June's garden. The sun beating down on my face.

I was playing ball with Jeorge.

I tossed over the ball to him, then looked over to see Hillary playing with some of her friends.

"Brook!" Jeorge yelled at me in a panic.

By the time I looked at him, the ball hit my right side and I dropped to the ground.

Holding my side, my eyes filled up with tears,

While clenching my teeth in an outrage, I replied,

"Why the hell did, you hit me! I wasn't even looking at you when you tossed the ball!"

"I -I am sorry. Thought you were paying attention." Jeorge said.

"I wasn't paying attention! I was watching Hillary!"

"Are you okay?" Jeorge asked getting upset.

I glared at him while I growled,

"Do I look okay?!"

"I am sorry. Wasn't trying to hit you." Jeorge said while he cried.

"Brook, come on. It was an accident. Jeorge, are you okay." June asked.

"Is he okay?! I got hit by the ball!" I growled at June.

June shoots me an irritated look then shifts her focus to Jeorge.

By this time, all the kids were watching us. My side hurt too much to care.

"I am fine. I want to make sure Brook is okay." Jeorge replies.

June then looks back at me and replies,

"Let's get you in the house and look at your side."

"I will go in the house myself, thank you very much! My side is fine." I told June while grabbing my hoodie.

I walked into the house holding my side and walked towards my corner. I put my hoodie on then I sat down.

About ten minutes later, June brought the rest of the kids in.

"Brook, I want to talk to you. Come here." June told me.

I got up from my spot and walked towards the kitchen.

"Yes?" I asked.

"Now, Brook and Jeorge. Are you both okay?"

We both gave her a nod.

When she was talking to the both of us, I was thinking to myself, If she only knew why I came across too harsh.

"Now, can you both apologize to each other and enjoy the rest of your day with each other?" June asked.

We both nodded again. Said sorry to each other. June then let us go play. Actually, she let Jeorge.

"Brook. Why did you come across so harsh? Mm."

"It hurt."

"What's going on at home? Where did you get these marks from?" She asked as she looked over my bruises on my face.

I looked away. Fighting the tears.

"Nothing." I whispered.

I heard her sigh before she replied,

"Okay. Go play."

I am sure June is catching on that something isn't right at Mom's house.

I went to play a little longer with the kids. Then Willie showed up. It was time to go home. To do chores most likely.

CHAPTER EIGHT

HOME/DAYCARE

At home:

"June told me you got hit by a ball today? How did that feel?" Willie asked me.

I gave him a disgusted look, while I replied,

"Yes, the ball hit me. On my right side to inform you. I dropped to the ground because it hurt like hell. So, I am grumpy."

"Oh, ouch. Your right side of all things." Willie said with a mocking smile.

Still, with my grumpy look, I replied,

"Yes. My side still hurts from you kicking me. From you pushing me into the wall, and now this. So, where's the magic list of yours and Mom's?"

"The magic list? It's called the chore list, Brook. Oh, before I forget. My friend will stop over tomorrow to help your Mom and I change the carpet in here. No thanks to you."

I gave Willie a confused/angry look,

"No thanks to me? I didn't beat myself up. If you didn't want blood all over the floor, ya shouldn't have beat the shit out of me."

Willie shrugs his shoulder and replied,

"Whatever. Here's the magic list."

I gave him an annoyed look as he handed me the list before walking out of the house.

I love that they leave me alone and give me a long list I need to get done in two hours. (Being sarcastic.)

Clean the kitchen, dust the whole house, and do Mom's room, plus dinner. It's only three, I can get it done by the time Mom gets home. NOT.

Anyway, I cleaned Mom's room first because her room is always the dirtiest. When I walked into her room, yep, a big mess. Personally, I don't mind cleaning their room. The part I hate is picking up their used needles. They do the drugs, they can take care of their own needles. But hey, I am just here to please them.

I made the bed, took out the garbage, cleaned the bathroom, dusted and vacuumed.

Since Mom's room is complete, I had to finish rest of the house and time was ticking.

I remember glancing at the clock in the living room and it read five o'clock. Didn't think much about at the direct second. So, I headed towards the kitchen. I came to a sudden stop as I realized what time it was.

Oh shit. I said out loud to myself as I hurried in the kitchen. For what reason? To super clean?! I wasn't thinking logically. I ran around the kitchen looking troubled. Dinner! I had to figure out dinner. I -I d-don't know.

"Brook?"

I turned around in surprise to see Mom. I didn't even hear her pull up or anything.

I gave her a nervous smile while I replied,

"Hi, Mom. How was your day?"

I then saw Willie walk in.

"Brook Harold, where is dinner?" Willie asked.

I gave them both a nervous smile, while I shrug my shoulders, with a reply,

"I was cleaning. Good news is that your room is clean. And I got the dusting done." I lost my smile. I looked down. "Bad news is, I didn't get the kitchen or dinner done."

I looked back up to Mom and Willie.

In disgust, they both replied,

"Yeah, we can see that."

After they went into their room, I felt like I could breathe. Plus, I knew I would be in trouble. Trouble or not, I had to get dinner made.

Dinner was an hour late. I let them know and went to my room.

While I was in my room, I picked it up. I had nothing better to do.

I changed the sheets. Took the dirty sheets to the laundry room. Went back to my room to empty the garbage, took the garbage outside.

"How was dinner?" I asked while walking back into the house.

They both said it was good.

"Why wasn't the kitchen and dinner done by the time I came home?" Mom asked me.

I looked at Mom while I replied,

"Willie was asking me what happened at daycare when we got home. Because of our little chat, I started at 3 instead of 2:45. I took from 3 to 5 to get two chores done."

"What happened at daycare?" Mom asked while looking at Willie and me.

"Brook wasn't paying attention when one of the other kids tossed the ball to him. So, he got hit by the ball. After that, he growled at June and this kid." Willie told her.

I looked down to the floor. Willie was right. I couldn't hide it.

"Brook. Is this true? You got short with another kid and June?" Mom asked.

I looked back up at her,

"For starters, the ball hit my right side. My side is trying to heal. It didn't feel the greatest when the ball hit me. Plus, June was trying to be snoopy and look at my side. She wanted to make sure the ball did no harm. But I thought it would be best if she didn't because what took place Monday night."

"Suck up the pain. Don't show your pain at daycare. Problem solved." Mom told me with a smile.

When I looked over at Willie, he was trying not to laugh.

I re-looked at Mom while I asked,

"I can't show pain here, because," I pointed to Willie." He makes fun of me." I crossed my arms. "I can't show it at daycare because of June. What the hell do you want me to do? Have no feelings."

"Yeah." Mom looks at Willie then back at me. "That would work on our end. Unless we are beating you, then we want to hear from you." Mom said with a smile.

"Great. You want me to be perfect and have no feelings unless you're beating me. Thank you, Mom and Willie. Now get out of my kitchen. I have to clean it."

"Uh, wait. Your kitchen?" Willie asked me.

I gave him a nod while I replied,

"You don't clean it. You only pay the bills."

They gave me a disgusted look while leaving the room.

I very much dislike those two.

"Hey Brook. Can I have your help to move things out of the living room?"

I turned to see Willie, and asked,

"Is that optional?"

"No. I am trying to sound nice."

"Hmm. Yeah, I will help."

Then Willie wandered back into his room. And I finished up the kitchen.

I had no choice to help plus, I had two broken ribs.

Shortly after Willie went back into the bedroom, Mom and he came out of their room.

Mom and Willie took the bigger items. Since I was the littlest, I took the small items while I sucked up the pain. But we ran out of furniture I could move.

But Mom went to sit down in the kitchen while Willie and I finished the rest. I remember thinking to myself that I should have been the one on the sidelines.

I remember I was trying to help Willie push a recliner, but it was hard to push it on the carpet. I thought to myself,

Couldn't Willie push it by himself?

10 minutes later, we got the recliner out the door to the storage unit then we came back in.

And the only reason it was taking longer to push because Willie was letting me do most of the pushing.

Willie went to go sit down in his chair as he asked Mom for his whiskey.

So, I thought I would be funny and ask for some.

Though, Willie gave me an odd look.

"You can't drink. But, you can have water."

I rolled my eyes with a smile, I replied,

"But a beer would help with the pain in my side."

"Brook Harold!"

I turned to look up at Mom and asked,

"What? Oh, wait. Wait. Brook, shut up about the pain. Because you can't express your pain. Nor are you allowed to cry."

"Who said you can't cry?" Mom asked.

I pointed to Willie while I glared at him.

"Yes, I told you that. Because your eyes were so bloodshot red the other day. It was hard to see your pretty blue eyes." Willie said with a smirk.

"What is it with you about my blue eyes? You didn't care that I had blood in my blond hair Monday."

"No, I didn't care. I have brown hair. I only love your blue eyes because we share the same eye color." Willie told me with a smile.

I gave him a disgusted look as I thought to myself of how creepy that sounded.

"We got work to do. So, stop talking about my blue eyes."

Then Mom walked over to hand Willie his cup.

"Thank you, my dear."

I stood there with an annoyed look on my face.

"Work!" I said firmly. "We don't kiss on the job." I told them.

"You are right." Willie pops up from his chair. "Thank you Brook." Willie hand me his drink. "Your Mom and I will go into our room."

I gave them a surprised look while I replied,

"Uh. W -wait. That's not what I meant! M- Mom? W- Willie?"

I watched them walk towards their room.

Not meaning to I didn't tell them to go to their room.

I stood there looking at the stuff in the living room. I can't move things by myself, was little and everything was big.

Looking at rest of the furniture in the livingroom. I could only move one end table. Because that was closer to my size.

I put Willie's drink on the counter and I went to move the end table.

It was a struggle to move it. Took me about five minutes when I realized it wasn't going to happen. Forget it. I can help, I can't move the furniture alone.

I went to go sit in Willie's chair to give my side a rest.

15 minutes passed.

Willie came back into the living room laughing.

"What's wrong, Brook? Do you need help?"

I shot him an annoyed look as he smiles at me.

"We will help you, honey. We both don't work tomorrow. You got to put up with us for tonight and Tomorrow." Mom told me.

"Fine. One thing though, don't get drunk and lay a finger on me." I told them.

"We can do anything we want, Brook. I can show you the belt." Willie said with a smile while picking up his cup of whiskey.

They both laughed.

"Nice Willie. That's why I love you." Mom told Willie.

And that's why I don't. I thought to myself.

It was a long night. We got all the furniture moved in the storage unit. Then it was bedtime.

The next morning I woke to my side hurting more than it did. I had to take a little breath at first.

I got out of bed and went to the kitchen to start breakfast.

"Good morning Brook." Mom said with a yawn.

"Good morning Mom. Sleep well?" I asked.

"Yes, I did. Feeling a little sore from moving the furniture around last night."

I grabbed a chair to used to stand on so I can grab the painkillers from the cabinet. Got off the chair and handed Mom the medicine over the breakfast bar.

"Here you go Mom. I will get breakfast started." I told her with a smile.

"Are you okay?" Mom asked while giving me a confused look.

"Yes. You said you were sore, so I gave you some pain meds to help. You and Willie have a long day ahead of you." I replied with a smile

"Okay. Thank you. I will go take a shower." Mom told me.

"All right. Breakfast will be on the table when you get out." I told her.

Mom gave me a strange look as she was walking out of the room.

By the time I got done setting the table, Mom and Willie were coming out.

"Good morning, Willie. How was your sleep?"

"Good." He replied groggy.

"Awesome. How was your shower Mom?"

"Fine." She replied.

"Great. Well, breakfast is ready. Come and eat. I will go clean your bedroom while you eat."

I gave them a smile while walking past them.

"Are you going to eat, hon?" Mom asked me.

"I had a piece of toast. I am good. Thank you."

I continued to walk towards their room.

Since I cleaned it the day before, it wasn't that bad.

Remade the bed. Straighten up the room. Straighten up the bathroom.

Twenty minutes passed.

By the time I got done, they walked into the room.

"Hello. The room is don, now I will go do the kitchen."

While I was getting the kitchen picked up, there was a knock on the door. I went to go answer it.

When I opened the door, a heavy-set guy about Willie's height was standing at the door.

"Hello? How may I help you?"

"You must be Brook. Hi. I am here for Willie and your Mom." This guy told me.

Must be Willie's friend. I thought to myself.

"Okay, come on in. I will let them know your are here."

I wandering down the hallway towards Mom's and Willie's room. I knocked on the door to let them know about the guy is here for them. I walked back out to the living room.

I saw Willie's friend looking at the carpet. At one spot in particular.

"They will be out in a minute. Would you like water while you wait?" I asked this guy.

"Sure. Thank you." He replied.

I went into the kitchen to get him a glass of water. Then brought it back to him.

"Here you go." I told him.

"Thank you. May I ask you something?"

I felt nervous for his question.

"What's up?"

"What happened here? With this red, brownish stain?"

"Uh. You see, I-"

"Hey Robert. I will tell you in the car."

I turned to see Mom and Willie standing behind me.

Phew. Thank god they came out.

"I will be in my room if you need me."

Once in my room, I attempted a deep breath as I fell backwards on my bed. I can stop with the, "Everything is good" act.

I was trying to act, perfect. Like what was mention in our talk the previous night.

"Brook, come here." Mom was calling me from the other room.

I got up off my bed to walk out to the living room.

"Yes? How can I help you?" I asked.

"Willie, Robert, and I will go look at carpet. We will drop you off at June's. Unless you want to come with." Mom told me.

I remember I felt confused by what she said. If I wanted to go with. She only said that because Willie's friend doesn't know about the abuse.

"Whatever you think is best."

"Well. Whatever I decide, get ready. I will talk to Willie."

I nodded while I replied,

"Okay. I will be right back."

I walked back to my room to get dressed. Then walked to the bathroom to brush my teeth, comb my hair. Then walked back towards the living room.

"I am ready."

"Hey babe. We all can't fit in either truck. I will ride with Robert." I over heard Willie tell Mom.

"I will go drop Brook off at June's. Which is down the road, remember? So, if you wait here. I will go drop him off then come back. That way we can ride together." Mom said.

"Yeah, true. Go drop Brook off. We will wait here for ya." Willie said.

Twelve o'clock PM:

Mom dropped me off at Junes. Told June the plans, then she left.

"Brook, you made it in time for lunch. Why don't you come sit down?" June told me.

"I am not hungry." I told her.

That's a lie, and we both knew it.

"Are you sure? Your Mom said you haven't eaten lunch yet. And when you were here yesterday, you scarfed down your food."

"Well, that was yesterday. Today is today." Me switching the topic. "Are we going back outside again? I liked it a lot from yesterday." I asked.

June let out a sigh.

"Yes. After lunch."

After the kids ate lunch, We all headed outside to the backyard.

I sat on the steps while the other kids played. I was watching Hillary. Again. I liked her smile, her green eyes. I looked down at my hands when I noticed she was looking back at me. I had this major crush on her growing up.

"Hi, Brook. I wanted to say this to you yesterday, but never did. Did you want to play with me yesterday? Is that why you were watching me?" Hillary asked me.

I looked up at Hillary and gave her a smile.

"I wanted to play with you and Jeorge. But you went to play with the other kids."

"Well, let's go over to Jeorge and find something to do." Hillary mention.

I nodded.

"Jeorge, Brook and I wanted to know if we could play in the sandbox with you." Hillary asked him.

Jeorge looked up at us, then he stared at me. Like he was thinking about yesterday. I gave him a smile. He finally nodded.

Hillary, Jeorge and I played in the sandbox with each other. Then we used chalk to draw on the sidewalk.

"Brook. It looks like your having super fun. And it makes me happy that you're playing with the kids. But your Mom is here for you now."

I looked up to see June then looked back down at the sidewalk.

"I don't want to go home. I want to stay. I am having fun here." I told her.

June kneels down next to me, tells the other kids to go play.

When they went away, June asked me,

"Why don't you want to go home, sweetie?"

CHAPTER NINE

HOME/DAYCARE: PART TWO

I looked away from her instead of answering the question.

"Brook. Is everything okay at home?" She asked.

"No" I mumbled under my breath.

I looked up to see Mom walking towards us.

I jumped to my feet while I replied,

"Yes. Everything is good at home. I love being there. I especially love my step-Dad."

June gave me a concern look. When she was getting up, she turned to look at Mom.

"Hi, Susie. Brook played well with the other kids today. Very proud of him."

"Good to hear. Willie told me how he was grumpy yesterday because he got hit by a ball." Said Mom.

"Yes. Brook wasn't paying attention when the other kid threw the ball. But, the other kid wasn't paying attention that Brook wasn't watching. Accidents happen. Say, I want to ask you something." Said June.

"Shoot. What's on your mind?" Mom asked.

I saw June looking around at the kids. Then she looked down at me.

"Come sit at the picnic table with me." June told Mom.

I was in earshot I could still hear what they were talking about.

"Um. Suzanne Susie. I want to make sure that Brook is safe, at home. He has come here more than once with a black eye and /or a fat lip, sometimes with different marks. Yesterday, he came looking horrible. Like did you slap him around before sending him to daycare? Plus, he distances himself from the other kids. Just recently he has been playing with the other kids. Also, he inhales his lunch like he hasn't eaten in days. It concerns me. Plus I have to report this." June seemed to struggle to say it.

Mom. Well, she sat there emotionless.

Mom clears her throat.

"Thank you for your concern. No reason to turn it in. My kiddo is a klutz."

A klutz? Thanks Mom. Want to explain my side then? Thought to myself.

"He's five, he's still in this awkward stage, you know. He's growing an inch, I swear every day. I can barely keep up with how much this kid eats."

She does?! When?! I thought to myself.

"The distant part. I don't know. Brook has been doing that since he came to live with me. I am wondering if Nathaniel did something to him. Willie and I have been trying to work with him. So, he won't be so shy."

Maybe Dad did something? I chuckled to myself. Unbelievable.

How June fidget with her hands, she was uncomfortable asking Mom.

"Thank you for this talk. Will I see Brook Monday?" June asked.

While walking towards my direction, Mom replied,

"Yep. He should be here."

She stopped in front me as she looked down at me; I look up at her. Mom gave me a smile. I remember not trusting her smile. I wasn't sure if it was a safe smile or your in trouble.

In the truck:

"What was June asking you about?" Mom asked me.

I gave Mom a nervous look.

"Brook. What did she want? Was she asking about home?"

I looked out the window.

After Mom parked the car in the driveway, I felt her gaze on me while she said,

"Brook Harold. Answer the damn question."

I looked back at Mom. The look on her face, the way she sounded, I knew she was getting angry with me. What she told June, about Dad. I didn't want to talk to Mom.

Mom smiled at me while she told me,

"Fine. Let's go in the house."

She got out of the car then she got me out, and into the house.

I watched Mom walk up to Willie and whispered something in his ear.

I went to stand in the kitchen while Mom talked to Willie.

Few minutes passed then he looks over at my direction, I gave him a smile. I watched Willie walk up to Robert, and he whispered something to Robert.

I watched them leave the house, didn't think much about it. Because Willie sometimes went out to have his cigarette. Turned my focus to Mom. When I heard the truck start, I looked left towards the window. I felt my stomach drop when I saw that truck leaving. I gave Mom a nervous smile.

Mom walked up and looked down at me with a disgusted look, I looked up at her. Studying her face.

She walked pass me to get to the table.

"Come sit Brook. We need to talk."

I stayed where I was, but I gave her a disgusted look.

"Why won't you talk? Are you afraid? Are you mad?"

I glared at her.

Mom sighed, walked over to look out the window.

"Brook, we got a half and hour to talk about this before they come back." Mom turned back to look at me while she crossed her arms. "So, talk."

I rolled my eyes as I looked away from her.

I heard Mom do a quiet laugh.

"Brook Harold Susie! I am getting furious."

I looked back her.

Mom points while she said,

"You are giving me the silent treatment. Aren't you?"

I smiled at her while I thought. Jeez Mom. You finally guessed it.

"I will take that as a yes. I know how to get you to talk. I will be right back."

Mom left the kitchen to go towards her room.

Brook Harold

I am not talking to her and she can't force me. Was my thought at that moment.

I went to sit at the table, looked down at my hands. I heard Mom walking back towards me but never looked up.

I heard the whip crack. I jumped to my feet. I looked at her with fear.

No, please no. I thought.

She could force me to talk.

"This should get you talking."

And she made that noise again.

I closed my eyes, shaking my head no.

"No? This won't get you talking. Hm."

When I opened my eyes, she was standing in front of me. I gave her an uneasy smile.

That noise. I hate, HATE, that noise.

"Enough Mom! Please, please don't." I beg her.

When Mom knew she broke me of my silence, she let out a loud, evil laugh.

"I got you to talk. It's so precious how you beg. I love it."

I looked up at her. Fear took over my body. I then switched my focus to the floor.

"June wanted to know what goes on here." I looked back up at her. "Like what she was asking you." My expression changed from fear to anger." It was not Dad's fault."

Mom's eyes widen with concern.

"The only thing I told her is that I love my step-dad."

Mom gave me a confused look,

"Your step-dad? You love your step-dad? I don't think love is the right word. I say hate would be a better word. Hell, you hate me too. Right?"

"Is that a trick question ma'am?"

Mom cackled.

"Yes, it is. Now, get up off your knees and start dinner."

"Right away, ma'am." I said while hopping to my feet.

I watched Mom walk back to her room.

I felt stupid for letting my weak side show. Growing up, I always tried to stay one step of my parents. There were days I could and others, I couldn't.

73

I made something quick and easy that night since Robert was there.

By the time dinner was ready, Willie and Robert were back. Which was longer than half an hour.

When I was setting the table, Robert walked towards me, and he stared at me.

I felt uncomfortable with him staring. I glanced at him as I asked, "Yes? Can I help you with something?"

"Nothing in particular. I'm - Wow. Your five and you take a lot. I am impressed."

"Brook," Willie said while walking towards me. "Lift your shirt up."

I gave him a confused look and asked,

"Why?"

"Just do it. Rob wants to see your side."

I gave them a puzzled look and showed them my side. Because if I didn't do it willingly, Willie would force it.

"See? Brook, how is your vision?"

"Better in my right eye than my left." I replied sounding annoyed.

"His left eye is taking longer for the vision to come back, which you heard because it swelled good. The day after, his face looked like a marshmallow." Willie told Robert.

Robert stood there in shock.

"Wow."

"Okay, okay. This is not a show and tell. I am not an object to show off. Yes, you kicked my butt but you don't need to be proud of your marks you left on me." I told Willie.

"Go to your room." Willie told me while he gave me a disgusted look.

He sent me to my room because I was rude to him. I could not be rude to my parents. They took that as me being defiant.

But I was happy to go to my room. I was not his trophy.

About an hour and a half later, Mom knocked on my door. I got off my bed to go see what she wanted.

"Yes? Are you done eating? Want me to come clean the kitchen? I asked.

"Yes. That's why I knocked on your door." She said.

"I will go clean it."

"Thank you."

I cleaned the kitchen while my parents plus Robert went to work on the floor. When I got done with the kitchen. I watched them lay down... wood.

"I thought you were getting carpet?" I asked.

Mom and Willie looked back at me then at each other. Willie looked back at me, about to speak, when Robert spoke for him.

Robert crossed his arms and said,

"They told me everything. I know what happens here. I told them it would best not to get carpet. That way it would be easier to clean up after your mess."

I looked at Robert perplexed. Unsure what to say at first.

"Uh, e-excuse me? M-My mess? To a point it is but there would-"

"If you listen to your parents, they wouldn't have to beat you." Robert said while he interrupts me.

"My parents? Only one is my parent. That would be Susie. Willie isn't my dad. My Dad lives out of town." I told him.

"I don't know. You look like both. Could be because of your blue eyes." Robert said with a wink.

I still had that confused look on my face as I told him,

"I have to do laundry. Before I get myself into trouble."

"Wise choice." Robert told me.

The reason Willie and Robert took longer to get back. Willie told Robert everything. If Robert had his head on his shoulders the right way, he would have done the smart thing by turning their asses in. But no, because it was his best friend, he wouldn't get his friend in trouble. Just take my parent's side and blame me for their sick actions. Plus that, my mom has brown eyes not blue. I take after my dad.

Ten minutes passed:

While walking into the living room, I saw them getting up.

"Pretty eyes, we are going outside to for a smoke. Go clean our room." Willie told me.

Pretty eyes? Oh, my goodness. I thought to myself.

"Yes sir, I will. Anything else?" I asked.

Willie shakes his head no. The three wandering outside and I went to make sure Mom's and Willie's room was clean.

I walked into their room. I stopped looked around. The room was clean. Not sure what he wanted me to do. I did a general pickup to keep myself busy.

After taking twenty minutes in their room, I walked back towards the living room. I looked at the wood flooring they got.

It was Cherry Amberwood color. It was pretty.

Even though I didn't want to admit they were right. The wooden floors looked better, plus it would be easier to clean and it scared me. Because I knew my hell was only beginning and more was to come.

I went to prepare my parents snack plate. Every night around nine o'clock P.M. They would have their snack plate and a drink.

When it's only Mom and Willie, they would hide out in their room doing whatever. But it was Friday Night, and we had an extra person in the house.

They came in laughing from being outside.

I asked with a hint of a smile,

"What happened? Did it rain on you?"

"Yes. It dumped." Mom told me

"Go change then I will come pick up the mess after your done." I told them.

I watched all three leave the room.

I picked up my mess, put their drinks and the snack plate on the table.

I went to grab the mop from the closet to mop up the dirt they drugged in.

I got done mopping the hallway and when I saw Robert; I told him to be careful because the floor was wet. I told the same thing to the other two when I saw them come out of their bedroom.

Dumped the water and rinsed the mop after I got done mopping.

I picked up the mess in the bathroom from Robert, then I headed towards Mom and Willie's room to get that mess cleaned up.

When I walked into the kitchen, I let them know if they needed me, I would be in my room.

"Thank you for picking up our mess. Thank you for the snack plate. We will let you know." Mom told me.

I told them, you're welcome. And headed towards my bedroom.

I was hoping they didn't need me for the rest of the night. It was a long day for me at a young age.

I put on my hoodie before I laid down on my bed.

My hoodie is my security blanket. It's the one thing that made me feel safe. It was soft, and it was warm. I could hide.

Anyway, I sat on my bed reading books while listening to the rain pouring outside. Plus, I could hear them laughing in the kitchen.

So I knew it was safe for me to close my eyes to rest them.

I remember that I dozed off and a loud clap of thunder woke me. When I realized that I was still safe, I rubbed my eyes, yawned while I stretched out.

Then I realized, it was almost three in the morning and I could still hear them.

I wandered out my room to see what's going on.

Almost to the kitchen, I stopped. They must have heard me coming out because they were all staring at me with an evil smile.

I got this funny feeling in my gut that something wasn't right.

I gave them all a nervous smile while backing away.

I ducked in my room as fast as I could. I shut my bedroom door.

Holy shit. I whispered to myself. They look like they have been smoking something and too much to drink.

I did not want to stop and ask. I don't even want to know why they smiled at me. Let's hope they stay out there. Because I don't trust Mom and Willie.

Now, I knew it was because I was jumpier than before and after they beating me good. I was unsure of them.

I curled up under my blankets. More like hiding under them, trying to get back to sleep. If I could fall asleep, I would feel better.

I tossed and turned, I could still hear them out there. I would feel better if they went to bed. I drifted off till I heard a noise out my door.

My eyes widen, my heart raced. Please, please, keep walking.

After five minutes, they were still outside my door.

Curiosity got the best of me so I listened closer to hear what they were saying.

Ten minutes later:

If I knew what they were talking about before I listened in, I wouldn't have. They kept a notebook to track how often I am obedient and disobedient. Which meant, I would be playing the perfect act more often.

I was happy they went to bed but after hearing that, I couldn't fall asleep.

I wondered how many marks they had written? When will I get another beating? Will they take me by surprise? Or are they going to hint at it like last time?

-Chapter Ten: Saturday-

When I got up in the morning, It surprised me they got the floor done. I don't want to admit it but the wooden floor made the living room look nice. However, the kitchen didn't look nice, it was a mess. They left their empty beer cans, and they left over drugs and used needles on the table.

I understood that I was their maid, their servant, whatever I was to them. But why couldn't they take care of their own damn needles. That was my biggest pet peeve growing up. My parents not taking care of their own used needles.

I remember after my fit about their needles; I realized, where was Robert? It bothered me I couldn't find him.

I didn't know if I should make extra breakfast or not. I got into this battle with myself that I should but then I panicked. When should I make breakfast? I kept questioning myself should I make it then, or wait till they get up. After a minute battling that question, I waited. But I thought of the notebook which sent me into a panic. So I changed my mind and made breakfast right then. They could heat it up if it was cold.

So, I made them pancakes with the works and put it in the refrigerator.

I however went to grab my book and go sit outside. Which lasted a short time because it rained.

I came back into the house and got dressed. Which reminded me that the dryer has been down for almost a week. I was hoping they would get it fix soon for my sake.

I went to the kitchen to finish cleaning it. Wiped down all the countertops, plus the table. Got the dishes done. Ran the garbage outside. Came back in to mop the kitchen floor.

Eleven o'clock A.M is when everyone woke up. I stood in the kitchen watching my parents come out of their room.

I told them good morning when they got to the kitchen.

"Brook Harold!" Mom said.

"Breakfast?" Willie said.

It didn't surprise me they scolded me about breakfast.

"Hi, Mom and Willie." I gave them a smile. "I was up at eight this morning to make breakfast. Though you two were still in bed. But I made it, and it it's in the fridge."

Out of nowhere, Robert slapped me. In confusion, I turned to look at him.

"This is why you get your butt kicked. You should have had breakfast warmed up for us and started lunch. I don't care if they weren't up. That's being rude." Robert growled while he pointed at me.

"Uh. A- again, Willie isn't my par-"

"He's dating your Mom. And when you date someone, you would like to marry them. So, consider them married. Willie is your Dad end of story. Your real Dad left. So, get over it." Robert said while interrupting me.

"Y- you know nothing about my past."

Robert gave me a disbelief look, while he told me,

"You think we were up late drinking for the hell of it? No. The three of us talked. I know your past."

Then Robert stormed off. I stood there stunned. Like what hell?

I looked at Mom and Willie and asked,

"Why? Where did he-? I am lost."

Mom and Willie looked as confused as I did.

"Robert stayed in mine and your Mom's room. But I don't know why he slapped you." Willie said with a hint of a smile.

"Look sweetheart, we will go out to eat. And when we get back, we will move the furniture in the house." Mom told me.

I nodded. Mom and Willie left to go back to their room. I went to stand by the kitchen window to think as I watched the rain fall outside.

One: I had breakfast made. I couldn't warm it up for them because I didn't know what time they would be up.

Two: If Robert knows my pass, he knows about the list. And that's why he hit me. My parents had him believe their lie that I was a bad boy. Or he could have been putting in his two cents. I don't know. But I know, Robert wanted me to call Willie Dad. This guy I never met before thinks he can walk into my parent's house and order me around plus he thinks he had the right to hit me because he was Willie's friend.

"Brook,"

I turned to look at Mom.

She smiled at me with a reply,

"Honey, we are leaving. I love you."

I re-looked out the window then re-looked back at her, as I replied,

"Okay. Have fun. I love you and-" Minute pause. "I love you and."

I couldn't get myself to say it. Mom looked at me waiting for me to finish my sentence. By the smile on her face, she knew what I was trying to say.

I took a deep breath and told her.

"I love you and D- Dad."

After I said it, I turned my focus outside.

I heard them leave; I watched them get into Willie's.... Dad's, somebody's truck.

I went to my room, put my hoodie on and hid under my blankets. I was sleepy.

I took a three-hour nap till Mom came home and woke me.

"Come on Brook. You got to wake up. We got to get the living room back to being the living room." Mom told me.

"(Yawn.) What time is it?" I asked.

"Two. Robert is here to help us."

"Why? I don't want him here." I protested.

"Brook Harold. Be nice. He's Willie's friend."

I gave her a disgusted look. I sat up while I stretched.

"(Yawn.) Okay, I am up. But I can't help a lot. I am still small."

Mom laughed.

"I know, darling. You will be okay."

I got out bed, told Mom I will be right out, running to the bathroom. After the bathroom, I walked towards the living room.

Mom, Willie and Robert were talking among each other. About where they wanted the furniture.

"Hi, Mom and Will-" I stopped talking because Robert was watching me.

I looked away; I swallowed and replied,

"Hi." It didn't want to roll off my tongue easy, but I forced myself to say it. "Dad. Hi."

I gave Willie a smile. I looked over at Robert.

"Thank you, Brook. I love you, my pretty eyes." Willie told me.

"Good job Rookie," Robert told me.

I lost the smile. Rookie? I thought to myself. When I looked over at Mom, she was smiling at me.

"What?" I asked her sounding annoyed.

She walked towards me to hug me and told me,

"It makes me happy that you call Willie that. Plus, Robert is your uncle."

She let go of me then walked over to kiss Willie.

I stood there confused. My uncle? I recently got a new dad and now I have an uncle. Nothing they said or did, surprised me. They were all nuts. I was the only sane one in the family.

"See, I told you we would be a family one day," Willie told Mom.

Oh dear. I thought to myself as I rolled my eyes. God, please help me.

"Are we going to move the furniture?" I asked.

"Yes. My son, my pretty eyes." Willie told me with a smile.

I rolled my eyes. Wonderful.

We got to work moving the furniture back into the house. Robert and Willie took care of the big items. Thank you, Uncle Robert. I still took the small items. And Mom? Making sure the two big boys had their beer.

We got half the furniture moved into the house when the three went out for a smoke.

It's seven o'clock P.M, two hours passed dinner.

I made mashed potatoes and steak for them while they told me I could have a grilled cheese sandwich. Very thoughtful of them. But hey, at least they allowed me to sit at the table with them. Bonus.

On any other day, I had to wait for them to eat first before I could.

After dinner, they finished moving in furniture.

I haven't been happier to clean the kitchen then I was that night. I didn't want to move the furniture.

After I got the kitchen done, I told them I like how the livingroom looks with the new floor.

All three of them gave me an odd look.

"What? Can't I say it looks nice?" I asked

"Yes, you can." Mom said.

"Then why did you all look at me." I said sounding offensive.

"No reason," Uncle Robert said.

"Okay. Do you three need me anymore? Otherwise, I will go into my room." I told them.

"No. Go in your room. We will let you know if we need you." Willie said.

When I got to my room, I sat at my desk. With my chin resting in my hands I looked out the window.

Willie is not my dad. Nor did I want to call him that. Plus, Robert isn't my uncle. That would be Jason, who's married to my Aunt Natalie.

Which then made me think when I lived with Dad. My Dad. Not the jerk who I grew up with. I hung on the good memories to help me survive the hell I lived in.

I lived with Dad for two years and he taught me the basic of life in a caring away.

I lived with Mom and her husband for thirteen years and they also taught me the basic of life... Just in a harsher way.

I was giving myself a headache thinking about when I lived with Dad so i we t to go lay down.

I laid on my bed for half an hour I heard someone open my door.

I opened my eyes; I sat up to look at Willie.

"Hey you. Will you come out here?" Willie asked me.

"Why don't you tell me that I have to come out. Instead of asking me if I want to. Because you and I both know I don't have a choice." I told him sounded grumpy.

Willie looked at me confused.

"Are you grumpy, Brook?"

"I am fine. Let's go."

We both walked out to the living room.

"What's up?" I said sounding annoyed.

"Some of our other friends are coming over. Go get a snack plate ready." Mom said.

I gave them all an angry look.

"I don't want to be out here if you all end up drunk."

"Um, Brook. Most of the time you're not out here when we have our friends over. We ask you to do things beforehand, other than that, you're in my closet." Mom said.

"And we are trying to get you more acquainted with our friends. So you know who is who, plus they know you. Minus helping out when we need you, I allow no one to lay a finger on you unless we say." Willie continued.

I gave Willie a disbelief look while I said,

"Then why did Robert smack me this morning, Willie?"

"Rookie!" Robert said.

I looked over at Uncle Robert.

"He is not my Dad. And I am not calling him that." I told Uncle Robert.

I looked over at Willie. I gave him a confused look. At that moment, I didn't understand why he was taking off his belt.

I looked over at Uncle Robert and he looked confused. The difference was, I knew what Willie was doing, Uncle Robert didn't.

I returned my focus back to Willie.

"Would you leave the belt alone if... If I call you it?" I asked him.

"Hmm. No. I want to know how it feels for you to beg while you call me it. Sassy over here says she loves how you call her mom while you're begging to her." Willie told me.

I looked at Mom and she had a smile on her face. Like she loved the fact her son is getting bullied. It's like she craves it. Feeds off of it.

I looked over at Uncle Robert, which he still looked confused.

"Robert, you look confused," Willie said. "Brook Harold Susie is afraid of belts. I was curious if I took it off and did that magic noise, which he hates, he would beg for me to stop by calling me, Dad." Willie finished saying.

"Ah. Well, that's outright mean." Robert smirked.

If I didn't already feel small, I did then. They were all smiling at me, looking down at me. I closed my eyes while I took a deep breath.

"Do what you have to do, to make yourself happy. I have learned this past six month living here, my thoughts don't matter. I am only here to serve you. Whatever you will do, do it. I have things I need to get done before your other friends show up. Unless you want to be that mean and hold that against me. What are two more ribs broken?" I told them while I gave them all an angry look.

We stood there looking at each other for about two minutes. I think I surprised everyone by what I said.

To be fair, it was a lot to say for a five-year-old.

He wants to hear it. I will give it to him.

"Mom, Dad, and Uncle Robert excuse me, I have things to do in the kitchen."

Feeling proud with a smile on my face, I walked past them.

"Brook Harold! Get back in here." Willie demanded me.

Being the innocent five-year-old I was, I walked back to the living room. But Willie snapped the belt.

I covered my ears quickly. I gave Willie an alarming look.

I did tell them to do what made them happy. I uncovered my ears.

"What do you want from me? Why are you so obsessed with me calling you Dad? Doesn't Willie work anymore? Because It did before Robert said anything." I told him getting upset.

"If you call me Dad, it gives me more power. And you squirm at it, only makes it better!" Willie said.

"Again, what do you want from me?! Are you going to stand there and intimidate me? Or would you like to beat me up?"

Willie smiles at me.

"I want you to get the snacks ready. And we may discuss this topic real soon."

Again, I was the only sane one in that house. I walked back into the kitchen, to finish making the snacks.

After I made snacks for this crazy group. I walked back towards, Mom, Willie, and Robert.

"I made the snacks. Is there anything else you need help with?" I asked, sounding grumpy.

"Nope. Go into your room. I will call you out when people show up." Willie told me.

I nodded and headed towards my room.

I remember I felt anxious about meeting my parent's friends I ended up pacing.

On the positive note, Mom and Willie were having their get together on a Saturday night instead of a Sunday night.

But why do they have to have the get together at night? Why can't they have it during the day? I asked myself this every time they had a party.

I didn't like staying up half the night worrying.

The pacing was getting tiring, so I went to sit in my chair. Which I sat there tapping my foot for five minutes. I got back up to pace more. But then I felt like I was getting cold, so I climbed under my blankets.

Chapter Ten

Saturday night

I was under my blanket for five minutes and I couldn't get warm. I didn't know it then, but my anxiety was causing it.

Because laying down wasn't working, I got up and paced. Again.

I figured I could read. Hoping that would get my mind off what will happen. But I couldn't find my book. So I went to my desk to draw.

It was midnight when I heard a knock on my door. I got up from my desk to open my door.

"Pretty eyes," Willie smirked.

I sensed there was something not right, but I played it cool. As cool as a five-year-old can be.

"Hi, Willie. How are you?" I asked

He laughed quietly.

"I'm great! But you need to come out here. That's an order."

"Yes, Willie."

"But." Willie points at me. "Your sweatshirt comes off first."

I gave him a questioning look as I asked,

"Why?"

"Because we all know it's your security blanket. Well, Brook, you're not safe. Not while you are living here. So, take it off."

I gave him a worried look while I hugged myself.

"I would rather leave it on, If I am not safe. I can still do anything you want."

Willie gave me a disapproval looked has he singled me to back up. I backed away from the door. Willie shut the door behind him after he walked in.

He rubs my face with his hand. I gave him a concerned look.

"Pretty eyes," Willie whispered. "You take that sweatshirt off." Back to a normal voice."Because if you don't do it yourself. You will regret it". Willie threated me.

I shook because of fear. I wasn't sure what this guy would do.

"Why do you look so afraid? I will not hurt you." Willie told me.

I bit down on my bottom lip while I looked away.

"Brook Harold! Look at me." Willie demanded.

I looked back up at him with terror in my eyes.

"You won't take it off, will you? Okay, I warned you."

Willie picked me up and tossed me on my bed. I bounced a little when I hit the bed. I was in shock. Back to, I didn't know what he would do. Nothing he did, surprised me. But for me being young he also scared me.

I watched him crawl on top of me. I groaned as he sat on me.

Feeling anxious, I whispered to Willie,

"What do you want from me?"

He smiled while he slowly unzipped my sweatshirt. I laid there shivering.

Willie stopped halfway, then leaned down and whispered in my ear. When he laid down on me, I felt a bulge in his pants. I closed my eyes because I was frightened.

"I want Brook Harold to suffer."

I re-opened my eyes to watch him sit back up with a smile to continue to unzip my sweatshirt. I was so scared that I cried.

"Pretty eyes. There is no reason to cry. Though, I need you to sit up, so I can take off your sweatshirt." Willie told me in a normal voice while he got done unzipping it.

"Get off of me first," I whispered to him through sniffles.

After he got off of me, I sat up with tears running down my face.

Willie walked up towards me, wiped the tears away from my eyes.

87

"Shh, shh. It's okay. Take it off and give it here. No reason for a meltdown. When you cry, your eyes turn red, and I can't see your pretty blue eyes then." Willie whispered.

While I took off my sweatshirt, I watched Willie look me over.

"Thank you." He said while I handed him my sweatshirt." Let's go into the living room."

Willie grabbed my hand, helped me off of my bed. Then we walked out to the living room.

"Brook! Willie! I was about to come in and get you two. What took so long?" Mom asked.

"Brook and I were having fun," Willie told Mom with a smile.

"What type of fun?" Asked Mom.

Willie puts an arm around me. I shift my eyes to look up at him.

"Brook and I were playing, let's take the sweatshirt off game. It was fun. I should show you how to play sometime." Willie said with a smile laugh.

"I would love to learn." Mom said with a smile.

I watched mom walk towards the kitchen. Willie grabbed my hand and made me walk over with him to Uncle Robert.

I stood next to Willie as he and Uncle Robert talked.

"Brook?"

I turned my head towards my left to see who was saying my name.

I looked up and saw a tall thin man looking down at me. He seemed familiar. I looked over at Willie. He turned to look at this guy.

"Teddy bear! How are you? When did you get here?"

"Half an hour ago. I should ask you the same thing. This can't be Brook. He looked less timid when I first met him back in January."

Willie laughs.

"Yes. I was in the other room, terrorizing him. Oh, my god. He becomes the biggest sissy. You don't have to lay a hand on him, you only have to look at him and he will break down in tears. So probably." Willie said sounding proud.

I gave him an angry look. Then looked back to the floor while I mumbled,

"I am not a sissy." Under my breath.

"What, Brook?" Willie asked me.

I gave Willie a disgusted look and told him,

"I am not a sissy. And you did more than look at me."

Willie smiled and did a quiet chuckle. He kneels down beside me while he told me firmly.

"Brook Harold, I will take you back into that room again and I will do worst to you, then what I did. Stop being lippy."

I glared at him as he stood back up.

I stood by him while he talked to his friends. Mom was in the kitchen talking to her girlfriends about how I call Willie Dad.

I remember I was standing next to Willie and he jerked my arm up.

"Thank you," I told him being sarcastic.

"Sassy!" Willie hurried into the kitchen.

I could barely keep up with him. Dude, the living room was next to the kitchen, you didn't need to rush into there!

And the only reason why he hurried because he over heard Mom telling her friends that I vall him dad.

"Sassy. We should totally show them! But we will have to force it out of Pretty eyes here." Willie told my Mom.

My eyes widen with fear.

"Wait. Show them what?" I asked looking at Mom and Willie.

They both gave me a sinister smile.

Willie overheard Mom saying I call him Dad. Let the fun begin.

Willie put me up against a wall in the livingroom.

I looked around at everyone. I felt worried.

Willie was talking to his boys and Mom was talking to her girls.

There was so much talking going on that I couldn't focus on one conversation. I felt overwhelmed. I looked down at my hands for a few minutes when I saw Willie standing in front of me.

When I looked up at him, he was smiling at me darkly. Then Uncle Robert and Teddy held me against the wall. I gave him a nervous smile. My anxiety skyrocketed.

"Okay, I now need," Willie stops in mid- sentence to look at Mom, for which she was handing him a wooden ruler. He smiled.

"Thank you, sweetie. Okay, you two, which one trust me I won't hit you?" Willie asked.

"I will do it. What do you need? Teddy asked.

"I need you to hold out his arm for me."

Teddy nodded in agreement.

Willie gave me a sinister look. I felt queasy. I didn't know why I am in this position. I looked around at everyone. What do they all want?

I look back up at Willie and gave him a dreadful look.

"Admire the ruler, Brook. For you will feel the sting from it." Willie told me while holding up the ruler.

Admire the ruler? How can you admire something when it causes pain?

I saw him raise his left hand; I closed my eyes.

After the ruler hit my right arm, I made a distressed look on my face.

"It didn't feel good, did it?" Willie asked me.

I shook my head no.

"You'll feel that pain till you show us all you can call me Dad. I won't stop till I hear that word. You have the power to tell me when to stop."

Willie continued to hit me and hit me. The pain was intense.

Mom stood by studying what took place. I kept asking myself why she didn't help me.

I then looked at everyone else laughing.

I knew I could have told him to stop sooner, but I wasn't going to give in.

"Stop. Stop. Robert and Teddy, let go of Brook." Mom said.

For a second I had hope. Maybe Mom came to her senses. I opened my eyes to see Mom whispering something in Willie's ear.

Willie gave me a terrifying smile. I lost that hope. I gave him a pleading look.

Willie continued to hit me. My arm was sore from being hit so many times. I wasn't sure if he hit harder this time around or because Robert and Teddy weren't holding onto me. But I dropped to the ground because I couldn't handle it anymore.

I never understood his obsession with me calling him Dad. If he went all that way to humiliate me, so he will get what he wants. I told him.

"Daddy enough!" I cried out.

Everyone laughed at my misery. They were all happy for Willie.

I sat there looking down at the ground, listening to everyone laugh.

"I didn't drop because of the pain. I dropped because I couldn't handle the humiliation anymore. Dad, if you wanted me to say it, you could have tormented me privately. "I said while still looking down at the ground.

-Chapter Twelve: Remember.-

The next morning I woke up alone. I felt scared. I sat up, looked around the room.

Felt confused as of why my mouth and butt hurt.

After looking down at my lap, it really confused me. Like why were my pants and underwear off?

I put my hands on my head as I thought. The only thing I could remember was him hitting me. Everything else was a blur.

The ruler he used was sitting on the nightstand. I got out of bed as I picked it up. Looked at it, there was blood on it. I looked at my hand, arms, and my legs. Figured the blood was from the cuts. Till I looked at my sheets. It shocked me to see blood on them. Plus, it confused me then because I didn't know if the blood was from me or Willie?

If I could, I would ponder the thought about what happened. But I had to get dressed and get breakfast going.

With my body being sore, mainly my legs and butt, it was hard to get dressed.

Though getting dressed was easier than walking to the bathroom.

When I got to the bathroom, I looked in the mirror.

I had a few scratches on my face. I remember I brought my hand up to my face, ran my finger across my bottom lip. It looked like I had a fat lip too. I took a deep breath and blow out slowly.

I looked at my neck; I had a mark on it. Like he was trying to strangle me, but why?

I remember when I walked into the living room, and I saw my parent's friends were zonked out. I shook my head as I walked toward the kitchen. Looked around the kitchen. They left their beer cans lying around. And this white powder stuff I ran my finger through. I didn't know what it was, so I tasted it. Thinking it was sugar or flour. I soon found out it was neither of them. Then I thought to myself why were they eating this disgusting stuff.

To this day, I still don't understand why people like to use coke. Its disgusting.

Even though everyone was asleep, I knew I had to start breakfast so Uncle Robert won't bitch at me about how bad, and disrespectful I was to my parents

I debated if I should clean the kitchen before or after breakfast. I choose after. That way, I would only have one mess to clean.

I made pancakes and eggs for everyone. Put it in the refrigerator for when they get up.

After I cleaned the kitchen, I went back to my room to clean it.

When I walked in, I felt uneasy. I felt puzzled of what happened.

The amount of blood on my bed didn't add up to my cuts. They were not that deep. I kept thinking it was from Willie.

I looked at the floor. Curious to why my pants were in the middle of the room instead of on the chair. Where I normally put them.

It's like someone took them off of me. Could Willie have taken them off? But for what reason?

And why am I sore when I walk? And why does my throat hurt?

Those two questions I kept asking myself over and over. But I knew how much I wanted the answers, I would not get them.

So, I cleaned my room. Had to get those gross sheets off my bed, anyway. But it was hard to focus. My young mind kept wondering.

Because of my wondering mind, it took longer to clean my room.

By the time I finished my room, I had to go figure out lunch.

Then I thought, what was the point, everyone was asleep still.

I laid down in my bed. Which felt funny. Strange.

I closed my eyes anyway. Thinking about the previous night.

What happened? I couldn't remember. Willie was in my room, but why? Why did I wake up the way I did? The only thing I could remember was Willie hitting me and sitting on me.

I remember I felt angry at myself because I couldn't remember what took place. Only thing I knew I felt scared and dirty.

I remember laying on my bed thinking about the previous night.

Five minutes passed when I saw Mom and Willie come into my room. I got scared and sat up quickly.

I looked at them both with fear.

Willie walked towards me, I backed into the corner on my bed.

I remember I brought my arms up, trying to guard my body. My whole body shook, and I began to cry.

"Are you okay, Brook?" Willie asked.

My breathing got faster as I replied while pointing to Willie,

"You were - you were - you were."

I cried, I closed my eyes tightly and hugged myself.

"I was what?" Willie asked.

I took a deep breath and tried to calm down. Breath. Say it again, I reopened my eyes.

"You were in- you were in my room last night. Why didn't I wake up with pants and underwear on? What happened last night?"

Willie looked over at Mom while he took a sigh.

"Brook, my dear. You won't understand till your much older." Mom spoke for Willie.

I looked at Mom wide eyed.

I didn't care if I would understand till I am older. I wanted answers.

"NO! Something happened last night. WHAT?! I am angry at myself because I can't remember. The only thing I remember was Willie hitting me."

I took a deep breath as I took off my sweatshirt. I showed Mom my arms.

"See, I have the same marks on my legs. And him hitting me shouldn't terrify me this much."

"Oh, Pretty eyes." Willie sounding guilty

I looked at him in surprise.

As I pointed to him, I told him,

"You kept calling me that last night! Get away from me!"

I backed into the corner even though I can't back up any more. I watched Willie walk out of my room.

"Brook. I love you and I am here for you if you need to talk." Mom told me.

I didn't reply to her. I hid in the corner crying.

I woke up from my nap I didn't mean to take. Looked over at my clock, 3'o'clock PM.

I stretched as I sat up. Put my hoodie back on. Then walked to the living room.

"Hi, Brook. How was your nap?" Mom asked me.

"It was good. I didn't mean to fall asleep. Did you guys eat?" I asked.

"Yes. I saw that you got the kitchen picked up, plus the bathroom. Thank you." Mom told me.

"Hi, Brook. Are you doing okay?" Willie asked me.

With an unsure look, I stared at him and nodded.

"You won't talk to me, will you?" Willie asked.

I shrugged my shoulders as I replied,

"I don't want to be rude. If not talking to you is being rude, then I will talk to you."

Willie gave me a smile. Then I saw Robert, and Teddy.

Then I question myself.

Do they know what happened last night between Willie and me?

"Rookie!" Robert said while putting his arm around me.

I flinched as I tried to pull away.

"Willie told us what happen last night. That lucky dog." Teddy said.

I looked up at both with an uneasy look. They know. I thought to myself as my stomach sank.

I felt uncomfortable with them standing next to me. Then Willie walked towards me.

"Come on Brook. Let's get you away from these two crazy boys." He said while taking my hand.

I jerk my hand away from Willie.

"Why don't you tell them to go, instead of taking my hand and leading me somewhere," I told him in a grumpy tone.

Willie gave me a confused look.

"Okay. Go on, you two. Leave him be." Then he looked down at me. "Brook, if you're going to be grumpy, go to your room. I don't want to hear whining."

"What for?!"

Willie gave me an angry look and pointed towards the hallway.

I returned the angry look and stormed off.

I walked into my room, fell on my bed and cried. I felt like I was on a roller coaster with my emotions. I wasn't sure what to feel.

I kept having flashbacks of the pervious night. Willie hitting me over and over with that damn ruler.

Did I ask for it? What did he do? Why didn't I have anything on when I woke up? I had all these questions I knew I wouldn't get an answer.

What made it worse, was when I came out of my room, everyone left. Okay, not a problem. Except for they went out to eat. That drove me insane. While they get good, tasting food, I am stuck here eating PBJ's or grilled cheese. Or nothing at all. Plus, I get to clean the house.

So, I got the chores done then made myself dinner. Then went to watch a movie.

After the movie, I went to take a shower.

While in the shower, the water stung my cuts. I let out a moan. But standing in a warm shower felt amazing.

I remember I leaned against the wall, watching the water hit the glass door. It was almost hypnotizing to watch. I let the tears run down my face.

I felt angry and terrified at Willie but I wasn't sure why. If he did something why doesn't Mom kick him out? Because she never cared about me. She only cared about her damn self.

After my shower, I got my pajamas on.

I was about to climb into bed, but I stopped myself. My chest felt heavy. At the time, I didn't know if I was safe sleeping in my bed or not. I felt like my heart would jump out of my chest. I let out a scream. I couldn't bring myself to lie down in my bed. I didn't feel safe. I thought of the couch. But then he could try to bring me back to my room. I hate him. I hate her. I hate being here.

I closed my eyes and took a deep breath. I climbed into my bed and laid there trying to fall asleep. But every time I closed my eyes, I thought about the previous night.

I laid there for an hour. Tossing and turning. I wanted to go to sleep darn it. I kept tossing and turning for another thirty minutes.

Then heard a noise outside. I looked over at my clock, ten o'clock PM. Good, they are home. Once they pass my bedroom door to get to their room, I would be happy. But that wasn't the case. They knocked on my door instead.

I sat up while Mom and Mr. Jerk (Willie) walked in.

"Yes? What can I help you with?" I asked them.

"We were checking on you before we went to bed. You seemed a little lost all day." Mom said.

I looked away from them and replied,

"I am fine." I re-looked at Mom and Mr. Jerk. "I am tired, I had a long weekend. Actually, a long week."

"Okay. We love you, you know that right? Get some rest, honey." Mom told me.

"Tomorrow the repair guy for the dryer will come out. So, I won't be going into my second job. Okay?" Mr. Jerk told me.

I nodded. They left the room.

Not the news I wanted to hear while I was trying to get to bed. I didn't want to be stuck in the house with him. No use worrying over it. I needed sleep. Which turned into a nightmare.

I woke up in a cold sweat. Heart beating fast, breathing hard. With wide eyes, I looked around my room in a panic.

Where is he? Where is he? I whispered to myself.

After I realized I was safe, I slowed my breathing.

I took a deep breath as I laid back down, hugged my pillow while I cried.

I heard my alarm go off. Crossed eye, I looked over at my clock, 6:30 AM.

I hit the snooze button and rolled back over, yawn, stretch.

I rubbed my eyes. Looked at my clock, then looked out my window. I re-looked at my clock in shock.

7:30! I told myself out loud.I needed to be up at seven! I continued to talk to myself.

I hurried out of my room to make breakfast. I set out the cereal for them. It was quick and easy.

I heard someone walking this way, look calm.

I turned and I gave him a sleepy look.

"Good morning Brook. You look sleepy, did you sleep well?" Asked Mr. Jerk.

"Yes. It's been a long week/weekend, remember." I replied back.

"Honey, you look like you didn't sleep." Mom told me.

"I am fine. Here is breakfast. I am going to go get ready."

I walked pass them to get to my room.

No, I didn't sleep well but they wont want to hear that. Even if they did, they wouldn't care.

After I got ready, I walked back out to the kitchen.

Huh, I chuckled to myself. I guess they didn't want cereal. Oopsie.

When they came out of their room, the three of us walked out to his truck.

I don't want to be sitting next to him, I don't care if it takes a minute to get to Junes. I don't like feeling trapped, and that's how I feel sitting between Mr. Jerk and Mom. Why can't his truck have a back seat?

When we showed up at June's house, she was waiting outside for us.

Willie put the car in park and then Mom got out and I followed her out. When I looked back at Mr. Jerk, he gave me a smile.

I got goose bumps at the sight of his smile. I turned to look at Mom, she also was smiling at me. I finally faced June.

"Brook, it's nice to see you without your hoodie on," June told me with a smile.

I gave her a sleepy smile.

"You might need a nap today, huh? You could take one when the kids go outside." June told me.

I shrugged my shoulders.

"Same plan as normal then?" June asked Mom.

"Yes, but Willie will be in my car. I get it back today, I am super excited." Mom replied back to June.

June laughs quietly and replies with a smile,

"You don't like Willie's car?"

"Our secret, Chevy's are better than Dodges." Mom smiled at June. "I got to run. Bye, Brook."

"Okay, our secret. Have a nice day."

June looked down at me with a smile then loses her smile when she looked at my arms and said my name in a concerned way.

I gave her a shameful look.

"Sigh, Come on Brook. Let's get you into the house." June told me.

We both walked into the house. I walk towards the living room.

"Hi, Jeorge and Hillary."

"Hi!" They both said at the same time.

I smiled at them.

I like being here. I love being here in a matter of fact. It's a place where I can relax. Where I can be a kid.

I tried to play with the other kids today but they kept walking away from me.

"Our parents said we can't play with you. They said you are trouble." One of the kids told me.

I looked at this kid, looking confused and replied back,

"Trouble? I am trouble? H- How? I am a pretty good kid. I don't understand."

"Our parents say that you are a freak and you do this to yourself to seek attention." The same kid said then walked away.

I do this to myself, to seek attention? So I am trouble? I am confused.

It could be the reason why Jeorge and Hillary are the only ones who play with me.

I walked up to Hillary to see what she was doing.

"My cousin doesn't want to play with you. You attention seeker, go sit in your corner." This kid told me.

"Hi, I am Brook. What is your name? And shouldn't she make that call?" I turned my focus to her. "Hillary?" I said.

I watched Hillary look at the both of us.

"Sorry Brook," Hillary told me.

"I am Ben by the way. The one that called you a freak, is my brother Chris. Bye.." He said while walking away with Hillary.

With a disbelief look on my face as I thought to myself,

really? She might be your cousin, doesn't mean you can boss her around.

On the bright side I still have Jeorge. I looked over at Jeorge, he was playing with other kids. Sigh, yeah not even going to bother.

Since everyone plus, Hillary is against me today, like Ben said,

"Go sit in your corner Brook."

I grabbed a ball before I went to sit down in my corner.

I sat down and rolled the ball between my hands, keeping myself busy till lunch.

I should take that nap when the kids go outside.

I am hoping, it goes well later with Willie. I mean Mr. Jerk. I rolled my eyes.

I am curious what chores awaits me when I get home.

I am sure if the repairman fixes the dryer, I will have to wash laundry. Yay.

It was finally lunch time, June called us kids into the dining room. Everyone sat down except for me. I didn't feel right at the table, after what Chris said. But then again, I should eat because I don't want to be an "attention seeker" by not eating.

"Brook, why don't you go eat. Are you not hungry?" June asked me.

I shrugged my shoulder and replied,

"I'm not hungry, I am sleepy. What about that nap, you mentioned earlier. I would love a nap."

June gave me a smile, and replied,

"Let the kids finishing eating. I will send them out to the backyard then you can lay down on the couch."

CHAPTER ELEVEN

AFRAID

One o'clock PM:

The kids were getting ready to go outside to play. I was getting ready for my nap. Much needed a nap to survive later at home.

I heard a faint voice calling my name as I started to wake up.

"No. Let me sleep," I grumbled.

"Brook, you got to get up. Willie is here." June said.

I squinted my eyes to look at June as I replied,

"Willie? No, I am happy here."

I re-closed my eyes.

"Brook Harold. You got to get up. We got to go home."

Either June's voice got rasper or that is Willie.

I re-opened my eyes to see Willie standing above me.

Feeling scared, I hurried to my feet and gave him a bothered look.

"Hi. We got to get home." Willie told me.

I looked at June and asked,

"Can I stay here longer? I don't want to go home. I can go home, I can go home- What time is it?"

"Two-fifty." June mention.

"I can go home when Mom gets home." I finished saying.

I saw June look at Willie then back at me.

"Okay, what's going on now? He doesn't want to go home with you but he is willing to go home when Susie is there. I am getting at that he doesn't want to be alone with you. Did you hurt Brook?" June asked.

"No. I don't know why he's saying this." Willie replied sounding surprised.

Confused, I looked up at Willie. Why does he sound so surprised? I thought to myself.

"Then where did he get these marks from?" June asked while pointing to my arms.

Willie snaps his fingers and replies,

"My friend did this. I just remembered. I brought Suzie out on a date and we came back home, Brook had these marks. Though, he is no longer allowed over."

I gave Willie an annoyed look.

June stood there for a minute before replying,

"You got to go home, Brook. Willie said no. Maybe next time."

I started to feel anxious.

"Okay. Thank you." I told June.

I followed Willie out to the SUV. I looked back at June, which she was standing at the door. She looks regretful. Like she knows that more is going on then Mom and Mr. Jerk say. Like they are always lying to her and she knows it.

"What are you telling June, that she keeps asking questions?" Willie asked me.

I turned my focus from outside to Willie.

"I am not telling her anything," I told him.

"Then why does she keep bugging Mom and me?" Willie asked sounding annoyed.

"Have you ever thought it's the way you send me?"

"The way we send you?" He asked.

"I keep going there with different marks. In this case, my arms. Because you kept hitting me with a ruler!" I growled at him.

I heard Willie mumble something to himself as we pulled into the driveway. He turned off the car and turned back to look at me, while he smiled,

"Should we go inside?"

I don't trust his smile. I gave him an annoyed look while I replied, "It's not like I have a choice."

"fair enough."

Willie got out of the SUV walked around to the passenger side to get me out.

"So, which of your friends are not allowed over anymore?" I asked while walking into the house.

"What?" Willie asked with a confused look.

I watched him hang up his keys on the key hook thingy.

"What you told June," I replied back.

"Oh, I was lying. I gave you those marks." Willie told me.

"I know. Thus the reason why I am afraid of you."

"Huh? That's the reason why you are afraid of me? Okay."

"But you also did something else, that I can't remember. Everything is a blur minus you hitting me!"

"And that's all you need to know, for now."

When the repair guy showed up, Willie sent me to go clean his and Mom's room.

When I walked in, I wish he didn't tell me. It was a disaster in there. Sigh, I finished walking into the room, looked around. Then I spotted a notebook on their bed.

I walked towards the bed, I open it up and started to read.

For the little amount that I can read. I couldn't believe what I was looking at! It was Mom and Willie's list.

Hmm. I should go put it in my room.

I hurried to my room before I get caught with the notebook.

Once in my room, I put the notebook under my bed.

Then went back to Mom and Willie's room.

By the time I finished cleaning, Willie walked in asking how it was going.

I looked up at Willie, I looked around the room then I re-looked back up at him.

"The room is clean," I said with a smile. "Is the dryer fixed?" I asked.

He nodded at me while he replied,

"Yes, I want you to go do laundry. We need clothes wash. This time, don't break it. And if you do, let your Mom or I know. Right away, instead of hiding it."

I gave him a disbelief look.

"After what happened last Monday, I will tell you anything. I don't need any more pain. Well, minus what happened on Saturday night. I want my side to heal but you need to stop picking on me!" I told Willie, getting angry.

He gave me a disgusted look while he replies,

"I can do whatever I want. Do you want to start arguing with me? Do you need a reminder about last Monday?" he snickered. "You shouldn't, you brought it up. If the answer is no to arguing with me, I want you go get your chores done."

I watched Willie walk out of his room, he walked back in. Realizing that it is his room.

He looked down at me, told me to get out of his room and go make dinner.

I glared at him while I was leaving the room.

No, I don't want to fight with Mr. Jerk but I don't need him to bring up the past about what I did not do when I did do it. I went to start a load of laundry then went to the kitchen to figure out dinner.

They have a frozen pizza in the freezer that I made for them. If it's not what they want, they will have to figure it out on their own.

I ran back to the laundry room to check on the washer.

When I was walking back to the kitchen, I saw Mom come into the house.

"Brook, where is dinner?" She asked me.

I gave her a confused look while I replied,

"It's only four - fifteen. You are early. Dinner will be done shortly, it's in the oven. Good news though, your room is clean and the washer is fix. The bad news is that June was asking questions again and Willie lied to her again. But I will let you talk to Willie about that topic."

"Oh great. Mom said while rolling her eyes. "What did you do now Brook?" She asked.

I looked at her, trying to figure out what to say.

"I, I did- what did I do? You mean what did you do? You send me to daycare with all these marks on me. Plus according to the two kids at daycare, I do this to seek attention. How does that make you feel." I replied back.

Mom started to laugh. Thanks, Mom. Make me feel better. I thought to myself.

"What is funny?" I asked

"What you said. You are an attention seeker." Mom said while still laughing.

"What is going on in here?" Willie asked.

"Our kid is an attention seeker. Mom told Willie.

"Oh? How so?" Willie asked.

"The two kids told me that they heard from their parents, I do this to myself for attention," I told Willie.

"Well, you should stop hitting yourself then," Willie told me with a smile.

"I am glad I am here to amuse you both."

I walked away from them to get the pizza out of the oven.

"Dinner is ready," I told them sounding annoyed. "Now, after you get done eating, I would like to talk to you both. But for now, I will be in my room." I told them while I walked passed them.

Once in my room, I grabbed the notebook and went to sit in my chair to read it.

They, Mom and Willie, keep track of every detail.

The words I use, the body language I use.

They plan when my next punishment is. They don't have a date for my next one. But it looks like I still have 10 strikes left till something happens. They only give me ten strikes? Hmm, weird.

Now, the question is, will I have another severe beating? Will they push me into the wall and use the belt on me? The ruler? Or how crazy they are, they could use both.

Huh, there's a page in here for when I can eat. I looked up from the book. When I can eat? Okay.

Oh look, a page that reads, what has been done.

I flipped through those pages and stop at one page that caught my eye.

Wait, what does S and A mean? The date on that was- Saturday!

I looked up from the notebook, gazed at my bed.

What do those two letters mean?

I sat there staring at the two letter on the page, S, and A.

I heard Mom call me from the other room.

I hid the notebook under my shirt and walked out to the living room.

Mom and Mr. Jerk were sitting on the couch when I walked in.

"Yes?" I asked.

"You wanted to talk to us. What on your mind sweetie?" Mom asked.

"Right. Umm. I overheard you two talking yesterday to your group about S and A? What is that? It has been on my mind since yesterday?" I asked.

Mom and he looked at each other.

He clears his throat and replies,

"Is that all you heard?"

I nodded

"Does S and A have to do with what happen Saturday night?" I asked.

"No. We were talking about, -"

"About our friends baby name. S and A means Seth Alex." Mom finished Willie's sentence.

He looked at Mom, she shrugged her shoulders at him.

"See, nothing to worry about," Willie told me with a smile.

I suspect their lying.

"Are you sure it doesn't mean anything else?" I replied

"Yes. And you were asleep when we talked to them. I even checked on you." Mom said.

"That you know of. Well, I am not believing you for the meaning of it." I pulled out the notebook from under my shirt. Mom plus Willie's eyes gotten wider. "Because, in your little booklet of yours, it says: The 12th of June of this year, Willie S. A. Brook. Correct me if I am wrong, but that isn't a baby's name. Willie Seth Alex Brook."

I looked away for a moment. Repeated the name to myself. Well, shoot. After I said it, it could be a name and I could be wrong.

No, something did happen.

When I looked back at Mom and Willie, they were both smiling at me. I shook my head no while I told them,

"No! That isn't a name. That means something, something he did!"

"Let's do this Brook. Take a seat, close your eyes and tell me what happened." Willie told me.

While I was grabbing my seat, Willie whispered something to Mom then she got up.

I watched mom walk over to the stereo, she turned on some relaxing music to help me relax and focus.

I sat down in the recliner, got comfy and closed my eyes.

"Good. Now, listen to the music and re-think about Saturday night after you and I went into your room." Willie told me.

"Once we got into my room, you told me to lay down. I questioned you at first but you gave me an angry look, I did what you told me to do. You turned off the lights then joined me in bed. You laid down next to me and wrapped your arm around me. Then you ran your fingers through my hair. Then down my arm to my hand. Which from there, you started to rub my hand. I started to panic, you told me to stop,"

"Right, keep going," Willie told me.

"I listened because I was scared. After that, you started to rub my leg. I started to whimper, again. You flipped me onto my back

and sat on me. You told me to knock it off plus you told me that, I kept telling myself how bad this was. And told me to tell myself how much I loved it. I told you no because I was scared. You told me that you had the ruler in your hand, and you threatened me with it."

"Continue."

"Because I sat there in silence, you hit me and told me you wouldn't stop till you heard me say it. I gave in because I was getting tired of being hit," I said while I started to panic.

"Calm down sweetheart." I heard Mom told me.

"And?" Willie asked me.

"You were still on top of me, I felt you put your hands down my pants. And, and, I can't remember. I can't." I finished saying while I started to cry.

I opened my eyes to see Willie walking back and forth.

"Calm down, sweetheart." Mom told me.

I looked at them in a frantic.

"Is that why I didn't have any pants or under wear on when I woke up?!" I said in a panic.

Willie clears his throat, looks at Mom and says while clenching his teeth,

"You had more off than just your pants and underwear."

Willie looked back at me. I gave him a shocked look while I asked,

"What?! What were you doing?!!"

"You tell me," Willie told me while walking up to me. "Re-close your eyes, and think hard," Willie told me while he put his hands on the armrest of the chair.

Feeling worried, I looked at him. I looked down as I took a deep breath. I closed my eyes as I exhaled.

I was trying to think real hard of what took place. I can still feel Willie's gaze on me. I ran both of my hands across my face while I sighed.

"Think real hard," Willie tells me, sounding annoyed.

"I am trying. Though, though, I can't remember."

Willie sighs, then he put his hand down my pants.

I gasp. It alarmed me when he grabbed my penis.

Feeling terrified, I respectfully asked him to stop. Willie took his hand out of my pants.

When I re-opened my eyes, I saw him walking away from me. He turned to look back at me.

"That's what I did to you in your room, Pretty eyes. Plus, I had sex with you."

Chapter Twelve

Obedience

I sat there very confused.

"Is that what S and A means?" I asked.

"It's another name for it." Mom said.

I bit my bottom lip. Still feel very confused.

"What is the point of the notebook then? You have things in here about when I get beaten and when I can have food. Plus many other things, that I don't need to tell you because you wrote it or he wrote it." I said.

"That is pretty much what the booklet is. To keep track of your obedience to us." Mom told me.

I got up from the chair, threw the notebook down.

"Well, what the fu- Who the hell am I to you two?! Obviously not your kid, Mom. And definitely not yours Willie. Am I here for your amusement? To use me? Am I your punching bag, when you two get pissed off?!" Enraged, I told them. I took a deep breath before speaking again. "Answer me this, I have lived here for six months. This past week, you both have beaten me up. Willie intimidated me." I point to Willie. "You are so obsessed with me calling you dad, you humiliated me in front of your friends. And I had to go through hell in my room because you had to have sex with me? I didn't even want plus I don't even know what that is?! What the fuck do you want from me?!"

Mom stood up from the couch as she told me firmly.

"You are here, Brook Harold Susie, for our services! For the good and the bad. I have full custody of you, Willie and I can do whatever we want to you. Like I told you when I brought you home from your Dads, I want obedience, no talk back. Chores have to be done. We may give you pain, but we don't want to hear it after the situation. We want to hear your cries during the beatings. Like Willie said, we will grab a drink or a joint to relax. The other way we relax is tormenting you. Willie may slap you around with ease but I need to be at my breaking point! Which I was when I whipped you. Hell, don't push me, I will do it again. And this little stunt is pushing me there. I have five strikes and Willie has five, ten total. I don't know where he stands, but for me, your down two. So, start kissing up to me honey!" I gave Mom a bothered look.

"I agree with Mom. You have two left. Four totally. You better be nice. By the way, I am the parent, don't tell me what I can't do, Brook Harold. We have full custody." Willie said.

I looked away, I chuckled to myself. I can't believe what I am hearing. I thought to myself.

"Not trying to be rude, but you are not my Dad. You don't have the full custody, my mom does. So, you don't have authority to use my middle name." I told him with a hint of a smile while I crossed my arms.

"What?" Willie asked me while walking back towards me.

I am standing my ground and not letting them see my fear. Even though on the inside, I am falling apart, feeling frightened. I don't want a repeat of last Monday. I really don't.

"You can't use my middle name," I told him.

"And you shouldn't have gone through our stuff, Brook Harold!"

"I didn't go through your stuff, I was cleaning the room and saw the notebook on the bed. Again, your not allowed to my middle name!"

"Brook, because it was on our bed, doesn't mean you had to look at it. That was being rude. You could have left it there or put it

-Page120-

somewhere else." Mom told me.

I looked over at her then back up to Willie. I wish he wasn't standing there with a dumb smile on his face. I don't trust him.

I closed my eyes, took a deep breath, and asked while re-opening my eyes.

"Why did I go through hell this week? Because I haven't listened? Because I am lippy. Because I am not showing my happiness? What have I done?!"

"You do listen, but you need to listen better. And knock off your lippy ness. Again, don't show us your pain. Be happy. You have a loving family that cares for you. You have food, a shelter, and clothes to wear. You have a lot compared to most. So, start being thankful. You ungrateful child." Mom told me.

"I agree with your Mother. We want you to be submissive to us. Be afraid of us. Show us the respect we deserve. Your Mom works a part time job and I work a full time plus a part time job to give you what you need. Again, be grateful." Willie said.

As he was walking by me, he shoved me over.

I looked over at him, and gave him a disgusted look. I turned my focus back to Mom.

She walked over towards me, pushed me into the wall, got into my face, and threatened me,

"Don't make me use the belt on you."

After she said it, I watched Mom walk over to Willie, for he had a smirk on his face.

When they walked out of the room, I slid down and sat on the floor and cried.

I am grateful, they are not. What do they give me? Nothing minus hardship.

I am sure they're sitting in their room, planning our next "Relaxing moment" between the three of us. Especially if I only have four strikes left. Good job Brook, get yourself in trouble.

It's bad enough that I have Willie walking around poking at me but now I have to watch Mom. Because I pushed her closer to her

-Page121-

breaking point. Plus, she already threatened me. I will have to be more careful now and play the good card. Again.

I suppose I should get up and get the kitchen cleaned.

Sigh, I only got one load of laundry done. I rolled my eyes, oh well.

After I got things done, I went to talk to Mom and Dad--, ugh, I mean, Willie. Why do I keep calling him Dad?

He must have drilled that into my head while he was having his "fun" with me.

I knocked on the door, they said to come in.

I walked in, looked at the floor. I believe this is how you're supposed to be submissive.

"What's up sweetie?" Mom asked.

Still looking down, I asked respectfully,

"May I talk to you two?"

"Brook Harold, look up," Willie told me.

I looked up at them both.

"Thank you, Brook." I know a way to make him happy.

"You're welcome Daddy," I told him with a smile.

Willie returns the smile.

"Now, what do you want, sweetie?" Mom asked.

"I re-cleaned the kitchen. Started a load of laundry. Do I have permission to go to bed?" I asked.

"From me, yes. Willie?" Mom said.

"Go grab me a drink, then you can go to bed," Willie told me.

"Yes, sir."

As I was about to walk out of the room, Mom told me to grab one for her as well.

"Yes, ma'am. Anything else?"

They both shook their head no.

"I will be right back."

I shut the door behind me as I was leaving the room.

I walked back to the kitchen, grabbed their whiskey. Brought it back to the room, knocked before entering. They told me to

-Page122-

come in.

"Here's your whiskey." With a smile, I told them while handing them their drink.

They both told me, thank you.

"Your welcome. Do I-, err, sorry. I mean, may I go to bed?"

"Yes. Good night, Pretty eyes. I love you." Willie told me.

"Good night, sweetie. I love you." Mom told me.

"Goodnight, Mommy, and Daddy. I love you both."

I left the room, walked towards my room.

Okay, I want to scream. I can't keep playing that, perfect act.

I took a deep breath as I ran my fingers through my hair, I exhaled. But you will, to stay on their good side.

I got ready for bed. Though, I still have issues getting into my bed. It might be easier to cope with what happened if he didn't do whatever in my bed. Don't think about it, just don't.

I took a deep breath, exhaled, went to turn off the light and climbed into my bed. Layed down on my left side, pulled up my blanket and tried to go to sleep.

I jumped awake, looked around the room, where am I?

I am confused, plus a little worried.

I saw someone open a door. After I was able to focus, I realized where I was.

"Pretty eyes, what are you doing?." Daddy asked a tired way.

"I- I fell off my bed. I guess." I replied to him.

"Well, get back into bed and don't fall off next time. Are you okay at least?" He asked me.

"Yes. Sorry for waking you, Daddy."

I heard him mumbled while he was shutting my door.

I pulled myself up off the floor. Felt a little unstable, walked out of my room towards the bathroom.

After the bathroom, I walked to the kitchen to grab some water.

While standing in the kitchen, I looked out the window while drinking my water. I was thinking about what happened.

Why did I fall out of my bed? I remember feeling like someone or
-Page123-
something was pinning me down. It bothers me. Did Daddy, only here a noise and come in to check on me? Or did he do something and acting innocent?

I went to lay back down. I actually have to get up on time this time. I have to stay on my, my, (deep breath), my parent's good side. There I said it, (Sigh), I said it.

The next thing I heard, was my alarm going off. I grumbled as I looked at my alarm clock crossed eyed, 6:30 AM.

I suppose I should get up. Remember Brook, happy face, happy face. You can do this!

Yeah, it's too early to for that nonsense.

I walked towards the bathroom, when I got there, I looked in the mirror. Trying to practice my, "happy face", still not getting into the right mood.

I walked towards the kitchen but I saw Daddy getting his shoes on.

Haha, that's right, he doesn't need to take Mom to work. He looks so tired.

"Hi, Daddy,"

He looked up at me, then back down to his shoes.

"You look tired. Take it easy at work today. I love you." I told Dad with a smile.

He looked back up to me and asked,

"Thank you Pretty eyes. How can you be this cheerful in the morning?"

"Oh, you know. I love getting up and making Mom breakfast," I said with a smile.

"I should get up extra early tomorrow and make you breakfast."

Daddy gave me a tired smile as he replied,

"I would like that. Thank you. I got to run, see ya later, Pretty eyes."

"Bye Daddy."

(Snort) You will get up and make breakfast for him. I chuckled to myself. What the hell did you comment to?

-Page124-

Well, let's focus on today. I went to start a load of laundry before I started making breakfast.

I walked back into the kitchen to figure out what to make.

I will make Mom oatmeal, which is on the top shelf. Oh boy, don't drop it this time.

I went to grab the step stool from the closet, brought it to the kitchen, stood on it to grab the oatmeal. Yay! I grabbed it! I chuckled to myself while getting off the step stool.

I went to go put the step stool back in the closet.

Made her breakfast, picked up my mess. Then I realized I never put the oatmeal away.

After that ordeal, I went to go throw the clothes into the dryer.

Went to take a quick shower. Got dressed, brushed my teeth.

"Good morning Brook."

I looked at Mom through the mirror, which she was standing in the doorway of the bathroom.

I was still brushing my teeth when I gave her a tooth pasty smile.

She at me over.

"Humph. Is breakfast ready?"

I nodded to her. I watched her walk away while I finished brushing my teeth.

Ran to my room to make my bed, straighten up a little bit.

Walked out to the living room, to make sure it was still neat.

I went to sit on the couch, I have been on my feet since I gotten up. Plus, I haven't eaten yet, and I am hungry.

"Brook, honey, are you ready to leave?"

But then again, food is over rated. I looked over to see Mom looking at me

."Yes, ma'am," I replied back with a smile.

"I love your smiles this morning. You seem so happy. It makes me happy." Mom told me with a smile.

I returned the smile.

At June's:

This time June wasn't outside waiting.

-Page125-

Mom and I got out of the car and walked into the house.

"Hello. Brook and Suzie. How are you, Brook?" June asked.

"We are good. Thank you." Mom replied.

June gave us a confused looked.

"Okay, good. The same plan like normal?" June asked.

"Yes. Brook could be tired due to him being up early." Mom replied.

"Well, he could take another nap."

"Another nap? Did he take one yesterday?"

"Yes, while the other kids went to play outside."

"Oh. Willie didn't tell me that. Okay, thank you. Have a good day, Brook sweetie."

"Bye Mommy. I love you. Have a good day." I told Mom with a smile.

Mom smiled at me then left.

"Hi, June. How are you?" I asked.

"I am well. thank you. How are you?" June replied.

"I am good, thank you. May I go play?" I asked.

"Yes, go on."

I walked towards the living room, I stopped, I looked around at everyone. I must be the last kid to get here and the first one to leave.

Jeorge and Hillary were already playing with other kids.

I looked over at my spot, then back at the kids.

Look, nobody is at the craft table. I walked over there and sat down to draw.

I was drawing out my thoughts of what happened last Saturday and my talk with my parents last night. I am trying to understand it.

"Hi, Brook. What are you drawing?" Hillary asked me.

I looked up at her, flip my paper over so she won't see my drawing.

"Hi, Hil-Hillary. Where's your cousins?" I asked.

"Over there playing. Care if I join you?" Asked Hillary.

-Page126-

"Go ahead. It's not my table." I told her.

So, Hillary sat down with me, across from me.

We sat there for five minutes when I realized Ben was looking at me. I looked up and asked,

"Yes?"

"We want to sit here with Hillary, so move."

I looked over at Hillary, she gave me a slight smile.

"It might be best if you listen to him. I don't want you to get into trouble." Hillary told me.

I gave her a confused looked.

"Wha-? We all can sit here." I said.

"Brook, it's best if you move."

"Can I at least finish this one part?"

After I asked, Ben took my paper from me.

"What is this?"

I jumped up from my seat.

"Hey, give it back," I said.

"Ben, give back his paper." Hillary said.

I watched Chris walk up to Ben and take the paper from him.

"Are you asking for more attention?" Asked Chris.

"No! Give me my paper back," I told him.

"Look, everyone, Brook is trying to get more attention," Chris said.

"No! Give me my paper!"

Chris and Ben started to laugh as they walked away with my paper. Feeling frustrated, I sat down, I looked over at Hillary.

"If you told them to buzz off, we wouldn't be here," I told Hillary.

"Sorry, but I did tell you it was best for you to leave," Hillary told me.

"Like that would make a difference? They would find a different way to bug me."

"Exactly what are you trying to draw that they are saying that you are seeking attention?" Hillary asked.

"It doesn't matter," I said while looking away.

-Page127-

"It does for you to be drawing it."

I looked back at Hillary.

"Do you want your paper back?" Ben told me while he waved the paper in my face.

I gave him an annoyed look.

"Yes, please," I said.

"Benjamin! Christopher! Give me the paper and leave Brook alone," June told them.

She took the paper from Ben then looked at it.

I looked at the table. I heard her sigh as she said,

"Alright kids, get along till lunch. Brook, come here."

I looked up at her, then looked away.

I got up from my seat, followed June out of the room, I heard Chris and Ben do quiet snicker. I shot them a them an irritated look.

I followed June to the dining room.

"Sit Brook. Tell me about your drawing. What's gong on at home?" June asked while sitting across from me.

I looked at her then turned my focus to the floor.

"Does this have to do with how you acted towards Willie yesterday?"

I looked back at her and replied, quietly,

"No."

I relook at the floor, while we sat there in silence for a couple of minutes. I heard June sigh.

"It was my Uncle Robert." I told her as I looked at her.

"Your Uncle Robert? I didn't know that you had an Uncle Robert."

"I do. He looks like Willie. That friend Willie mention about yesterday. Yeah, my uncle." I said with a smile, she returned the smile.

"Go play Brook."

"Can I have my picture back?" I asked

"I am going to hold onto it. I want to ask Willie about it." June replied.

My eyes widen with fear as I replied,

"You can't, pleases don't."

"Why?" June asked sounding concerned.

"Be-because I don't want my parents to worry. They don't know that Uncle Robert, hurt me." I said in a panic.

By June's expression, it looks like she was thinking.

"Okay, go play Brook. But I am still going to hold onto it." June told me.

I wandering back into the living room. Should I go play, so someone can tell me to get lost and take my toys from me or should I go sit in my corner?

"Bookie!" I looked over to see Jeorge walking towards me.

"Are you avoiding me." He asked me.

I gave him a smile.

"Hi. No, I am not avoiding you. You were playing with the other kids. Same as yesterday. So I left you alone." I told Jeorge.

"Oh. Well, you could have at least said hi." Jeorge told me.

"I know. I replied.

"Do you want to find something that we can do with each other?"

"Like what?" I asked

"I don't know. June as a lot of toys, so pick something. Unless you are not in the mood."

Before I could respond, one of the other kids walked up to get Jeorge to play with him.

"I- umm," I was trying to think of what to say. "I am not in the mood. Go on and play." I told him.

Jeorge gave me a confused look and asked,

"Okay. Are you okay, Brook?"

"Uh- huh," I told him while a nodded.

I gave him a smile then walked over to my corner.

I sat down and watched the other kids play. I hate feeling alone.

I try to play with the other kids but they push me aside.

Then Ben and Chris tells me that I am trying to seek attention because I sit by myself. It doesn't matter, I suppose.

"Kids, lunch time. After lunch, we will go outside." June told us kids. I watched all the kids follow June to the other room. Then I looked back down to my hands.

-Chapter Fifteen: What's not allowed-

"Brook,"

I looked up to see June standing in front of me.

"You know, ever since you started to come, you claimed this corner has your own." June smiled at me. "I can move a chair over here so you won't have to sit on the ground," June told me.

"I am fine," I replied to her.

"Well, come eat."

"Not hungry," I told her as I look back at my hands.

June got down to my level.

"Brook,"

I gave her my attention.

"You haven't eaten here since last Thursday. I am afraid that your not going to anymore. Because everyone stopped eating to look at you while you scarf down your food. Plus, your losing weight. Your five, Brook, you shouldn't be losing weight." June tells me quietly.

I looked away from her as I replied back,

"Oh." I replied sounding sad.

"Another thing, I am not your mother. Let's go eat." June said while taking my hand.

I got up with her, followed her to the dining room.

"Sit Brook," June told me with a smile.

I watched her walk away.

I sat down but I stared at my plate while everyone ate.

Half an hour passed when June came back in.

She gave me a disappointed look.

"Alright, kids all you guys can get ready to go outside."

All the kids let out a cry of excitement while they hurried to get ready.

"Brook?"

I looked up to June while I replied,

"What?"

-Page130-

June sighs while smiling at me. And asked me while opening up the sliding door to let the kids outside,

"You're not going to eat, are you?"

"I said I wasn't hungry," I told her.

"Are you telling yourself that because your Mom won't feed you."

I looked away from her for a few minutes before returning my attention to her.

"Do you want to know the truth?" I asked June.

"Yes."

"I am not hungry. That's the truth."

June smiles at me and tells me to go play.

I walked outside onto the patio.

"Come play, Brook," Jeorge told me while walking up to me.

I shook my head no.

"Come on Jeorge, let's go join the other kids at the sandbox." A kid told Jeorge.

Jeorge looked at me, then at the kid.

"Yeah, I will come." Jeorge looks back at me. "But, Brook comes too."

Then Jeorge re-looks at the kid. The kid looked at me, I gave him a nerves smile. He turned his focus to Jeorge.

"My parents tell me that I can't play with him."

"Why?" Jeorge asked.

"He's a freak who's trying to seek attention. According to Ben and Chris. Didn't you see his picture that he drew?"

"Yes, but do you understand what he drew?"

"No, but look at him. He has a black eye, fat lip, and scratches on his face."

I felt worried after he said that, the only thing I could do was to look at Jeorge. Like I was pleading for Jeorge and this kid to go away. Jeorge looked at me.

"Jeorge, go play. I am fine." I told him with a smile.

As Jeorge was walking away, I went to sit at the picnic table.

I saw Jeorge looking back at me. I gave him an assured smile.

-Page131-

I looked over at the other kids playing.

Hillary and I made eye contact, I gave her a smile.

"Alright, alright, you win."

I looked over to see Jeorge standing next to me.

"What?" I asked sounding confused.

"You win." He told me again.

"I won?" Still confused.

"Yes. No other kids want to play with you, so I will sit here with you."

"Oh. You don't have to. I am fine."

"Honestly Brook,"

"What?"

"You always say your fine, yet your always sitting by yourself." While crossing his arms, Jeorge said with a smile.

So, he sat down across from me.

I sat there with Jeorge, watching the other kids play for about 20 minutes.

"This is boring."

I looked over at Jeorge, I laughed quietly to myself.

"What are you laughing about?" Jeorge asked me.

I smiled at him as I replied,

"If you're bored, go play."

"No. I am gong to sit here with you. How do you not get bored sitting by yourself?"

I am amused by this kid.

"I am not allowed to play at home, so it comes naturally, I guess." I told him.

"Wait. Why are you not allowed to play at your house?"

"Long story," I said while looking away.

"Does it have to do with the marks on your arms, plus your black eye, fat lip, and scratches on your face?"

With an uneasy look, I looked back at Jeorge then down at my arms. I looked away while replying,

"I guess some parents are more loving."

-Page132-

"My parents love me. Don't your parents love you?" Jeorge asked.

After he asked that question, I felt my heart ache. Like someone ripped out my heart. My eyes starting to fill up, I looked at back at him and replied,

"They do.... They are, they are strict, that's all."

I watched him look away. I closed my eyes as I felt the tears roll down my face.

Trying not to cry. I wiped the tears from my eyes as I opened my eyes I looked down at my arms.

We sat there in silence for about half an hour.

"Brook?" Asked Jeorge.

I looked over at him and replied,

"Yes?"

"Would you be ok if I went to play?"

I quietly laughed to myself. I smiled at him as I nodded to him.

I watched Jeorge wonder off and I sat there watching the kids play. Some of the other kids ran by me. Hillary came to a stop in front of me. She looked at me and gave me a smile. I returned the smile. Then one of the other kids told her to run. I watched her take off.

I like Hillary's bright smile. Her eyes are a deep intense emerald green that light up when she smiles. It sucks that she doesn't want to hang out with me.

I decided to grab some chalk and went to color.

Ten minutes passed:

"Brook. Willie is here."

I heard June tell me from behind me.

Sigh, of course, he is.

I got up and followed her into the house. I saw Willie standing in the kitchen.

Breath and smile Brook. I told myself.

"Hi, Daddy," I told Willie with a smile.

"See, he wouldn't call me that if I did something."

I overheard Dad tell June while giving me a hug. I looked up at

-Page133-

both of them.

"Does he know about the picture?" I asked.

"Yes Brook, I told him. And he agrees with you. It was Uncle Robert." June said.

-Page133-

"See, my Daddy wouldn't hurt me. He loves me." I said while hugging him.

I can't believe what I am saying. Why did I even hug him? It wasn't Robert, it was Willie. My new Dad.

June gave me a smile while she said,

"I know. Thank you for coming over and playing. I will see you tomorrow. Thank you for picking Brook up. Bye."

June handed Dad the picture I drew.

Dad and I walked outside and got me into the truck.

"Really Pretty eyes. Couldn't find anything else to draw? Mom isn't going to be happy." Daddy said while buckling me in.

I watched Daddy get into the driver seat and turned on the engine.

He looks over at me and asked with a smile,

"What is Uncle Robert going to say?"

"What are you going to tell him? You agreed with me that it was Robert in the picture." I replied with a smile.

"Huh, fair enough." Daddy said while driving away.

Once at home, Daddy told me to finish laundry, do the dusting, and make dinner.

"Are you heading off to work?" I asked.

"Yes. So make sure everything is done before Mom gets home. For your safety." He told me.

"My safety?" I asked.

"Yes. Your mother is still not happy about yesterday. Plus she isn't going to be happy about the picture you drew. So, if she comes home to a messy house, you better kiss your life goodbye."

"Right. Yes sir, the house will be spotless. Have a nice day at

-Page 134-

work. I love you."

Daddy gave me gave me a quick smile before leaving the house.

I went to start a load of laundry before I started the dusting. I worked fast to assure that I got all the dusting done in plenty of time to make dinner. Because I don't want to kiss my life goodbye, yet.

Though, after Mom sees the picture, I will be kissing my life
-Page134-
goodbye.

Anyways, I went to make dinner. While dinner was making, I went to switch the load of laundry.

Went back to the kitchen to check on the food. Set the table, turned off the stove. Went back to the laundry room, to fold the clothes.

"Hi, Brook."

I turned around to see Mom behind me. I gave her a smile.

"Hi, Mommy. How are you? How was work?" I asked her.

"I am okay. Work was busy. How are you?" She replies.

I looked down at the floor. I was slow to responding due to me thinking about my day.

I looked back up at Mom, and replied,

"My day was good."

"The house looks nice. Did you dust?" Mom asked.

"Yes, ma'am."

"Good. Well, I am going to go change. Your Dad should be here soon."

"Okay."

I don't want Daddy to come home from work. He's going to show her my drawing, then she is going to be pissed. I only have four strikes left. But after she sees it, I will have... I don't know.

God Brook, why did you have to be stupid.

"Brook?"

I looked over towards Mom with a blank stare.

"You okay? Your spacing off. You did that when I asked about
-Page135-
your day." Mom asked.

I nodded to her.

"If you don't need anything else, I will be in my room," I told her.

"Alright."

While in my room, I was pacing nervously for Daddy to come home. I grabbed my book and went to sit down in my chair.

Hoping that reading will get my mind to focus and not to worry.

About five minutes later. I have the book in my hand but not focusing on it.

Page135-

Sigh, as I was getting up, I put the book down on my shelf.

I should go check on the laundry.

Once in the laundry room, I switched the loads around.

Walked out to the living room.

I saw Mom sitting on the couch watching T.V. while she had a can of beer in one hand and a cigarette in the other.

"Hi, Mommy."

Mom looks over at me.

"What are you doing out of your room?" Mom asked like I was annoying her.

"I was putting a new load in the washer."

"The washer is down the hall, not in the living room."

"I know. Sorry Mommy, not meaning to annoy you. I thought I would come out to see how you are doing. Plus, to make sure everything is still neat."

"(humph) Well, the house is clean and I am fine. Now go away."

"Yes, ma'am."

I turned around to walk towards my room.

"Brook Harold?"

I turned to look at Mom.

"Yes, ma'am?"

"Come here."

I walked over to her and stood in front of her.

"Checking the laundry is fine, but don't come back into the living
-Page136-
room till your allowed to. Now go." Mom growled.

"Yes, ma'am, sorry ma'am."

I continued to walk towards my room.

I went to lay down in my bed. I looked at my clock, 6:05.

Daddy will be here soon. I got off of my bed, walked over to my desk, sat down to color.

Mom seem mad. She must have had a bad day at work. If she is already mad due to work, its going to be a blast when she talks to me about the picture.

Fifteen minute's later, I heard a knock on my door. I turned around to see Daddy walking in.

"Hi, Daddy. How are you? How was Work?"

"I am fine. Work was annoying." he rolled his eye. "Like always. But my attitude will be better once Mom looks at the picture and deals with you. I have a feeling she won't be nice about it. She already has a bad attitude." He told me.

"Yes, sir. I know sir."

"I love you, Pretty eyes. Talk to you after dinner." Daddy told me with a smile.

As he was leaving the room, I told him that I love him too.

I don't actually love him but it's what he wants to hear.

Breath Brook, breath. It might not be that bad. Daddy will show Mommy the picture, the three of us will have a nice conversation and go on our ways.

Ha! Only if my parents were brainwashed. Anyways, I went back to coloring till they wanted me.

-Chapter sixteen: Submission.-

An hour later:

I heard my door open, I turned to see who was at the door.

"Your mother awaits you." Daddy said.

"Is she mad?" I asked in a concerned way.

"Why don't you come out and see for yourself."

I followed Daddy out to the living room. I saw Mommy sitting on
-Page 137-

the couch, looking at my picture that I drew. She doesn't look happy either. I cautiously walked over to Mom.

Once in front of her, I told her,

"Hi, Mommy."

I watched Mom stand up as she glared at me. Her whole body language said that she was furious. I gulped as I gave her a terrified look. Either I shrunk, or she got taller, but I feel smaller.

"What the fuck is this? What the hell were you thinking? God, Brook, why do you have to be so fuckin stupid."

"I am s - sorry, Mom," I said while starting to cry.

Mom looked at me in surprised as she replied,

"You're sorry?" Mom pushed me into the wall.

I felt afraid for what would happen next.

"You're sorry?! For what? For drawing this and making a fool of your father?! And telling June how it's Uncle Robert? God, I hope she never meets Robert. Your father and uncle Robert doesn't even look the same."

Mom grabs my shirt, pulls me away from the wall, to only shove me back into the wall.

I groaned.

"Why do you have to be so senseless?! You annoy the crap out of me."

Once again, pulls me away, to shove me back. About three time being shoved into the wall, I closed my eyes, I was trying to turn from her. To protect myself but Daddy told me to look at her. I opened my eyes to look over at him, He had a smirk on his face.

"Are you mad at me, Mommy?" I asked fearfully through sniffles.

Wasn't sure what else to say.

"Am I mad?" Scoff. "No, Brook Harold, I happy. What are you, an idiot? That was a dumb question. Of course, I am mad! If I wasn't mad, I wouldn't be here yelling at you!"

Mom pulled me away from the wall, to shove me into it. Again! Mom got into my face. I was afraid to breathe at that moment.

-Page138-

"I told you, you have two strikes left. Two! And that you better start kissing up to me." Mom told me quietly while she clenched her teeth. "Well your not kissing up to me, You are pissing me off!!"

After she said it, she backhanded me. Twice! Plus, she slammed my head into the wall like three times.

With tears running down my face, I opened my eyes, to see Mom facing Daddy.

I felt weak from being shoved into the wall plus my head being slammed into the wall. So, I sat down on the ground, with my knees close to my chest to protect myself from any more harm. I hid my face in my arms, trying to stop crying.

"What the hell are you doing Brook?!"

I looked up at her and replied,

"I am trying to protect myself from you. I can't take your hits anymore."

Scoff. "I will make sure you can't sit down anymore."

I felt worried by what she said. What does she mean?

"William my dear, I Love you. Can I use your belt? I don't have mine on me." I overheard Mom tell Daddy.

"I love you too, you're my girl."

I watched Daddy remove his belt and handed it to Mom. I watched Mom walk over towards the couch.

"Brook Harold, please come here."

I slowly got up off the floor, walked over to her.

"Yes?" I asked.

"Willie, will you come here and hold him down for me?"

"Sure thing," Daddy said while walking over to us.

He sat down on the couch and gave me a smile.

"Pretty eyes, bend over." Daddy told me.

"Huh?"

"Bend over."

I gave them both a tense look as I started to shake, and I went to lean over Daddy's lap. After I did, I felt Mom pull down my pants

-Page139-

plus underwear, then she struck my bottom with the belt. I gasp as I closed my eyes. I bit down on my bottom lip as I started to cry.

She kept on hitting me over and over. With each hit, the pain grew worse. I want her to stop! I can't even struggle because Daddy is holding me down so tightly.

The whimpering, the heavy breathing, tears rolling down my face.

I cried out to her,

"Stop Mom!"

I laid there, moaning. The pain was unbearable.

"Brook Harold, stand up. Pull up your pants and underwear." Mom told me.

I stood up, did as she told me. I looked at her as the tears still rolled down my face.

"I didn't give you permission to sit down. Because you didn't ask, now you can't sit down. I mean, you could try, but it might be painful. Why don't you try."

So, I tried to sit down on the couch but quickly got up. The pain was sharp.

I heard Mommy and Daddy snickering. I looked over at Daddy, he sat there with a smirk on his face, same with Mommy.

"We are going into our room now. Get the kitchen cleaned." Daddy told me.

I watched both of them head toward the hallway.

"Pretty eyes, stop crying. Smile." Daddy told me.

I shifted my eyes to look at him. I gave him a weak smile

"Atta boy, I love you." Daddy told me.

"I love you too."

Daycare should be fun tomorrow. Plus, I didn't think sitting on the couch would hurt that much. I mean, did she have to hit me that hard?

Is this because I sat down without her permission? So this is my punishment, not able to sit down. That doesn't even make sense.

-Page140

Using my hand, I wiped the tears from my eyes. Looked at my hand, blood?

Oh, then accord to me. I bit my lip harder than I meant to.

I suppose I should get the kitchen cleaned. I got that room cleaned plus I straightened up the living room.

I went to knock on my parent's bedroom door.

They told me to come in. I walked in looking down.

"What do you want? Did you come in here for another beating? Because I will gladly give you one." I heard Mom say sounding angry.

I shook my head no. I got down on both knees, put my arms out, to show the I am no threat.

Still looking down, I told my parents,

"I have come before you, to humbly ask for your forgiveness. I have sinned against both of you. In which of doing so, I have angered you both. I made a fool of Daddy, for everyone to see. If you think beating me more is best, then do so. I have learned that I am not your kid, I am your slave, there for, I have no say. I only obey."

There was a moment of silence before I heard Daddy speak.

"Um, kind of speechless at the moment."

"Out of curiosity, how obedient will you be?" I heard Mom ask.

"I will do anything you tell me to do," I replied.

"Then repeat what you mother told you out in the living room." Said Daddy.

My eyes got wider, I took a deep breath, I exhaled as I closed my eyes.

"I am disobedient. I am rude, I am ungrateful. I don't listen, which goes back to being disobedient. Plus, I am disrespectful. I am always giving you talk back. I am always grumpy. I will no longer be an attention seeker. I am stupid, senseless. Again, goes back to being stupid, along with me being an idiot. I annoy you both, and I anger you both."

"Good boy. So, with all that you said, are you going to try to be
-Page141-
perfect?" Mom asked.

I can't be perfect. If I try, I will screw something up, then they will be pissed. I thought to myself.

"Trying, no. Going to be, yes. I am here to serve you both and make your life less stressful."

"Pretty eyes, why don't you look at us?" Daddy asked.

What's with all the questions? I came in here to apologize and was hoping to go to bed. Again, I thought to myself.

I took a deep breath, exhaled.

"Because I am not" short pause." worthy enough to look my....." I stalled at saying it. Breath Brook, breath. Say it. "At my master and mistress."

OW. That was painful to say. Suzanne Susie is supposed to be my mother, not my mistress, nor am I suppose to be her servant. I am supposed to be her son. And William Tyler is supposed to be a loving stepdad, not a jerk.

I want to go. I don't want to be on my knees anymore. I want them to speak! I can't breathe.

Dad laughs.

"That's right. You are not worthy enough. Brook Harold Tyler! Look up at us." Daddy demanded.

Tyler? Oh, okay.

I slowly looked up at them. They gave me an angry look.

"Yes, sir? Yes, ma'am?" I asked.

"What do you think we should do, Sas?" Daddy asked Mommy.

"I don't know. Let him go to bed. Mommy replied back to Daddy.

What do you mean what you should do to me? Bed seems like a good plan. I thought to myself.

"Why would we allow that? I mean, it's so tempting to do something."

(Still thinking to myself.) You should allow me to go to bed because I feel overwhelmed, I called you my master for heaven sakes! Heck, I recently called you my Dad, before that you were Willie. Let me go to bed. Please.

-Page142-

"Yes very Tempting. Or we can let him to bed now, and torture him all week."

"Oh. That sounds even better."

Thinking to myself again. What?! NO!

"Right. Brook, get up and go to your room." Mom told me.

"Yes, sir, yes, ma'am," I replied while getting up.

Once in my room, I was trying to figure out how to sit on my bed without sitting on it. I could fall onto my bed and sleep on my stomach.

I wish she didn't whip me that hard. My butt is sore. Obviously, next time, I will ask her permission before sitting down.

I looked at my clock, ugh five o'clock Am. I hit the snooze button.

"Daddy, I will get up extra early to make you breakfast...." Me and my stupid ideas. I thought to myself.

I decided to slide out of my bed. Haha, it was easier.

God, my butt plus my back didn't hurt this much last night. While on my knees, I buried my face into my pillow. I can stay here longer. I have headache. I was about to closes my eyes when my second alarm went off. (Grumble) Fine, I will get up.

Turned off both alarms before moving. I got on all fours and crawled to the bathroom. Laughing at myself, though.

Got to the bathroom. I used the tub to push myself up. Groan OW. My head is pounding.

I went to look into the mirror. Positive note, my lip looks better.

Went to the bathroom, washed my hands.

Went to the kitchen to start breakfast. Daddy is very picky about his breakfast. Hmm, looked at the clock, 5:32. I will make him and Mommy pancakes and eggs. Mom might be up.

While cooking, the smell of the pancakes was torture.

I want food, I am hungry.

Pretty sure that I started to drool while watching the pancakes cook...

Okay, Brook, wake up. You need to watch the pancakes so they won't burn. Not dream that you are eating them. Oh, they won't

-Page143-

notice one gone, would they? If I go brush my teeth and use mouthwash, they may not notice. Oh, it's very tempting.

No, no. no. Can't do that, because that will piss them off.

Especially since Mom already threatened me, so I shouldn't test her.

Anyways, got done making breakfast, put it on a couple of plates. Put the plates on a tray and walked towards Mom and Dad's room.

Knocked before opening the door. I walked in with a smile.

"Good morning Daddy. Good morning Mommy. I made breakfast."

They both sat up and looked at me tiredly.

"Good morning Pretty eyes. I am surprised to see you up this early." Daddy told me.

I looked at him and was trying to figure out what to say.

"I said I would get up and make you breakfast. It's my job to make my master happy." I replied to him.

My master? Ha ha ha. More like he's a loser.

Daddy smiled at me and replied,

"Thank you, but do we get something to drink?"

I gave him a surprised look as I replied,

"Uh. Yes, sir. I forgot it in the kitchen, sir. Excuses me, sir."

Oh, shoot, shoot. I Backed out of the room. I walked back towards the kitchen. Grab their milk, which I forgot to grab. Went back to the room, knocked before entering.

"I am sorry. Here you go."

"Pretty eye, why do you seem so nervous?" Asked Daddy.

I gave him a blank stare, then looked over at Mom.

It's too early to deal with them. I returned my focus back on Daddy.

"Who's nervous?" I did a nervous a chuckle. Then I sighed. "Oh. I don't want to disappoint you or Mommy," I said with a hint of a smile.

Daddy gave me a smile then looked over at Mom.

"Sweet Brook of mine, we love you. Try not to make any mistakes, -Page144-

okay?" Mommy said.

"Yes, ma'am. Enjoy your breakfast with Daddy."

I walked back out of the room. Headed towards the living room.

Try not to make mistakes. Ha ha. Right.

I went to go look out the window.

I hope it gets sunnier outside. I don't like cloudy skies. God, I still have a pounding headache.

I should go pick up the kitchen and start a load of laundry.

Laundry first, then the kitchen.

I went to start the laundry, came back into the living room.

I picked up the living room, I re-dusted and mopped the floor.

"The living room looks nice, but the kitchen needs to be done."

I turned around to see Daddy.

"Thank you. Yes, I still have to work on the kitchen." I replied.

I watched him walk up towards me.

"Oh, Pretty eyes." Whispered Daddy.

I looked up and gave him a smile.

"Your smile, I love it. Your hair is so soft."

I lost my smile and gave him a worried look. He ran his hand across my face and down to my neck. Loosely, he put both hands around my neck.

"You have such a beautiful neck." He whispered.

He leaned down and started to kiss my neck.

I closed my eyes. I heard him moaning in pleasure.

I started to shake with fear.

What does he want? Why is he kissing me?

He started to kiss down my arm towards my hand.

"Oh, Pretty eyes." Daddy whispered while holding my hand.

We looked at each other.

"I love you. Your my boy, you know that right? I got to go to work. Talk to you later."

I nodded at him.

"Yes, sir. Talk to you later."

Daddy smiled at me before leaving the house.

-Page145-

I went to look out the window to watch him get into his truck.

I sighed as I turned from the window. What was that about? I asked myself.

I looked up at the time. 6:45. He's running late now, not my problem. Though, I could see him blaming me later for it.

I don't want to come home him with later, now.

I better get the kitchen cleaned before Mom gets up.

Everything I did in the living room, I did in the kitchen plus the dishes.

Went to my room to get dressed. Made sure the room was neat.

Went to brush my teeth, comb my hair. Thanks to Daddy for messing it up.

As I was about to leave the bathroom, I saw Mom come out of her room.

"Good morning, again Mommy," I told her with a smile.

"Hi. Are you ready?" She asked me.

"I only need to get my shoes on."

She nodded in agreement.

Instead of putting me in the backseat like normal, Mom put me in the front seat.

"We are going down the road, you should be fine for that minute."

Though, it didn't feel like a minute drive, because it was an uncomfortable drive.

"Are you uncomfortable? You look like it." Mom asked me.

I gave her a painful smile.

She returns the smile while she asked,

"Are you going to ask if you can sit down next time?"

I nodded and replied,

"Yes, ma'am."

"Then you learned your lesson."

"Yes, ma'am. Though my punishment isn't over yet."

Mom looks at me.

"Hmm. No, it will be over in four weeks, though."

"Yes, ma'am."

-Chapter Seventeen: Fitting in-

We got out of the car and walked into June's house.

"Come on in. How are you both doing this morning? Brook, you look tired." Said June.

I gave her a smile while I shrugged my shoulders.

"We are both good. Brook didn't eat breakfast, so he may be hungry. Plus he was up at five this morning." Mom said.

"What is it with kids getting up so early?" Asked June.

"Yeah, I don't know. I always asked myself that when I was with Nathaniel."

"Yeah, Hillary was always up early too. I mean, I know that's what they do. But depending on how many times she was up during the night or the time she went to bed, I wanted to sleep."

"Right. And Brook was colicky when he was a baby."

"Oh dear. I was lucky on that part.

"Yes, you were. I got to run. See ya later Brook. Thank you, June."

"Yeah, no problem. Buh-bye. Well, Brook, since you stood here listening to your Mom and I ramble, you can go play now."

We smiled at each other.

When I walked in the living room, I saw Ben and Chris playing with some cars. So, I decided to go say hi.

"Hi, Ben and Chris. Are you having fun?" I asked them.

They looked at each other then at me.

"What do you want?" Asked Chris.

"Nothing. Trying to be friendly, that's all." I told them.

"Well, we are busy. So leave us alone." Said Ben.

"Oh, okay. Wasn't trying to bug you."

Okay, they don't want to play. Next kid.

"Hello. I haven't met you yet. I am Brook Harold. Well, Brook for short." I said to this girl.

She looked up at me.

"Hi, I am Cali. Nice to meet you." She replied back.

"Can I play with you," I asked.

"No. I am playing by myself."

-Page147-

"Okay, have fun."

Sigh. Next one, but this girl is coloring with Hillary.

"Hello. What pretty pictures. I am Brook Harold, Brook for short. Do you care if I color with you?"

"I don't care. Jill, do you mind?" Hillary asked her friend.

"No. I am Jillian by the way. Jill for short."

We smiled at each other.

"That's a pretty name."

"Hey, attention seeker, get lost. We want to do some coloring ourselves." I heard Chris say.

I rolled my eyes in disgust. I turned to look at him.

"We can all share," I told him.

"Nah. We don't need you to be drawing something stupid again," Ben told me.

I gave him an annoyed look and walked away.

I will go sit in my corner. Correction, I will go stand in the corner.

Sigh, I tried playing with other kids but they all told me, no.

On my right side, with my arms crossed, I was leaning against the wall while looking out the window. I am curious what will happen later with, Willie, Dad, my master. Whatever name he wants me to call him. Mr. Jerk, the name I like. I smiled to myself. Anyways, I wonder what will take place later between me and him. I don't understand why he kissed my neck this morning. Plus, what was with the moaning he was doing? Does he get pleasure from kissing his son? Hell, I am not even his son.

He's like, what in thirty's? And I am five, that's a big age gap. And Mom allows this? Why?

I looked over at the kids playing. They seem all happy. I must be the only one living in hell. Because I don't see any other kid show up with the bruises and looks like they are starving.

(Scoff) And Mom this morning:

"He didn't eat breakfast this morning, he may be hungry."

When does she feed me?! She Never feeds me. Heck, she doesn't even cook, I do the cooking.

-Page148-

I have to stand there and be tortured by the smell of the food. Like this morning.

135

Oh, wait, they do feed me, peanut butter sandwiches. Oh, that's real filling.

While Mom and Dad get to leave the house and go have fun, I have to stay home and clean their damn house. Plus, on top of that, I have anxiety bad when there not home, so I can't fall asleep till they get home. Well at least till Dad gets home. I don't trust him.

God, I don't want to go home with him. I don't want him to be kissing me again. At least he's dropping me off, demanding orders, then leaving.

"Brook?"

I turned my focus from the window to look at Hillary.

"What?" I asked

"Do you want to come play with me? Can we find a something to do? My mom has plenty of toys." She said.

"Why do you now want to play with me? Are you feeling bad that I keep getting pushed into the corner?"

"What? N-no. You look lonely."

Hillary sounds like Jeorge. What do they do, talk to each other about me?

"I am used to it. Thanks." Being Sarcastic, I replied with a smile.

"I am sure you are but I am willing to come play with you."

"Why now? Why? I have tried to play with you all week and you push me away. Like rest of the kids do."

I watched Hillary walk away. Then I saw Jeorge looking at me. I gave him a, questioning look. Then I re-look out the window. I was watching the rain fall.

"Brook?"

I looked over to see Jeorge looking at me.

"Yes?"

"Why don't you sit down? Like you normally do. You look uncomfortable." Said Jeorge.

-Page149-

"I am fine. I get tired of sitting." I told him.

Yeah, that's a lie. Nor does he need to know. I thought to myself as I looked down.

"You know, I sat down with you yesterday."

Surprised, I looked up at him.

"That's why you looked over at me."

Jeorge nods.

"Well, I am sorry. You are at least trying to make me feel welcomed."

We both smiled at each other.

"Do you want to go play?" Jeorge asked.

I looked around the room before I answered.

"Brook,"

I turned my focus back to him.

"What?"

"Stop scanning the room. I am not playing with the other kids, I am asking you to play."

This kid is getting to know me. I am not sure if I like it or not.

"Sure. I would love to play with somebody. I get tired of being alone."

Jeorge and I went off to find something to do. Though, I can't exactly sit down next to him. Shoot. I could sit on my knees, I could squat. I can't sit down.

"Brook?"

I gave him a blank stare while I replied,

"Yes?"

"Did you hear the question?" Asked Jeorge.

"What question?"

Jeorge gave out a quiet laugh.

"Sigh. I asked if you want to play with Legos?"

"Oh."

"Yes or no?"

"Yes or no what?"

Jeorge gave me a confused look.

-Page150-

"You are not listening. The Lego's, do you want to play with them."

"Oh! Yes. Sorry, my mind is wandering."

"I noticed."

I watched Jeorge sit down at the Lego table.

"Are you going to sit? Or are you going to stand?" Jeorge asked.

"Um. I- I was going to sit on my knees."

"Suit yourself."

Jeorge and I played with each other till lunch.

I joined the kids for lunch. I figured I don't get a lot of food at home, might as well enjoy lunch while I am here.

Though, I stood and ate my lunch. Ignored all the looks and whispers. I especially ignored June.

After lunch, June told all the kids to go play except for me, because she wants to talk to me.

Probably ask me why I am not sitting. Sigh. Here we go.

"Brook, is there a reason why you're not sitting?"

Nailed it. Ha ha.

I gave her an annoyed smile while I told her,

"Because I don't want to. Stop asking me things. You don't drag any of the other kids to the other room and ask them questions. Everything is fine, I am fine. Plus when you ask, I tell you the truth, then you go to my parents, to confirm everything that I told you. Which that gets me into trouble. I don't want to be in trouble tonight."

June gave me a worried look.

"Brook, I am concerned about you. I am not trying to get you in trouble."

"Thank you for caring but I am not answering your questions anymore. And please, don't go to my parents."

June nods and tells me to go play.

When I walked into the living room, Jeorge rushes over to me.

"What was June talking to you about?" He asked.

I looked at Jeorge while I gave him an upsetting look.

-Page151-

I shook my head while I told him.

"I don't want to talk about it. Leave me alone."

I walked over to my spot. Again, using my right side to lean up against the wall. I stared outside.

Shortly afterward, I saw June walk in. My eyes followed her.

"Alright kids, it's movie time. So pick up your toys."

June looked over towards me. I quickly turned my attention to the floor. I relooked out the window.

"Brook, why don't you come join the circle and sit next to me?"

I looked over to see Hillary.

Sit. I thought to myself. I would love to sit but I can't. I guess she hasn't been paying close attention today. I haven't sat down all day. Well, minus being down on my knees.

"Sure."

I saw her smile ear to ear.

"Great!"

I guess I made her day.

Like earlier, when I played with Jeorge, he sat down but I didn't. Yeah, that's what I was doing with Hillary.

Though, I sat down with my legs tucked under me. Trying to ignore the pain.

I can't wait till I get to go home. Sigh.

Out of the corner of my eye, I saw June smiling at me. I shifted my eyes towards her and gave her a smile.

Not even fifteen minutes later I heard June call for me.

I turned my focus to her.

"Willie is here."

I smiled at her and told her.

"You mean my Dad?"

June looked confused.

"Yes, your Dad."

I slowly got up off the floor. Walked into the kitchen. Act like you like him.

"Hi, Daddy," I told him with a smile.

-Page152-

"Hi, Pre- Brook." Said Dad.

I looked up to him still with a smile on my face then hugged him.

I hate hugging him.

I saw him smiling.

"Brook was good today. He played with the other kids and joined circle time this time." June was telling Dad.

"Good, good. Well, let's get ya home. Thank you, June." Dad replied.

"Bye, June," I told her. "Buh-bye."

Dad picked me up and put me in the truck.

I moaned.

"You okay, there Pretty eyes?" Dad asked.

I nodded to him.

Dad got into the truck, started it up. And pulled out the driveway.

"Why are you going right? We go left?" I asked.

"Because we are taking a long way home," Dad looks over at me with a smile.

"Why?" I asked sounding concerned.

Though, he never answered. He kept his gaze on the road.

(Whining)

I kept shifting around in my seat to get comfortable.

By the time I looked out the window, I saw Daddy passing our street.

I looked at him and asked,

"Daddy, can we please go home? I don't want to be in the car anymore."

Daddy looked over at me and asked,

"Why are you so eager to get home?"

"Because I don't want to sit anymore," I told him.

"Why?" He asked.

I gave Daddy a pleading look.

He laughed to himself.

We finally made it home. Thank God. I hurried out of the car.

"Brook, relax. The chores aren't going anywhere." Daddy told

-Page153-

me.

I looked up at him and replied,

"I know. But I can't sit down. Mom whipped my bottom pretty hard."

He gave me a smile along with a chuckle.

"I know, I was holding you down, remember? Plus, that's why I took a long way to get home."

I looked away.

"Let's get you inside."

We walked inside. He handed me the list of chores.

"Oh, chores. So exciting." I said sarcastically.

I looked up realizing that Dad had a raised eyebrow expression.

"Right. Brook, get your chores done. Plus, your Mom and I will be going out for dinner. So make sure it's done by eight tonight."

I nodded.

Aaand Dads gone, phew. At least I can relax now. I'm glad there was no more... Kissing. He's a freak. Sigh. Now, let's hope, there's no problem later on.

Because, they, well, Dad, wanted it done before 8, I was taking my time.

I went to clean the bathrooms, my parent's room plus mopped the hallway.

At five, mom came home.

Though she didn't say much. Just went into her room.

An hour later, Dad came home.

He walked in, walk towards me.

I tensed up while I gave him a worried look.

Oh no. No, no, no. I thought.

"Pretty eyes, relax." Daddy told me with a smile.

He patted me on my head and walk towards his room.

I breathed out.

About 20 minutes later, Mom and Dad came out of there room.

Told me to finish up any left over chores and they will see me later.

-Page154-

I did the remaining chores, got ready for bed.

No body is here, so I put my hoodie on. Oh, how I missed wearing it.

Then I went to lay down on the couch to watch a movie.

It felt so good to be off of my feet. I have been going since five this morning.

I pulled my hooded part of my sweatshirt over my eyes.

I heard a faint voice call my name. It sounds like Daddy.

I whined in a tired way. I barely opened my eyes to see Daddy smiling at me.

I yawned. Trying to open my eyes.

"Hello, Pretty eyes. You fell asleep on the couch. Why don't we get you moved to your bed?" He told me.

"Uh, I will bring myself there," I told him.

I finally got my eyes to stay open. I looked at him, then around the room.

"What time is it?" I asked.

"Ten." Daddy replied.

"In them morning? Where's Mom?"

"No, at night. Your mother is at my sister's house staying the night. It's only you and me, Pretty eyes."

I jumped off the couch.

"WHAT!?" I asked in Surprise panic.

Dad turned to look at me. He looked as surprised as I did. Mainly by my reaction.

"Everything okay?"

"NO! I don't want to be alone with you!" I said started to get scared.

"Why?"

"Because you kissed me this morning!"

"(Chuckle) Correction, I kissed your neck." Daddy rolled his eyes. "It's not like I kissed your lips."

After he said it, he walked towards me.

-Page155-

I froze, I gave Dad a terrified look.

He grabbed me and was trying to kiss me. I fought him. I don't want to kiss!

When I got free from Dad, I ran towards the hall. But him being bigger then me....

I made him mad, so he chased me. When he grabbed me, he pushed me into the wall.

He pinned me there and pushed for the kiss even more. I was still trying to fight my way out of his arms.

"Quit fighting me! You agreed to this. You told me last night it's your job to make your master happy. That you will do anything that I tell you to do, and not to disappoint me. Plus, you said, you will make sure my life is less stressful. Well, I am disappointed and stressed at the moment!"

"I never agreed to kiss you! I meant it for being your servant! I liked it when you were beating me up. Not this forcible kissing game." I said while getting upset.

"Oh really."

He punched me in my nose.

"Like that? Plus, you also said, how you have no say, and that you will obey."

"Yes, like that," I said while I started to tear up.

I felt the blood dripping from my nose.

"I don't have a say because I am your servant."

Wait... I thought of what I told him. Oh, fruit loops. Not what I meant.

While holding on my nose, I looked up at him as he puts his hands on the wall. He gave me a sly smile.

When I removed my hands from my nose, he leaned down to kiss my nose.

He removed one hand from the wall. With that hand, he was unbuckling his belt, and undoing his pants.

"NO! Just no." I said sounding desperate.

"No what? Do you even know what I am doing?"

-Page156-

"No. But the last time you undid your belt plus your pants, you - you...." I looked away. "It doesn't matter."

"Your right, it doesn't matter. Plus, it's not like you have a choice. Remember? With that been said, get on your knees-"

"For what!"

"Let me finish! Get on your knees and-"

"I am not getting on my knees! I don't know what you want!"

"Because you won't allow me to finish!" Daddy growled at me.

He forced me to get down on my knees.

OW, I mumbled to myself.

Before he could go anywhere else with his little plan. There was a knock on the door. Saved by the door.

Daddy sigh in frustration.

"Stay!" He told me firmly while he pointed to me.

He walks over to answer the door.

I saw Teddy come in.

Daddy walks back over to me. He puts his hands together while he put them up to his mouth.

"You make me so furious. Just wait till your mother hears about your disobedience towards me! Get up, take off your sweatshirt, then give it to me. And go put your butt in that chair over there. Now! This is not over with." He demanded me.

I hurried to my feet, took my sweatshirt off and went to sit in the chair. Still shaking, on top of my bloody nose.

I sat in the chair while Daddy and Teddy played video games and got drunk. Yeah.

Then we went to bed. Daddy put me on the couch, so Teddy can sleep in my bed.

I didn't sleep at all that night. I wasn't sure if Daddy would come back to finish what he was trying to do to me before Teddy showed up.

Chapter Thirteen

LIFE

The next morning, I woke to Dad standing over me. He startled me. I wasn't expecting him to be up....Looking at me.

"Hi, Daddy. What time is it?" I asked.

He points to the clock. I looked at the clock. Eight o'clock AM.

Feeling confused, because he should have been at work by now.

"Are you not going to work?"

He shakes his head no.

"Is Teddy still here?"

He looks over towards the hallway. I looked that direction, Teddy is still here, hmmk.

"Have you had breakfast?"

Dad shakes his head no.

"No. Okay, do you want me to make you breakfast?"

Again, he shakes his head at me.

"Are you going to talk to me?"

Dad gave me an angry look and walked away.

Guess not. What did I do to piss him off now?

"Brook,"

I turned to look at Teddy.

"Your Dad said to go sit in your room. He wants the couch. Plus he doesn't want to see you." Teddy told me.

"Okay. But why isn't he telling me this?" I asked.

Teddy shrugs his shoulders and he too walks away.

Good. I made Dad angry and now he won't talk to me.

Anyways not much happen today. I stayed in my room. Because Daddy wanted me to stay in here.

I colored, I read, I drew and took a small nap.

About one o'clock, I left my room to see if Daddy wanted lunch.

"Hi, Daddy. How are you? I know, I didn't have permission to leave my room but I came in here to see if you wanted lunch."

He shakes his head no.

"What did I do to make you mad? Does it involve last night?"

He gave me angry look.

"Sigh. I am sorry Daddy. I love you."

-Page158-

I can't believe that I am about to say this.

"I can give you whatever you wanted last night. If that's what's going to take for you to talk to me."

Dad still has an angry look. And points towards the hallway.

"You want me back in my room?"

He smiles.

"Okay."

So, I went to sit in my room. Again.

An hour later, I heard some one open my door. I turned around to see Teddy.

"Yes, can I help you with something?" I asked.

"Your Dad and I are heading off to work. Also, be nice to your Dad. Give him what he wants without fighting him. He's the Dom and you are the submissive. Yeah, he told me. If I hear anything like this again, I will personally come after you." Teddy told me.

"Yes, sir."

Then he left my room.

Sigh. I leaned back in my chair. I have him and Robert after me. Great.... My two uncles. Actually they are not my uncles.

Not much happen after those two guys left for work.

Besides keeping up with laundry, plus doing a re-pick up, the house was clean.

I did some cleaning then made dinner.

I heard Mom drive up. I kept my focus wiping the counter top.

"Hi Brook. Feeling better?"

I looked up at Mom with a doubtful look.

"No." I told her.

Mom gave me a confused look while she shut the door behind her.

"Are you actually not feeling good, is that why your father took the day off?" Mom asked.

Still gave her a doubtful look.

"What's wrong, Brook?"

"Whoever said there's something wrong?"

-Page159-

"Your doubtful look."

I looked away before I spoke.

"I - I, may have been a bad boy," I relooked at her, "And Daddy wants to talk to you after work."

"Great." Mom said while rolling her eyes. "What did you do this time?" She asked while giving me an annoyed look.

"It's best if you talk to Daddy. On top of that, he hasn't talked to me all day."

"Then go sit in your room till your Dad gets home. I will finish dinner."

"Yes, ma'am."

I went to sit in my room to wait for my punishment.

Two hours later, about seven o'clock. Mom called me out of my room. Breathe, just breathe.

I walked out to the living room. I looked up at Daddy. He looked away from me. Okay, he's still not going to look at me.

I looked over at Mom, she was holding the belt plus she looks mad. Bad combination.

She snaps the belt. It made me jump, I gave her a worried look.

She signaled me to come over. I creep over to her. One foot at a time, till I was in front of her.

I glanced at her then looked at the floor.

Mom pushed me over, which made me fall on my butt. OW! I let out a screech.

She snapped the whip again.

In fear, I hurried to my knees. I used my arms to protect myself because I wasn't sure what she was going to do.

"(Quiet laugh) You are a fool. I could still hit you." Mom told me.

"Yes, but I don't want you to use the buckle part across my face." Anxiously, I told her.

"Should I try?"

"I don't have a say."

"Sigh. Brook Harold Tyler. Do you understand what two strikes left mean? I gave you mercy so you could make up your mistakes -Page160-

from the second time. Either your stupid and don't understand or do you like the fact that I yell at you. When you came into my room and got down on your knees and asked for forgiveness. Because you sinned against me and your Father. I had hope, your starting to understand." Mom chuckled. "Then I lost it. For your Dad to come home from work and tell me that you disobeyed him! I regret giving you compassion. I should have finished beating you right there and then. Didn't you tell us, that you are our servant, you have no say, you only obey? Am I wrong about this?"

I let my guard down, still on my knees, keeping my focus on the floor.

I replied to her quietly,

"No ma'am"

"No what?"

"You are not wrong."

"Hmm. You even told us that, your Dad is your master and I am your mistress. So, you have no say. What do you have to say for yourself?"

"I have nothing to say for myself. Because.... Because I have sinned a-against you both. Though, Uncle Teddy told me that Daddy is the Dom and I am the submissive and I should listen."

"Yes, Teddy's right. Because you weren't allowing Dad to have the control, you have angered him, you have hurt him. Let him have his fun. You are the servant, the submissive one. Make your master happy. Like he always tells you, smile Pretty eyes."

I looked up at her, and asked,

"Ma'am?"

"What?" Mom asked.

"Not trying to be rude. But doesn't shoving me into the wall, backhanding me, and slamming my head into the wall, count as a beating? H- How did you give me mercy?"

"Yes, but that was the sweet version." Mom said.

Then she walks over to Dad.

-Page161-

"He's all yours, my bad boy." Mom told Daddy.

I looked down. I felt like I am not breathing. Yet at the same time, I am breathing too fast. I started to cry.

My mother gave her boyfriend permission to have sex with me! What is wrong with this picture?

When I looked up, he was giving me a furious look.

Nope, I can't breathe. I continued to cry. I gave him a terrified/pleading looking. I returned my focus back to the floor.

The second time seemed worse than the first time when Daddy raped me. Like how did I allow him to do this a second time?! It hasn't even been a week since the first time!

I felt every touch, every kiss, I felt all the pain, plus I felt humiliated.

Daddy smiled at me while he guides himself into me. I made a distress look, because I can feel the pressure plus the pain while he slides himself into me.

Daddy is enjoying himself, while I laid there uncomfortable, whining and in tears. I can feel him thrusting faster and faster.

With each thrust, the burning became more intense. I swear the pressure keeps getting worse too.

I let out a painful whimper. I heard Daddy laugh in a mocking way.

I want him to stop torturing me! I can't handle the intense pain.

On top of that, he kept repeating the four letter word with the three-word sentence. "I love you."

Is that how you show your kid that you love him?!

Or do you show it by starving him and pulverizing him? Or locking your kid in his room, because the house wasn't cleaned to your standards!

When Daddy got done, while he was getting up, I asked him,

"Are you happy, Daddy?"

"You bet I am." Daddy told me with a smile as he looked down at me while he was zipping up his pants.

"So, the next time we do this, no fighting. I have Sassy and Uncle
-Page162-
Teddy on my side."

I gave him a tired look as nodded while I replied,

"You are my master, I must obey. It's my job to make you happy not angry."

"(Scoff) About time you learned your place. Now get up, get your pants on. I will be in the other room with your Mom."

Still laying on the ground, my eyes followed him out of the living room. I closed my eyes as I took a deep breath.

My question is, what is love? How does it feel to be loved by someone that doesn't call you names, who doesn't hurt you?

I am not their kid, I am their servant. I am Dad's toy, my parent's punching bag.

Hell, are they are my parents anymore? No! They are my master and mistress, according to Mom because what I said.

They don't love me, even though they say they do.

They tell me when they want something or after they torment me.

Is that what love is?

Weeks passed. And I am still getting up every morning at five.

I walked into the bathroom every morning. Look in the mirror pull myself together, breathe, focus on today's agenda.

Remind myself that I am.... Their servant, that I am here to please my master and mistress.

Pull myself together again, and smile. Time to get the morning chores done, and make breakfast. Plus, make sure Dad is up and not running behind for work.

95% of the time Dad is on time to work.

According to Daddy, the other 5% is my fault. Either he didn't want to get up, or he was playing kissy face with Mom.

Or he's running late for work because he wanted me to give him a....... (Long pause). Anyways, I let Mom sleep a little longer, while getting the kitchen cleaned, plus I get myself ready. Then I make sure Mom is up. For the most part, she is up by the time I am getting ready.

She drops me off at daycare, then she goes to work.

-Page163-

About seven hours being there, Dad picks me up, brings me home. Give me chores to do, then he leaves to go back to work.

The chores need to be done by four and dinner made by five.

From there, I sit in my room till they need me.

The next day, I repeat it all.

As far as beatings go, they jot things down in their notebook throughout the day.

Most days, I either get pushed into the wall when they walk by me or if I walk by them. Because they are mad about something.

Or I get slapped, that's where I get my famous black eye(s) from. Thank you, Mom and Dad. Being sarcastic.

In July, Daddy official moved in. All along, I thought he was "official" living here.

I mean I know mom mentioned once that he has his own apartment. It had to do with something about the lease. I don't know, it didn't make sense to me when they were trying to explain it.

I also got to spend the day at the zoo to celebrate Hillary's birthday along with the other daycare kids.

Mom wasn't a fan of it though. Because the house wasn't getting cleaned.

Oh my gosh, what will we do? The house isn't getting cleaned! Sarcastically, I thought to myself.

Though, after I came home from the zoo, I had work to do.

Other then that, not much happened in July.

August came and June planned something small for Jeorge's birthday.

Which Mom had the same issue like she did with Hillary's birthday.

Because I wasn't going to be home to take care of the house.

Oh my god Mom, relax!

That's what my thought were. Haha, yeah.

Mom and the gang celebrated Dad's birthday.

-Page164-

And Mom was trying to get me ready for kindergarten that starts in September.

Which I am nervous to go. A new place, new people, and teachers I haven't met before.

Plus new people for my parents to lie to.

They can put on their act like we are some happy family. Sigh.

What scares me, will the kids accepted me or will I not be accepted, like at daycare.

Positive note, Hillary..... Well, at least Jeorge will be there. He plays with me, verses Hillary.

She plays with me when she feels like it.

Do we get lunch there? That's my other concern.

Hmm, I had to think about food. Now I am hungry.

Any ways, August went, September came.

It was the first day of kindergarten.

While in the car, Mom was going over the new house rules.

She will get off of work then come get me. Then I have chores to get done before Dad gets home. Somewhere in there, I have to make dinner.

Yep, glad my life hasn't changed. I am only here to please my master and mistress.

Once at school, I looked at all the other parents dropping their kids off. Most of them showed some sort of emotion.

We walked by one kid that looked upset and his mother was trying to calm him.

At that moment, Mom looked down at me, I looked up at her. There was no reassurance in her eyes. Does it concern her at all that I am terrified?

What is she feeling? Is she happy? Is she scared? Is she mad?

We got to my classroom. Mr. Howard greeted us in the hallway.

"Hello. Come on in." He told us.

Mom knelt down to my level and told me,

"Honey, have a good day. I will be back later for you. I love you."

"Okay. Have a good day Mommy. I love you."

-Page165-

I watched her get while she patted me on the head.

I watched her walk away. I turned around to see Mr. Howard smiling at me.

"Would you like me to show you your locker?" He asked me.

I nodded to him.

So, he should me which locker was mine.

I put my stuff in my locker and joined rest of the kids for circle time.

We went over what day it was. We got to know each others name through a song.

After the songs, we had some free time to play.

With happened at daycare, I didn't want to play with toys. I wanted to find somewhere to hide.

But with there being two teachers, there shouldn't be a problem.

I saw Jeorge and decided to go say hi.

"Well, well, don't you look all fancy." I told him with a smile.

He looked at me in surprise while he replied,

"It is special day."

"You always were dress better then us kids at daycare. I doubt because its a special day."

He let out a quiet laugh.

"Yeah, I suppose your right. I dress to impress. Well, I hear my dad say that a lot. But it's also the job he is in."

"Oh, that makes sense. My parents don't get all fancy for work. But then again, one is a janitor and the other is a nurse." I replied.

"That's cool. My dad is a business man and my mom is a stay at home mom. Sometimes she volunteers at the church."

"That's awesome."

"Yep. I can't believe that we are in kindergarten. Can you?" He asked.

I looked at him in surprise. Looked around the room then back at him.

I leaned in while I quietly told him,

"I am lucky that I get to live another day. Everyday to me is a

-Page166-

gift."

Jeorge gave me a worried look.

I saw him looking around the room then back to me.

"But you look okay." He replied.

"For now. It all depends on if I am good. Actually, it depends on what mood my parents are in."

Jeorge gave me another worried look.

He shrugged his shoulders while he looked away.

"Are your parents going to lie to the teachers like they did at daycare?" Jeorge asked.

I gave him a perplex look.

Has he being listening to our conversation when Dad picks me up? I thought to myself.

Plus, how does he know they are lying?

"H-how do you know that?"

"I am sorry. Did I cross a line?" He asked.

"N-no, but maybe. It's not like I tell you a lot, plus I want to know how you know they are lying."

"Over hearing when June talks to you and when she talks with your dad.."

Oh great. If he was listening, who else was?

I was deep in thought that I didn't realize that Jeorge was talking to me.

"Can you repeat that? I only got half of that." I told him.

"I said, are you okay? You look like your lost in thought."

"I am fine." I told him while I hugged myself.

"Alright kids, one minute to play." Mr. Howard told all us kids.

"That time already. We spent our time talking." Jeorge told me.

I nodded in agreement.

I mention to Jeorge about going sitting down. He nodded in agreement.

We both sat down on the rug. A few minutes later, the rest of the kids joined us.

When I looked up, I saw Chris smiling at me. I returned the smile.

-Page167-

Where's Ben? I thought.

When the teacher sat down, he opened the book that he held, and began to read.

I looked down at my hands, tapping my fingers against each other.

When I looked back up at Mr. Howard, I saw Chris still looking at me through the corner of my eye.

I shrugged my shoulders and gave him a questioning look. He gave me an annoyed look.

I turned my focus to Mr. Howard.

After story time, we went to have lunch.

I look around and saw rest of the kids eating their lunch.

"Well, this is not a surprise that your not eating. After all, you are an attention seeker." Chris told me.

I gave him an annoyed look, while I replied,

"What do you want? You have been watching me all morning."

He shrugs his shoulders and replies,

"If you noticed, Ben isn't here. I have to report to him when I get home."

"Report to him? Is he your master or something."

"No. But he is missing out on the first day. It's my job to tell him what happened."

"Like the fact I am not eating. Because that is so important to tell your brother. Hmm." I told with a smile.

Chris gave me a dumfounded look.

"Uh, yeah." He replied

I chuckled to myself as I was getting up.

"Look, I have a reason why I don't eat. So drop it." I told him while walking pass him.

"I am surprised that you don't have any marks on you. You must have been a good boy for your Mommy and Daddy."

I stopped in my tracts and turned to look at Chris.

He laughs as he shakes his head.

"What is the surprised look for? Am I right?" he asked.

I walked up to him, got into his face, and told him with a stern voice,

"You don't know anything about me or my life."

Then walked away from him. I stop to look around the room, there was no place I can hide.

"Brook, did you bring lunch?"

I turned to look at Jeorge. Then away while shaking my head.

"Here,"

I relooked at him. He was giving me half of his sandwich.

I looked at the sandwich, then back at him.

"I can't take your lunch. I will be fine." I told him.

"I am sharing it with you. I have the other half."

I leaned into Jeorge, and told him a low voice,

"I don't have my parents permission. I need to have their permission to eat."

I looked away feeling embarrassed.

"What? We are at school. If you don't eat, the teacher will tell your mom, then what?" Jeorge mention.

Hmm. I thought to myself. He has a good point.

"Thank you." I told him while talking the other half of the sandwich. We smiled at each other.

After lunch, it was time to play out side on the playground.

I watched the other kids play while I sat on the bench.

A few minutes passed when I saw Chris walking towards me.

Why does he have a sinister smile on his face. I thought to myself.

"What do you want? I have nothing to offer you." I told Chris.

He laughs to himself, and replies,

"Offer me? Who ever said that I want you to offer me something?"

"I don't know. Every time I am sitting down by myself, you think you can pick on me. And you know, thinking about it, I know why you pick on me." I told him.

"Oh? What is the reason then?" He replied.

"I am the shortest kid here. I was the shortest kid at daycare. All the other kids are your heights or around it."

"Hmm, good point. You are right. With you being the smallest, it is easier to pick on you."

I gave him an annoyed look while I replied,

"But now that's not fair is it. Because I am the smallest doesn't give you the right to pick on me."

Chris shakes his head and walks way.

I chuckled to myself. I guess he didn't know what to say.

Sometime passed and it was time to come in.

"Hi Brook."

I turned around to see Hillary behind me.

"Oh. Hi Hillary. How are you?" I asked her.

"I am good. Thank you. Though you look like your having a bad day. You okay?" She asked.

I look passed her to Chris.

I am glad he is playing with a toy. I thought.

I put my focus back to Hillary.

"I am fine. Your cousin is being his normal self." I told her.

"You got to learn to ignore him. Half of the time he doesn't know what he's talking about." She replied.

"Yeah, I'll try that. But it's hard when he starts in of how I am an attention seeker. I am not an attention seeker. I have rules that I have to follow. Plus he thinks he can pick on me because I am the smallest one of the group." I told her.

"Again, ignore him. He and Ben don't know what they are talking about."

I nodded in agreement.

It was time to do an art project. It was fall theme.

So, we glued some leaf cut outs on a piece of paper.

After that, we could color a picture.

I found my self drawing Daddy's truck. For some odd reason.

After the crafts, we had snack time.

I look around and saw rest of the kids eating their snacks.

"Brook, aren't you hungry?"

I looked up at the second teacher, known as, Peggy.

Only if you knew. I thought to myself. I don't have my parents permission to eat.

"No. I want to go home." I replied.

I saw Peggy kneel down to my level, and she told me,

"Your Mom will be here soon."

I nodded.

I want to go home. That's the last place I want to be. At least I won't be home alone with Daddy.

After art, we did a couple of songs. Then it was time to leave.

I watched as all the parents came into the class room.

Again, all the parents seem to have some sort of emotion.

Then there was my mom, no emotion.

I saw Mr. Howard walk up to mom and they were talking about something. I kept my focus to the floor.

When I heard Mr. Howard call my name, I looked up at him and Mom.

I got up off the floor and walked over towards them.

"Hi Mommy. Did you see the picture that I drew?" I asked her.

She smiles at me and replies,

"Yes. Your dad will love that you drew his truck."

I smiled to her.

Went to grab my stuff from my locker, then Mom and I were heading home.

Once we pulled into the driveway, Mom asked what the issue was between me and Chris.

I sighed before replying,

"He calls me attention seeker because I don't eat. He thinks he can pick on me because I am the smallest one in the class. Plus, he made a remark about how I must have been a good boy to my parents because I have no marks on me. That's why I growled at him."

Mom gave me the death stare look. She looked at me for a couple of minutes. Her look is making me uncomfortable.

Her look lighten up before she spoke.

"I see. Well, I will or you will have to make sure you bring lunch. As for as the marks, hmm, you have been a good boy and you still are a good boy but your father has had a bad day. You might want to be prepare yourself."

She smiles at me while she walk away.

I followed her into the house.

"If I am a good boy, why would Dad beat me? I didn't cause his bad day."

Mom looks at me like she's confused.

"Yes I know. Your point?" She asked.

I shook my head before replying,

"I got chores to do."

-Chapter Nineteen: End of '99-

Mom nods in agreement.

I started on the chores right away. Got dinner goin, finished the remaining chores.

After I got dinner on the table, I went to sit on the couch waiting for Dad to come home.

Half an hour passed and I heard his truck outside.

I got up and walked over towards the door. I heard his keys rattling as he was trying to unlock the door.

When Daddy walked in, we locked eyes for a moment. He broke the connection to put his keys and his cell phone on the counter.

Then he looked back at me with a dark smile.

"Pretty eyes, are you waiting for me?"

Before I could say anything, he pushed me into the wall.

I gave him a nerve look.

Before I knew it, I was looking at Daddy straight in the eye instead of looking up at him.

I looked down at the ground then back at Daddy. Realizing my feet are no longer on the ground.

I gave him a terrified look along with a nerves smile.

Dad returned the smile, then he threw me to the ground.

I let out a whimper, and Dad laughs about that.

I shook my head while sitting up.

I looked up at him while he was taking his belt off.

-Page172-

"Get up. Take off your shirt and face the wall." Daddy told me with a firm voice.

I listened quickly.

I gave him a terrified look before taking my shirt off.

I faced the wall while taking my shirt off. I heard Dad snickering.

I took a deep breath, exhaled while I put my hands on the wall.

"You are home. I thought I heard you." Said Mom.

"Yes. May I continue?" Asked Daddy.

I looked at Mom out of the corner of my eye.

She smiled at me while she replied to Dad,

"Don't let me stop you. Continue."

After Mom said it, I felt Daddy strike me.

I got 24 lashes. For what? I didn't do anything. I only got it because Dad had a bad day at work.

I don't turn around till they give me the cue to turn around. But Dad never gave me that cue.

Instead, I felt him breathing on my neck.

He ran his fingers through my hair.

My heart started to race. My breathing got faster. I was afraid of what he might do.

"Pretty eyes." Daddy whispered.

I felt him run his fingers across my burning back. I flinched.

I asked myself my normal thought. What does he want?

Dad wrapped his arms around me. He let out a quiet moan while he ran both of his hands down my pants.

"Pretty eyes," He whispered. " You are my boy. I love you."

While removing his hands from my pants, he told me to get my shirt back on and go to my room.

I hope he doesn't follow me. I thought to myself.

I turned around and gave Daddy an nervous look. He smiled at me like nothing happened.

Then he changed his focus to the hallway. I turned my focus to the hallway to see what he was looking at.

"Hi Mommy. I will be going in my room now. So you and Daddy

-Page173-

can eat."

"I love you, pretty smile."

I turned to look at Dad.

Isn't pretty eyes? I thought to myself.

He gave me a sinister smile.

I turned around and continued towards my room.

And that's how my day ended.

Which makes me angry. I didn't get 24 lashes because I growled at Chris.

No! I got them because my father was pissed off at something at work.

In one way, I would been happier if I got punished for me getting into a fight with Chris,

Minus fighting with him, my day went well.

Sigh, (Chuckle) But who I am kidding.

I am Brook Tyler. William and Suzanne Tyler's servant. They can use me anyway they please. I only must obey.

(Scoff) Today I was on my best..... Not exactly best behavior but I didn't get punished because I was a bad boy.

Dad used me to get his anger out.

I have been putting up with their crap for almost a year. I am tired of it.

Sigh, but it won't change.

-Page 100-

November came and Daddy's truck died. Which means, Mom and him will be riding together to work. Till Dad gets new car.

That also means, I will be getting picked up by Jeorge and his mom for school and they will drop me off at home.

Then a special day came. My sixth birthday.

Most six year olds get gifts, maybe have a few friends over.

That morning Dad and Mom went to go buy that truck they were looking at the other day.

How did I spend my birthday? Not like most six year olds.

Daddy wanted me to go for a test drive with him in his new truck.

-Page174-

"What do you think, Pretty eyes?" He asked me.

I looked at Dad, for he had a smile on his face. Then I looked at the truck.

To me, it looked like the same truck he had before.

Only thing what was different about it, was it had a back seat and it blue instead of red.

I looked at Dad and replied,

"It's nice. It's blue like our eyes color."

"I know. I thought of you when I looked at it. You have such beautiful blue eyes." He told me with a smile.

If that doesn't sound creepy. I thought to myself.

"Thank you." I told him.

"Let's go for a test drive." Daddy mention.

My gut told me something is wrong. But when I get that feeling, I can't listen to it. If I do, I get into trouble.

"I don't want to go for a test drive Dad." I told him, getting nervous.

He gave me an angry look and points to the truck while he told me,

"Get in the damn truck, Brook Harold."

I gave him a surprised look and said,

"Uh, y-yes sir. Right away sir."

After I got into the truck, he got in and started it up.

We drove for a little while till we got to a spot that looks like nobody drives by often.

He pulled over to the side and turned off the engine.

When I looked at him, he was giving me a unpleasant smile.

Did I forget to mention that most kids get cake for their birthday?

How did I spend my birthday that evening?

Sitting on the side of the road with my Dad. My superior.

He exposed himself and told me,

"Happy birthday, Pretty eyes."

Then forced me to give him a blow job.

He told me that it was my, "birthday cake."

-Page175-

After that, he told me to get out of the truck.

Feeling scared, plus him being my master, I listened. I had to listen.

When we were both outside the truck, he pushed me into the side of it and told me,

"Oh, Pretty eye." He clicks his tongue." Here's your birthday gift."

Dad called it, birthday sex.

That's how I spent my fucking sixth birthday. Taking a test drive with Dad.

A week later was Thanksgiving but it was three days before it that got me into trouble.

We didn't have school but parents still had work. So, I had to go to daycare.

June had us kids draw a picture for what we are thankful for.

I ended up drawing a picture of my parents beating me. Saying I am grateful for discipline

I was proud of the picture. But when June saw it, she told me that I drew nice yet took my picture.

Did I do something wrong? I thought to myself.

When Mom came to get me, June and her talked for a little bit. Then she told me its time to go.

Though Mommy didn't seem happy.

When we got home, she told me to start my chores and she will talk to me after her and Dad talk.

She knows about the picture, means I am in trouble. I thought to myself.

After Dad got home, him and Mom talked.

They called me out of my room about 20 minutes later. So we all could talk.

Sigh, then they both took turns beating me.

They found the game more entertaining then me.

The only thought I had during the wiping /the beating was
I don't want to die.
They were both furious. And with them both going at it, I wasn't
-Page176-
sure anymore.
I remember laying on my side coughing up blood after they felt better.
It hurt like hell to cough.
Though, I coughed something up or so I thought.
Wasn't sure what it was till I slid my tongue over my teeth.
Wait... Slowly, I brought my hand up to my mouth.
I am missing my two front teeth.
Oh, they must have came out while I was coughing.
"Don't worry sport. They are only your baby teeth."
I looked up at Mom, she was blurry. And she sounds like she is in another room, yet she is in front of me.
I nodded.
I laid down on my back and closed my eyes.
I let out a groan. My whole body hurts. I thought to myself.
When I reopened my eyes sometime later. I saw, I believe it was Daddy standing over me.
"Pretty eyes. Now you look like your drawing. The reason why we did what we did. Happy Thanksgiving."
I gave him a weak smile. I reclosed my eyes.
Ah yes, the picture. The reason why I am laying here in pain.
After that night, I stopped drawing at school and at daycare.
Because I work out my feelings through my drawings and when I draw like that in public, it gets me into trouble.
-Page 102-
Mom and Dad spent Thanksgiving with his family. Because I am their servant, they left me home.
They said I can take the day off from work. Mom told I can a peanut butter sandwich.
According to Mom, a Thanksgiving dinner would contain to much calories.
By the way, Mom keeps tracks of my calorie intake. Which is stupid.
Her reason or what she tells me, if I get to fat, no one will like me.

-Page177-

Why would you tell your kid that?! For real Mom?

Because of that, I need their permission to eat. And I am grateful for the little food I do get.

Anyways, December came, not much happened. The same stuff, only different days. Chores and school. Make my master and mistress happy. Not always easy though.

Christmas came fast. See, my family doesn't celebrate it. Not in this house anyways.

My parents do with Dad's side.

Actually, Mom doesn't have family to celebrate Thanksgiving and Christmas with, minus Dad's.

With Mom growing up in an abusive home, and no family she can think of, minus her dad that passed away. She only has Dad's side to celebrate with.

My parents went to spend time over there and told me, relax. Take the day off.

Then there was New years eve.

They, as in my parents, spent it getting high and drunk with the gang.

Best part of it, Mom had HER friends over.

Which of course means...... Mom and Dad put me their closet and told me not to make a sound. If Mom's friends found out about me, I could kiss my life goodbye. According to Dad.

Mom's friends seeing one beating, was enough for my parents to talk about who they trust.

They decided they don't trust Mom's friends but they trust Dad's friends.

They have faith in Uncle Teddy and Uncle Robert that they won't tell any one.

CHAPTER FOURTEEN

THE FUTURE

It is the summer of 2005. I am 10 now.

(Scoff) I am surprised that I am still around. I mean, how Mom and Dad beat me, there are days that I shouldn't be alive. But here I am, 10 years old.

As Jeorge would say,

"I can't believe we are 10."

He's a silly boy.

Right now he's starting puberty. He's starting a little early then most boys.

Me? Still the same heights since first grade. Still need to use stepladders. I hope I get taller some time. Maybe when I hit puberty, I will shoot up.

For now, I better not drop anything when I am on my stepladder because that would make a mess, which means, Mommy will be pissed.

Plus, Daddy thinks I am the right size for..... things.

He thinks he can back me into a corner and have his way.

I didn't think being a, "servant" meant that I have to be Daddy's, what do you want to call it? His sex toy? His boy slut?

I mean, after all, I don't only do it with Daddy. No, there is Uncle Teddy and Uncle Robert. But it's not my choice after all nor do I have a say.

Anyways,

Hillary plus her cousins are still stuck up.

She is not as bad as them, but she is also hitting puberty. Which could be making it worse right now.

Hey, positive note, I got my girl. Hillary is my girlfriend.

Wait? Am I allowed to have one at age ten?

I guess so, because she is mine. Which makes me happy.

But Ben and Chris believe they need to protect her from me.

Though, I only get to see her at school or if I go over there.

But my parents don't know that.

While my parents are gone at work, I get half the chores done, then go hang out with Hillary some times Jeorge, or both.

I have to make sure I am home by 2:30 to be there before Mom plus to finish the chores before Dad gets home.

Because I don't have my parents permission to leave, I hope that

-Page179-

they don't come home early.

I will be...... I don't want to ask what would happen.

Hillary will drag me to church with her once in awhile.

Let's say, that we don't get along when she does that.

Just because you are the pastors daughter, doesn't give you the right to drag your boyfriend to church.

Enough of Hillary, now let's talk about Mom.

Mom is her normal, grumpy self. Only towards me though.

I get the feeling I bug her, not trying to but I don't know how to make her happy someday.

Oh! It's her turn to get a new car. That Blazer she owns currently, is as old as me.

In 2003, Mom and Dad got married. So Mom and I are officially a Tyler.

Even though they were using that name for me before they got married but now its official.

The story of how Dad asked Mom is funny. Now it is not then.

My mom is known to use the belt on me. She doesn't normally use her hands to beat me but that day she did.

She was having a bad day and I was not helping being sarcastic about everything she told me.

She started with the belt first but ended up tossing that to the side plus me.

She kicked me at first then ended up sitting on me to punch me.

And that's when Dad walk in, she stopped to look at him then continues to hit me. Three more times!

"Suzanne Alex, my love."

Mom relooked at Dad.

"I love you. This may not be the right time to ask you. Suzanne Alex, my girl. Wanna be mine, forever?"

Mom chuckled as she was getting up.

"You don't ask a girl to marry you when she is beating up someone. But if you promise to help me keep him in line, then

-Page180-

yes." Mom told Dad as she was running her hands over his groin area.

After she did, she smiled at me then left the room.

She pretty much signaled to Dad that I need to be finished off. In his way.

I couldn't find it funny then like I do now.

But this year is going good so far. That doesn't mean it can't turn bad.

One day, I went to hang with Hillary.

Most of the chores were done and it was noon. So I have an hour and a half.

Grabbed my sweatshirt off my bed before leaving the house. Yep, still wear my good old sweat shirt, even though it's summer. My security blanket, I can't help that.

Any who, it's roughly a five to ten minute walk to Hillary's from my house.

Once I showed up at her house, I knocked, and June answered the door.

"Hi honey. Come on in."

"Thank you. Is Hillary here?" I asked June.

"Yes she is. Hold on a minute, I will go grab her." Replied June.

"Thank you."

I walked in the living room where she use to hold the daycare at when I was growing up. I looked around the living room while I let out a sigh.

"Hi Brooks."

I turned around to see Hillary.

"Hi Hill. How are you?" I asked her.

"I am pretty good. Thanks for asking. How are you?" She replied.

"I am alright. Teaching myself not to be stressed out when I leave the house." I told her.

She laughed before replying,

"Yeah, I suppose. They still don't know that you sneak over here during the day?"

-Page181-

I shook my head as I told her no.

"Dang. Hope you don't get caught. You don't need another black eye."

I gave her a surprised look and nodded in agreement while I replied,

"Yeah, me too. Me too."

She smiled at me before she replied,

"Should we go for a walk? Or should we go sit on the patio?"

"Backyard might be safer." I told her.

"Hmm, I suppose."

We went to go sit at the picnic table.

"I remember sitting outside at this table watching you play with the other kids. Hoping one day that I would have you." I told her with a smile.

She returned the smile.

"Mm-hmm. Me too." Hillary said while looking down.

"How did I get so lucky?" I asked her while resting my arms, criss cross on the table and putting my head on my arms.

She looked back towards me.

"You need some good luck in your life. You know, to keep you going."

"I know. Your my luck charm." I smiled at her. "So, does your Mom still have the daycare?" I asked her while I brought my head back up.

"Yep. She runs it at the church now. That way she can help more people." She replied.

"Makes sense."

"Yes. You look like your getting around pretty well since last month. Are you every going to tell me the truth of how you broke your leg?" She asked.

I looked at her, trying to think what to say.

I shrugged my shoulders while I replied,

"I told you, I fell off my bike."

Hillary gave me a disbelief look.

-Page182-

"Brook, you don't ride a bike. Let alone own one. That's why I don't believe you." She told me.

I looked away feeling ashamed while I replied,

"I know." I looked at her, "Besides, it's been 12 weeks since I broke it. Of course I am getting around fine."

"True. Now we got to do something about that sweat shirt." She mentioned.

I looked at her in shock while I replied,

"What do you mean WE got to do something about my sweatshirt?!"

Hillary started to laugh.

"What is with the look? When it's 90 degrees outside and your wearing your sweatshirt, you look silly."

"Your point?" I asked her.

"We live in Kentucky not Antarctica." She told me.

I gave her an annoyed look while I replied,

"I know where we live." I looked away chuckling, then back at Hillary. "Your silly and I like you."

She smiled as she replies.

"I like you too."

We both smiled at each other.

"Brook,"

I turned to look at June.

"It's two o'clock."

"What?! That can't be right." I told her in a panic as I was getting up. "I g-got to go. Thank you for having me over. I will talk to you later, bye." I told Hillary and June.

I hurried as fast as I can go. But with my leg still healing, I can't run on it. Actually, with my short statue I can't run easily.

I mean, it's only two, Mom doesn't get home till 2:30. So, what is the rush.

Before hitting my street, there was a certain blue Chevy Blazer that drove by.

Huh, that looks like Mom. And it seems to be heading in the

-Page183-

direction where my house is.

My stomach sunk. Shoot, it is Mom. I am so dead. Why did she come home early?

I cut through our neighbors back yards to reach my back yard.

I am hoping it looks like I have been sitting outside on the patio.

Finally got home.

I looked into Mom's window but didn't see her. So, I peaked around the corner to see if she was still in the car.

Nope. She isn't in the car. She could be in the kitchen.

At that moment, I saw her come out of her bathroom.

I quickly dropped to the ground.

I did an army crawl back to the back yard.

When I made it to the back yard, I stood up and walked towards the door.

Breath Brook, breath. I told myself before entering the house.

"Brook?"

I heard Mom from the hallway.

When I saw her walk into the living room, I smiled at her, while I replied,

"Yes ma'am?"

"You weren't in the house nor outside. Where were you when I came home?"

"Where was I? I was...." I lost my smile while looking away. Shoot, I didn't come up with an excuse.

"Brook Harold, where were you?" Mom asked, getting inpatient.

I looked back at her and continued to say with a nervous chuckle,

"I - I, was in the shed."

"Huh? What were you doing in there?"

I looked away while I quietly replied,

"Eating."

I heard Mom sigh.

"That's fine. You won't be getting dinner now." She replied.

I looked at her while I gave her a surprised look.

"But ma'am, I only had breakfast."

-Page184-

"I thought you were in the shed eating?" She said while crossing her arms with a hint of a smile.

"I - I was... In the shed eating." Realizing what I told her. I sighed. "Oh yeah." I chuckled to myself. I lowered my voice. "I snuck lunch in. Which means, I won't get dinner. Makes sense."

Mom nods in an agreement.

I watched her leave the room.

Great. That was a lie, and because of it, I won't be getting dinner.

Which sucks, because I am hungry. I barely got breakfast this morning because of Dad.

Any who, got the chores done, got dinner made.

I walked towards Mom's room, I knock and she told me to come in.

When I walked in, she was laying down with a pillow over her eyes. She lifted it to look at me.

"What do you want?" She asked while putting the pillow back over her eyes.

"I am sorry about eating without your permission." I told her.

"I am not worried about it. You gave your self natural consequence." She let out a quiet chuckle. "You won't get dinner that's all and there is that possibility, you might not get breakfast. But I will have to talk to your dad when he gets home."

"Yes ma'am. By the way, I got the chores and dinner done."

"Excellent. Now go to your room."

"Yes ma'am.

My room looks so different then it did when I was younger.

With me having the title, "servant", they, my parents or my master and mistress, believe I don't need a proper room. Having a room like most kids would be consider a luxury.

The only thing that I have in my room is my desk, to do homework on and the bed is only here for my dad's purposes.

I don't even have carpet in my room. I am not saying that all kids have carpet in their room. But I don't even have wood floors in my room. Hell, I have concert as my bedroom floor. Sigh. But that is

-Page185-

my Master and Mistress choice after all.

I laid down in my bed, thinking about my day.

I was cutting it a little close today but she did come home early.

Sometime passed before I heard a knock on my door.

I sat up while Daddy was walking in.

"Yes sir?" I asked.

"Pretty eyes, What is this I hear about you sneaking food? I am disappointed in you. I was hoping to have dinner with you." Daddy told me.

"Uh," I look down then relook at him. "I am sorry sir. I was hungry."

"I get that. But I had to hear it from your mistress that you were sneaking food. Plus you were hiding in the shed? Honey, we were both at work, you could have ate it in the house."

"W- Well, I was trying to hide the evidence from both of you. I- I am s-sorry. I agree it wasn't the smartest idea." I replied.

Dad looks towards my window as he blew out.

"Honey," He looks at me. "It makes me angry that your sneaking around. I and your mistress are trying to taking care of you, we love our boy. But I am sorry, you don't get any dinner tonight, plus no breakfast tomorrow. We will talk about this again tomorrow about if you get lunch. or possible no food at all tomorrow. Then you might learn to be grateful."

My eyes widen,

"A -A whole day without food sir? Isn't that a little harsh? It's not like get a full meal sir, like you and Mom-"

"Your mistress." Dad told me after interrupting me.

"Sir?" I asked with a puzzled look.

"She is your mistress."

"Sir?" I questioned again.

"You are our servant. So she is your Mistress and I am your Master." He replied.

"But you called me your boy. I am yours and my," Minute pause. "Mistress boy." I told him.

-Page186-

"Mm-hmm, I did. You are our submissive boy, our servant. So your mistress and I deserve a full meal."

Am I hearing this right or am I making it up? That's it, I am having a nightmare! I thought to myself.

"Sir. Why are you so gentle?" I asked.

"Gentle?" He asked with a puzzled look.

"Your words. Your not yelling at me sir, your calm." I replied.

"Ah." He laughs quietly. " Pretty eyes, it's always calm before the storm." He told me with a smile. Then he left the room.

What storm is he talking about? I asked myself, starting to get concerned.

With not much happening the rest of the night and my parents...... Well, my Master and Mistress hasn't called me out. I went to sleep. Whatever mess is out there I can take care of tomorrow.

I kept on tossing and turning. Dads words are still on my mind plus I am hungry. It sucks that I don't get breakfast in the morning. I hoping I get lunch. A natural consequence for sure. I wasn't sneaking food, I snuck out of the house and was trying to sneak back in. I rolled my eyes.

It's not like a get a lot of food in this house anyways. It all depends on their mood. Plus it depends on if I was good boy.

"Pretty eyes, it's six o'clock. It is time to start waking up."

I groaned in a tired way. When I rolled over and opened my eyes, I gave Daddy a surprise look.

"Hi. Um, sir?" I asked.

"Yes Pretty eyes?" He replied with a smile while playing with my hair.

"I am asking respectfully sir, why are you in my bed?"

"Trying to wake you up."

"By rubbing yourself against me, sir?" I asked.

I am getting worried why he is in my bed. Hell, I shouldn't be worried. This is how I wake up most mornings.

"Your awake aren't you?" He replied with a smile.

"Yes sir, I am." I gave him a nervous smile. Cleared my throat.

-Page187-

"Now, is there something I can help you with, sir?"

"No. Only trying to wake you. Oh. I talked with your mistress, and she agreed that you don't get breakfast or lunch. If you behave yourself, you can have dinner." Daddy told me.

"Y- Yes sir. I will behave myself today sir." I replied back with a smile.

"Are you hungry?" He asked me.

"Very much so, sir."

"Then take that hungry feeling" As he pokes me in the stomach. "And stay out of trouble today. Be Daddy's little good boy. Hmm."

I gave him a force smile.

Before I could get up, Dad climbed on me and I felt his lips against mine. Plus I felt how hard he was.

I looked at him with a anxious look.

"Kiss me damn it!" Dad demanded.

I gave him a terrified look while I replied,

"B-But you have work sir?"

He does a quiet laugh as he looks away. Few seconds pass when he relooks at me.

"Pretty eyes, give me the damn kiss. Or kiss your meals goodbye, sweetheart."

"Yes sir."

What other choice did I have? I gave him what he wanted now or I will be punished later. Hell, I could still be because I fought him or didn't listen right away. I hate when he threatens me.

A few minutes passed then I felt him rubbing against me. Again!

I moved my eyes frantically.

Dad picked up on my heavy breathing that he stop kissing me to look at me.

"What is wrong Pretty eyes? Don't like the rubbing?" Daddy sneered.

"Sir, out of respect, you're going to be late for work." I told him feeling concerned.

"Well, I guess that's the risk we will have to take. I won't be -Page188- suffering from it later, you will be." He told me with a sinister smile.

"Sir, I don't want you late. It's not going to make your boss happy."

"My boss? Who the hell cares about my boss. To be honest, I have him wrapped around my finger. I am one of the best employees he has. I am not concerned. Maybe you should be concerned about your boss. Hmm?"

"The only thing I am concerned about is that your not going to allow me to have dinner because I caused you to be late."

"Then please me. Your stalling is making me late. Make your Daddy happy and kiss me. And let me rub against you without you freaking out." He said with a smile.

"Yes sir."

This guy is annoying. Stop messing around with your kid and get to work damn it.

He only wants a reason to beat me later. Or sick Mom, Mistress, whatever she is called now, after me.

For real, you have work. Kissing me and rub dry humping me isn't helping neither of us.

After a few minutes, still laying there playing kissy face, I felt Daddy run his hand down my pants.

I felt my heart starting to pound faster.

He grabbed my penis and squeezed it tightly.

I stopped the kiss with a whimper.

I laid there wining while giving him a pleading look.

It hurts, I want him to let go.

"Make your boss happy. Remember? Speaking about bosses, I made mine happy this morning. I called him before laying down with you, told him that I will be an hour late. By the way, did you see what time it is? 6:45, Pretty eyes. I don't leave till 7:30. We still got time. Time for me to be cruel to you." He starts rubbing my penis. "We haven't had this much fun with each other for a while." Daddy told me with a smile.

-Page189-

We haven't?! I thought to myself. I am pretty sure this happen every other morning.

"Please Daddy. Please let go." I told him in a winey voice.

He just laughs and give me a sinister smile.

He continued for another five minutes before letting go.

I laid there panting. It hurts.

"Your cute when you pant. I love to hear your whimpers." Dad said with a smile.

"Why do you hate me?" I asked him.

"Hate you?" Dad gave me a questioning look. "Who ever said I hate you?"

"Because your always picking on me."

"I do it because I love you." Dad replied with a hint of a smile.

"Love me?!" I gave him a surprised look. "This is how you show your love? By kissing me while rubbing against me? Then grabbing my penis and hold onto it tightly. So you can hear me whimper! That's love to you?! I would hate to see what hate is to you."

Dad started to laugh before replying,

"You have seen my hate. You were five and didn't tell me or mother about the dryer being broken. I kicked your butt pretty good that night. There was Thanksgiving of that same year, where I kicked your butt again. And recently when I broke your leg because you were trying to run away. Plus other things I didn't mention but you already know them. There is my hate Brook Harold."

I nodded before replying,

"Just because I nodded, doesn't mean I totally agree."

"You don't have to. Just telling you what the difference between love and hate." He replied.

I nodded and replied,

"Your version at least."

-Chapter twenty-one: Planning-

Lets jump a month and half to middle of July. The time I made a huge mistake.

I have been dealing with my. (Minute pause.) Master and Mistress abuse for six years. So, I attempted to runway. Again. But this time without failing. Like the first time.

My punishment from the first time, resulted me getting my leg broken by my Master and bars on my window.

The only reason why I got caught the first time, because I was stupid enough to think that I could escape while my Mistress was outside having a cigarette.

What do my owners think I do when they are gone? Clean the house? Hahaha, right.

No, I plan my escape route. A better one then the first time.

It started out like any other day. My owners went to work. I cleaned the house. Honestly, with me cleaning the house everyday, it doesn't take that long to clean. That's why I sneak over to Hillary's or Jeorge's. Or sometimes, I sleep. And that's what I did that day, I slept.

I got up an hour before my Mistress got home.

I laid there thinking of how I want to escape. I will do it after they are in bed sleeping. Hmm, I wonder how easy it is to take one of the cars.

My Mistress's car isn't running right, I may not get far with that. But my Masters truck.

They always hang up their car keys by the door, so that shouldn't be a problem.

What about food? Hmm, if I have one of the cars, I will make it out of here faster.

I rolled over to my side and was staring out the window.

I can't go out the window for obvious reasons.

I closed my eyes as I covered them with my hands.

I was thinking about the first time I attempted this. Then I started to think of how my Master broke my leg.

He first busted my knee with a hammer. Then processed with breaking my leg. But during the whole process my Mistress was I

-Page191-

holding me down trying to muffle my screaming.

I started to cry thinking about this. I can't fail this time around. I can't endure that type of torture again. I could get something worse if I fail this time.

I removed my hands and started to get up. My Mistress will be home soon.

I sat up and looked around the room. I then looked at my floor. It is stupid that I have concrete for my floor. Having carpet or even wood floors would be, what? A normal thing that most kids have in their room. But then again, I am not a normal kid. Most kids have parents. I have owners.... Sigh.

I walked around the house to double check if the house was clean. Making sure I didn't miss anything.

I figured if all or at least if most chores are done before my Mistress gets home, I can focus on dinner.

When I looked up at the clock it read, 2:27 P.M.

Any minute now. I went to sit at the table to wait for her.

While looking out the window, I saw her pull into the driveway.

I got up to go unlock the door and opened it.

"Hi sweetie. How was your day?" My Mistress asked while walking up to the door.

"My day was good. Got the house cleaned. I got to get dinner ready still." I replied.

"Good, good. With it being Friday night, Uncle Teddy, Uncle Robert plus some of my friends are going to be coming over. You know what that means don't you?" She asked.

Unfortunately. I thought to myself.

"Yes ma'am. What time are they coming over?"

I watched my Mistress light up her cigarette before replying,

"Uncle Teddy and Uncle Robert will be over the same time your Master gets home. My friends a little later. So make extra dinner." She told me.

"Yes ma'am. Do I get dinner ma'am?"

"Mhmm, you will get dinner. Then you will have time to take care
-Page192-
of the dinner mess. Then it's the closet for you sweetheart." She replied.

"Yes ma'am."

We both walked back into the house. Mistress went to her room to change out of her work uniform. I went to the kitchen to figure out dinner.

Sigh, great. Every body is coming over. Depending on when every one leaves... I don't want to fail sneaking out this time. Hopefully my owners will be completely drunk they pass out. That way, they won't hear the car leaving.

I don't want to be sitting in the closet. I hate when my Mistress has her friends over. I thought to myself.

I got busy with dinner and before I knew it, it was that time.

When my master pulled up outside. I looked out the window and saw Uncle Teddy pull up on his motorcycle and Uncle Robert in his truck.

By the time they were coming in, I was setting the table.

"Rookie! My bo,-" Robert started to say

"Your boy?" Master question him.

Robert looked at him.

"Yes, my boy."

My master laughs

"No, he's my boy." he said walking up to me while he putting his arms around me.

I looked up at my Master and smiled at him.

"Hello sir, how are you?" I asked.

"Doing better since I am hugging my boy."

"Good to hear, sir. But you got to let me go so I can finish with dinner sir."

"I will after I feel you up." He snickered." But it would be easier if you weren't so damn short."

I looked up at him as I replied,

"Sorry sir. I didn't choose to be four feet tall."

"Yeah, I know. " He replied while he patted me on my head.

-Page193-

"Oh Brook, we love your shortness. It's easier to pick on you." I heard uncle Teddy say.

I looked over at him. He gave me smile, I returned the smile.

Then my Mistress came in.

"Honey!" I heard my Master telling my Mistress.

I laughed to myself as my Master hugged attack her.

"Hi dear." She told him.

"Your both cute together." I told them with a smile.

They both looked at me.

"At least she is a foot shorter then verse two." Master told me with a smile.

I shrugged my shoulders as I replied,

"Should have married some lady with a taller son."

My master rolled his eyes at me.

Because I am the servant, I eat after everyone else does.

"While you guys eat I will go check on the laundry." I told them.

I walked toward the laundry room, halfway down the hall, I stop and turned to look at everybody in the kitchen. They all look happy. Talking among each other and laughing. Uncle Robert and I locked eyes for a brief moment.

I broke the connection by turning away. I continued towards the laundry room.

As I was switching the loads, I can still hear them talking and laughing among each other. I don't want to sit in the closet.

With the laundry room being in the bathroom, I looked in mirror before leaving. Hopefully that will be the last bruise I see on my face. I took a deep breath and blow out as I shook my head.

I waked back towards the kitchen,

"Pretty eyes!" My master jumped up from his chair while putting out his arms.

I gave him an unsure smile. He walked up to me, hugged me lightly then started doing circles around me.

"You're going into the closet. You're going into the closet."

I watched him doing circles around me.

-Page194-

"Sir, not trying to be disrespectful but why are you happy about that?"

My Master stopped in front of me, kneeled down to my level.

"Because I am William Tyler." He said while he started to laugh.

I raised my eye brow at him with a puzzling look while I replied,

"I don't understand sir."

He continues to laugh while getting up.

"I still feel confused." I said.

I looked at my Master and my Mistress then towards my uncles. They were all smiling at me. I gave them a weak smile.

"I am going to get dinner then get the kitchen cleaned. After that I can get your snack plate ready."

They all nodded in agreement.

They all left the kitchen to sit in the living room.

This group is nuts. And they only become worse when they drink and use drugs.

So, I ate then cleaned up the kitchen. Afterwards, I made their snack plate, I set it on the table. Then I went to clean up that mess.

"Brook,"

I turned my head towards my left to look up at my Mistress standing over me. I smiled at her.

"Yes ma'am?"

"It's time."

After she said that, I lost my smile while I looked down at the counter that I was wiping off.

"Brook Harold,"

I relooked up at her, then passed her to look down the hall.

I slowly looked back at the dish rag that I was holding in my right hand.

I looked up at her, while I replied,

"One minute ma'am."

I walk passed her towards the sink to rinse out the rag, wringed it out and put it over the sinks edge to let it dry.

-Page195-

I let out a long sigh then turned to face my Mistress who was behind me. Realizing that my Mater, Uncle Teddy, and Uncle Robert were standing behind her.

Jeez guys, I am going into the closet not to prison. The again, prison might sound better.

"You ready now?" My Mistress asked me.

I looked around the kitchen to make sure everything was done.

I turned my attention back to my Mistress and nodded.

No but I couldn't tell her that.

"I'll come get you out after everybody leaves." My Master told me.

I did a slow nod to him.

I followed my Mistress towards her room. When we took a step into her room, she turned to look down at me. She knelt down to my level and told me,

"Alright, you sit in there and be a good boy for your Master and I. I don't want to punish you later."

I looked passed her to the closet. I felt my chest get tight.

Trying to hide the fact I am upset.

I don't like.... Going in that.... Small dark room. It's darkness is like a monster, ready to swallow you up.

I returned my focus to my Mistress.

I took a deep swallow and replied,

"Yes ma'am."

She got up to open the closet for me.

"I am trusting that you will be quiet and I won't have to put a gag around you mouth, right?"

I looked up at her in shock. In fear, I stood there studying her face for a couple of minutes.

She broke the silence when she laughed to her self.

"But that also means I will have to tie your hand behind your back. I am positive you don't want that."

She left me speechless that I could only look at her. My thoughts raced.

-Page196-

"Brook." She raised her eye brow at me." You need to speak." She said with a hint of a smile.

"I -..... Um," I looked away from her. "N-No ma'am, I wouldn't like t-that." I relooked at her. "But, I am only the servant, it's your call."

"Hmm, that's true. Since you ran away back in May, June, I should tie you up. We haven't had my friends here since then. Normally we go over there or meet up at a bar. Yeah, I'll tie you up and gag you. We shouldn't take any chances." She told me with a wink.

I nodded in agreement.

So she tied my hands together behind my back and tied my ankles together and put a gag over my mouth.

My mistress smiled at me, I gave her an anxious look.

"Now, I am going to go join the fun and your Master will be back later to get you."

The whole room went dark as I heard the bedroom door close.

I search the closet, letting my eyes get adjust to the dark.

I let out a sigh. What's the worst thing about being in a dark closet? Being tied up and gaged in that dark closet.

I leaned my head back against the wall as I closed my eyes.

The only I can do is sleep. Catch up on sleep before my big escape.

Every time I felt my head to start to bob, I lean my head back against the wall.

I startled my self awake when I jerked my head.

Hmm. I grunted. I think my Mistress tied the ropes to tight. It's cutting into my wrist and ankles. Plus I am getting sick of this gag in my mouth.

I can still hear their music on. How long was I sleeping for? What time is it? I thought.

A few minutes passed then I saw the bedroom light come on.

Some body was in the room. Then the closet light came on.

I squinted my eyes. The light was bright. When I looked up, my Master was standing before me. Though he had a puzzled look on

-Page197-

his face. I gave him a sleepy look.

"Alright Pretty eyes. Lets get you untied and that gag out of your mouth." He said while he knelt down. "She tied the ropes to tight that its cutting into you. (Sigh)" My Master looks at me and smiles.

After untying the ropes, he took the gag out of my mouth.

"Does that feel better, honey?" Master asked in a calming voice.

His voice seems comforting. For some odd reason.

"Thank you sir.

He smiled at me and hugged me.

"Hey, come here. Just lean into Daddy. I got you." Master started to run his fingers through my hair. "Shh. Daddy's here. It's okay."

He looked at me, I looked at him.

He smiled at me while wiping the tears away.

"There is no reason to cry. Remember, when you start to crying, your eyes turn red and-"

"And you can't see my pretty blue eyes. Plus crying is meant for sissy not young boys. I know." I finished his sentence for him through sniffles.

"That's right. You know Daddy like your sky blue eyes." He said while he put both hand on my face.

I nodded.

"Alright, I suppose we should go out there before your Mistress comes in looking for us." He said while standing up.

Before I got up, I looked at my wrist and ankles. There was a red line where the ropes was.

I shook my head while I let out a sigh.

When I look up, I saw that my Master was holding out a hand to help me up.

I grab his hand but felt shaky when I stood up.

My leg fell asleep when I was sitting there. I shook it to wake it up.

We both walked out to the living room.

"Hey Rookie. How was the closet?" Uncle Robert asked.

I looked at him with a puzzling look.

-Page197-

What's with the smirk on his face. I thought to myself.

I cleared my throat before replying,

"It was good. You know, got time to myself. To think."

"I think you get enough time to yourself to think but ok." Uncle Teddy said sounded annoyed.

I looked at Uncle Teddy, who was on my right side.

"True. But I know better saying anything negative."

"Smart boy. That's why you are Daddy's boy." My Master said.

I turned my head to my left to look at him and nodded in agreement.

I watch my Master walk over towards my Mistress and whisper something in her ear.

I watched them for a brief moment till I looked down at my wrists.

"Let me see your wrist."

I looked up and Mistress was standing over me.

I showed her my wrist. She nodded then knelt down. She rolled up my pants to look at my ankles.

"Hmm. Yeah, I did tie the ropes tighter then I meant to but at least you couldn't escape." She said with a smirk.

"Yes ma'am. So what are the sleeping rearrangements?" I asked while I watched my Mistress stand up.

"Teddy bear and Robby on the couch." Mistress said.

"If Da- um, my Master is okay with it. Uncle Robert in bed with you, Mistress and Uncle Teddy in my bed. And I can share the couch with My Master."

I don't really want to sleep with him but that way I can take his truck.

Make Daddy, Master, my owner, happy for one last time.

"I am up for that. I love cuddling my boy." My Master said while hugging me.

I looked up at him with a smile.

Hopefully my plan doesn't fall through.

"Well goodnight boy." Uncle Teddy told me while patting me on my head.

-Page199-

"Night Sweetie." Mistress told me.

"Night Mistress and Uncle Robert."

I watched them leave the room,

I saw my Master walk pass me to where uncle Teddy was sitting to pull out the futon.

He sat on the edge of the futon smiling at me. I returned the smile.

I walk in front of him, study his face. He looked at me.

I leaned in to kiss him. To my surprise, he pulled me in closer.

He wasn't suppose to do that.

I was trying to keep my breathing steady. Remember the plan Brook, the truck. I thought to myself.

I pulled away from the kiss. We looked at each other.

"What would you like to be called sir? Master or Daddy?" I asked while I looked him in the eyes.

"Daddy is fine Pretty eyes." He replied with a smile.

"May I give you a blow job Daddy?" I asked while biting my lower lip.

He nodded and started to undo his pants.

I watched him take off his pants and boxer, then he laid down on the couch.

I sat down on the couch. We smiled at each other.

When I looked down he was rubbing himself.

"Well? I am waiting." Master told me.

I relooked at him with a nod.

The night started with me giving Daddy, my Master a blow job and it ended with Daddy having sex with me.

Afterwards we laid down cuddling with each other.

I felt his hairy chest against my bare back. The warmth I felt with his arms wrapped around me.

"I am sorry Daddy." I whispered to myself when I knew he was asleep.

I carefully got up, got dressed, slipped my shoes on. Grabbed the truck keys that were hanging up by door. Before leaving the

-Page200-

house, I turned to look at my master sleeping.

I smiled to myself while leaving the house.

Still smiling to myself as I walked up to the truck.

I took a deep breath and let it out slowly.

Unlock the door and climbed into the truck.

I sat there in the driver seat feeling proud of myself.

I turned the engine on and the truck growled.

Sheesh, I forgot how loud the truck was. I am hoping no one in the house woke to the loud engine.

One problem though, If I look out the windshield, I can't touch the gas pedal. If I touch the gas pedal, I can't see out of the window. Sigh, short problems. I hate being short.

I looked out the back window to make sure no was coming.

Put it in reverse and I gentle put pressure on the gas pedal, turned right out of the drive away.

Made my way slowly towards Main Street. When I got to the intersection, I came to a stop.

Wasn't sure if I was suppose to go, right, left, or straight.

I.. Um.. I kept shifting my eyes towards the right to the left and straight ahead of me.

I put my hands over my eyes.

The only thing I could think of, is I am free.

I smiled to my self. Sigh, Straight. I go straight. I hope.

Ten minute out of town, I realized there was a truck that was following me.

My heart stop, I started to tremble. I pulled the truck over to the side of the road and turned it off. Sat there gripping the steering wheel, hoping it was no body from the house and he should pass me.

I gripped the wheel tighter when I saw the truck pull over as well. I started to cry, my breathing got heavier, closed my eyes.

-Chapter Twenty- two: Hell-

When I heard the truck door open, I closed my eyes tighter.

-Page201-

"Master isn't happy. You know better then to run off. Hell, you know better then to take his truck. I am very disappointed in you." Uncle Teddy told me.

I let go of the steering wheel, opened my eyes, wiped the tears from my eyes.

"Am I in trouble?" I asked through sniffles.

"You took his truck and ran off!" quiet laugh." Trouble no. He's going to kill you."

"Kill me?!" I asked sounding concerned." I - I don't want to go home if he's gonna k-kill me."

Uncle Teddy scoffs,

"We have to get you home. Scoot over."

"B- But I don't want to die." I looked at Uncle Teddy.

"Boy, you should have thought about that before running off and taking his truck. Now scoot over."

Uncle Teddy as a point. The truck is Daddy's baby. He takes pride in his truck.

"Yes sir." I said while scooting over.

Uncle Teddy got into the truck and started it back up.

He did an U-turn on the road to ahead back into town.

I sat there staring out the window. So much for freedom. I thought to myself.

"Your daddy broke your leg the last time for running off. Except you never did. Because you were dumb enough to try it with your Mother outside." He clicks his tongue. "This time you actually ran away and took his truck. He may not kill you but he isn't going to be nice about it like last time."

"Breaking my leg was nice?" I asked under my breath.

I felt his stare. I kept my gaze outside.

"Here we are boy. Got any last words to say before you meet your maker?" He sneered.

I gave him a nerve look.

I got out of the truck and stood there unable to move.

"Come on boy. Master is waiting." Uncle Teddy growled.

-Page202-

"Are you going to start crying Rookie? I thought Daddy doesn't like that. You got to go face him. Be brave." Uncle Robert said with a smirk.

I closed my eyes while I took a deep breath, and exhaled slowly. I was trying to calm myself. I walked slowly up to the door.

Once at the door, I turned the nob of the door.

One of the guys pushed me in that I fell to my hands and knees.

"Get up boy. Your Mistress is waiting for you in your room."

I never had the chance to get up, when I felt Uncle Teddy grab the back of my shirt and pick me up.

"Walk!" He growled.

I didn't really walk on my own towards my room, more like Uncle Teddy dragged me there.

Once at my bedroom, I peeked in to see my Mistress waiting for me.

She stood there with her arms crossed, while giving a halfhearted smile.

"Come on Brook Harold. Face up for what you did."

I creep towards her. When I got in front of her and she asked me,

"What the hell were you thinking Brook Harold? Running off like that and taking your Master's truck."

She held her gaze at me for a brief moment, till she shift her eyes pass me.

I turned to see who she was looking at.

I looked at my Master.

I felt sick, I don't recall ever seeing fire in his eyes before. Plus I never saw him wearing his holster before either.

He stomp towards me and shoved me into the wall.

For your information, I was about three feet maybe four away from the wall.

He came at me like a bulldozer. I just know that I went flying backwards into the wall. Once I hit it, I slid down to a sitting position.

I sat there dazed for a couple of minutes.

-Page203-

I saw Master walk up to me and grab me by the collar of my shirt, lifting me to my feet.

I gave him a terrified look.

"What the fuck is wrong with you?! Running off and stealing my truck?! YOU," He slaps me with his pistol" Know better then to touch my fuckin truck! You obviously didn't learn from me breaking your leg."

I looked passed Master to my Mistress and my uncles.

They all look amused by this.

Master puts one finger under my chin to make me look at him.

"Pretty eyes. The only reason why you.." He starts to snap his fingers. "What is the word I am looking for."

"Surrender?" Uncle Robert ask.

Master turned too look at him.

"YES! Thank you." He told Robert.

Master turned to look at me.

"As I was saying, you only surrendered yourself so you can steal my truck?"

I looked away from.

"Answer me Pretty eyes!" Master demanded.

I re looked up to him.

"N-no."

He pistol whips me across the face. Again.

I felt my nose started to bleed. My eyes started to get watery.

"Don't lie to me boy." Master said harshly.

"I am not l-lying sir. I wanted to show you how much I loved you." I said with a quiver.

"It makes sense now. I will surrender myself to you for sex for the trade of your truck. Except you never told me about your plan, Pretty eyes."

"You weren't suppose to know to my plan, sir." I said while I used the back of my hand to wipe the blood from my nose.

Master chuckles to himself.

"Boys, would you come.... Well, I need to strip him down to his

-Page204

underwear first but I need you guys to come hold him." he said while putting his gun back in the holster.

After Master stripped me down, the boys came over to hold me.

Mistress and Master walked out of the room to talk in privet.

"I told you boy, he's going to kill you." Uncle Teddy sneered.

"Because you took his truck. Even I know better not to touch his truck." Uncle Robert finish saying.

I look up at them both.

A few minutes later, Mistress and Master came back in.

I looked at them both, fearing for what they had in mind.

Master still had his gun with him.

"Are you going to kill me like Uncle Teddy says?"

They didn't say anything. Though I watched Master take off his belt.

My breathing got faster, I started to cry.

I closed my eyes tightly, biting my lip.

Then I felt Master strike me. I let out cry.

He kept on thrashing me over and over.

I couldn't do anything. I had no choice. It was completely up to him how long he wanted to whip me for. And I knew whether I liked it or not, he wasn't done.

This went on for about 15 minutes.

"Pretty eyes. Look at me." Master said.

I was shaking with tears running down my face while I opened one of my eyes to look at him.

"Sir?" I quivered.

"You got to turn around now."

I gave him a scared look, I watch him hand the belt over to my Mistress.

I whined while turning around.

Mistress did the same thing that my Master did. Just on my back,

After Mistress turn, Master walked back up to me, grab back of my head, slammed the front of my head into the wall. I felt the gush of blood from my nose. Turned me around to punch me in

-Page205-

the face!

Master smiled darkly before punching me in the stomach.

I gasp I tried to lean over but couldn't with the two boys holding me. I was trying to breath but couldn't.

Then Master punched me again. He kept on hitting me over and over again. Not caring where he punched me. I got hit in the stomach, the chest and the neck.

When he stop, I gave him a questioning look, trying to catch my breath.

I stood there retching.

When I looked down at the ground, I saw the blood droplets from my nose.

After they were done Uncle Teddy and Uncle Robert let me drop to the floor.

I closed my good eye as I sat against the wall for few minutes, trying to catch my breath. When I opened my eye, the room was spinning. I saw them standing there looking at me with a slight grin.

When they left the room, I closed my eye.

God, I want to throw up.. I wished he killed me. It would feel better.

I open my eye when I heard them come back in.

Master walked up to me and knelt down to my level.

"I see that you have your gun on you. Just shoot me. Kill me right now. Is that why you have it out?" I asked in a low wheezy, raspy voice.

I started to cough as I leaned forward. Took deep a breath as I leaned back against the wall.

"I am not going to kill you." Master told me.

I sat up and grabbed his gun.

"Hey! Give it here." Master pleaded.

I gave him an furious look with a dark smile while I put the gun to my head.

-Page206-

"I want to die!" I growled while looking at Master then passed him to the rest of the gang.

They all look concerned. Why are they concerned?

"Honey. Give me the gun." Master said while reaching for it.

I love the fact that he has terror running through him.

"Then kill me!" I wheezed, "Or I will do it. I don't want to be here anymore!" I said while clenching my teeth. "Do you even know what Brook means?" I asked.

They all shook their head no.

"It means stream, it runs freely. I want to be free! So just kill me." I said while dropping the gun as I started to cry.

Master grabs the gun from my hand.

I leaned my head back on the wall and brought my knees up to my chest. I sat there and sobbed.

A few minutes passed when Master told me to reach out my hands. I did as I was told.

"Come on Pretty eyes, get up on your knees. Atta boy."

I looked up at Master, then look at my hand that was cuffed to the wall behind me. Then I looked back at him with a questioning look.

I dropped my head, stared at the ground as they shut off the light and shut the door behind them.

Is this what my life has come to? I ain't their kid, I am their servant. Who's currently chained to the wall, and is still sitting my boxer. Awesome!

Instead of feeling sad, I felt angry.

I am tired of being here, dealing with their crap! The physical and the sexual abuse, I can't handle it anymore! Actually I can't handle the sexual abuse. Because I can't mentally escape.

It goes back to my one question that I asked once before, what is love?

I just want to feel like some one appreciates me for me. The young boy I am suppose to be not the servant. I want parents not owners.

-Page207-

With me standing on my knees, the concert started to hurt them. So I tried to sit on my knees, realizing that won't work either. Because I would pull my arms out of my sockets. Great.

I went back to standing on my knees.

When I started to relax, I felt my body aching.

I groan, it wasn't necessary to hit me with the gun.

"You don't touch my truck." I whispered to myself, mocking Master. I roll my eye is disgust.

What is wrong with my left eye any ways? It must be that swollen that I can't open it.

You know, Mom, um, Mistress never checked me over. Probably because she isn't a parent any more. She is an owner.

Sigh, try to get some rest. I have a feeling that I am not going anywhere, anytime soon.

Moan. I open my eye, to look around the room.

My whole body hurts, Especially my knees.

As I was about to close my eye, I heard my door open.

My Mistress walked in and gave emotionless look.

I gave her a weak smile.

"Why did you run of Brook? Don't you like us anymore? For all the things we do for you. This is how you show us how grateful you are, by running away?! What else are you going to steal? How can we trust you?"

I looked down.

"I am s-sorry Mistress." I said in a low voice.

She walks up to me, and puts a mirror in front of me.

"Look at yourself. Your a mess." She said while forcing the mirror at me.

I wasn't surprised by my looks. Though, it explains why I can't open my left eye. Minus it being swollen, there is this red line across my face. Either from Master hitting me with his gun or the whip.

She's right though, I am a mess.

"That's what happens to thief and bad boys." Mistress told me.

-Page208-

I looked away from the mirror while I replied,

"Wasn't trying to be bad. I wanted to be free."

"Hmm. Your Brook Harold, you'll never be free. Your job is to serve us."

I kept my focus on the floor while she left the room.

Serve them? I must have done something bad enough to end up being their servant. And losing that privilege for being their son.

With me being held as a prisoner in my room, I won't get my chores done. I could see them beating because I am not getting my chores done. Because they are jerks.

I might as well try to rest again. I wish they would give me something for under my knees. The concert hurts.

"Pretty eyes. Hey, you got to get up."

"(Groan). I have a headache and I want to throw up.." I replied in a tired way.

"I know honey."

I squinted my eye, and gave Master a puzzled look.

"No you don't. You don't know nothing. You have no idea what I am going through." I growled at him.

He gave me a surprised look while he let out a laugh as he crossed his arms.

"You are a trouble some kid. Aren't you? Just because your 11, doesn't give you the right to be lippy."

I look up at him, while I replied,

"I always have been lippy. That's how I survive this hell."

Master walk up to me and backhands me.

With my face already being sore, the sting of the hit hurt twice as much.

"Don't look at me!" He backhands me again. " I never gave you permission That is being disrespectful. You got to learn your place boy. You are the servant. You'll only speak when giving permission to do so.

Keep your eyes towards the ground, unless one of us tells you to look up."
He get up close to my face and whispers. "We put your through hell when
your were five to

-Page209-

make you learn your place. Looks like we are back to that step.
Welcome to hell Brook Harold."

I kept my gaze towards the floor while he shut the door behind him.
I bit my lip as I started to cry.

"Stupid Brook. Why do you have to be dumb." I scold myself.

I closed my eye as I was still crying.

Sometime later Master came back in.

I bowed my head and stared at the ground.

"Pretty eyes. I got some water for you." He said as he walked up to
me. "Look at me please."

I looked at him as he was kneeling to give me a drink of water.

I was so excited that I gulp down the water.

"Take it easy Pretty-"

Before Master could finish is sentence, I threw up all over him.

He threw his arms in the air with a shocked expression.

I whispered I am sorry before I threw up on him again.

"Suzanne!" He yelled for my Mistress.

"Now Suzanne!" He yelled for her again by the time I got sick on him
a third time.

Mistress came rushing into the room.

"What the hell do you want?!" She asked.

"Your kid threw up on me." Master whined.

Mistress burst out laughing.

"Its not funny!" He snapped at her. "Can you grab Pretty eyes
something."

I looked up at master then dropped my head in shame. I wish I could
hold my head.

"My head is pounding sir." I whispered.

"I know honey. " Master said.

When Mistress came back into the room, she wiped my face off and
told Master to go shower.

After Master left, my Mistress sat on my bed watching me.

The whipping, the pistol whipping, the punching, and the kicking went on every three days for a month.

Along with the drill session that contained how I am not their kid, I am their servant. So they can do whatever they want to me. Don't speak nor look at anyone unless I have permission to do so. Also a bunch of name calling and put downs.

Plus I barely ate that month. For two reason:

1. Because they didn't believe in feeding me.

2. I wasn't feeling good a lot of times.

Sigh, when Master said welcome to hell, he meant it.

When they put me through hell back when I was five so I would learn my place, that was nothing. I came out worse this time around.

CHAPTER FIFTEEN

THE ACCIDENT

When my Owners came into my room, I gave them a terrified look as I shook.

"Please don't hurt me." I pleaded as I looked down.

"Pretty eyes, we will not hurt you. We came to get you out. It has been a month. Punishment is over." Master told me.

I kept my gaze to the floor as I nodded.

"Brook Harold, look at us." Mistress told me.

I cautiously looked up at them.

"Yes?" I said in a low voice.

Master walked over to me to un-cuffed me from the wall.

It felt so good to have my wrists out of those cuffs.

"You need to go take a shower then get dressed." Said Mistress.

"Yes, ma'am." I said while getting up.

When I stood up, I was wobbly. I had to stable myself before moving.

Carefully walked towards the door of my room and down the hall towards the bathroom.

I looked into the mirror when I got into the bathroom; I didn't recognize myself. I look.... A minute pause. Like shit.

I was thinner than I was before. A month without or little food can do that to you. I was dirtier because I haven't showered for a month.

"Where is Brook?" I asked myself.

He doesn't exist anymore.

I am the servant to my owners. A boy toy to my father.

I looked down at my wrist; the cuffs were cutting into them. I tried to tell them that, but they told me to stop complaining.

I shook my head as I got into the shower.

The warmth of the water felt AMAZING.

Along with no food, no shower, I couldn't have any clothes on. Easy access for Master to rape me.

It felt amazing to be warm and clean again.

Beatings every other day and getting raped every night, I don't know who I am anymore.

After that month in hell, I learned my place in that household. Again.

My owner's puppet. Because puppets don't talk or look at people, I have to wait for their command.

When school started, Hillary and Jeorge noticed I was quieter than normal.

I didn't get into fights with Ben and Chris like I have done in the past.

I hated going to school. The teachers noticed more that something was wrong with me. But like always, they stayed quiet about it. So did I when they asked questions.

Didn't care to see the school nurse. She knew I stayed quiet with the teachers, so when I was with her, she always tried to pry me open.

I didn't want to talk to her either... So, I came up with the best excuses and lies. Which didn't always work.

When Mistress noticed I was gaining weight, she barked at me to tell her where I was getting the food at.

I couldn't tell her. HA! More like I wouldn't tell her.

I told her she was imaging things. She can't keep things straight when she is using her drugs and alcohol.

She got furious with me because I told her that.

Haha, go figure. She doesn't like to face the truth.

So, I got my butt severely whipped that day.

At school the next day, I couldn't sit down. I tried my best to ignore the discomfort. But because I became wigglier in my seat, the kids started noticing.

When Mistress found out that whipping me didn't stop me from sneaking food.

She tried a new technique, Induced vomiting. So, mistress could see if I was lying to her.

I had to make myself throw up. If I didn't do it, she did it for me.

Every day when I got home from school, that was the first thing we did. Go stand in the bathroom and........ Force myself to throw up. To prove to her I wasn't lying.

Now there were days I put up a fight about doing it. But that's when she would stick her own finger down my throat. The one of many issues I have about being a little person, I can't fight people off.

There were a lot of times I bit her finger to stop her from gagging me. Though that always got me a slap in the face.

Mostly, Mistress saw I wasn't lying to her when I told her I have eaten nothing.

But when she caught me lying, I paid my price.

She told me if I am so hungry to.... (A minute pause. Clear throat.)

Go give my Master a..... Uh.... Blow job. Till he cummed into my mouth.

I was hungry for food! Not my Master... Hmm, it's so hard to say. My Masters cum, my Masters penis.

Was Mistress that obsessed to keep track of my food intake, that - that she turned to induce vomiting?! And if you're hungry to give your father a BJ?! What the hell?

I refused to take any food from the teachers, the nurse, and the principle after that.

When my owners left, Mistress locked all the cabinets and the fridge plus the garbage.

That's why, from a young age, I have learned to shut that feeling off. If I ignore the hunger pain, it would go away. So, I thought.

One day in November, after thanksgiving, I went with Master to Uncle Teddy's house.

I was a little skeptical. Because I don't get to leave with Master while Mistress stays home.

It turned out my Mistress was throwing a baby shower for one of her friends at the house and I would have "guy" time for my late birthday present.

Guy time means the three boys get high and drunk while playing video games.

For me? I was their sex toy.

When we got to Uncle Teddy's house, they led me to a spare room. From there, they directed me to strip naked and to lie on the bed.

I wasn't stupid to argue with them. So, after I striped down and laid on the bed, Master tied me to the bed.

Oh, I had an outstanding night. (Clears throat.) Correction, the boys had an exceptional night. I was trying to escape mentally.

We stayed the night because Master was too drunk to walk straight, let alone drive.

The next morning, Master and I left around noon.

When we walked outside, the ground and the truck had snow on it.

"Looks like it snowed last night." Master observed.

I nodded in agreement.

I held my breath as I slowly got into the truck and sat down. I breathed out before putting my seat belt on.

"Did you have fun last night, Pretty eyes?" Master snickered.

I looked at Master with sleepy eyes. I turned my focus to outside, watching the snow fall.

Fun? I thought to myself. If fun is being tied to a bed and forced to have sex, then yes, I had a blast.

Note the sarcasm.

My train of thought came to an abrupt end when I heard Master say my name.

I gave Master a weary look. I study his face before he returned his attention to the road.

Master's tone and his expression said that he was waiting for an answer.

"Y-Yes s-sir. I had a-a lot of f-fun." I forced a smile.

He looked at me out of the corner of his eye.

"Good." He replied as he looked back at the road. "How do you feel?"

"I f-feel f-"

Master looks at me with a raised eyebrow.

"When did you become a stuttering freak?" Master interrupted me while turning his focus on the road.

"S-Sorry s-sir."

I re-looked out the window as I rested against it.

I am wonderful. I love having sexual intercourse with three men.

One would perform anal sex; one did oral sex on me while I give the last guy a blow job.

DOGGY STYLE! Yep! I am great.

To be honest, everything hurts down there plus I am exhausted.

"S-Sir?" I asked while giving him a questioning look.

Master looked at me with curiosity in his eyes.

"Yes, Pretty eyes?"

"Uh... N-Never mind." I replied while looking back out the window.

"What is it, Pretty eyes? Talk to Daddy."

"I-It's n-nothing, sir."

I stared out the window. I can't wait till we get home.

All suddenly everything became foggy. Then there was silence.

I didn't move; I kept my focus on the airbag in front of me. I slowly looked up at the cracked windshield. I noticed blood on it, half curious if it was mine.

I could smell the coolant from the engine. Something smelled like smoke, but didn't know where it was coming from.

I said Master's name, but he wasn't responding. When I looked over at him, he was leaning forward with his head resting on the steering wheel, the air bag under his face.

The accident knocked Master out cold.

He had blood dripping down his face. He must have hit the steering wheel?

I don't know; I wasn't sure what happened.

When I looked out the window, we were facing the wrong way, plus I saw it wrecked two other cars from the accident.

I looked down at my leg it didn't look right; blood was gushing out of it.

I jumped to someone pounding on my window.

I gave them a question look before opening my door.

"Are you all, right? Help is on the way."

"N-no. My ma- my dad isn't responding." I told the man.

"It looks like you have a nasty cut on your leg. Don't move. Again, help is on the way."

I watched him scamper off.

I couldn't move if I wanted to.

I looked back down at my leg, watching the blood flow out of the wound.

I need to get the bleeding to stop. What can I use though?

I looked around the truck, then at my shoes.

Uh Ah! My shoe laces!

I tried to bend down and reach for it. When I did, I carefully got it wrapped around my leg.

After I got it tied on, and the flow slowed down. I leaned my head on the headrest of the seat and closed my eyes.

CHAPTER SIXTEEN

AFTERMATH

When I opened my eyes, I looked around?

Where am I? (Groan) Why I am so sleepy?

"Hello. How are you feeling?"

When I looked over towards my right, there was a lady standing there looking at some machines.

"Where am I? Where is my Master? Uh, I mean, my dad?" I asked in a raspy voice.

"You are in the hospital. You recently got out of surgery. We will have to move you up to your room soon. Your dad? We will find him. He might be in the waiting room." The nurse smiled.

"Why am I so tired?" I groaned. "Wait? Surgery?" I asked.

"You had surgery to fix your leg. The anesthesia will wear off and by the time we get you moved to your room; someone will give you pain medication."

"Oh." I said as I closed my eyes.

"What is your name, sweetie?" The nurse asked.

I opened my eyes and gave her a tired look. I turned my focus to my injured leg.

"You don't... You don't know my name?" I hesitated.

"No. When the paramedics brought you in, they said you had no ID on you. So we labeled you as a John Doe."

After the nurse said that, I smiled to myself as I thought.

That means no one knows who I am. I could change my name. That way my owners won't find me.

I looked at the nurse with a weak smile as I replied,

"Harold Jenkins ma'am."

"Hello Harold. How Old Are You?"

"Twelve."

"Okay. We have to move you up to your room now." She smiled.

I nodded in agreement.

Once in my room, I was giving more pain medicine and because it was late; I tried to go to bed. After laying there for about guessing half an hour, I gave up on sleeping.

I kept on thinking about what took place at Uncle Teddy's. I looked at my wrist; I have red marks where the rope was at. Master tying the ropes tighter to prevent me from escaping.

Master. My mind wondered. I hope Master is okay.

The next morning, I woke to a nurse checking my vital signs.

"My leg, it hurts." I told the nurse in a groggy tone.

"You are due for your medicine. But first, we should get you some breakfast."

My eyes widen.

"Food? I get food?" My eyes lit up.

The nurse raised her eyebrow while giving me a question look.

"Yes. You should eat something before taking your pill. We don't want you to get sick."

"D- Did my owners give you permission to feed me?" I asked with caution.

"Owners?" The nurse asked, sounding confused.

"W- Well, my p-parents. I can't eat till I get their p-permission."

"Yes, we got their permission." She smiled at me.

"That means you saw my dad. H-How is he?"

"He's good. I will be right back with your food." The nurse smiled.

I nodded with excitement.

It was a great way to start of my day. I get food, and Master is doing well.

After a short time, the nurse returned with my breakfast and medicine.

I was eager to eat.

The nurse smiled at me.

"Here you go, Harold."

"Thank you!"

She brought me scramble eggs, toast, a side of fruit, and a glass of milk.

I didn't know where to start first. If I get fed, it's not this much food.

"So," The nurse said while pulling up a chair. "Tell me about your Owners?"

I gave her a puzzled look. Then I took a bite while thinking.

After I swallowed my food. I took a deep breath and asked,

"What would you like to know?"

"Do your owners hurt you, Harold?"

When I heard the question, I choked on my food.

After a minute of coughing, I grabbed a drink of milk.

"Sorry."

"It's okay."

"Do they hurt me?" I asked, sounding concerned.

The nurse nods.

I looked down at my plate.

I re-looked at her with concern in my eyes.

"Sorta...... I mean my own-, my parents, I mean. They get unhappy with me, but I deserve it."

"Why do you deserve it?"

"I don't know." I shrug my shoulders. "I mean, I get into a lot of trouble at school." I said while looking away.

"Like what type of trouble?" She asked.

"Fights mostly."

"You don't look like the fighting type."

"Not fist fights." I looked at the nurse. "I use my words to fight. Which if you're not careful with your words, you could offend someone." I finish saying while I looked away.

"That doesn't mean you deserve to be hurt. Do you know why they hurt you?"

I nod slowly before replying.

"I am a bad boy, I guess."

"Okay. Thank you for our brief chat." She patted my hand.

I turned to see the nurse leaving my room.

I looked down at my plate as I pushed it away.

I laid down and looked out the window; it is snowing again.

I felt like I did something wrong. I didn't understand why she was asking me those questions. Did I act too eager for food? Did I give the wrong answer? It worried me, but no point worrying about it.

I dozed off and on throughout the day. Skip lunch because I wasn't feeling well.

I laid there watching T. V when another nurse; I didn't recognize, came in.

"Hello. I am your nurse now. If you need anything, just give me a ring." The nurse said.

"Okay, thank you." I replied.

The nurse smiled at me. I returned the smile.

Then her smile disappeared.

"What's your name, son." She asked.

"Harold Jenkins, ma'am. It says it on the chart board." I told her as I pointed to the board.

After she checked me over, she left the room without a word.

I looked up at the monitors; I hope everything was okay. The previous nurse should have updated her.

About ten minutes later, I heard talking outside my room.

I opened my eyes when I heard someone clear their throat.

I looked over towards my left where the doorway was.

I did a double look at the guy standing in my room. Was I dreaming? I had to be. Because I couldn't believe my eyes. I felt them getting watery as I smiled.

"Dad? Is that really you?"

He smiles at me while he replies.

"I can't stay long. Heard you were in the hospital. Had to check on you." Dad said in a low tone.

"How did you know I was here?" I asked.

"A friend of mine. So, how are you?"

"Doing okay."

"Look at you." He said as he pushed my hair out of my eyes. "What has she done to you?"

I looked away.

"She has been treating me well. Along with.... My stepdad."

"Stepdad?" he questioned.

"Yes." I looked back at dad. "Willie, Mom's boyfriend, now her husband. After they got married, he legally adopted me."

Dad had worried written all over his face.

"Look, I got to go. I am not supposed to be here. I could get in trouble if your mom catches me."

I gave him a surprise look.

"Please take me with you." I pleaded.

"I-I can't."

"I can't go back home. You don't know what they do to me." I cried.

"I am sorry."

Dad turned away and left the room.

"Dad!" I yelled for him.

He gave me one more glance before walking away.

I hung my head as I cried.

Three hours after dad left, there was a voice that I recognize. But with the curtain pulled shut, I can't see who it is.

"Harold Jenkins." The lady said in a bitter tone while walking in.

Shit, it's Mom! I held my breath as my heart pounded faster. I looked at her with bug eyes.

"W-What a-are you doing here?!" I panic.

"Calm down Brook, or should I say Harold Jenkins." Mom said with a smirk.

I looked at my injured leg.

"I ch-changed m-my n-name so you w-wouldn't f-find me." I said, feeling ashamed.

"I gathered that. But I work here, like your father does. You couldn't hide from me." She said coldly.

I felt her ice icy stare on me.

I didn't know they worked here.

I returned to my focus to her while I replied,

"How is M-Master doing? One nurse said he's fine, but she doesn't know I am his."

"That's because YOU changed your name so no one knows who you are. I couldn't even find you myself. I got wo-"

I raised my eyebrow at her.

Mistress clears her throat.

"Your master isn't doing well. He's in a coma." Mistress reserved herself.

"Coma ma'am?" I asked, sounded worried.

"Yes. Meaning, he's sleeping and hasn't woke up yet. And I am sure YOU have something to do with it."

I shook my head, no.

She walked up towards me, got into my face and told me in a lowered voice.

"You put my husband in a coma. Once I get you home, you're dead."

"Oh good. You did you find your son." The nurse said.

Mistress clears her throat while she turned to look at the nurse.

"Hi Beth, he looks like he's ready to go home. I mean, what could happen? I am a nurse." Mom giggles nervously.

"Harold came in yesterday. So, let's see what the doctor says. But I am sure your eager to get your son home with Willie being in a coma."

The nurse, Beth, looks at me and smiles. I gave her a sad smile. Then she left.

Mistress turned back to me with a heartless stare. And hand singled, "You're dead" then left the room.

My eyes got watery. There had to be away for me to stay here longer. I looked around the room, then looked at the IV in my hand.

I could pull that out, I thought. Would that be enough to keep me here? I looked passed my hand to my injured leg.

Better plan, I could re-open my leg.

I look towards the curtain. There are different conversations going on. Things being said over the PA system.

I looked back at my leg.

I need something to cut off the bandage. I looked around for something sharp.

Except I couldn't walk on it. However, I walked on it when I broke it.

I looked over at the curtain again. Shifted my eyes to my leg, then turned my head.

I leaned back into the bed. Forget it. It won't matter what I do, Mistress will bring me home, anyway.

An hour later, the nurse, known as Beth, came back in to check up on me.

"How are you feeling, Harold?"

"My name isn't Harold." I mumbled as I turned away.

"I know, sweetie. Your mom told me everything. Why did you change your name? I know the nurse before me was asking if you're safe at home. And the doctor was wondering about the marks he found on you. In a particular spot."

I gave her an uneasy look.

"Harold, has somebody touched you inappropriate." She asked with concern.

I turn my head slowly away. Then look down at my hands. Thought about the previous night.

"Like, have they have raped me before?" I asked while I re-looked at her.

"Mm-hmm" Beth nodded.

"Yes." I desperately wanted out of the house, I let it slip out of my mouth. I paused. Trying to rethink of something to say.

"I- I have been." I said as I choked up.

"By who?" She asked with concern in her eyes.

I turned away as the tears ran down my face.

"By my da-." I swallowed hard. "By my dad." I said as I sobbed.

I put my hands over my eyes.

"Your dad, as in your mom's ex?"

I nodded.

"Okay, thank you."

I was stupid. Blaming the one person who cares about me.

I slammed my hand down on the bed. I was furious with myself. With my Mistress.

"Oh, honey. It's okay."

I turned to see Mistress.

My lip kept on quivering as we stared at each other.

When I cried again, I turned away as I closed my eyes.

I felt Mistress hug me while she strokes my hair.

"It's okay, baby. Nathaniel won't hurt you anymore."

"Nathaniel? "I questioned her with a raised eyebrow.

Mistress nods.

I pushed her away.

"Nathaniel did nothing wrong! It was you and that Jerk! You two are putting me through this hell, not him." I raised my voice.

Mistress quickly covers my mouth.

I gave her a surprised look.

"Shut up, you little shit." She let out a low growl. "Why do you have to be so ungrateful? I can't wait till I get you home." she whispered while clenching her teeth.

Then she slammed her hand down over my injured leg.

I bit my lip to stop from me whining.

I glared at her.

She removed her hand while she replied,

"This is just a taste of what you will get when you get home. So, pipe it down."

Then she left my room.

I fucking hate her. She kept blaming dad for her actions.

I threw my hands into the air.

I haven't been with him since I was five!

I was getting a headache. I put my pointer finger to my temples as I shut my eyes...

Wait. I popped my eyes open, removed my hands. I never got dinner.

I called the nurse in and asked about where my dinner was.

"You said you weren't hungry." Beth said.

I gave her a surprise look. I wasn't hungry. I had to think about that for a moment. Then I realized Mistress canceled my dinner. That mother f....

"Yeah." I said while scratching my head. "I just don't remember." I let out a chuckle. "This medicine and I am tired. When do I get to go home?"

"Tomorrow. If the doctor clears you." She smiles at then leaves the room.

The next morning when Beth came in, I asked about seeing my dad.

"We can rearrange that." Beth replied.

I smiled at her; she returned the smile.

"But first let's get you some breakfast." She mentioned.

I nodded in an agreement.

I went to go see Master after I got done eating breakfast.

I had to use a wheelchair to get to the ICU floor.

When I rolled into Master's room, Mistress jumps out of her chair. She gave me an unsure look.

"I came to say hi." I told Mistress.

She nods.

"I will leave you two alone." Beth told me.

"Thank you."

"I will be right back, sweetie." Mistress told me as she was walking out of the room.

When I looked at Master, they hooked him up to different machines.

He had a breathing tube; he had an IV. And other machines, I wasn't sure what everyone did. But I took comfort in seeing him with bruises, yet I felt sad for him.

I rolled up to his bedside.

"Hi master. It's me, Pretty eyes. I am sorry for putting you through this. I hope you come back soon. Mistress is worrying about you, along with Uncle Teddy and Uncle Robert. I love you, Daddy."

I picked up his hand and held it between my hands.

I got out of my wheelchair and climbed into bed with him.

Laid my head down on his chest as I closed my eyes.

I was on the brink of falling asleep when I heard Mistress say my name as she put a hand on my shoulder.

I looked up to Mistress with a questioning look.

"You got to get up and go back to your room. If the doctor clears ya, you will go home today."

I looked at Master, then re-looked at Mistress.

I gave her a nod.

I got off of the bed, back into the wheelchair, and Beth brought me back to my room.

I watched some T. V while waiting for the doctor to clear me.

About an hour and a half, he came in. And told me they will keep me one more day.

I was a little disappointed, but on the positive note; I got more food.

Not much happened that day, just slept and watched T.V.

The next morning after breakfast, the doctor came in.

"How are you feeling, Brook? Ready to go home?" The doctor asked me.

"I am feeling great sir." I smiled at him." I am so ready to go home. I miss my bed." I said with a quiet laugh.

He returns the laugh as he replies.

"All right. Like I went over with your mom, you will need some physical therapy to help with the injury. So, for now, use the crutches to get around with. We will send you home with some oxycodone. Take when needed only."

"Yes, sir."

"All right, let me go grab your discharge papers." The doctor said while he patted my hand.

After my discharge, the doctor told me I could get dressed except I had no clothes.

"You don't?" The doctor acted surprise.

"No, sir. My mom hasn't left my dad's side. And the clothes I had on when I came in were all bloody." I told him.

"True. Let me go talk to your mother."

About fifteen minutes later Mistress came in.

"So, you need clothes." Mistress said while sitting at the foot of the bed.

"Yes, ma'am, I do."

She clicks her tongue as she looks over towards the curtain.

"I will run to the store which across the street, to get you," Mistress looks at me." A new outfit. That you don't deserve." She coldly stated.

"New outfit, ma'am?"

"I don't want to run back and forth to home. It's a twenty-minute ride there and back, plus with it snowing."

"Yes, ma'am. I understand that. T-The part I don't, is why I don't deserve it."

"Because you're the servant. No slave deserves a new outfit. Or at least that is what my father told me."

"Your father?"

Mistress nods.

I chuckled to myself as I replied,

"Are you trying to follow your father's footsteps?"

She laughs.

"I am an angle compared to my father. My father treated me worse than how I treat you."

I gave her a disbelief look as I thought to myself.

That's because you are not going through the abuse anymore. You are now the abuser.

"Yes, ma'am." I agreed with her.

"Good boy. I will be back shortly." She said with a smile.

I nodded to her as I waved her out of the room.

About an hour later, Mistress showed up with my clothes.

"I got you pant, a t-shirt, underwear, and socks." She told me as she tossed the bag at me.

I became butterfingers, trying to catch the bag.

"Thank you."

She gave me a disgusted look as she rolled her eyes.

She turned around snobbishly as she left the room.

Jeez, what is her problem? I asked myself.

After getting dressed, said goodbye to Master, then headed home.

When we got home, Mistress took my crutches away. She told me; I don't need them.

I shrugged my shoulders at her and said,

"Yes, ma'am."

I limp to my room.

Once in my room, I stood by the middle of my room looking around.

Bars on the window, cement flooring, and charcoal-colored walls. According to my owners, it's hiding the blood splatter.

Barely any clothes in my closet, and a desk where I can do my homework. The only reason I have a bed is because of Master.

I don't deserve new clothes, let alone decent room.

My train of thought came to an abrupt end when I heard a booming voice behind me.

"You sly little dog."

My eyes widen, I could feel my stomach flip.

Uncle Teddy!

Before I could turn around to look at him, he pulled me close and put his arm across my throat. Pulling my chin up so he could look at me.

I couldn't shake my head or talk with the pressure against my throat.

"What is wrong, boy? Can't you breathe?" Uncle Teddy mocked.

I was clawing at his arm to get him to release his grip. But that only made him put more pressure on my neck.

I was about to lose conscious when Uncle Teddy released his grip. I fell to my hands and knees, coughing and gasping for air.

Before I could finish catching my breath, I felt a painful blow to my left side, which I fell over. Laid on my right side, holding unto my injured side.

Wasn't surprised when I looked up and saw Mistress towering over me.

"Is this why..." I coughed "I don't need my crutches wheezed.

She didn't answer, she just kept on kicking me. I tried to block her, though failed big time.

I tried to crawl away from her.

"Oh, no you don't!" She warned me while she grabbed the back of my shirt.

Which knocked me off balance, and I fell on my face.

I let out a whine.

"Come here Rookie." Uncle Robert demanding me as he grabs my hips.

Then I felt him slip off my pants and underwear, and he forced himself into me.

I let out a howl as the tears run down my face.

"Is this what you wanted, Rookie? Is this what you were trying to get Daddy to do with you? Do you like this?" Uncle Robert asked as he thrust faster.

I could only whimper as I continued to cry.

"You flashed him, didn't you? Is that how your Daddy wrecks his truck? You are the one who put him in a coma. Come on, say you did it. We all know you did it, Rook. You can't hide it." He said, while he keeps increasing his speed.

I let a moan; I can't handle the pressure.

"Um, y-you s-see, I did-"

"Exactly! You did it." Uncle Robert said while interrupting me.

"N-No!" I protested.

After I said that, Mistress kneeled down in front of me with a skeptical look.

"No? My husband is in the hospital, in a coma because of you." She jabbed her finger at my face. "You should be the one laying in the hospital, not him." She was bitter with her words.

I gave her an exhausted look, then dropped my head as I continued to whimper.

This torment went on for another five minutes.

"I d-did it!" I shouted.

When Uncle Robert heard me say this, he pulled out, and I fell down.

"Good boy Rookie." Uncle Robert said.

I laid there looking at the three of them. They all wore a nasty smile with pride. My eyes are getting heavy that I couldn't keep them open. I eventually closed them. And heard them laughing as they left the room.

CHAPTER SEVENTEEN

MASTER COME HOME

I jumped awake in a panic, looked around the room in a frantic. When I realized I was alone, I took a deep breath as I closed my eyes.

I popped my eyes open again; I was so sleepy. I had to force my eyes to stay open.

The little strength I had, I tried to get up. On the fourth attempt, I finally got up on all four. I let out a whine. I used my bed to stable myself so I could stand up.

Heavy breathing, along with me still wheezing, I groaned. My whole-body aches, plus I was stiff from sleeping on the ground all night.

I carefully got dressed before leaving my room. After I got clothes on, I headed towards the bathroom.

Holy shit. I thought to myself as I looked in the mirror.

The bruise on my neck, my bloody face. I don't even remember bleeding. But there was so much going on at one time, everything was foggy.

"Good, you're up."

Still looking in the mirror, I saw Mistress standing at the doorway of the bathroom.

"Can I help you ma'am?" I asked, sounding pouty, as I turned around to give her my full attention.

"Yes!" Mistress clapped her hands together." Get your chores done and I will see," She points to me. "You after work." She told me with a smile.

I raised an eyebrow to her. She seems lively this morning. I thought to myself.

I took a deep breath before replying,

"Yes, ma'am. Have a good day at work." I forced my smile.

"Thank you! Have a good day yourself."

After she spoke, she hurried away.

I walked into the hallway and watched her gather her things as she was walking out the door.

I tilted my head towards the right as I scratched it.

Was I missing something? I thought to myself.

I shrugged my shoulders as I headed towards the kitchen. Doesn't matter, I guess.

Once in the kitchen, I walked over towards the window and looked out.

Sigh. Let's see what chores Mistress cooked up for me.

Wait. I turned back around to look out the window.

"Uncle Teddy's car?" I said to myself.

"That's right, buckaroo."

I spun around to see Uncle Teddy standing behind me.

Looking up to him, I felt small.

"W-What a-are you d-doing here?" I panicked.

"To torment you. Why else?" He said sounding cocky with a half-smile.

I swallowed hard as I shivered.

"It's cold in here. Do you agree?" I asked as I rubbed my arms.

Uncle Teddy looked around the kitchen, then back to me.

"No. You're just nervous."

I hung my head.

He laughed and replied,

"Your pathetic. Look up at me." I slowly looked up at him as he was lighting up a cigarette. "I love the mark I left on your pretty neck. Is that why you are having issue speaking?"

"Yes, sir, and breathing." I kept my voice low.

"Hmm. What a shame. Remember, your mom doesn't want you. That's why she said that you should be in the hospital, not my brother."

"I know." I whispered as I hung my head low.

Uncle Teddy laughed as he walked away.

"Wait?" I asked as I popped my head up.

Uncle Teddy stops in his tracks to give me a questioning look as he replies,

"Yes?"

"Why are you here?" I asked again.

"To torment you. I said that boy. I shouldn't have to repeat myself, right?"

"Right" I replied as I looked at the floor.

"Excuse me?" Uncle Teddy said while he lifted my chin up to make me look at him. "Is that being respectful?

"No, sir."

He removes his finger, taps my face, then points to me as he orders me.

"Watch your mouth, boy. You got chores to do before your Mistress comes home at noon with Uncle Robert."

"Yes, sir."

"Also, don't look at or speak to me or any of us unless you are giving permission. Isn't that what Daddy told you?"

"Yes, sir. Sorry, sir." I replied as I looked down.

"Good boy. Now get your chores done." Uncle Teddy said while he patted me on the head.

"Yes, sir."

Between trying to get chores done, I also was Uncle Teddy's little gopher.

Brook do this, Brook do that. Brook, get your chores done.

I took a minor break. Resting my elbows on the countertop as I rest my head in my hands.

I was thinking about; what was the real reason Uncle Teddy was here? And why is Mistress and Uncle Robert coming home together at noon? Was he the reason she was so perky this morning.? But she wouldn't cheat on Master, would she? Then again, she cheated before.

I stop my thinking as I gave Uncle Teddy an annoyed look.

"I repeat myself. Why are you slow, boy?"

"I am not slow. My leg is killing me." I growled at him.

"Quit your complaining. Or I will give you something to complain about. Now work faster."

"Yes, sir." I mumbled.

I stopped leaning on the counter and walked around the breakfast bar to get to the hallway.

"Oh, Brook Harold."

I turn to look at him as I replied.

"Sir?"

"You got to figure out lunch."

"Yes, sir."

"Now."

"I will, sir, after I take care of my owner's room."

I turned to continue walking that direction.

The clock in my owner's room read ten o'clock. I still had time to finish this room. Plus, I still had to clean the kitchen, anyway.

It was eleven o'clock by the time I got done with my owner's room. Now lunch.

I headed towards the kitchen but stopped in front of my room.

I peered around the corner to see Uncle Teddy in the living room.

He is drinking and watching T.V. I should be safe to sneak into my room.

When I walked into my room, I threw myself onto my bed and buried my face into my pillow.

"Brook Harold Tyler!"

I came flying out of my bed. I stood before Uncle Teddy. Giving him a freighted look.

"What the hell are you doing?!" He yelled. "You have chores to do and you are supposed be starting lunch."

I looked down at my holey pants and replied,

"S-Sorry s-sir. I was t-tired."

"(Scoff) I believe you deserve a punishment."

"Y-Yes sir."

"Take your shirt off, turn around, and put your hands on the wall."

I listened right away.

"Count for me. Out loud boy, till I tell you to stop."

I let out a sigh as I replied,

"Yes, sir."

With each number I counted, I took a deep breath. I found a spot on the wall and held my gaze on it while I counted.

I went up to 25. Twenty - five! Twenty-five lashes because I laid down without his permission.

"Look at me, boy."

I turned to look at him with watery eyes.

"Get your shirt on and get your butt in that kitchen." he firmly said.

Yes, sir."

When I knew it was safe, I let myself cry a little. I try not to, but sometimes it gets to you.

When I came out of my room and headed towards the kitchen. I saw Uncle Teddy with his arms crossed, standing by the breakfast bar waiting for me.

"Boy, were you crying?"

I turned my eyes away as I used my sleeve to wipe my runny nose, and I replied,

"So, what if I was?" I said, sounding pouty.

"You're such a baby."

I re-looked at him as I replied with sniffles,

"I got work to do."

I walk past him to get into the kitchen.

Lunch. I thought to myself. Looked up at the clock: Noon.

Because I fell asleep, and of the time, I had to find something to make that was quick and easy.

I didn't know what to make. But when I opened up the freezer, I saw a pizza.

When I look around the kitchen / living room, I wasn't sure where Uncle Teddy went to.

I shrugged my shoulders. They are getting pizza.

After the oven got preheated, I put the pizza in. Then went to fill a bucket of warm water to mop.

Brook Harold doesn't have the privilege to use an actual mop. I thought to myself sarcastically. So I had to hand mop the damn floor.

I was half a done when I heard Mistress pull up.

"Brook. Brook. Brook. Mistress is home, and the kitchen has not been clean yet."

I looked up to Uncle Teddy with a puzzled look.

"What do you mean, sir?"

Then he poured two buckets full of dirt around the kitchen.

My eyes widen.

"W-What a-are you d-doing sir?" I panicked.

When he didn't answer, I pleased for him to please stop.

Uncle Teddy stood in front of me with a grim smile. I looked at him helplessly.

He then poured the remaining dirt on my head.

I closed my eyes so I wouldn't get any dirt in them. Plus, I held my breath.

"I am disappointed in you." Uncle Teddy said while he kicked over the bucket of water.

I froze as I watched the water spill out of the bucket. My pants became wet as the water ran by me.

I couldn't look up when I heard Mistress come in. I knew she would be furious with me.

About five minutes later, I heard her yell my full name.

I tightly closed my eyes while I clasped my hands together.

Uncle Teddy and Mistress were talking among each other. Then I heard Uncle Teddy tell Mistress that I was a troublemaker.

That word rang threw my head. I was a troublemaker. A bad boy.

With my eyes still close, I could hear Mistress' heavy breathing next to me.

Before I could do anything, she grabbed me by my left ear and yanked me up. I let out a whimper.

"Stand up, boy!" She growled harshly.

Once on my feet, she grabbed a fist full of my hair and slammed my face down on the countertop. I let out a squeal. I could feel the blood gush from my nose and my mouth.

Then she pulled me up by my hair and stared into my soul. I let out a smile with a quiet laugh. Which only got my face slammed back into the counter.

"Don't be disrespectful, Brook Harold! You had a job to do, and this is how you left my house?!"

After she said it, she tossed me to the floor like I was some rag doll.

She shoved a mirror in my face.

"Look at how hideous you are. No one will ever love you like we do. Now, get your ass off the floor and get this damn house cleaned. The right way."

"Yes, ma'am." my voice was low.

When I looked up at Uncle Teddy, he wore a smile like he just won a million dollars.

I shook my head as I was trying to push myself up.

I only knew about the kitchen being a mess, till I walked down the hall and realized he poured dirt everywhere! I was in shock.

Where the hell did he get the dirt, anyway? I thought to myself as I walked down the hallway.

I chuckled to myself, just like his brother.

For all the things I do for them, they could be a little grateful, but no.

I cleaned the damn house. I felt the anger build up. It was clean till Uncle Teddy poured dirt everywhere and trash the house!

What the hell is wrong with him?! Like I said, he's like his brother or trying to replace him. All four of them are jerks. Ungrateful bastards.

Using my hand, I was trying to shake all the dirt out of my hair. Then used my sleeve to wipe my bloody nose.

I got to work on the house. Trying to work fast, but still trying to make it look nice.

I first started picking up all the trash. Then went to my owner's room to straighten up. Vacuumed all the rooms.

By the time I was hand mopping my bathroom, I heard one of them walking down the hall.

"You're not finished yet?"

When I looked up, I saw Mistress standing before me.

"No, ma'am."

"I didn't give you permission to look at me."

I glanced down at the rag in my hand.

"Sorry ma'am."

"Better. But I thought you would have this house cleaned by now. Why isn't clean Brook Harold?"

"It was clean. Till Uncle Teddy-"

"No, no. Uncle Teddy had nothing to do with it. Stop blaming others for your lack of responsibility. Now, come to the living room."

"But the bath-"

"Move it!" She said clenching her teeth while snapped her fingers.

I quickly got up and headed towards the living room.

When I walked into the living room, I looked at Uncle Teddy and Uncle Robert.

"Can I help you?" I asked.

They shook their head no.

"Brook Harold. What are we going to do with you?" Mistress asked.

I shrug my shoulders as I looked down to the floor.

"I thought I would go another round with him." Uncle Robert mentioned.

I looked up as I growled,

"You're not my Daddy. And you can't replace him. Neither of you can."

It took me a few minutes to understand every one's surprised reaction.

I dropped my head, more out of embarrassment. Oh shit, I can't believe I said that.

"Oh, how cute? The boy misses his daddy." I heard Uncle Teddy mocking.

Then they all laughed. I closed my eyes.

I missed my dad, Nathaniel. Not Willie. He wasn't my dad; he was my nightmare.

"If you miss him so much, let me do what I did to you yesterday." Robert mentioned.

"I have no say, I only obey." I said, still looking down.

"(Chuckle) You only obey? Then why did I come home to my house trashed?"

I couldn't answer. After a few minutes of me not answering, Mistress forcefully turned my head left to make me look at her. But my eyes were still looking down.

"Look at me, Brook Harold," she demanded.

I picked up on her, angry that I brought my eyes up slowly.

"Ma'am?" I said, trying to control my breathing.

"My house was a disaster when I came home! I told you to clean it, not trash it! I doubt that you only obey."

After they got done, they joined Mistress in the kitchen.

I was shaking so badly that I collapsed. Lying flat on my stomach with my right side of my face against the cold, hard floor.

I saw the three of them standing in the kitchen. They were all talking among each other.

They act like nothing happened. I tried to, but it's hard when you are the one feeling the pain and being humiliated.

When Mistress looked at me, she had this dark smile on her face. She walked over towards me. I popped my head up to look at her.

"Your pitiful and no one will ever love you. Your ugly, I mean look at this."

I tensed my body, for I was unsure what she will do.

She kneeled down and put a mirror in front of me.

"See? You should smile." Mistress mentioned.

I looked at her confused.

"Do it."

So, I did.

"No. Show your teeth."

When I did, I saw I chipped my front teeth.

"That was from me slamming your face into the counter. Twice!" She cackled.

I gave her a fearful look while I study her face.

"Oh. Master is waking up and should be home in two weeks." She smiled at me. "He also misses his boy."

After she spoke, she stood up and walked back to the kitchen.

"Brook," Mistress said while she picked up her whiskey, "Get this damn house clean."

I watched her take a drink while she gave me an icy stare.

I slowly got to my feet. Then got redressed.

Before leaving the living room, I gave them all an upset look, for which they returned an annoyed look.

Got the house cleaned. Again. Not much happen rest of the day. Mistress and the boys went back to the hospital. I took this time to, (sigh). drown my sorrows.

Sat down on the couch with a beer in one hand and my pain killers in the other.

Took a sip of my drink, then popped two pills in my mouth, took another sip to swallow the pills.

Before I knew it, I already drank three beers. Oh man, it felt nice to feel nothing. I smiled to myself as I closed my eyes.

A knock on the door startled me out of my daydream. At first, it worried me it was my Mistress, but I peeled myself off the couch to go answer it.

When I answered it, my excited girlfriend was standing there along with Jeorge.

I groaned at the sight of them and told them to come in.

"I haven't' seen you for a while and this is how you greet me?" Hillary said sounded disgusted as she put her hands on her hips.

I raised a brow at her.

"Look, "I put my hands out in front of me. "I have a headache, and I am tired. I apologize." I said before Turing from her.

I plopped my myself down on the couch.

"Brook!" Hillary gasp as she covers her mouth. "You aren't taking your medication with alcohol?" Hillary expressed her concerns.

I gave her an agitated look as I replied,

"And if I am?"

"It could kill you. This is not the way to deal with your depression."

I looked at Jeorge, which he was sitting in the chair across from me.

"You could have left her home." I whispered to him.

He mouthed the words,

"Sorry." As he shrugged his shoulders.

"I know your life is hell but you can find better ways to coupe." Hillary said.

Somebody shoot her or me. I thought to myself.

I stood up and pointed a finger at her while I growled at her,

"You do not understand what I have been through these past couple of days. Don't tell me what to do."

"Brooks, I am not meaning to. I am just concerned you'll overdose."

I folded my arms in front of me and replied,

"I thought you came over to say hi. Not yell at me. I get enough of that the way it is."

"We came by to say hi. But you know Hillary, always have to be snoopy." Jeorge chimed in.

I looked over at him, and I nodded in agreement.

I visited with them for a little while. Till I told them they better get home because I am not sure when my mom will be back.

Shortly after Jeorge and Hillary left, the Owners showed up.

I was still drunk when they came home, so I didn't care if they saw the empty beer bottles. Fuck them.

When Uncle Robert walked into the living room, he saw them. And question me about it.

I gave him an annoyed look and explained to him I've been having a bad time since I got home from the hospital.

He reminds me I shouldn't be stealing.

I rolled my eyes, got off of the couch and walked pass Uncle Robert. Stopped three feet away from him, turned around to look at him as I told him.

"Fuck you."

Though I didn't get far. Uncle Teddy stopped me while I was walking towards my room.

"Where do you think you're going, boy?"

I gave him an annoyed look.

"Hi, I am Brook Harold. I believe we haven't met before." I said as I reached out to shake his hand.

Uncle Teddy gave me a puzzled look.

Because of my attitude I gave them, I paid the price. Though, I was too drunk to give a shit.

After they got done beating me, Mistress handcuffed me to the wall.

She told me it was for stealing. So, that's where I stayed while my mistress and uncles went to work. And when they were home, I had chores.

Time passed and on the day my master was coming home, Uncle Teddy and Uncle Robert made me drunk.

In Uncle Teddy's words,

"You can handle three beers, why don't we give you six beers. That way you would be drunk enough that you won't fight us when we torment you."

After I was completely drunk, they stripped me naked and tied me to my bed.

To my surprise, Uncle Teddy and Uncle Robert did nothing, they just left the room.

Because I was drunk, I dozed off and on. And when I heard the front door close, I knew I was in trouble. When I opened my eyes; I wasn't sure if I was dreaming about my master or he was actually in front of me. Whichever the case was, Daddy was home and wanting his fun.

CHAPTER EIGHTEEN

BIG NEWS, YET BAD NEWS

September 2007, a new year of school.

Back in May, Hillary broke up with me. Her reason was because I wasn't giving her enough attention. She could have ripped my heart out. It would have hurt less. I tried my best to be the best boyfriend, but we were young and I didn't know how to be a boyfriend.

Now that Hillary and I are no longer together, I'm praying Ben and Chris leave me alone.

On the morning of the first day of school, Mistress was grumpy and a little drunk. So, she was ordering me around. I was trying to do every fast and accurate; I didn't want to be late on my first day back to school.

I figured I got everything done. So, I went to go put my school clothes on, ran to the bathroom to brush my teeth and comb my hair. Grab my backpack from my room before slipping my sneakers on.

I wrapped my fingers around the front door handle, about to turn it, then Mistress yelled my name.

I sighed as I dropped my head while letting go of the door handle.

"Where the hell are you going?" She yelled.

I stared at my holey shoes.

I first thought to myself, did she forget it was the first day back to school?

"I want an answer, young man?" She demanded.

"School ma'am. It's the first day, I don't want to be late." I replied while keeping my breathing steady.

Mistress scoffs before replying.

"I never gave you permission to leave. Who do you think you are? Someone special?" She sneered.

"N-No. I -"

"Ba, ba, ba, nor did I give you permission to speak." She interrupted me.

"Looks like someone one needs to be taught a lesson."

Before I could say or do anything, she grabbed me by my shirt and dragged me to the living room. Where she smacked me around.

"Now, Mr. goodie two shoes, this is a little reminder when you think you are someone special." She snickered as she jabbed her finger at me. "Get out of my sight. Go to school." She said while she pointed to the door.

I kept my focus to the floor while heading towards the door.

Once again, I grabbed the door handle. Before opening the door,

I heard Mistress tell me to tell the teachers I fell getting out of the shower. I just rolled my eye as I thought to myself, Whatever.

Then she told me to have a good day.

I opened the door slowly. When I walked out and shut the door behind me, I looked up and saw Jeorge.

He gave me a concerned look.

I shuffled down the sidewalk towards Jeorge.

"Don't speak." I snapped at him as I looked at the ground.

"I only wanted to ask you about the weather."

I shot him a disgusted look.

"(Sigh) Since we are late, my mom will take us to school."

"Is she meeting us down at the corner?" I asked as I felt the anxiety hit me.

"Yep." Jeorge gave me a reassuring smile. "Let's go."

Approaching his mom's car, I stopped five feet away.

Jeorge stopped to look at me.

"What's up Brook?"

"Nothing. I don't want to go."

"Why?" Jeorge asked.

"Look at me."

He looked me over.

"You look cute." He smiled.

I looked away from Jeorge.

"Honey." Becky (Jeorge's mom) said.

I looked at her with tired eyes.

"It will be okay. I will walk in with you."

"I-I don't know. I didn't want to be late on the first day. I didn't want to make Jeorge late either."

She smiled at me while she replies,

"I know, sweetie. Let's go."

I nodded as we got into the car.

It hasn't been my first time running late, nor will it be my last. But I normally walk myself in. But with Jeorge been late...... It makes sense.

By the time we arrived at the school, we were twenty minutes late.

Becky walked in with us, explained the situation to the reception. She wrote Jeorge a note to give the teacher.

Me? She sent me to the nurse's office.

Becky walked with me. At the office, Becky hugged me before she left.

I took a deep breath before opening the door.

"Good morning, Brook. So, what happened this morning?" The nurse asked as she picked up her notepad.

I shuffled in my seat.

"Well, you see..." What did Mistress tell you? Remember. I screamed to myself.

"I fell getting out of the shower."

"I see" she nodded as she wrote things down.

She looked me over. Mark things down and told me to get to class.

I have a feeling my excuses are running thin.

I walked into my classroom sheepishly. Ignored all the looks and gave my note to my teacher. Then I took my seat next to Hillary. Looked down at my desk, noticed her looking at me out of the corner of my eye. I turned to look at her, while giving her a questioning look before returning my focus to my desk.

At lunch, I found a table away from everyone. I sat down and fold my arms on the table, then buried my face.

"Aren't you going to eat, little one?"

I looked up to see Jeorge standing there with his lunch tray.

"No." I shook my head. "I am not hungry."

"You sure?" Hillary asked.

"I am positive. I had breakfast this morning." I smiled at them both. That was a lie, and they both knew it.

"Hillary?" asked Jeorge.

"Yes, Jeorge?" Replied Hillary.

"Have you noticed how Brook finds excuses for everything? My opinion, I don't think he ate this morning."

"Yes, I agree."

"Knock it off, you two." I said under my breath.

They both smiled at me while they were sitting down. We talked a little while they were eating their lunch. And I daydreamed about food as I watched them eat.

"Brook!"

"Huh?" I gave Hillary a blank stare.

Hillary let out a chuckle as she replied,

"I said your drooling."

"Oh." I gave her a surprised look. "Am I? Sorry." I used my hand to wipe my face.

"Here." Jeorge said while handing me a napkin.

"Thank you." I replied while taking the napkin from his hand.

"See," Jeorge said while he took a bite out of his sandwich. "You are hungry."

"That's why you are drooling." Hillary finished his sentence.

"I don't know what you are talking about." I said acting innocent.

Honestly, I didn't have permission to eat. And Mistress will know I lied to her when she forces me to vomit later.

After lunch, went back to class. Blah blah blah. Then it was time to go home.

Home... To do that ridiculous number of chores in a short time frame. Yay. I groaned when I thought about it.

When my owners feel generous and if I finish my chores, my reward will be dinner.

"Look, it's Brook."

"Hey Ben, I wonder if Daddy beat his ass because he didn't listen." Chris taunted.

"It looks like that." Ben snickered.

I glared at Chris and Ben while walking past them.

"Hey, where do you think you're going?" Chris said while he grabbed my backpack.

Which I almost lost my balance.

"Hey! I need to get on the bus." I said while I steady myself.

"We don't want a loser like you," Ben pushes me. "On our bus." He said while he finished knocking me down.

I used my hand to slow my fall, but I ended up hurting my hand. I laid there holding my throbbing hand.

Since I was down, Chris kicked me. I let out a whimper when I felt the kick to my side. Then Ben joined in.

"Christopher and Benjamin! Lay off of him." I heard Hillary's voice break through the cheering of the other kids.

"Are you going to send your girlfriend on us if we don't?" Chris asked.

"We have been over this more than once. I am a boy much like you. Don't let my looks fool you, I can still kick your butt. Now buzz off." Jeorge growled.

"Here, take my hand." Hillary mentioned.

"Just get away from me!" I barked at her as I held my side.

"I was only trying to help." She snapped back.

When I looked up, the bus driver had an impatient look.

"Do you kids need a ride?"

"We're coming. Give us a second" Jeorge got short with the driver.

I got myself off the ground and onto the bus. I took a seat at the back of the bus.

I plopped myself down and stared out the window.

"You don't have to sit down next me." I told Jeorge quietly.

"We get off at the same stop." He reminded me.

The bus stopped at Hillary's stop first.

She looked back at me; I looked at her. She smiled, then got off.

Chris and Ben mocked me before they got off. I rolled my eyes in disgust.

Then it was our stop. Jeorge's, and mine, plus couple of other kids.

"Brook, take care of yourself now." The bus driver told me.

"Thank you. I will." I replied.

232

When we got to Jeorge street, I told him, I will see him tomorrow.

"Do you need any help with your chores?" Jeorge asked.

I shook my head no.

"All right, talk to you later than."

We went our separate ways.

I stop in front of my owner's house. A faded blue house with vinyl siding. It's showing its wear and tear through the years. There are more weeds than grass.

I shook my head as I was about to walk around the house to the back door.

Then I saw Jeorge walking up towards me. I cocked my head to the side while I gave him a puzzled look.

"Brook, I know you hurt your hand. You just don't want to show it."

"Oh." I looked down. "I would love the help." I looked back up at him. "Come on in."

Once inside, Jeorge was scanning the living room.

I smiled to myself as I told him,

"I'll be right back."

I head towards my room. When I got into my room, I dropped my bag on the floor. Was about to change when Jeorge walked in.

While changing my shirt, I heard him gasp.

"Brook!"

I finished putting my shirt on, then looked at him.

"Yes?"

"Your back!"

"What about it?" I asked, sounding concerned.

"I-I didn't realize how many scares you had."

I shrugged my shoulders as I replied,

"Don't worry about it."

"Why is your room so dark and why are there bars on your window?" Jeorge questioned.

I rolled my eyes in disgusted as I growled,

"Look," I put up on hand." You came to help with the chores, not examine my room."

"Okay, okay. Calm down."

I shook my head before replying.

"Come on."

When I got to the kitchen, I grabbed the list. I let out a disgusted sigh as I read it.

"Are you sure you want to help?

"Yes. What needs to get done?"

I breathed out when I showed Jeorge the list. His eyes widen as his mouth fell open.

I let out a laugh as I ask,

"What's wrong?"

"We only have an hour and a half? There is no way we will get this done."

I nodded with a smile.

"Oh, we will. If we don't, I will be in trouble. But hey, with the two of us, it will go faster." I told Jeorge.

"We better start then." He told me.

I gave him the easy chores. Like; vacuuming my owner's room, taking out the garbage, and cleaning the kitchen and living room.

While I did the dusting, cleaned the owner's room plus picked up the bathroom and hand mop.

When we finished, it was 5:15 P.M.

"Well, thank you. You better leave before my mas,- " I cleared my throat." My dad gets home."

Jeorge nods in agreement and replies,

"Okay, I'll see ya tomorrow."

We said our goodbyes, then he left.

After some time, while I was washing dishes, Master walked in.

"What did you do?" He asked.

"Sir?" I replied, sounding confused.

"Where is the mess? There is no way you got the house cleaned before I got home."

"It is, sir." I replied while I looked at him with a puzzled look.

He scolded me to look down because he never gave me permission. I quickly changed my focus to the dish rag I was holding.

Master kept on drilling me about the house because he didn't believe it was clean. To be honest, there wasn't much of a mess to clean, anyway.

He stops asking and told me to grab him a beer.

After I gave him his beer, he disappeared to the living room.

An hour later Master called me into the living room.

I walked into the living room. Once I stood in front of him, I got down on my knees. (My submissive form.) It changes with whom I am with.

"Pretty eyes, did you eat at all today?"

"No, sir."

Master leaned forward and made me look at him. I gave him a terrified look.

"Should I believe you?" He questioned.

"Yes, sir."

He nods while he replies,

"Well, I don't know if you are telling the truth or not." He smiles. "Come here."

I took a deep swallow while he leaned back on the couch and undid his pants.

This has nothing to do with the truth or lies. He just wants a fix. (Sometime later.)

"Good boy." Master said while he pulled himself out of my mouth.

I looked at him with cum dripping off my face.

Master chuckles as he replies,

"You're too cute. Now, you are daddy's little fuck toy."

Now? I have always been his toy.

"Yes, sir. I am here to serve you." I forced a smile.

"Atta boy. Now, turn around."

"Yes, sir."

After his fun, he told me to go to my room.

I asked about dinner because I got the chores done. In theory, I should get my reward.

He gave me a disbelief look while he said that I already had dinner.

I made the mistake to question him because I didn't understand.

He repeated himself then smacked me across the face while he called me different names. Sigh.

December:

When I walked up to my owner's house after getting off the bus, I saw both cars were home. Which made me confused. Because I don't remember them saying anything about being home early.

I shrugged my shoulders before I walked into the house.

"We need to talk. Now!" Master was stern.

I looked at him. His body language showed that he was madder than a hornet.

I looked over at Mistress, which she was sitting on the couch crying.

"Yes, sir." I turned my focus back to Master. "Let me go put my stuff in my room and let me change." I finished saying.

When I got to my room, put my backpack on my bed and got changed out of my school clothes.

When I walked back into the living room, Master was sitting on the couch hugging Mistress. He was talking to her, trying to reassure her.

"Sir, you wanted to talk- " I stop mid-sentence when I saw the look that Master gave me. His look sent chills down my spine.

Out of habit, I dropped myself to my knees and hung my head.

I apologized over and over. Though I wasn't sure what I did wrong.

"Enough!" Master snapped as he back hands me. He sighs. "Your mother is pregnant."

I slowly looked at him with a puzzled look as I tilted my head to the side.

What does that have to do with me? I thought to myself.

"Why did you rape my wife?" Master sputtered.

After those words left his mouth, I felt like throwing up.

When I looked up at Master; he was looking at me, waiting for an explanation. I just let my head hang lower than it was before. My mind flooded with thoughts and what if's? When and how did I get her pregnant?

"Oh, my god." Master said while he walked away.

"I didn't get her pregnant! I don't even know how to get a girl pregnant." I stated.

"You may be mad at Nathanial for abusing you every day before we rescued you. Doesn't mean you had to take that anger out on me." Mistress said through sobs.

"I didn't rape you!" I pleaded.

"Lies!" Master shouted as he pointed a finger at me.

I tensed my body as Mistress ran past me while still crying.

I watched her leave the room, then I looked back at Master.

He sighs in disgust as he went after her.

I stayed where I was, letting my mind wonder.

Two days ago, Master left me in the woods overnight because I wouldn't make out with him. So, he tempted to run me over with his truck, then took off and left me outside. To teach me a lesson. The only thing that I learned was that my cough got worse by sleeping outside during a cold winter night. Because I didn't know where I was, I couldn't make it home. I prayed Master would come back for me. When I realized it was getting later into the night and he wasn't coming back for me. I found a clear spot free from snow and tried to get some rest.

The next day Master woke me by nudging me with his foot. I was so happy to see him, but; he didn't share that excitement. He gave me an emotionless look and told me to get into the truck.

Once back at home, Mistress released her wrath on me. Accusing me of hurting her husband. I didn't know what she was talking about because he looked fine when he picked me up. But then again, I never looked at him closely.

My thoughts came to an abrupt end when I heard Master yell my name.

He picked me up so swiftly, that you think I was a rag doll, as threw me against the wall.

Master whipped me with an extension cord. I howled with every hit.

Then he moved to kicking me and punching me. He told me this is payback for hitting him the other day.

When I got away from him, I hurried behind the futon where he couldn't reach me. I laid down and shivered.

I heard him leave, but I didn't dare come out. It might be a trick.

After hiding for five minutes, I figured it was safe to come out. I thought wrong, when a blow to my head knocks me off my balance.

I fell to the ground holding my head. When I could focus, I looked up to Master; he was pointing his gun at me. I looked away in fear.

Back in 2005, a week after Master came home from the hospital. Uncle Robert showed him the damage the truck took in the accident. Oh, Master was furious. And since they were blaming me for the accident. In Master's rage, I got a severe beating that ended with me having a gun wound to my upper arm.

"Just shoot me. You have before." I said in a soft tone.

"I can't kill you; you have a baby on the way. No. I will have to talk to the boys about finding you a job." Master said while putting his gun back into his holster.

"A job, sir?" I questioned.

"Someone has to pay for the baby. And it isn't going to be me." Master sighs. "Come on, get up." He said while reaching out his hand to me.

I took his hand cautiously as I got up. I followed him to my room. I stopped at the doorway to my room as Master continues to walk in. He stopped and looked back at me.

"Come here Pretty eyes, come to Daddy."

I walked up to him slowly. Once in front of him, he pulls me in for a kiss. Then pulls away and smiles at me.

He picks me up and tosses me onto the bed. I bounced a little when I hit the mattress. Which only made my head hurt more.

I watched him crawl on me where he processed to make out with me.

If I knew he wouldn't get mad at me, I wouldn't kiss him. I hated when he made out with me. But I would rather have a make-out session verses having sex with him.

After five minutes, Master rolls off of me and gave me a proud smile. I gave him an uneasy look.

"Don't you ever forget that your Daddy's boy." He said while playing with my hair.

"Yes, sir. I won't."

"Good boy. All right, you got to go to the wall now."

"Yes, sir."

I got up and walked towards the wall where I got down on my knees, then he cuffed me to the wall.

He gave me another kiss before he left the room.

The next morning when Mistress came in to un-cuff me from the wall. I couldn't look her in the eyes without feeling ashamed of myself. I mean, I couldn't look at her anyway, but now I am telling myself not to look at her.

I couldn't focus on anything that day. Chores, school, homework, not happening.

Just make it through the day. I kept on telling myself. The night wasn't any easier.

But I can tell you this, I looked at my mother differently.

Not only was she pregnant, she was pregnant by me, her son.

No mother should have to carry her son's kid.

After all my mom, my mistress, has done for me, this is how I thank her, by raping her. How fucked up is that?

CHAPTER NINETEEN

WSTR

"Sit down, Buttercup." Master demand as he pushed me into a chair.

Then Uncle Robert walked up to tie me to the chair.

I looked at Master and Uncle Robert with a confused look.

I am felt anxious. What did they want? What did I do? I thought to myself.

"I am sorry." I whispered.

Master gave me a furious look and replied,

"You're sorry?! My wife is pregnant because of you! You filthy dog, forcing your mother to have sex with you. You make me sick."

I hung my head before replying,

"I am sorry. I still feel the pain from you beating me last month."

"Yeah, well, I am considering doing that again. Plus, I have some awesome news for ya."

Master got into my face. I can smell the alcohol on his breath. I looked into his red, tired eyes. Like I was trying to search for sympathy.

"Uncle Robert found you a job. You will be a sex slave. A male escort."

My eyes widen as Master took a step back. He reached out his arm as he said with a dark smile.

"Welcome to the WSTR Brook Harold Tyler."

"The WSTR sir?" I questioned.

He nodded in agreement. Then he looked passed me.

Out of the corner of my eye, I saw Uncle Teddy walk up to me, then put a scalding medal to my forearm.

Master covered my mouth when I let out a squeal and he gave me a warning look to be quiet.

"Ah, that looks beautiful." Master said with a smile.

I looked at my left arm.

"Welcome to the team, Rookie." Uncle Robert said with a smile.

I looked up at him with a questioning look; I changed my focus to Master and Uncle Teddy.

"You official belong to us." Uncle Teddy told me with a smile.

"Oh." I forced a smile at them before turning my focus to my arm.

"What does it mean?" I asked.

"Willie, Susie, Teddy, and Robert." Master said.

I looked up to see Master grab a beer.

"Boys." Master said while he opened up his beer.

"Bring the toy," He looked at me dead in the eye. I swallowed hard. The toy? I didn't know if he was talking about an actual toy, or was I the toy.

"To the spare room." He finished saying, then he ventured down the hallway.

"Come on, boy." Uncle Teddy said with a sneer while he untied me. "Daddy wants his toy.

I got up from the chair and walked to the spare room.

Before going in, I peeked into the room. Master was looking out the window.

I crept into the room so he wouldn't hear me.

I froze when the floorboards creaked under me.

Master laughed. I saw him shake his head.

Without warning, he spun around and threw his can of beer at me.

I gave him a disgusted look when it whacked me in the forehead. Plus, it wasn't empty.

"Please lay down my Pretty eyes." Master said while he pointed to the bed.

My entire body shook as I kept my eyes on him while I climbed onto the bed.

After I laid down, he sat on me and smiled at me.

"Oh, Pretty eyes." He said while he rubbed my face.

He lost that smile as his eyes grew dark.

"I am going to fucking kill you!"

My heart stops along with my breathing. I became paralyzed with fear.

He took a turn for the worse. I didn't understand why he is so upset.

Master took off his belt before getting up. I watched him timidly.

I flinched at the snap of the belt. I covered my face.

He knows I hate that sound. Why was he persistent in making that awful noise?

I begged him not to hit me. But he whipped me like there was no tomorrow.

After the whipping, he beat me up.

I cried out in pain with every hit.

I felt so weak after that, that...... Whatever Master did to me. I kept zoning out. But I was afraid to close my eyes in fear of me not waking up.

Laying there in a pool of my blood and urine, Master climbed on me and started kissing me. I cringed every time he came in for a kiss.

Then the kissing turned into a gang rape.

I was too weak to fight them off. So, I laid there and took it.

Yet, this time when they raped me, it felt different from the past times; I didn't know why. I couldn't explain it.

Maybe because Master beat the shit out of me? Mistress being pregnant by me or the fact that I will be a sex slave to whomever the boys desire to hire.

After they got done, I kept apologizing over and over through sobs.

I kept my face buried into the mattress with my hands over my head.

"You got to learn that the house servant can't be sleeping with the Master's wife. You did this to yourself." Uncle Robert mentioned.

I lifted my head to squint at him. But then Uncle Teddy raised his hand. I closed my eyes tightly in fear of him hitting me.

"You stupid boy, I ain't going to hit you. But you know better to look at us. You need permission, which we never gave."

I apologized again as I dropped my head.

One of the boys grabbed a fist full of my hair while he pulled my head back.

"Don't you ever touch my wife again." Master hissed. "If you do, I will remove your manhood then kill you." Master breathed heavy in my ear. "I am your master and your future. You will obey me. Do I make myself clear?" He said while clenching his teeth.

I let out a whimper as I replied,

"Yes sir, I am sorry, sir."

He shoved my head back into the mattress.

I laid there shaking as I cried uncontrollably.

"You are pitiful." Master muttered while he shut the door.

Within my five minutes of crying hard, I felt like I was going to throw up.

I hunched over the bed trying to throw up but because I haven't eaten in two days; I dried heave.

That went on for a minute, which hurt like hell, then I laid back down.

I curled up into a fetus position and continued to cry.

It exhausted me, and my entire body ached. Every time I breathed, it felt like someone is stabbing me.

My eyes were heavy. No! Stay awake Brook, stay awake. I screamed to myself.

"Brook Harold Tyler!"

I immediately sat up and gave Master surprise look. Then I changed my focus to the bed.

"Get dressed. We have to get home."

"Sir?" I my voice was shaky.

"Yes?"

"Do I have permission to speak?" I asked in a raspy voice.

"Go on." Master says.

"W-What will happen now?"

"You have clients in two days at my house." Uncle Teddy said as he walked into the room.

I nodded slowly as I took in everything, he told me.

"Yes, sir."

I got dressed, then Master, and I left to go home.

"Oh, Pretty eyes. I am so proud of you."

"Proud sir?" I questioned as I looked at him.

"Yes. I have faith you'll do good on Tuesday." He smiled at me.

"Thank you, sir."

I think that's the nicest thing I ever heard from him.

It was eleven P. M when we arrived home.

Master told me to go shower before bed because of school tomorrow. Unless Mistress says otherwise.

I took a warm bath instead.

The warm water stung, though. But once I got passed that, I melted into the tub. It feels nice on my aching body.

Tuesday.... That soon? That's not enough time to get mentally ready for the job. But then again, can you be ready for that job?

I put my hands over my face as I cried.

In god's name, what type of father puts their son into prostitution? I don't remember forcing my Mistress to have sex with me. Are they sure that it's my baby? I was just hitting puberty.

I read somewhere how teen males sex drive are high. Was that what caused it?

I didn't crave sex like most boys my age did.

Got out of the tub 45 minutes later, bandaged up any cuts I have. Then walked into my room to put on my, my.... I looked at the little clothes I had. The only decent outfit I had was my school outfit.

I should toss my other clothes out. They were more like rags than clothes. I shook my head as I put my pj's on.

Monday, I was sore and stiff when I woke.

I got up, started the chores, made breakfast.

"Brook Harold, let me see your arm." Mistress said while she walked up to me.

I showed her.

"Nice. Not only your arm, but all of you." she smiled. "You're not going to school today, not how you look."

"That means he can do extra chores." Master chimed in.

Mistress agreed with him.

They went off to work; while I did my normal chores on top of extra chores.

By the time they came home around 5:30 P. M, I made dinner.

After they got done eating, we had to run to the store for new clothes for me.

They instructed me to keep my hand on the shopping cart and my eyes to the floor.

I didn't care. I was excited to go shopping. Even though Mistress picked out my outfits, and Master helped me try them on.

I took in all the new smells and sounds. And I even looked up twice while Mistress was busy picking out my clothes.

We spent an hour in the store, so by the time we got home, it was bedtime.

The next morning, Master was in bed with me.

How normal people have coffee in the morning, Master coffee is having sex or making out with me. Isn't the reason why he has a wife?

After that, I started my morning duties. My owners had to approve before I could quit.

Then it was time to get ready for school.

School was hell. I didn't want to play 20 questions with the nurse, so I avoid her. I didn't want to deal with all the looks from the kids.

I kept getting yelled at by the teachers because I kept spacing off.

Ben and Chris tormented me at lunch and the walk to the bus.

By the time I got home, I had to do my chores, make dinner and try to fit homework somewhere in that mess.

I dreaded the fact that my owners came home. Because that meant I was going to Uncle Teddy's soon.

Watching my owners eat made me realized how hungry I was.

I first asked them if I could have food, I told them I got everything done.

They looked at me like I asked them for a million bucks. When they turned me down, I got down on my knees and beg them.

"Haven't I been good? I got my chores done. I have been trying my best to be a good boy." I pleaded.

They only snickered at me while they continue to eat.

"Brook Harold, your principal called and told me how you kept on spacing off during school. NO food." Mistress said while she threw her food away into the garbage.

I watched in surprise as I replied,

"But I ha-"

"Pretty eyes!" Master barked.

I looked over at him with a question look.

"You heard your mother. No food." He was stern.

I hung my head in disappointment.

Mostly, I was good at shutting the hungry feeling down. But it's hard when you haven't had food for 4 days. Only water and water don't really fill you up.

"Open wide Pretty eyes."

I looked up at Master.

That stupid evil grin with his cigarette hanging out of his mouth. Like he gets amusement out of it.

Before I could do anything, he shoved himself into my mouth. Made me gag.

Food. I wanted food. Do they know what food was? You know, potatoes, pizza, candy.

No, they didn't. Because my step dad's penis was not food!

"Sallow it."

I looked at him with pleading eyes as I tried my best not to cry.

"Atta boy." Master said while he smiled at me. "Now, you got to get ready."

I got up, went to my room, got dressed.

After I got dressed, I walked towards my Owner's room. Knocked before entering.

Master gave me a smile while I walked in. He looked me over.

"Damn. I have a good feeling about tonight. Honey, look at our kid."

Mistress looked me over as she said,

"Very handsome." She smiled.

I walked over to the full-length mirror.

Dress shirt, dress pants, and new shoes. If it weren't for the bruises, I wouldn't recognize myself.

I rolled up my left sleeve to look at my tattoo, re-looked back in the mirror. Let out a sigh as I closed my eyes.

God, I don't talk to you normally or ask for help, but I need help tonight. I am asking for your help. I don't know if you can hear me or not, please be with me.

I opened my eyes and turned to face my owners.

"I am ready." I said while rolling down my sleeve.

"Go make us money." Mistress told me.

"Oh," Master chuckled, "He will. He will. All right, Honey, I'll talk to you later."

He leaned in to kiss Mistress bye.

Then we walked towards the truck and then we were on our way to Uncle Teddy's.

It felt like it took longer to get to his house because fear paralyzed me.

When we pulled up at his house, Master had a talk with me before going in.

After our talk, Master got out of the truck, but I couldn't. Still paralyzed with fear.

"Pretty eyes, we got to go inside." He said before shutting his door.

"I know." I whispered to myself.

I opened my door and got out. He took my hand as we walked into the house.

Uncle Teddy laughed when he looked at me.

"Well, lookie here. Brought us a new toy." He said while walking up towards me. "Boy, I never recall seeing you all this dressed up before."

He ran his hands over me.

I bit down on my lower lip.

"Hmm, yeah. Let's go over here."

He got me over to a clear spot, turned me around, and pushed me into the wall. Where he proceeded to dry hump me. I looked over at Master as he lit up his cigarette. He had an amusement smile on his face. I just looked away.

That it went on for about five minutes till Uncle Robert pushed Uncle Teddy out of the way.

"Boys, stop fighting over the toy. He's not new, he's just not looking like a bum. Besides, he needs to look presentable for his clients."

I looked over at Master with a worried look while he gave me a dark smile.

Uncle Robert grabbed me by the collar of my shirt and shoved me towards Master.

"Come on pretty eyes, let's get you to your room."

I nodded in agreement.

"All right, like I told you in the truck, the boys and I will take care of the money. You just do your job."

"Yes, sir."

I looked around the room,

"What is wrong Pretty eyes?"

I looked back at him with worry in my eyes.

"W-What do I do?"

Master chuckles to himself.

"You got your pretty eyes; you got your looks. You do great with me and the boys. You have a job to do, go impress your clients. After all, you have a baby on the way. Welcome to the WSTR Brook Harold."

From 8 o'clock to midnight I was having sex or anything sexual with people I didn't even know. Five-minute breaks between each client to re-focus myself.

After it was over with, I sat on the foot of the bed, still in my underwear, gripping my t-shirt in my hands.

I saw Master and the boys come in; I couldn't hear them though. They were like miles away from me but in reality; they were in front of me.

Master was trying to make me look up at him, but I only brought my hands up to protect myself from him. I didn't know what he wanted or what they wanted.

After sometime trying to get me to respond, they left.

After I knew it was safe, I laid down in a fetal position and cried and cried.

The next thing I remember was waking to a car door shutting. When I looked around, I was still at Uncle Teddy's. I sat up slowly, looked over at the clock, 6 am.

Got dressed and walked towards the bathroom.

My eyes were so bloodshot and swollen and god, it hurts down there. That I kept whining when I walked.

Using the bathroom was painful. While washing my hands, there was a knock on the door.

I opened it to see Master standing there. He looked like he didn't sleep at all.

"Did I do wonderful daddy? Did I make you proud?"

He smiled. But it differed from his normal smiles. It was like a relief to him I was talking to him.

"Yes, you did. You made Daddy proud and worried."

"Worried sir?" I question as I cock my head to the side.

"Mm-hmm. You didn't seem like yourself last night. When I looked you in the eyes, you had no life in them."

He leaned down and kissed my forehead.

"I love you Pretty eyes. Your daddy's. Remember that." He said while he poked my nose.

"I know, and I won't. I practically have your initial on my arm. WST. Willie Seth Tyler. My Master's name. The R could go for red, your favorite color." I smiled at him.

"That's my boy." Master's eyes shined with pride. "The boys already left for work. Let's go."

Once at home, Master got ready for work. Mistress was already ready.

"Mistress?"

She looked at me with a questioning look.

"How are you feeling? Is it normal to be throwing up in the morning?" I asked.

She smiles at me before replying,

"Yes. It's normal and I am doing okay. Hey, so Willie told me how you made $340 last night. Good job, proud of you."

She pats my head before leaving for work.

"Have a good day at work. Both of you." I told my owners as they were leaving the house.

I looked out the kitchen window as they both got into the truck. I watched them pull away before I went to get ready for school.

I got dressed really quick, grabbed my school bag, then headed out the door. To see Jeorge standing in my owners' driveway.

"Hey, we will not be late for school this time." He said teasingly.

"Shut up." I told him with a smile.

He laughs to himself.

We walked to the bus stop in silent. Once on the bus after we sat down, Jeorge whispered to me, asking if I was okay.

We looked at each other; he had concern in his eyes.

"I'm fine." I assured him in a low tone.

I leaned my head back and closed my eyes.

"Brook. We are at school."

I opened my eyes and looked around.

"Did I fall asleep?" I asked.

Jeorge nodded with a smile.

"Oh, wasn't trying to." I sighed "Let's go." I said while grabbing my bag from the floor.

I slowly got off the bus. Correction, I was slow getting anywhere.

The morning dragged on. I was sore and tired and trying my best to stay focus, to stay awake.

When it was lunchtime, I glanced around the cafeteria. Found a table away from everyone.

I sat at the table watching all the kids.

Must be nice to have normal lives. Having parents instead of owners. Sharing the household responsibilities. Sitting down, having meals with your family instead of being treated like a dog. Sigh.

"Want some food Brook?"

I gave Jeorge a tired look as I shook my head no.

"Don't feel like being forced to throw up later." I whispered.

"Huh?" He questioned.

"Nothing."

"Okay? So, you sure you're, okay?" He asked again.

"Didn't I already answer that?" I said with a hint of frustration.

"Yes, but you-"

"Drop it, Jeorge. I am fine." I hissed at him.

Then I turned my focus to the table.

"Okay. I am sorry. Do you mind if I sit with you?"

"If you must."

Jeorge sat down across from me.

After lunch, it was back to class. History class. Because the teacher was reading, I kept dozing off.

"Mr. Tyler."

I jump awake when the teacher called on me. I looked around at the other kids, who were giggling.

"Yes?" I asked, putting my attention to the teacher.

"I would like to see you after class."

"Yes, sir."

Once after class, I tried to sneak out with rest of the kids.

"Brook Tyler."

I froze as I replied,

"Yes?"

"I wanted to speak to you. Please take your seat."

"Yes, sir."

I went back to my seat.

Hillary and Jeorge gave me a concern look before leaving the classroom.

"So, I understand you're tired from last night." The teacher said as he leaned against his desk. " But, for the safety of both of us, you got to stay focused in class."

"I don't know what you are talking about, sir?"

"Don't play dumb, Brook. I couldn't care less what happens to you, but I need to stay under the radar. Do I make myself clear?" he asked.

"Yes, sir." I replied quietly.

"Good. Now, have you seen the nurse today?" He asked while taking a seat in front of me.

I didn't like him in front of me. It made me nervous.

"No, sir." I said while looking at him.

"Well, let's take a walk down there."

"Do we have to?" I asked with a nervous smile.

"Yes." He was stern.

So, we walked to the nurse's station.

"Thank you, Mr. Gerald, for bringing him. Now Brook," The nurse looked at me. "You can't keep avoiding me. We are here to help. Now, they can't keep on hurting you like this."

"Like what?"

"This." Mr. Gerald put out his hand.

Isn't nice how concerned he sounds now that we are not by ourselves? I don't know why he even brought me to the nurse. It's not helping me, it's only helping him to stay under radar. With him being a teacher, he should know better to have sex with his students.

"Like I told you. They don't do it out of anger, I cause them to be angry with me."

"Brook, when was the last time you ate?"

"I don't know." I said while I shrugged my shoulders, "Why?"

"Because you look too thin. Here I will get you some food." The nurse mentions.

"No." I said, sounding too eager.

"No?" The nurse looked at me, puzzled.

"I have...." I looked away from the nurse and Mr. Gerald.

"I have yogurt every night." I gave them a confident smile.

They both sighed.

"Get to your last class." Mr. Gerald told me with a dark look in his eye.

"Thank you."

Yogurt? I have yogurt every night? How the hell did that come up? I thought to myself.

Sigh, so I went to my last class.

Couldn't focus there either, but I tried. Lucky this teacher didn't have sex with me. So, it was easier to deal with.

Then it was home time. I rolled my eyes.

While I was walking to the bus, someone pushed me down. I fell to all four, my books scattered in front of me.

"Hey loser. Can't you walk?"

I didn't need to look up to know who it was.

"At least being a little person, I don't have far to fall."

"Do they trip easily too?" Ben asked.

I looked up at Ben and Chris with a mischievous smile while I sat on my knees.

"Only when someone is knocking them down. AKA, you two jackasses."

"Hey, Ben. When did he start calling us names?" Chris asked.

"Now." I said with a hint of a smile.

They both looked at me.

"Brook!" I heard Jeorge yelling.

When Ben and Chris heard him, they hurried away.

"Brook, are you okay? Here, let me help."

"Thank you."

Jeorge smiled at me. I returned the smile.

CHAPTER TWENTY

WSTR PART 2

May 2008, I have been working for WSTR for 5 months. Five months! Having sex to whoever the boys hire and giving oral sex to more men and women then I would like to admit. Men and women giving me oral sex. Which made me uncomfortable. It's a feeling you don't get used to.

When I have clients, I am at Uncle Teddy's and when I don't have clients; I was walking the streets.

To be honest, I liked it much better at Uncle Teddy's. It was in a controlled environment. The boys set up the time and dates. The only thing I had to do was wait in my room and do my job. It was easier, didn't have to deal with creeps. Or a lot fewer verses being out on the street.

Now being on the street. You got to stand there and look cute, look available. Walk back and forth till a car pulls up to you or you flag down a car. When you get a car, you got to walk over to them and talk to them. Tell them your prices. If they accept, you get in the car with them and go to the location of their choice.

Some clients weren't that bad, they offered you a drink and small talk before jumping into the action. And then there were some that were royal jerks. Those people treated you like you were not human.

Just because I was a sex worker, didn't mean they had to treat me like crap. But since I am not doing this by choice, the ones who could be jackasses to you, paid better. Sometimes.

And the night wasn't complete till I'd face Master.

My goal was to hit $500 every night. Bonus if I could make more.

"Where is the money Pretty eyes?" He repeated till I gave him the money.

My biggest problem I had with him was when I gave him the money. Somewhere between the truck and the house, he either "lost" all or half of it, then blamed me for stealing it.

Every time we got back to Uncle Teddy's house or my owner's house; I got questioned, then I got a severe beating.

There was one night that I was walking the streets for two hours before I got someone.

Honestly, I didn't want to go talk to them; I wanted to go home. I was tired and hungry.

So, I stopped walking and looked at the driver; he singled me over; I went over to him.

"What's your prices boy?" The driver asked.

I looked into the car and saw three other men. I turned my attention back to the driver. I smiled as I replied.

"That depends on what you want."

"We want two hours. Can you give us that?"

"Yes, sir."

"Get in."

I walked around the car and got in the front seat.

"How much do you charge?" The driver asked as he pulled away.

I faced palmed myself.

Shit. I forgot to tell him before getting in the car.

"$100 an hour, sir." I said with a smile.

"Not bad."

"Nope. I also have no limits."

"Yeah?" The driver asked while he looked at me.

I nodded.

"I like that."

"Good. Then we will have a wonderful evening."

No limits. Master choice, not mine. I thought to myself. To make $500 or more each night, I had to have no limits.

I got $200 off that job. So, I hoped that the other $300 would come easy.

While at my client's house, the driver offered me a drink while we talked for a little while. Then we got to.... Work for me and pleasure for the guys.

After the two hours, the driver kindly dropped me off where he picked me up at.

Shortly after I got dropped off, another person showed up asking what I charge. I went over with her like I did with the last person.

She only wanted to blow me. So, I got in her car; she found a place to park the car and let her get her fun out of it.

"Can you lick me?"

I looked at her puzzled as I replied,

"Ma'am?"

She started laughing.

"I want you to lick my pussy dear. I will pay extra."

"Oh.... I... Um... I can try." I acted baffled.

"Have you ever done it before?" She asked.

"Yes." I smiled.

I wasn't good at it. It's easier with guys verses ladies.

We attempted it, but I think I offend her. Because she yelled at me and pushed me out of the car, then drove away.

Did I do something wrong? I thought to myself as I sat on the ground.

I got up, brushed the dirt off from my pants, then was trying to find another client. I was desperate to find anyone.

But it was getting late, so I called it a night and headed back to the truck.

It made me nerves to face Master. He won't be happy to know that I only made $200.

I breathed out slowly as I approached the truck.

"The money Pretty eyes. Where is it?" Master asked.

I looked down at the money in my hand.

"Here, sir." I said with a shaky voice.

"Thank you. Get into the truck."

"Yes, sir."

I got into the truck. Then he pulled away.

"C-Can we stop somewhere to get food?" I dared to ask.

I saw Master give me a scowling look through the review mirror.

"Excuses me?"

I looked over at Uncle Robert who was sitting next to me, then I looked down at my hands with my fingers interlaced.

"Haven't I been an obedient boy? I did the job and I haven't eaten in two days."

I waited for his reply, but he never did. He only pulled over and trade spots with Uncle Robert.

"Everyone ready?" He asked before pulling away.

"Go." Master told him.

"I want actual food." I protested.

"It's daddy cock or nothing, Buttercup." Master said with a stern look.

"Come on boy," Uncle Teddy said, *Give your daddy what he wants."

I looked toward the front seat to see Uncle Teddy looking back at me. Then I re-looked at Master.

"But sir, haven't I been good? Don't I deserve a treat?"

Once again, I waited for his reply, which he never gave.

Two minutes passed when he finally told Uncle Robert to run through McDonald to get a cheeseburger.

Master then looked at me with a cunning smile.

I returned the smile with a nervous smile. He's never gotten me food before.

After Uncle Robert ran through McDonald's, he handed the cheeseburger back to Master.

"You want this?" He asked.

YES! It smells so good that I drooled.

"Yeah?" He was teasing me with the food.

I licked my lips. Which made him laugh.

I changed my focus from the food to look at him.

Trying to fight back the tears, I turned to look out the window.

"I'll make you a deal Pretty eyes."

I turned to look at him with curiosity in my eyes.

"Every ten sucks, licks, whatever. You get one bite of this cheese burger."

I study his face. What type of game is this? He is gambling my chances of getting food.

I am stuck. If I deny his deal, he will still force me, but then I won't get food. Or I gamble my chances.

I took a deep breath, let it out slowly. And I accepted his offer.

I got half of the cheese burger before Master finished in my mouth.

"Thank you, Daddy." I said while he whipped off my face.

"Any time Butter cup, anytime." He said while zipping up his pants.

After we got to Uncle Teddy's house, I went to go sit on the couch.

I was shaking. I knew when Master counted the money, he would be furious with me.

"200 dollars!" I heard Master shout from the kitchen.

I closed my eyes tightly as he stormed in the living room.

"Stand up now!"

When I opened my eyes, I slowly looked up to him. You could see the fire in his eyes.

I didn't have time to stand up before he yanked me off the couch.

And forced my mouth open to gag me. Which I ended up throwing up.

I stood there hunched over. With my knees bent slightly, I rested my hands on them as I coughed.

"Obedient boy, my ass. You made 200 fucking dollars! Where's the rest of the money, Brook Harold?!"

I sat back down before replying,

"I-I am-sorry, sir. I was out there for t-two hours before I got my first job, and he wanted two hours. When I got done with him, it was midnight. I had another client, but I offend her."

Master looked at me, confused.

"How? How do you offend someone?" Master questioned.

"By not knowing how to eat a pussy the correct way." I muttered.

I heard him laughing. Then he was laughing hysterically.

"You don't know how to eat a girl? He said while still laughing.

"I understand now." He took a deep breath. "Pretty eyes, you have a job to do that you have to make 500 dollars each night. I am missing 300. Let's move on from tonight and I expect you to make 800 tomorrow night. Do I make myself clear?"

"Yes, sir." I whispered.

"Boys. Why don't we have some fun?"

I looked up at Master with a pleading look.

He gave me a devilish smile.

The boys had their fun. Then we went home.

For the next day, I repeated it all.

Morning chores, school after school chores.

While I getting ready for work, I heard a knock on the door. Wait a second, we don't have many people that show up. So, who's at our door. I listened while Mistress answered the door.

It was Jeorge! I panicked. What was he doing here?

Five minutes later, I heard mistress walk towards my room, then my door opened.

"Your friend is here. You know I don't like people over."

"I know ma'am."

"Go tell him he needs to leave."

"I will ma'am.

"Your father won't be happy about you seen someone else." She said while I walked pass her.

I turned to look at her with a confused look.

"Ma'am?"

"Your daddy's boy. You don't belong to anyone else." She stated as she looked me dead on.

I looked into her red, swollen eyes.

"I know ma'am. I-I will give rid of him." I said without showing I was getting annoyed with her.

"Better." She said while she lit her cigarettes.

"Hey, what are you doing here?" I asked Jeorge.

"I am sorry. I had to come tell you the news."

"What news?" I asked, sounding confused.

I watched him play with his hands nervously.

"I am moving back to Canada."

"What?! Why?" I stammered in disbelieve.

"My grandparents.... They got into an accident and they have a very low chance at Survival." He puffed.

I couldn't believe what he told me. Was I dreaming?

I needed him. He was always there for me. He checked up on me regularly. The main thought went through my head was, could I survive without him.

Since the first day I meant him in daycare, we have been best of buds.

Sure, I still had Hilliary, but she didn't listen like Jeorge. She didn't have the patients to deal with me.

She's only good for telling Chris and Ben off.

"Brook?"

I looked back up at him with tears in my eyes.

"You can't leave. I won't make it without you." I said while I cried.

"Please don't." He said while he cried. "I don't want to leave. But I have to. I will be back for you once I turn 18."

I turned away from him.

"I understand." I whispered.

I felt him hug me.

I allowed him, and I normally didn't.

I felt safe in his arms. I didn't want him to let me go. Ever.

I felt him let go.

"Brook, look at me, please."

I turned to look at him. He held my face, then I felt his lips pressed against mine.

I surprised myself when I pulled him in for a longer kiss.

I had so many emotions running through me I haven't felt before. It scared me, but I didn't want to let go. It felt so right.

Jeorge pulled away. I looked at him, confused.

"I love you, Brook Harold." He let out a slight smile. "Keep your head up. I got to go now."

"I love you too, Jeorge. And I will." I smiled at him.

He returned the smile.

I walked him outside and watched him walk away.

When he was a house away, he turned to look at me. I gave him a smile as I waved goodbye to him.

"I love you Brook Harold Tyler!" He yelled to me.

I nodded in agreement.

I whispered; I love you too.

When he turned and continue walking towards his house.

I dropped my head as I turned to go into the house.

"So. Jeorge? He seems nice, but you only need your daddy. Plus, you already got a girl pregnant."

I gave her annoyed look.

"Isn't daddy your boy? He married you, not me. I am only his son...." I shook my head no. "His stepson."

"He married me. But be real Brook, you are not going nowhere. You will always be daddy's fuck toy." She said with an evil smile. "Oh. Guess who is home." She said as she got excited.

"I'll go warm up his food."

When Master walked in, Mistress told him they need to talk. So, they went into their room.

I was picking up the mess I made in the kitchen when Master came out.

"So, what's this I hear about you finding someone one else?"

"Only a friend, sir." I said while I roll my eyes.

"Friends don't kiss each other."

I shrugged my shoulders.

"Neither do dad's and sons." I said under my breath.

He walked up to me and put his hands around my waist as he kissed my neck.

"If you didn't have work tonight, I would fuck you hard right now. In doggy style. Because I know my boy likes it rough. Ruff ruff ruff."

The only thought came to mind was, what the hell is wrong with him?

"Sir, out of respect, you got to eat so we can get going."

"Oh. But I need to show you some love. Because apparently I am not showing you how much I love you." He said while ran his hands down my pants.

"Why don't we have some fun later. After we get home?" I said anxiously.

"Hmm. I can't wait." He whispered in my ear.

That makes both of us. For two different reasons. I thought to myself.

So, after Master got done eating, we left.

While driving into the city, he reminded me I have to make 800 tonight.

I told him I know, but that was the wrong way to answer it. I just earned myself a hit to the back of my head.

"Excuse me?" Master questioned.

Ow. I rub my head as I replied,

"Yes, sir. I will bring you the money."

"Atta boy. Now get out." He told me as he dropped me off on a corner street.

I got out of the truck and found a place that seemed to be busy with people.

The night seemed to start off well.

Got a client right away. An easy 150 dollars.

Next client I only got 50, but that's okay. It's still early in the night.

I was doing anything and everything to keep my mind off of Jeorge and what took place between us.

And eager to earn the money I owe Master.

I made a thousand easily. Feeling proud of myself. Master should be proud too.

"The money. Give it here."

I handed Master the money; I saw him glance at it. Then he told me to get in. After I got in, I told him,

"I was aggressive tonight, sir. To make you proud. I earned a thousand dollars."

He glanced at me before he replied.

"Good. I'll count it when we get home."

"Yes, sir."

Once we got home, he wandered to the kitchen to count the money while I went to my room to get out of my work uniform.

"I am missing 300." I heard Master say from the other room.

What? That doesn't seem right. I thought to myself.

"Sir?" I question as I step out of my room.

I walked into the kitchen to see what he was talking about.

"The money." He stood up. "Where is it?!" He slammed his hands on the table. Which made me jump.

"I-I know better than to steal the m-money, sir."

He walks up to me and knocks me to the ground then threw rest of the money at me.

"Take it. Take it all. I'll just go wake Mother and tell her you have been stealing again."

I scrambled to my knees and pleaded to him.

"Please don't wake her, she will be mad. No. She will be furious with me."

Master smiled at me before leaving.

"Please don't wake her." I whispered to myself.

"Why do you have to torment me?!" I yelled at Master.

I was angry. I made him the damn money.

"Why do you hate me?" I asked as he walked back into the kitchen.

I kept my eyes on him while he went to grab a beer from the fridge. Master stayed quiet.

"Why am I a male escort or whatever at 13?!" I saw him sipping his beer. "What have I done to you? Am I not good enough to be your stepson? I was three when I met you and even back then you pounding me, for whatever reason. Two years after that, you raped me. What type of stepdad does that?" I scoffed, "Are you afraid that I will leave you?"

"Are you finished?" Master asked with an annoyed look.

I nodded.

He took his last sip of his beer before he threw it away. He was thinking.

He clears his throat.

"It's like a drug. Once you feel the power, the control.... You can't go back." Master looks down as he puts his hands in his pants pocket. "I didn't understand it myself when I was your age. When my uncle was doing it to me, but now I do." Master looked at me with a hateful look.

I looked at him, puzzled.

"If you have gone through the same thing and know what hell I am going through. Then what's the point of repeating it? You know firsthand how I feel. You can stop this cycle, yet you won't. Because you are so power hungry. Uncle or stepdad, don't make it right. Once I am free, I will stop this vicious cycle. I will not put my kids through the hell I have been through."

He stood across from me, arms crossed over his chest, still with that hateful look.

"Buttercup, you'll NEVER be free. Look at your arm, stupid." He said while he lit his cigarette. "You work for the WSTR, and my god, I can sell you to another pimp if I want." he points to me. "Which means, you'll be a sex worker till you die." He smiles at me. "Now, shut the fuck up and get over here and suck daddy's cock like a good little boy you are."

My breathing got heavy as I glared at him.

Master started laughing as he replies,

"Have to do it the hard way. All right."

"Go ask your wife to suck you. I quit." I said while getting off the floor and walked away.

But he has longer arms then me and grabbed the back of my shirt. Pulled me back to him.

"Do you really want to test me?" He whispered in my ear as he wrapped his arm around my throat.

I glanced up at Master.

"Go fuck yourself." I hissed at him.

Wrong answer... He shoved me to the ground, and I fell flat on my face.

I pushed off the ground to get on all fours.

While turning myself around to face him. I got a harsh slap across the face from the belt buckle.

My face stung.

"Who do you think you are being a smartass? I am your master, you listen to me, you little punk." He growled.

I nodded to him as I held onto my face.

"I will do as I am told. I will give you that blow job now." I whispered.

"Hell no. We are going to the bedroom, Pretty eyes. You just earned yourself a rough night."

The next morning, after I woke up, I looked around the room. Realizing that Master was still next to me. I looked at my clock, nine o'clock A. M, Saturday.

I looked at Master.

What pleasure does he get out of always hurting me?

I carefully got up so I wouldn't wake him.

When I stood up, I was a little stiff from being thrown to the floor. And sore in other places. I think he got too rough last night. By the time I got my pants on, Master was changing position.

"Pretty eyes." he said in a groggy way.

I froze as I replied,

"I'm here, daddy." Trying to keep my voice from breaking.

He looks over at me. He smiles at me and replies,

"You did great last night. I am proud of you. Now go make breakfast."

"Thank you, sir."

CHAPTER TWENTY-ONE

THE NIGHT MY LIFE CHANGED

July 14th, 2008.

In this house, the weekends meant different things. Like extra chores, if it's the school year, catch up on any homework. Plus, I always had to get ready for my owner's party. I was told it wasn't the normal party. Master told me we are going to some guy's house. It confused me. I asked what he meant because I thought I didn't work that night. He said it was a friend of Uncle Roberts and this guy was rich. I got told to shut up indirectly.

Later that night we drove up to a mansion. I was in awe at how big it was. It made my owner's house look like a shed.

"Here comes Robert. Go with him and listen. Oh, Pretty eyes. This guy will pay us a load of money if you make him happy. So please listen to him and do as your told." Master told me.

"Yes, sir." I nodded to him.

He leans over to kiss me on the forehead.

"Now get out of the truck." I gave him a half smile as I opened the door to the truck.

"Rookie!" Uncle Robert said while he stretched his arms.

"Hi Uncle Robert." I forced a smile.

"Don't worry, Will, I'll take care of him."

"I know. I will see you guys in three hours."

I walked into the house with Uncle Robert and my mouth dropped opened.

One word, Wow!

"Rookie, close your mouth. It's not polite."

"Sorry. Just amazed how big the house is." I told him quietly.

"I know." Uncle Robert said while he patted my head.

"He'll be right down, Robert. Please go sit in the living room." The house Maid said.

"Thank you." Uncle Robert replied.

I followed him into this majestic living room. The ceiling must have been ten feet tall and you could easily put two, maybe more of my owner's house in there.

Uncle Robert turned to look at me as he straightens up my shirt.

"Thank you."

He smiled at me.

Now, I am sure your Daddy told you this on the way here. I will go over it again. This guy is rich. If you could tell. Plus, he pays outstanding money for my dad's company. Hell, he helps promotes my dad's busy and WSTR. So please, make him happy and do everything he tells you to do. Do I make myself clear?" Uncle Robert told me in a low but firm voice.

"Yes, sir. Though, I have one question."

"What is your question?"

"Why did he want me?"

Uncle Robert lets out a quiet laugh as he replies.

"Because your uncle was eavesdropping on his conversation." He said as he slightly poked my nose.

"Oh."

"Is that all?"

I nod to him.

"Steven!" This guy said while walking up to us.

"Why does he call you Steven?" I whispered to Uncle Robert.

He didn't answer my question, he only shushed me.

I shrugged my shoulders as I saw the two guy's hug.

"Roger, this is Brook."

I smiled shyly at him.

"Don't be shy. We won't have time for you to be shy. But your uncle is right, you are a cute kid." Roger tells me. "Follow me."

I looked up at Uncle Robert; he motioned me to go.

So, I followed him down this long hallway, into a room that was half the size of the living room.

I felt my anxiety hit me as I watched Roger take off his robe, realizing he had nothing on under it.

He gave me a look like he was hungry for fresh meat. I gave him a nerves smile.

"C- Could I use your restroom. Please?" I asked.

He pointed over to a glass door. I told him thank you as I walked past him.

When I got to the bathroom, I felt like throwing up. I had to slow my breathing. Focus Brook, focus. Just another client. I splashed water on my face, dried my face. Then walked out of the bathroom; Roger was sitting next to the fireplace. He singled me over. I took a deep breath and joined him. When I sat down next to him, he rubbed my face. I swallowed hard before I asked him if he wanted me to undress. He looked at me like a lion looks at its prey. He never answered. He removed my shirt for me. While he was kissing my neck, I saw other men enter the room.

I panicked. Therefore, Master and Uncle Robert told me to listen. They know I don't do well in groups. I remember things got heated quickly, but I don't remember what took place.

"Rookie?"

I looked up at Uncle Robert with a blank stare.

"Are you okay, buddy? I have been trying to get your attention for the past five minutes." He told me.

"Oh. Am I done?" I asked.

Uncle Robert nods to me.

I looked over at Roger. He doesn't look too happy.

Shit. I knew I screwed something up.

"What did I do?" I whispered as I looked down.

"What do you mean?" Uncle Robert asked, sounding confused.

"Roger." I pointed out.

"We will talk later. Get dressed."

Nodded to Uncle Robert.

After I got dressed, Roger walked us to the front door, then gave Uncle Robert the money.

"What the hell is wrong with you?!" Uncle Robert asked as he slaps my arm.

"W-What did I do?" I asked nervously as I looked up at him.

He gave me a disbelief look as he growled,

"What did you do! Were you in la-la land the entire time!"

I shrugged my shoulders.

He opened the truck door for me.

"Get in the damn truck. Very disappointed in you." Uncle Robert said as he slammed my door. Which made me flinch.

I tried not to listen in on Master's and Uncle Robert's conversation. But I was curious. Where did I go wrong? I did everything right up till Roger...... Oh.

I jump to Master saying my name.

"Sir?"

"We'll talk when we get home." Master was stern.

"Yes, sir."

I felt like I was carrying a load of bricks as I dragged myself out of the truck and into the house. It was after one AM and sleep was the only thought in my head. Though before I entered my room, I felt Master put his hand on my shoulder. I didn't dare look at him. I could feel the hate he has for me.

I didn't fully get where I messed up for the three men to hate me.

Master broke me out of my trance when I heard him say my name.

"I want you to go sit at the table. We need to talk. I'll meet you there." He told me.

I didn't move till I knew he was in his room. When I heard his bedroom door shut, I let my breath out slowly.

Never mind for sleep. I thought to myself as I walked into the kitchen.

But stop short of the table. I tilted my head with a puzzled look.

"Why is Master's pistol out?" I asked myself.

"Pretty eyes, please go to the couch." Master told me.

I grabbed the gun off the table and put it in my pants before going to the couch to sit down.

I sat on the couch, keeping my gaze to the floor while waiting for Master to punish me.

"Pretty eyes, do you know what you did wrong?"

I shook my head no.

"I told you, Uncle Robert told you, to listen to Roger. Why didn't you?"

"Be- Because he br- brought out wh- whips sir." I told Master, sounding nervous.

"Shut up." He said while smacking me across the face." I told you in the fucking truck, if you can't talk right, don't talk at all."

I looked at my hands as I rubbed them on my pants.

Master sat down next to me and kissed my neck.

I felt the fear leave and the anger take over.

I pushed him away as I stood up. He pulled me back down and removed my shirt. I pushed him away again and hurried away from him. With him being bigger than me, he ran after me and tackled me to the ground.

"Thought you could get away from me, didn't you? Did you forget I out weight you?"

I groaned under his weight.

"Now," Master said while putting my hands behind my back. I let out a whimper.

"If you don't fight me, we can get done with this faster." he continued to say while tying my hands behind my back.

He flipped me over to my back before he stood up to remove his pants.

But he didn't tie the rope tight enough. I could get my hands out and get to my feet while he was removing his shirt.

"Hey!" Master said in surprise.

I took the pistol out of my pants and held it with both hands as I pointed it to him while I said

"Don't you dare come near me!"

Master started laughing.

"What are you doing? Going to shoot me, Pretty eyes?" He said as he took a step forward.

"I might." My voice was shaky, my hands were shaky.

I watched Master walk into the kitchen to grab his beer.

"I'll tell you this Buttercup, you try, but my wife will call the cops on you and charge you with murdering your father. They will charge you as an adult. Then they would lock you away. No freedom, no life. Hell, you hate it when me and your uncles use you for sex. It will be worse in prison." He takes a sip of his beer. "Now, you can go ahead with your little plan, or you can put the gun down and continue working for WSTR. Your choice, your life, sweetheart."

I study his face as he leaned in closer and taunted me.

With my hands being shaky, it was hard to hold the gun steady.

The gun going off startled me as I drop the gun. My heart sank when I saw Master.

Chapter Twenty-Two

Alec Willow Tyler

I stood there in shock as the blood gushed from Master's stomach.

He let out this evil laugh.

Why was he laughing? He just got shot. I don't understand why he laughed.

"What the hell is going on?!"

I turned around quickly to see Mistress standing behind me.

I could not speak. I dropped my head in guilt as Mistress walked over to Master.

"Wiliam my dear, what happened?" she asked sounding worried.

I looked behind me to see Master leaning over the counter holding his stomach.

Mistress grab a dish rag so she could put pressure on his wound.

"Your pathetic." Master whispered as he clenched his teeth through shallow breaths. "You hate me, why didn't you kill me?" He hissed.

"I do, you and Mom. B -But I couldn't kill you, b-because it wouldn't be fair for her. Sh-She is pregnant and needs you. Plus, I don't want to be in prison for the rest of my life. At least here, I got little freedom." I said as my voice broke.

"Freedom?!" Mistress questioned in surprise.

I looked at her as I nodded.

"You are not free. You are a slave. You are your father's fuck toy." She sighs. "You put your father in a coma a while back, you raped me, which got me pregnant and now this?" She pointed with her hand. "You shot my husband? I could easily call the cops on you and tell them you attempted to murder my husband." My eyes widen, "But I got someone better than the cops."

I put my hands in my pocket as I looked at the gun that was lying on the ground.

"Brook Harold!"

I looked up slowly at Mistress.

"Yes, ma'am?"

"Room, now!" She demanded as she snapped her fingers.

I walked into my room, Mistress followed me in and directed me to the wall.

I looked over at the wall, then back to her.

I stop to study her face. She wasn't only mad, but she also looked like she was in discomfort.

She broke me out of my trance by calling my name.

I re-looked at the wall, closed my eyes as I took a deep breath. Then walked up to it and got down on my knees.

Then she walked over towards me and cuffed me to the wall.

"One of your uncles will take care of you." She said coldly. Then she left.

An hour passed when I heard my door open.

"Bro, what is this I hear about you shooting my brother? Not cool, man. What did he do to you anyway?" Uncle Teddy asked.

I glanced up at him.

"He, he,"

"Speak, boy. What did he do to you to make you shoot him?" Uncle Teddy asked, getting angry.

I swallowed hard as I looked at him.

"He was trying to have sex with me." I blurted out.

Teddy laughs in disbelief as he looks away. Then looks at me while he replies,

"Are you stupid or something? What's branded on your arm, boy?" He questioned.

I looked at my left arm, then back to Uncle Teddy.

"Well, my master's name. Including my mistress, yours and Roberts." I shook my head. "I mean Uncle Roberts."

"Exactly." He points to me." WSTR. Which means your daddy's little boy toy. He can use you anyway, he pleases. But you had to shoot my brother, which sent my sister-in-law into premature labor." I gave him a surprised look.

That explains her look. I thought to myself.

"That's right. We wouldn't be in this mess if you only gave your daddy what he wanted. Now, you will pay the price."

I gave him a worried look.

The last thing I remember was Uncle Teddy un-cuffing me from the wall and offering me a drink. Then waking up naked next to him in my bed. My eyes felt heavy, the room was blurry. I moaned in pain as I looked at him, Uncle Teddy gave me a concerned look. I shook my head as I turned away as I closed my eyes.

When I woke up again, Uncle Teddy wasn't next to me. I slowly sat up while the room spun.

"What the hell did he do to me?" I mumbled to myself.

My entire body trembled as I tried to stand. I used my bed as a guide to leave the room.

When I walked out to the hall, I looked towards the kitchen and saw Uncle Teddy sitting shirtless at the table drinking something.

I felt so light-headed then I had to lean against the wall while I held my head.

I continued walking towards the kitchen. I saw him lit a cigarette.

"Hi princess." He chuckled.

"Hi." I whispered.

"Come, take a seat next to your favorite uncle." Uncle Teddy sneered. I shot him a disgusted look.

"Have you looked at yourself, boy?" He asked with a smile.

I shook my head no.

He looked me over before he replies,

"You look wonderful." He snickers as he takes a puff.

"What happened last night?" I asked as I tilted my head towards the right.

"I drugged you. Then beat the shit out of you." Uncle Teddy said, sounding proud.

I slowly nodded my head as I took it all in.

"But go get some clothes on." He said as he put out his cigarette.

"Oh yeah," I said as I felt my face get hot.

"You don't have to feel embarrassed, Brook."

I shrugged my shoulders.

We both looked out the window when we heard a car pull up."Lookie, who is here." Uncle Teddy said as we both put our attention to the door.

"Mister Roberts Steven." Uncle Teddy said as he stood up and reached his hand out to shake Uncle Robert's hand.

They both looked at me with a goofy grin.

"Hey guys." Uncle Robert said sleepily. "I see what type of fun you two had." He continued.

"Yes, sir." Uncle Teddy said as he slurred his words. "But uh, how are Willie and Annie?" He asked, being serious this time.

"Well," Uncle Robert said as he scratched the back of his head. "Will is..." Uncle Robert paused. "He is fine. They have him in the ICU. The bullet missed his liver by a hair." He let out a nervous chuckle." Annie is fine. The umbilical cord got wrapped around the baby. So, they had to do an emergency c-section. And now she is up in the NICU."

"She?" I asked.

Uncle Robert nods as he replies,

"Yes. You have a sister. Alec Willows Tyler."

"You mean I have a daughter."

They both look at me in surprise.

"Right." They both said.

"I - I have to go get some clothes on." I told them.

"Before you do that, I need to release some stress."

I sighed before replying with yes sir.

How rough he went. He released his stress on top of anger. Which didn't feel great. Thrusting fast and doing it hard is one thing but is shoving my face... Into the counter? Is that necessary?

"Thank you, Rookie. Go get your clothes on now." He told me.

"You're welcome, sir."

When I got to my room, I threw some clothes on. Then I went to start my chores while Uncle Robert took a nap.

Uncle Teddy? (scoff) I became his little gopher again.

After I got my chores done, I checked in with the guys about dinner.

"I don't know, Rookie." Uncle Robert sighed.

"We were talking about running to the hospital." Uncle Teddy mentioned.

"All right. Do I have permission to go to my room?" I asked.

They both looked at me like they were thinking.

A few minutes passed when they both let out a sigh and said, "Yes."

I laid on my bed as I stared at the ceiling with my hands resting on my chest.

Alec Willows Tyle. A daughter. I have a daughter. She'll be a part of this family; they will love her. I was hoping. Master should love her. He has been excited about being a father. Which hurts. He could had been a dad, but he became a psycho.

A knock on my door woke me from my daydream. I sat up as Uncle Teddy was walking in.

"We are running to the hospital. And you are coming with."

I looked at Uncle Teddy in surprise. Was it some threat?

I nodded in agreement.

On the way to the hospital, the boys grabbed dinner on the way. I hated smelling the food from the back seat of Uncle Robert's pick up. To ignore the hungry pains; I put my focus outside. Thinking about Alec, plus what I might see with her and Master. I have seen Master hooked up to machines before. But Alec was too little to be out of the womb. She was born two months early. It concerned me she wouldn't make it.

We finally showed up at the hospital. I felt nervous to go in. That I was taking my time walking to the entrance.

"Boy, we want to go before visiting hours are over. Move it!" Uncle Teddy growled.

I knew he meant business, so I hurried my pace.

We first hit the NICU, where Alec was. Uncle Robert led the way to Alec's room. When we got to her room, I let the guys go in first. I heard them talking to Mistress plus the machines beeping. I took a deep breath and let it out slowly as I walked in.

I only took five steps in, and I saw Alec laying in an enclosed case. The doctors had her hooked up to different machines. She was so little.

It overwhelmed me. I took a few steps back and backed into a nurse without realizing it. She gave me a sweet smile. I couldn't help letting the tears fill up in my eyes. I ran out of the room looking for a safe place to hide.

I couldn't believe what I did to my daughter. I wanted her to have a better life than I did, but this was not an excellent way to start out.

I stopped walking short of the nurse's station and leaned up against the wall.

I had to slow my breathing, clear my head. I couldn't think straight.

"Is everything okay?" A nurse asked me.

I looked up at the nurse as the tears rolled down my face.

"Do you know where my dad is?" I asked.

The nurse looked down the hall, then back to me.

"Did you lose him? Is that why you're upset?" She asked in a concerned tone.

I looked at her alarmed as I replied,

"Lost? I - I don't think so. They admitted him to the ICU. I hope I didn't lose him. That's the last thing my mother needs at the moment."

She gave me a surprised look.

"Not the loss I meant, sweetie." She gives me a reassuring smile. "What is your dad's name?"

"William Tyler." I said through sniffles.

"I know where he is." She smiled at me.

So, I followed her to his room.

"He's in here. Just be quiet. He needs to rest. Even though he keeps fighting it."

I gave a half-hearted smile and told her,

"Thank you."

"Daddy, are you awake?" I asked quietly.

Master opens his eyes to look at me.

"Pretty eyes!" He smiled at me. "How is my boy?" He asked.

I felt my lip quivered.

"What have I done?" I said as I cried.

"Shh, Shh. Come here." He told me.

I walked over towards him and crawled up next to him.

He played with my hair as I cried.

"Okay, now that is enough. Look at me, Pretty eyes. What is going on?" He asked.

I looked at him, trying to calm myself before I spoke.

"Alec." I said as my voice broke.

"What about her?"

"She is so little. I wanted to hurt you, not my daughter." I said as I looked down at the IV in Master's hand.

He lets out a quiet chuckle as he replies,

"Then you shouldn't have shot me."

I nodded in agreement.

"Well," I said as I wiped my nose. "I will make it up to you." I finished with a smile.

He smiled with pride. And told me he loves me.

"There you are. We have been wondering where you went to." Uncle Robert said.

I hung my head as I whispered,

"Sorry, sir."

I heard him sigh.

"It's okay. I should have warned you. Hey, look at me."

I slowly looked up to see Uncle Robert smiling at me.

I returned the smile.

So, after visiting Master for a brief time, Uncle Robert and I went back to Alec's room.

"Hi, sweetie, come look at your sister." Mistress said.

I watched Alec breathe

"Will she make it?" I asked, not taking my eye off of her.

"She has an 80% chance." Mistress told me.

I nodded.

"Stay strong, Allie. I love you." I whispered.

I turned to look at the boys.

"Uncle Robert and Uncle Teddy, we should go home. We got things to take care of." I said with authority.

All three of them looked at me with a confused look.

"Remember?" I asked the boys.

"Yes, but you don't tell us what to do." Uncle Teddy told me.

"Sorry sir, I was stepping out of line."

"Just don't do it again." He warned me.

"Yes, sir."

We said our goodbyes, then headed home. So, I thought, but an hour and a half, later, I realized we weren't going home.

And my stomach flip when I saw a mansion come up. I knew better than to ask what was happening, because I damn well knew what was happening.

We pulled up to Roger's house after the gate opened; we drove up the driveway.

"Uh, Sir?" I asked, trying to keep myself calm.

Uncle Robert looked back at me through the rearview mirror,

"I am not wearing my work clothes."

I saw him look over at Uncle Teddy as he smiled. Then looked back at me as he told me,

"That's okay. Your clothes won't stay on, anyway."

I sunk in my seat when my door opened.

"Come on, boy. You got work to do." Uncle Teddy said.

I gave him a dread look as I got out of the truck.

"This is not what I meant by things we got to take care of." I whispered as we were walking up to the door. But Uncle Robert shushed me.

I slumped my shoulders as I put my hands in my pocket.

"Stand tall boy." Uncle Teddy whispered to me.

I listened as Roger opened the door.

"Brook! I am glad to see you."

"Hello, sir. It's nice to see you again." I replied with my game face on.

"All right, Rookie. Talk to you tomorrow." Uncle Robert told me.

I turned to look at him in surprise.

"To- Tomorrow?"

He nods to me.

"Come on, Brook. We got work to do." Roger told me.

I turned to face him with a nervous look.

"Here, take this." He said while he handed me a pill.

"What is it?" I asked.

"Just take it. It's supposed to help you relax."

I gave him an unsure look as I took the pill. He handed me a glass of water to swallow the pill.

"Good." He said with an ominous smile.

After Roger led me to his room, and I laid down on the bed, I don't remember what happened. I only remember waking up next to him, feeling sore everywhere.

I laid there looking around the room, then looked over at Roger.

I took a deep breath and let it out slowly.

Hopefully, I passed this time. I am sore enough the way it is; I don't need anymore... Whatever he did to me.

I slowly got up and carefully walked towards the bathroom.

When I looked in the mirror, I didn't see any marks. So obviously it wasn't my face that hurt.

I went to the bathroom, washed my hands afterwards. Then quietly walked back towards the bed.

I sat on the edge of the bed as I watched Roger sleep.

I wonder what time he went to bed.

Man, I am sore. I thought as I rubbed the back of my neck.

I laid back down next to him.

I woke to someone nudges me.

I pushed whoever away as I mumbled,

"Let me sleep."

"Rookie, you got to get up. We have to get home." Uncle Robert told me.

I opened my eyes to look at him. Then looked at the foot of the bed, where Uncle Teddy and Roger were standing.

I nodded as I rubbed my eyes.

"Did I pass?" I asked as I sounded worn out.

"Pass? This isn't a test." Uncle Robert said with an amused smile.

I shrugged my shoulders.

"You earned a thousand." Roger smiled." You deserved it, kid. The guys loved you." Roger finished saying.

I felt proud of myself. A thousand in one night. Even though I didn't earn a damn cent of that thousand.

"You're welcome." I said with a smile.

Guys? I thought as I felt my smile disappear.

"What guys?" I asked nervously.

Uncle Teddy told me not to worry about it. Yeah, because it's not him who will have the nightmares about it. It's not him who feels ashamed for whatever reason.

So, we went home, and I had a surprise waiting for me. When we got home, the boys led me to the backyard.

"Uncle Teddy and I agreed on to put you in the shed. Because you are a threat to this family. You have hurt our brother more than once. And raped your mother. We can't have you in the house when Annie brings Alec home. We have to protect her."

I looked at the shed and then back at Uncle Teddy and Uncle Robert with a questioning look.

"You don't have that say. It's not your house." I stated.

"Boy, who the hell cares if it's our house or not. What Robert said is the truth. And your owners won't argue that."

So, for the next four days, I cooked and cleaned while Uncle Robert plus some other men were helping build the new shed. And when Uncle Robert didn't have his construction buddies here, him and Uncle Teddy work on. "My shed".

They built a sound proof torture room.

The fifth day they, my uncles moved me in. It surprised me when I looked into the shed. It looked dingy compared to the outside. Low lighting, the cuffs on the wall, a chair with chains, and a wall where they put their "tools".

"Where is my bed?" I asked.

They led me through another door, which led to another room encased in cement.

"Is that my bed?" I asked as I pointed to a blanket on the floor as I looked at my uncles.

They both nodded.

I returned my focus to the bed.

It looked pathetic. I thought while I took a step towards it.

"Well, enjoy." Uncle Teddy said.

I turned my focus to the door and shouted, "No!" as he was closing it.

"Don't leave me!" I said while I banged on the door.

I got nervous. I turned around and took everything in.

I don't believe it. I just don't. I thought as I leaned against the door. It was darker in here than in the other room. I looked around for the light switch. But there wasn't one.

After twenty minutes passed, I knew they weren't coming back, so I laid down on my.... Bed. A blanket to lie on and one to cover up with, plus a hopeless excuse for a pillow.

I tossed and turned all night long. I came from sleeping on a mattress to a cement floor. And the blanket doesn't make the floor any softer.

I was about to fall asleep when a loud bang woke me up.

I sat up quickly and looked around. There was this rumble that kept continuing.

Thunder? I thought. But it was hard to tell in this cement block.

I woke to a bright light shining in my eyes. I squinted to see who was there.

"You look tired. How did you sleep?" Asked Uncle Robert.

"I didn't." I said, sounding annoyed as I sat up.

Uncle Robert let out a laugh.

"Sorry to hear that, kiddo. But you got to get up now and start chores."

"Why? I cleaned the house last night. There is nothing to clean." I protested.

"Fine, fine. You can come in and be mine and Teddy's fuck toy." Uncle Robert said with a smile.

I gave him a disgusted look.

"But seriously, Uncle Teddy and I are running to the hospital."

I nodded to him.

"And yes, the house is clean. So, I am just going to leave you in here." Uncle Robert said before closing the door.

Since they left me in here, I might as well catch up on my sleep. Nothing better to do.

When I woke up, I saw a plate of food next to me. Which I thought was odd.

I sat up and looked at it. It was a slice of pizza with all the topping on it.

I poke at it to see if I was dreaming. It felt real; it looks real. I brought it up to my nose. It even smelled real.

I put it back down and stared at it for two minutes. This must be some kind of trick. Because they wouldn't leave food for me.

I turned my focus to the door when I heard the keys jingle outside.

"You haven't eaten. You know you can eat, right?" Uncle Teddy told me.

I gave him a skeptical look.

Now I know I am dreaming. Food plus Uncle Teddy being nice to me. I shrugged my shoulders.

If this is a dream, that means I can hurt him and get away with it.

I gave him a smile as I was standing up.

I am dreaming, correct? That means I can hit him.

And I threw a hard punch to his stomach.

I watched him drop to his knees as he holds his stomach, trying to gasp for air.

"You little shit." He wheezed.

"What the hell is wrong with you?" Uncle Teddy asked.

"I want to be free. And since this is a dream, I can do whatever." I said proudly.

"Dream? This isn't a dream.

"He hissed as he rose to his feet.

"It isn't? Then why are you being nice to me?" I asked as my stomach did backflip.

"How?"

"By bringing me food. You never bring me food."

He first gave me a surprise look, then smiled.

"Because you haven't eaten in three days. You know we wait three days to feed you." He reminded me.

Ah shit. That's right.

"Look sir, I was out of line. I thought I was dreaming." I told him in a shaky voice.

"Hmm. Well, let me return the favor." He said before punching me in the stomach.

Yep, not dreaming. That felt real.

I tried to breathe but couldn't. Then he backhanded me.

"Are you dreaming, boy?" he asked furiously.

I shook my head no as tears ran down my face.

"Eat your damn food. I will be back in half an hour." He said then, slamming the door behind him.

I curled up into a ball, still holding my stomach.

After ten minutes passed, I forced myself to take a bite of my pizza. But couldn't eat after getting hit.

It was thirty minutes when Uncle Teddy came back with a glass of milk.

"Here." He handed me the glass. "You barely ate your food."

"Wasn't that hungry." I told him.

He only rolls his eyes at me.

"Well, I got some news for you." I looked at him with a curious look. "Annie, your Mistress is coming home today. Uncle Robert went to go pick her up."

I nodded as I drank my milk.

I had to get some chores done. That included giving Uncle Teddy, "a treat". Making up for hitting him.

After Uncle Robert and Mistress came home, the boys showed her the changes. She seemed excited knowing that I now sleep in the shed.

Thanks, Mom. You shouldn't get excited about your son sleeping in a torture chamber.

Anyway, a week and a half later, Master came home. He also got to see the changes. He too was happy about it.

Since he is home, he wants to go for a drive with me. Great.

Dude, if you just got out of the hospital, go have sex with your fucken wife. Sigh. But then again, it's more of keeping control over me.

So, we went for our "brief drive."

After we got back home, I did some chores. Made them dinner. Then back to the shed I went.

Chapter Thirty-Three

Life Sucks

The months passed and Alec ready to come home. She weighed seven pounds when my owners brought her home. Everyone was glad that she could at last come home.

Even though I cleaned the house throughout every day, I had to clean the clean house from top to bottom. And my goodness, my Mistress stood over me, literally...

"You missed a spot." She told me.

I stop mopping to look up at her with a confused look.

"Right there. There is still dirt on the floor."

I looked where she was pointing at.

"I cleaned that already. It may be your floor." I replied.

"Excuse me?"

Shit. I thought to myself.

"Out of respect, ma'am." I lowered my voice.

"I don't give a damn if you meant it out of respect. Do it again." She said as her voice got louder.

"Yes, ma'am."

So, I cleaned the floor again.

We were up at 6 AM and didn't finish until 11 at night.

"Outstanding job, Brook." She smiled at me." Now excuse me. It's my last night to have a drink."

"Am I excused to go to my shed?" I asked.

She pointed to Master, who was behind me.

I looked up to see Master smiling at me. I looked back down at my hands.

Master had a list that Mistress wrote him stating all the things I did wrong.

Which meant we took a trip outside to the torture room.

God, I hated that room. They have tortured me all of my life, and my owners never needed a padded cell to torture me. But now since they have one, its Master's new entertainment center.

And his favorite game to play is, BDSM.

What I don't understand is, why is he doing all his sex fantasies on me? Doesn't my Mistress allow them? Or maybe she does and Master just enjoys tormenting me? I don't like sex and I dislike BDSM. But hey, it's not my life to say what I like or don't like.

As I am tied to the wall with a gag in my mouth, I'll stay quiet. It's safer that way. So I won't get hurt even more in his horror sexual fantasy game.

I watched Master closely as he gathered his supplies. I was half curious what he planned. What wicked idea has he came up with now.

He looked up at me and smiled. I gave him a blank stare. I didn't know how to react sometimes, and I was better off with an emotionless stare.

Heard the keys jingle from outside. Figured it was Mistress so didn't put too much thought into it. I was wrong. Uncle Robert and Roger stood at the entrance. My eyes widen with fear. I breathed faster. I looked at all three of them.

Now what? I thought.

Master walked up to me with an evil smile. I looked at him unguarded. His eyes were red from whatever drug he is on, and I can smell the alcohol off his breath.

He pressed his hand to my throat. Each press made it harder to breathe. Plus, the gag in my mouth and me going into a panic attack wasn't helping.

My body responded to being choked and was trying to fight him off. Which I could not. Before I lost consciousness, he let go.

I kept on coughing. Middle of one of my coughs, Uncle Robert walked up to me and used a whip on me. Through lashes, I could see Master and Roger getting excited.

After Uncle Robert had his turn, it was Roger's turn. He untied my legs from the wall so he could fuck me better.

But that didn't last long. He removed me from the wall and told me to get on my back. Where he finished having sex with me. I was told to play with myself till I cum. When the other two boys heard this, they got even more excited. Master couldn't handle it anymore. Watching what Roger was doing, watching what I was doing, Master had to come face fuck me. Even Uncle Robert got a turn.

When Master put me to bed for the night, I couldn't be happier.

I was about to fall asleep when I heard someone outside my door. I held my breath. Hoping whoever was there would go away. The door swung open, and I hurried into the corner of the room.

"Please let me be. I'm tired. I won't have the energy to perform." I beg.

Scoff. "You think you have a say?" Uncle Robert asked.

"No, sir. I only obey. But I'm too tired to obey."

"We don't need you awake to have sex with you. So don't worry about it. Now, come here." He told me.

I stumbled towards him. He caught me before I fell.

"You're not tired. You're sore. And your night is only beginning."

I didn't want to hear those words. I anxiously waited for him to tell me he was only kidding. Except he wasn't. He led me back to the torture room.

I squinted at the bright lights that shined on me. I didn't see Master. I looked up at Uncle Robert with a questionable look.

"Where is Master?" I whispered to Uncle Robert.

"Don't worry about it. Uncle Teddy and I got everything under control." He said as Uncle Teddy walked in with Roger and three other men.

Six guys and one toy? Which I'm the toy. I don't see this ending well.

"Why can't I go to bed? Can we reschedule this for another night?" I protested.

"Rookie!" Uncle Robert growled. "That's enough. Now quiet."

I crossed my arms in disgust.

I stood back while the six men set things up and talked with each other.

I tiptoed backwards as careful as I could to sneak back to my room. Backed up to the door, gripped the doorknob and carefully turned it.

CREAK! I stopped as everyone was looking at me.

Both of my uncles let out a quiet laugh as they looked at each other.

Their looks paralyzed me. I wasn't sure if I was breathing or not. My heart pounding out of my chest.

"Boy, you have work to do. Uncle Robert told you that. We'll let these other guys take care of you."

After Uncle Teddy gave them the go single. It was full swing gang rape. They tore at me and all wanted a piece of me like I was a piece of meat and they were lions.

Afterwards.

"C - can I go to bed now?" I trembled.

"Yes." Uncle Robert said.

"You did great buckaroo." Uncle Teddy told me.

While standing up, the room spun. I felt like throwing up.

"Before I go to bed, may I go outside?" I panted.

"Yes. Let's go." Uncle Robert said.

Once outside, I breathed in the fresh air like you do on a spring morning. In attempts to slow my breathing.

After being out there for a couple of minutes, Uncle Robert asked if I was okay.

I gave him a skeptical look as I replied,

"Why the fuck do you care? You put me through hell then ask if everything is fine?"

He gave me a surprised look and replied,

"Excuse me? Yes, we may put you through hell, but we also know that you're a human with feelings. Time to go inside."

While we were walking in, Roger and his crew were leaving. Which meant it was time for me to go to bed. Finally.

The next morning Master woke me, letting me know my uncles are still here and that him and Mistress are on their way to the hospital.

"Do I have any clients today?" I asked.

"Maybe, but the boys will be in charge of it and will get you ready. I love you. Be good. Because if you're not, "He points to his belt. "You and I later."

"Yes, sir. Hug Allie for me."

Master smiles at me before leaving.

I couldn't fall back to sleep after he left. I could only think about Allie. Today is the day she comes home. I got the house ready for her. So did rest of the family.

But thoughts raced through my head. How this family will treat her? Will they love her? Will they treat her kindly?

I could only see her for brief visits whenever I came in to do the chores, otherwise, I was in the shed. It was better in there, anyway. It hurt too much emotionally to see how they treated her with kind hands and being respectful to her. The only time I got that was when I lived with my dad.

October

I woke up on that crisp fall morning with a strange feeling. Like I couldn't place my finger on it. But I knew, somehow, something might change.

Since I have been spending a lot of time over at Rogers, I figured it had to do with something along that line.

Plus, I overheard my Owners and uncles talk about. (Minute pause) Selling me to Roger. With Alec being around and getting older, they don't want me near her. They don't want to risk losing her.

Master will still be part of it and still will have contact with me but won't be my "owner" anymore.

If that is true, my chances of getting out of this, this, whatever you want to call it. The sex business? I don't know. My chances of getting out of it would be very low.

But I am hoping, praying that I am wrong. And this strange feeling might be something better. Maybe they will allow me back into the house. Maybe they've stopped their bullshit and we all can work on being a family.

I am only looking for a positive outcome. I don't want to be in the sex trade anymore. It's demanding, it's tiring. Someone is always in your personal bubble. Hell, you don't have that personal bubble anymore. Go here, go there. Stand this way, do this, do that. I am only a toy for Master to show case me. To make money off of me. I have been told many times I am cute; I have the right look, the right body. The list is endless. I would like to hear how I am cute because of me, my personality. Someone who likes me for me and not lusting over me or what I can do in the bedroom.

I couldn't focus on school. It didn't matter how hard I tried. But I knew I had to or I would get in trouble.

After school, it was chores, make dinner and get ready for work. Yay.

"Sir, I respectfully ask, what the plan is tonight?" I asked Master.

"You have two appointments tonight. Both at two different hotels. I already got a big tip from the one guy. So, I am hoping you'll do outstanding and they like you." Master replied.

I nodded in agreement.

When we showed up at the hotel, the hotel looked rundown and shabby.

"How much did he pay you? The hotel looks cheap." I asked while looking at Master.

He gave me a disapproval look as he replied,

"You don't need that information. Just go in there and do your job."

"Right. Sorry, sir. Wasn't trying to be disrespectful." I said while turning away.

"Pretty eyes," He made me look at him. "Make Daddy proud." He smiled.

I returned a force smile.

Went up to the door and knocked. A guy answered it and I told him who I was. He acted excited and pulled me in the room as he was shutting the door behind me.

There was no introduction, just got tossed onto the bed and strip down. Then bondages and gaged.

There were too many guys, I couldn't keep up with all their commands. And it's not like I could move or anything.

I was doing my best until one guy brought out a whip thingy. Then I lost it. Made a complete fool of myself. But my crying and pleading only aroused them more. Then I realized they had more "toys" with them. Sigh: My night was hell.

Three hours later. I laid there thinking I won't have enough energy for the next guy.

"Just stay there, your master is coming in."

"So, how did he do?" Master said.

"He's a cutie and does well with BDSM." The guy said proudly.

"Good." Master said.

After the guys left, Master climbed on the bed with me.

"Pretty eyes." He forced me to look at him.

I study his face, trying to find any sympathy. Any answer to why he does what he does.

"We get two, three hours before we meet the next guy." He told me.

I nodded.

"But, since we have extra time, it's my turn with you."

I mouthed the words, "Why?"

"I don't need a reason. Now, up on all fours."

I listened quickly. However, I couldn't handle our session. I was sore and tired from my last session.

I don't know if Master had his satisfaction met or not with me on all fours, but he told me to lie down on my stomach. Which only made it worse. He could get more speed and go harder. I didn't need faster and harder right then. I needed a fucking break... He kept pushing my face into the mattress to keep me quiet. This was round two of my night in hell.

By the time he had enough, I looked like a mess.

Hand marks across my face, my face stained with tears. My hair was a mess. I don't look presentable for the next guy. But we still had time to kill, so Master told me to take a quick shower. I wasn't even sure the shower would work in this shabby-looking hotel.

Hotel number 2:

This hotel looked like a normal hotel. A lot nicer than the first. And since I technically don't know, the big tipper could have come from this guy.

Knocked on the door and got a surprise for a lifetime when the guy answered.

"Uh. I may have the wrong room." I said in shock.

"No. No, you got the right room. Please come in."

"I can't. "I stutter.

"Brook, please come in so we can talk." He told me.

I went into the room. Felt a little unsure about this whole thing.

"I should apologize. I didn't act professionally when you answered the door, but I wasn't expecting you to be one of my clients, Dad. Master wouldn't have approved how I acted. I am sorry." I told my dad.

"Don't worry about it. I am not here for that. It's the only way I could think of to get close to you. Without your mother freaking out."

"How do you know about WSTR?" I hated to ask.

"I have my resources. It's the only way I could think of getting you out of your mothers without a fight. I told your stepdad this would be an overnighter. That way we have time to get further away." Dad said.

"Won't work. Master doesn't go back home. We are too far from home for him to drive back home and then back here. He'll end up sleeping in his truck. Or get a room."

Dad had worried written all over his face.

"Are you positive?"

"Positive." I walked over to the window to look out. And there sits Master's truck. "His truck is sitting outside. He won't go far. He keeps a close eye on me. To make sure I don't run away. Because I have attempted it more than once before."

Dad sighs before replying,

"Then how do we get you out of here. Without him knowing. I hate to ask this, but would he know what room number we are in? I didn't tell him."

"You won't have to. He's a creep. He will find out in his own way. Trust me, I have tried over and over to escape. But whatever I do, he still finds me."

Dad and I sat there trying to come up with a way to get me out. But nothing was working. I know how Master thinks, like he knows my thoughts. There was no tricking him. Dad told me to get some rest while he figures out a plan. Which I gladly accepted because I need sleep. I slept for three hours.

After waking, I realized. Master knows the room number. He told me which room to go to, but Dad said he didn't tell him.

"Dad, you said you didn't tell Master what number, but he knew what room you were in."

I watch Dad let out a long sigh.

"You are right. It must have slipped my mind. The plan to get you out worked in my head. But it's not working in actual life. I was hoping the big tip would be enough for him to disappear. I was wrong."

"May I ask how much you paid him?" I asked respectfully.

Dad put his hands over his face as he replied,

"$5,000" He put his hands down and looked at me with exhaustion.

I was speechless. He paid 5 grand to help me escape, and now his plan is backfiring on him.

We sat in silence as I study his face.

He looks like he hasn't slept in days. His blue eyes that once sparkled with life, no longer have life in them. He doesn't have a smile on his face that once brought me joy. His face now hangs low with sadness. He looks defeated.

We were both startled by Dad's phone ringing.

"It's him." Dad said.

"Master?" I asked.

Dad nods to me.

"Hello?" Dad answered the phone as he put in on speaker phone.

"So, how is it going?" Master asked.

"It's going wonderful." Dad replied.

"Good. Thought I would give you a ring, letting you know I am on my way up. See you soon."

Before Dad could respond, Master hung up the phone.

I watched Dad grip his phone out of anger. His facial expression changed from sad to anger.

"You tried dad." I said.

Dad sighs before replying,

"I know. I hate to do this but take something off and lay on the bed."

I didn't question. I hopped to it.

Took my shirt off, mess my hair up and laid on the bed.

Then there was a knock on the door.

Dad went to answer the door.

"Hi, I'm Nathan. We haven't official meet." Dad said while reaching out his hand.

"Hi, I am William." Master said has he shook Dad's hand.

"Not to ruin your make-out session, but I searched your number and made a few phone calls. I know you weren't making out with him. You 're his dad, you wouldn't do that. And I am here to take him home now. Paying me 5 grand would not make me get lost. I am his Master; I know what's best for the boy. You don't." Master said.

"Having him work as a sex worker is best for him? How so?" Dad asked.

"Because he is paying off his crime."

"What crime?"

"His crime of raping his mother. And now because of what he did, we have a baby to take care of."

"He would never do such a thing. No, Brook is coming with me."

"I am his master. I own him. We both have the WSTR marking. Plus, he's still thirteen. He's coming home with me. Unless you want me to call the cops for breaking the court order?"

They both looked at me with different expressions.

Dad looked defeated again. And Master looked proud.

"Daddy, don't cry. I'll be okay." I hate myself for what I am about to say. "In fact, I am in love with him." I said as I kept my breathing steady.

"In love with him? But that's - "

"Yes, yes, it is. I know it sounds crazy, but I love him and being in the sex trade makes him happy. I want to make him proud." I interrupt my dad.

Dad gave me an unsure look.

I gave him a reassuring smile.

"No need for the cops. I'll leave without a fight. Keep the 5 grand. Use it to take care of Brook. Bye, kiddo."

I said goodbye, which was hard to do. Then dad left.

Since I said out loud that I am I in love with my Master, I might as well please him.

"Sir, we have the motel for the night. Why don't we make good use out of it?" I asked.

Master smiles with joy.

"Gladly." he said as he pulls me closer for a kiss.

Printed in the United States
by Baker & Taylor Publisher Services